THE FORGOTTEN FARMHOUSE BY THE SEA

CAROLINE YOUNG

Storm
PUBLISHING

This is a work of fiction. Names, characters, business, events and incidents are the products of the author's imagination. Any resemblance to actual persons, living or dead, or actual events is purely coincidental.

Ebook ISBN: 978-1-80508-219-4
Paperback ISBN: 978-1-80508-221-7

Cover design: Emma Rogers
Cover images: Shutterstock

Published by Storm Publishing.
For further information, visit:
www.stormpublishing.co

'But one man loved the pilgrim soul in you,
And loved the sorrows of your changing face.'
W.B. Yeats

For my family, without whom this story could not have been written.

PART 1

TIME TO GO

ONE

CAMBRIDGE

"How can I possibly bear to say goodbye to all this?" Nan murmured.

She looked out at the postbox, topped with chewing gum; a wheel-less bike frame chained sadly to the fence and a burger box impaled on the railings of the house opposite. People scurried past, phones to ears, collars up against the rain. This had been her view for six years, but today was the day Nan Green and her family were moving to Anglesey, the little island off the northwest coast of Wales. She had banked on blue skies and a final glass of chilled white wine in the garden when the house was empty, but instead, rain dribbled down her grimy windows like sooty tears.

"This was not the plan," she said. "It's *June*, for goodness' sake."

Nan was prepared to accept cold, rainy summer days on Anglesey, but it really mattered that everything went swimmingly today, because this whole thing was all her doing. The reality of that had yet to hit her, but when it did, she knew it would hit her hard. Her husband Robin had warned her of that this morning, as he left her to manage the move on her own.

"Too late to change your mind now. All boats are royally burnt. See you later."

She had not dared to admit any real doubt yet, but today, Nan allowed herself to see that she was taking a huge, *huge* risk. Anglesey could not be more different from the perfectly proportioned grandeur of Cambridge. The island's landscape was ruggedly beautiful, its glorious coastline renowned for its beauty, stunningly varied wildlife, and the air, glacier-cold, was the cleanest Nan had ever breathed. Birds she saw nowhere else cruised above hidden coves and sandy stretches as if they owned them, because they did. But there were none of the comforts of city life that her family had grown used to.

Her planning for today had been faultless. The house had sold in days, her five-year-old twins, Ceri and Elin, had been stowed with Robin's parents in Putney for a week and a supermarket delivery had been ordered to the new house for tomorrow afternoon, by which time, she and Robin were due to be in and sorted. Fang, the semi-feral cat they had adopted during their last trip to the island, was already hissing resentfully in her basket. All that could be done, had been done, and yet Nan was shaking.

She walked into the empty kitchen and looked around her. Her waters had broken over there, by the sink, where the floorboards were stained slightly darker; she and Robin had saved for months for that six-hob oven and spent so many hours stripping those pine window frames, but soon she would never, ever stand in this room again. There was a huge guffaw of laughter from upstairs, and Nan wondered whether the removal men had found a used condom under their bed. It would be pretty dusty, if so.

The panic began, as it always did, with a feeling of powerlessness that lapped at her toes, her legs, her hips until, within minutes, it consumed her.

"Oh, please no," she gasped. "Not now. I haven't got time for this today."

As the walls began to buckle and billow around her, she grabbed the granite-topped kitchen island, knuckles white, breathing in so deeply that her chest hurt. She tried to focus on her breath, but one stubborn thought would not let her. Was this momentous upheaval another whim, like the potter's wheel that had ended up on eBay or the architect-designed "writing space" she had not written a word in? Was it another pilgrimage in search of something that always slipped away the moment she grasped it? Nothing could undo what had been done to her years ago, and in her heart, Nan knew that no amount of beautiful beaches or bracing mountain walks could erase that. It had happened and was embedded in the fabric of her life, a row of slipped stitches she could never go back and make good. Her only hope was that she could learn to live with it and find some peace within herself.

Closing her eyes, she forced herself to do the "relax and visualise" technique her friend Ella had taught her. Breathe in, long and slow; hold, then breathe out, longer and slower. After a couple of rounds of this, Nan could see the sea, the wide sky, a peppering of oystercatchers on the rocks and the waves hitting the sand with a pulse that never stopped, day or night. She whispered the affirmations that had got her through so many sleepless nights since the house had been sold:

It is right, for all of us.

I can make it work.

I need to do it.

Her heart rate slowed just as Andy, one of the removal men, came up behind her.

"Just the plants and the last of the 'fragiles' to go, Mrs Green." He paused, running his hand over his head. "Oh, shall I let you have a minute... on your own, like?"

"Sorry. No, it's fine, Andy. Just having a *moment,*" she said, adding, "And please, I keep telling you, call me Nan."

"*Nan,* yes, right you are. Just sounds a bit... err..." Andy petered out.

Yes, she knew, the name made him think of a grandmother, not the mother of twins, nearing thirty, who still rocked a size 28 Levi's® and a battered leather jacket. She preferred it to "Nansi", the Welsh spelling of "Nancy" that her mother had saddled her with. She had spent her childhood longing to be called Judith, Sophie or Claudia, but by the time she named her own children, she had embraced her Welsh roots and called them Ceri and Elin. Robin could not resist reminding her of how hypocritical this was – however much he liked the names – at any opportunity.

"Right, I'll tell the lads to do the last bits, OK?" Andy said, touching her shoulder gently before almost tiptoeing out of the room.

Nan flushed. She had almost forgotten how it felt to receive kindness. The atmosphere in their house had been so *officious* for the past few weeks: lists, the ruthless culling of stuff, urgent calls, checks and double checks, goodbyes, change of address notifications. Robin kept his distance, buried himself in his work, snapped at her as his doubts flared, subsided and then festered. He had said 'yes', but his coolness told her every single day that *this was all her doing* and he was *not at all happy about it*; the responsibility was sometimes unbearable. Then she tried to imagine her children's cheeks turning pink in the salty breeze that blew off the sea as they explored the island together, and it calmed her. As a child, when she had visited the island, she hadn't washed between her toes after their last day on the beach so that she could bring some sand back home to Hanwell and feel it in her bed. Exploring Uncle Dewi's farm, burying her face in Auntie Manon's apron and inhaling her baking-doggy-farmy smell remained one of her happiest childhood memories, the distillation of joy. She needed her girls to feel that joy too, but she could still see their faces when she told them that they would be leaving their bedroom, Tumble Tots, and Zillah – their childminder – who gave them cubes of fresh mango or pineapple after lunch. Telling them they would not be going to school with their nursery friends had been even worse, their wide eyes and little "o" mouths had been the definition of "heartbroken". She had promised them a wonderful new life, a beautiful home by the sea, lots of visits to Uncle Dewi's farm, a new puppy to be collected next week... She closed her eyes and murmured:

It will be fine, Nan. Just believe.

TWO

ANGLESEY, A YEAR EARLIER

Nan sat in their holiday cottage, looking out over the bay. It was a beautiful, clear-skied morning and the expanse of blue above them was marred only by a speckling of white gulls floating effortlessly on the breeze. The horizontal rain which had greeted them the previous day and drummed on the roof all night had finally stopped. The world was washed clean, the windows wide open and Nan had tied the net curtains firmly to one side; she despised them almost as much as she did overhead lights. Both of them "stifled joy" in her view.

"Robin, come and look at this, will you?"

Her husband ambled over, his eyes on his phone, and almost tripped over the rug on the floor.

"For Christ's sake! This place is a health hazard!" he yelled. "Why can't we find a holiday rental that isn't, well, so *basic?* I mean, that mattress – Jesus, it was like sleeping on a sackful of turnips. And the Wi-Fi signal is *sporadic*, to put it mildly."

Nan sighed. Her public-school educated husband kicked off every holiday on Anglesey with at least a day's worth of complaints. Secretly, she called this time The Moanathon, and it was as much a part of the annual routine as a) having a row about how to pack the car, b) forgetting to bring wellies, and c) getting lost when the satnav mangled the Welsh place names. Robin's idea of a holiday was a five-star hotel with a pool or a villa in Tuscany, but he had promised to let her come back to Anglesey every year when they got married, and so they did. She paid her dues in other ways.

"Breathe in that air, love," she said. "It's *edibly* fresh, and you look so pale and pasty."

Taking a melodramatically deep breath, her husband started spluttering. "Fresh, perhaps, but full of dust as well. I thought you said this place was rated 'immaculate' on Airbnb? It's filthy."

"It's fine, love. Remember we could always have stayed with Uncle Dewi on the farm," she said, grinning. "That would have been free, and the kids would have loved it."

Her husband winced. "We would all have risked botulism if we had."

Nan took his point. Dewi Jones was her uncle, her mother Eira's twin brother. He had inherited the family farm in his late twenties when their parents had both died suddenly of 'flu, and he and his wife Manon had always been Nan's absolute favourite adults. She remembered sitting on his knee as he told her about him and Eira camping out in a house they'd made from bales of straw in the barn, and scrambling down cliffs to spot slick seals bobbing in the shallows. This carefree Eira bore no relation to the mum Nan knew – the timid woman who kept her head low at all times – but it had made her long for such a childhood for her own children. The downside of this bucolic paradise was that Dewi's farmhouse was verging on squalid. When his only son, Wyn, left home for Manchester University at eighteen, he had gloomily told Nan that the livestock lived in more comfort than his parents did, and she believed him.

"They don't own a hoover, they never put anything away

and they don't believe in cleaning," he told her. "It's disgusting, but they say it doesn't matter to them."

"At least they are kind to you, unlike my parents," Nan replied.

But she saw Robin's point about the risks of her little family staying on the farm. The farmyard was always littered with liquid-topped cowpats and having the pig pen very near the house meant that the kitchen buzzed with fat bluebottles. When Auntie Manon died of breast cancer six months after Wyn had left, things had got even worse. Wherever Dewi went, a miasma of unwashed clothes and stale sweat followed. The only time Nan and Robin had stayed on the farm for their holiday, they had found a thriving colony of earwigs in the bottom of the fridge, feasting on a brown liquid that had once been a cucumber. Rhian Owen, a strikingly pretty teenager from the nearest village, came and did nothing very noticeable in the house once a week, but Dewi paid her more out of goodwill than because he wanted any help. He sat each evening with his memories, surrounded by dogs and grime.

"Dewi, I don't know what she does, but it isn't cleaning," Nan had told him, when Rhian arrived, vape in mouth, during their holiday.

"Her family have had some difficult times," Dewi replied. "And it's my money."

"Then you need to spend it more wisely, Dewi," Robin had said. "Rhian, come with me, please. We need a chat about standards and reliability."

Later, he told Nan that he had given her a "motivational chat about the importance of a good work ethic", and she did seem more cheerful afterwards, shaking her glorious golden curls and promising to "try harder". Despite this, they rented a cottage whenever they visited the island from then on, at Robin's insistence, but he was never happy with her choice.

"Perhaps Rhian's cleaned this place too," he said, looking

around at this year's pretty converted boathouse. "It's about as disgusting as Dewi's."

"Oh, stop being such a *snob*, Robin. Rhian is a sixteen-year-old girl who doesn't like housework, but Dewi employs her to help her family. She told me she wanted to be a model anyway, and she's certainly pretty enough. And suitably flirty, wouldn't you say?"

"*Glamour* modelling, she wants to do, she told me," Robin continued, ignoring her question. "Do you know what on earth *that* is?"

Nan did not feel like explaining bras, basques, crotchless panties and thongs. Robin might get expectations she certainly did not intend to fulfil.

"Underwear, or rather 'not much wear at all'," she said. "And why are you discussing Rhian's career aspirations with her?"

Her husband shrugged. "Just being kind. She looked a bit gloomy when we called the other day, and she's *such* a lovely girl. Did you know she's a fabulous folk singer? A strange mix, that and modelling, but she does lots of gigs, apparently. She needs some care, some *guidance*, that's all."

"Well, we're on holiday, and it's one week out of fifty-two and that's all I care about today, to be honest. And I know you love it here really," she added with a wink.

Robin grunted, but there were things about what he called her "annual pilgrimage" to Anglesey that her husband *did* love, and she knew it. He loved being able to go for a run on soft sand rather than hard pavements. He loved donning his Barbour and Hunters and "looking rustic". He loved the fact that a pint was cheaper; that gorgeous fresh fish cost "peanuts" and that the mussels from the Menai Straits were "second to none". He liked the lack of traffic, and that driving on the one dual carriageway that crossed the island was quick and easy. He had even admitted one year that he felt a nicer person when he had been on the island for a few days and allowed himself to turn off what Nan called his "need to achieve", which had been driving him since about the age of five. Above all, however, her husband liked the sex they had there, so she always ensured that lots of it was part of the deal whenever they visited. Indeed, she had duly obliged last night, *despite* the mattress.

"*One* thing I love is that you're different here," he'd said. "Calmer, more relaxed."

"So are you. You are far more chilled, which has to be good for your blood pressure. You even *smell* more real!" she'd murmured, nuzzling into his neck.

They both laughed, but Nan knew she had hit gold by reminding him of his health. Robin was a terrible hypochondriac: a diagnosis of slightly raised blood pressure the day before the twins' third birthday party had seen him take to his bed. The party, which she had managed alone, had been carnage. If she could convince him he would be *healthier* here...

"You're right, actually. I do relax here, if you can call being bored witless 'relaxed'."

"Oh, stop it! Look at the kids – they're in paradise, Robin. It's such a part of their lives, coming here, and they know how important this place is to me."

"Shame your mother will never join us. We could have gone *out* occasionally," Robin said with a sigh.

Nan bridled. "Yes, I know, but she doesn't like coming back."

"She doesn't like looking after her grandchildren either, does she?"

They both looked at the twins, who were squatting in the garden of the cottage, studying a patch of scrubby grass with fascination. They were still in their pyjamas, hair tousled and eyes gummy from sleep, but there was no gobbled toast and crawling in the traffic to nursery, or Zillah the childminder today. Here, there was all the time in the world to stare at the ground if they wanted to.

"Hey, what you are looking at, you two?" Robin shouted out of the window. "You're getting mud all over your trousers." Two perfect little faces turned to look up at him, like open flowers.

"Ants!" Elin, the older of the twins by a few minutes, yelled back. "They are coming up out of the ground and carrying eggs."

"White eggs," Ceri added. "Bigger than nit eggs."

Robin turned to Nan with a horrified expression. "Nit eggs! Don't tell me we are paying those astronomical nursery fees for our kids to get nits?"

"Robin, most young kids get them," Nan replied.

"Don't touch them, kids," he called. "And move back a bit. Ants can sting you. Horrible little buggers."

His daughters looked at him, puzzled, before shuffling back a centimetre or two and returning to their close scrutiny of the ground.

"Let them be," Nan said. "If they get dirty, we can wash their clothes in that astonishing thing called a *washing machine*, Robin, and if they get stung, they'll remember it next time they meet an ant."

Robin harrumphed. "No wonder you've got a reputation as a risk-taker at nursery."

"I just believe that kids need to *experience* things, to get stuck in, which often involves mess, noise and getting dirty. If that's my reputation at that prissy nursery, I'm proud of it!"

"Give me stainless steel, white surfaces and a fake pot plant any day of the week."

Nan shuddered. His smug words reminded her of a childhood spent constrained by the litany of her father's rules:

Put all that stuff away and sit quietly.

Don't scuff your shoes on the lino.

Clean up that God-awful mess.

Turn that mindless rubbish off.

Plump the cushion when you leave a chair.

... and the most frequently repeated of all, whenever Nan asked to go out and play:

No. Staying home means you're safe.

Which was very, very far from the truth.

"Fancy a coffee?" Robin said. Getting up, he kissed her on the head, which made her want to purr with happiness. It always surprised her, unexpected tenderness from her husband. It was pretty rare these days. Holiday sex had softened him.

"You read my mind."

"Right, I'm going in. Wish me luck!" He held his nose and headed into the kitchen.

Out in the bay, dozens of gulls rose up from the sand in a soft, white cloud that pulsed across the sky until they landed as one. The tide was so far out that the sea was just a glimmering blue line on the horizon, which made the beach a paradise for feeding birds and dog-walkers. Nan watched as a dog, released from its lead, shot off, tail windmilling with joy. As it raced across the huge expanse of rippled sand, she could almost *feel* its bliss. How she envied it.

She picked up the local paper to see what was news on the island. Out of town shopping developments and a growing furore about second homeowners seemed to sum it up. But when she reached the property pages, she gasped.

"Oh my God. *Coed Uchaf* is for sale!"

Her breathing quickened as her heart began to pound. The photo had been taken on a drab day, but *Coed Uchaf* was just as beautiful as she remembered it. A slate-roofed Welsh farmhouse with a ramshackle outbuilding to one side that had an undulating soft lime-plaster roof that, as a girl, Nan had thought looked like a horse's back. The hawthorn tree was still by the gate, curved like a hunch-shouldered old man by many years of withstanding the winds that blasted off the sea. As a child on the beach below, she had watched the farmer on a tractor ploughing the field behind it, followed by a congregation of hungry seagulls. Hunkering down in the elbow of the coastal road, the house had always seemed an organic part of the landscape, as "meant to be there" as the clifftop, the green sward of headland and the waves that beat against the shore below. Here it was, as it had always been, as if it was quietly waiting for her. It was now or never.

"I'm coming," she whispered, running a finger over the photo.

"Oh Jesus. Surely there's a cafetière in this place?" Robin yelled.

Nan closed the paper, rolled her eyes and took a long, deep breath. How was she going to manage this? How was she going to persuade Robin to let her view the house? If it was right for them, as she knew it would be, how would she persuade him to make the leap?

"Nan, I refuse to drink instant coffee!"

"Left-hand cupboard," she said.

"I know you're dog-drooling. I can tell."

He was right: she did drool over dogs, and always had. She was as desperate for her own dog now as she had been as a child, when her father had always called them "smelly, filthy animals" and refused to let her have one. Uncle Dewi had had a succession of energetic, flea-infested collies, with mesmerising grey eyes and good Welsh names like Nel, Hâf and Siân, and she treasured memories of being greeted with licks and frantic tail-wagging by these quicksilver dogs. They then spent the entire week of her holiday either following her around, dropping a ball in her lap for her to throw or trying to round her up and take her somewhere "safe". Nan, unused to such devotion, never resented the fleabites.

She wanted her children to have a dog – one that would love them utterly, romp for miles and snuggle muddily with them on the sofa when she wasn't looking. Central Cambridge, with its countless pedestrian crossings and spindly rowan trees that designer breeds resignedly peed against if they couldn't hold on until they were let off the lead, was a pretty poor substitute for what she was looking at today.

"I want us to live here. We need to live here... with a dog," she murmured.

"What was that?" Robin came back into the room holding two mugs of coffee. Nan knew from the look on his face that he had not found the cafetière.

"Just talking to myself," she said.

"Fine with me. Means I don't have to listen to you." He smirked. "So, what's the plan for this week then? Take in a show? Dip in the pool?"

Nan paused. Whatever they did, they were going to have to drive past *Coed Uchaf*, but she could not tell him that. "No big agenda. Time to slow down and recharge, as usual."

"Well, I hope this weather lasts, as there's precious little to do if it doesn't. It is April, so I anticipate showers. Remember that wet week a few years ago? God, it was never-ending."

Nan felt a flare of anger in the pit of her stomach. It was April, but it wasn't raining, and Robin was already dampening the mood.

"Look, you can all snuggle up and watch TV here if the worst happens and some rain falls, and I'll go out on my own, but let's dare to hope it will stay SUNNY, shall we, like it is RIGHT NOW?" she said, glaring at him. "Please cheer up."

"Nan, I know how you love being here, in the back of beyond, but I can understand why your mother left and never looked back." Slurping his coffee, he grimaced. "Revolting."

"Oh, Robin, do stop *moaning*."

He reached across and patted her hand. "Sorry. I know it's pretty when the sun shines and you always came here as a kid, but it's just, well, it's *every* year, and, you know, there are other places we could go on holiday."

"I need to come back every year," Nan said quietly. "And you promised I could."

"Yes, I know I did, but you have to admit it's a bit odd. I mean my family rented a house in St Ives for a few summers when I was small, but I don't feel a lemming-like draw to go back there. From the bare bones you've told me, Eric made your childhood a bloody misery. Why was it all so much better when you came *here*? I just don't get it."

Nan blew on her coffee, playing for time. Yes, it had been better here because she had felt *safe* here. She had stopped wondering why her husband never guessed that fact.

"Just call me a creature of habit. I like familiar places," she said.

Robin stood up with a snort and left the room. When she heard him nagging the kids to come inside, wash their hands and change out of their muddy pyjamas, she sighed. Sometimes, she was sure she could actually visualise the dark cloud that followed him around, like poor old Eeyore. He was so lucky, didn't he realise? Yes, the death of his older brother in an accident years ago must have been terrible, but he had only talked to her about it once so it couldn't explain his sheer *joylessness* at times. Yes, she had accepted that he didn't want to discuss it – she kept her darkest secret from him, after all – but it troubled her that he was deeply unhappy with his lot in life, and so, she assumed, with her.

He had rescued her once, from a morass of drink and despair; now it was her chance to rescue him, if he would let her, and for them build a better future together. All she had needed was a sign – and she had received it.

THREE

Nan had often compared getting ready to go out with two young children with planning Hannibal's march over the Alps, elephants and all. By noon, they were still not on the road. The local paper listing *Coed Uchaf* was almost a week old already and such opportunities were rare, she felt sure. She had googled the estate agent's details: an empty six-bedroomed farmhouse, outbuilding and roughly one acre of land was on the market with no chain for about a quarter of what their terraced house in Cambridge was worth.

"What's up?" Robin said. "You're as white as a sheet."

"Can we please just GO OUT!" she wailed. Robin headed to the bathroom – again. Only Robin could complain of having "Delhi belly" in North Wales.

Nobody asked Nan where they were going each day on Anglesey; she was boss, but there were things she insisted they did. They had to walk along the glittering expanse of Llanddwyn right to the lighthouse that guarded the rocks at one end of it. The twins had to catch crabs with lines baited with chunks of fatty bacon off Beaumaris Pier, shrieking with horror as Nan pulled the wriggling crabs out of the water. A boat trip around

Puffin Island was another main event, but more to see the seals sprawled on the rocks than the puffins, who were only there for their breeding season and shy, even then. Robin was always on his phone on these boat trips. It distracted him from feeling sick, he told them.

"So, where are we going today, Nan?" Robin said. "Do tell."

"Today is Tyn Tywyn day," she replied, holding her breath in case he objected. He didn't.

Tyn Tywyn was a sand and shingle beach on the west of the island. Nan had always loved exploring it while her parents snoozed, read the paper or ate their picnic, completely ignoring her. She'd crouched by the water's edge to watch hermit crabs scuttling to escape an outgoing tide, kicked gobbets of sea foam with her bare feet or done a sneaky wee in the shallows, all unseen. These were rare slivers of light in a very dark childhood, and she held them close.

* * *

As she saw mile after mile of the ragged Anglesey coastline laid out ahead, Nan felt her heart lift. This drive, along the west coast, was her favourite, a meandering route along tiny, tall-hedged roads ablaze with periwinkles, celandines and hawthorn at this time of year.

"Oh, look at that, girls. Stunning."

In the back, her daughters looked pale. The road was very winding, but neither had complained about feeling sick, as both were far more stoic than their father.

"Nearly there, sweethearts. We're nearly at the beach," she said.

"Is it the good beach, with the tiny crabs in the pools?" Ceri added. "I love that one."

"Well, we're at the *sea*," Robin replied. "*Beach* could be a bit of an overstatement. A strip of sandy shingle more like. I wish we could go to Trearddur Bay or Benllech, where there at least is a proper esplanade with, you know, some actual *sand*."

Nan saw the "For Sale" board the moment they crested the final hill... and there was no red "*Gwerthwyd*/Sold" notice on it. It was still on the market!

"Oh, Robin, slow down! Look – *Coed Uchaf* is for sale!" she cried. "It's such a wonderful old house."

Robin tutted. "It's a sizeable pile, for sure, but a money pit no doubt. It'll be snapped up and listed on Airbnb before you know it."

"Can we stop, please?" Nan said, hoping they had not heard the tremble in her voice.

"Oh, Mum, we want to get to the beach," the twins chorused as one.

She hesitated. Playing this right was vital and she had to get them all on board.

"OK, sure," she said. "I'll walk back myself and take a look later," she said.

"But why do you want to?" Robin asked.

"Well, it's such a glorious spot, and a fabulous house. I remember visiting it as a girl. I wonder what happened to the family that farmed it. The mother was Mum's old school friend, called Annie Hughes, I think. The kitchen was so..."

"Don't get any ideas, please, Nan," Robin cut in drily. "I know that look in your eyes. I've seen it before, remember? Think 'potter's wheel'..."

They drove on, but she craned her neck to look back at the farmhouse, taking in its soft outline, the stunning view of the sea from all its windows. Robin parked, and the twins raced down onto the warm shingle as soon as he released the child lock.

"Girls, wait!" he shouted, but they ignored him, scampering down to the water's edge. He put the cool bag down with a plop and began to walk after them. "I'm going to keep an eye. We can't let them run wild."

"Why not?" Nan muttered. "We can still *see* them, for God's sake."

She picked up the cool bag, the swimming stuff, the picnic blanket, beach toys, macs, sun cream and books and staggered down to the beach. Robin hovered over Ceri and Elin, but she could see him yelling into his mobile. It would be to James, even though they were on holiday. A poor signal wouldn't go down well with either alpha male.

* * *

The day was a warm one, and only a few egg-white clouds scudded across the sky. Sun-creamed and sun-hatted, the twins were soon happily occupied making pools in the shingle, lining up big stones to make a wall "to keep the sea away from us when the slide comes in". After lunch, Nan tucked them into an envelope of towels and encouraged them to have a nap under the parasol. Within minutes, Robin was snoring next to them, Booker Prize winner open at page 3 on his chest.

"Robin," she murmured into his ear. "I'm going to look at *Coed Uchaf*, OK?"

He grunted, turned over, and resumed snoring with gusto.

The path back to Cable Bay followed the gentle curve of the cliff. Nan had walked the same route every year with her mother or with Wyn, her cousin, and it was always just as beautiful as she remembered it. As she strode through the soft, tussocky grass past the Neolithic burial mound and alongside the bay, *Coed Uchaf* lay straight ahead of her like a beacon. If the farmhouse was for sale, what had happened to Tomos Hughes, the farmer who had tended the fields all those years, and his lovely wife, Annie? Surely his two sons should now be ploughing the same land? One was very ill when they had visited, she recalled, but what had befallen the family in the intervening years for this to happen to their home, their land?

This was not the way things were in farming families. And why had Uncle Dewi not mentioned it to her? There was sadness hidden here, she could feel it.

The farmhouse looked forlorn that day, as if it had been forgotten by the world. There were cracks in several of the smaller panes in the old sash windows and buddleia seedlings in chinks in the rendering. The traditional long, low roof of the outhouse had several large holes that gaped like wounds. The entire structure looked as if it was simply giving up, and slowly collapsing in on itself.

"I hate to think of nobody taking care of you," Nan said. "You've always been here, *Coed Uchaf*, through everything that's happened to me. You need rescuing, and so do we."

A crow, its blue-black feathers gleaming in the sunshine, took off from one of the outbuildings and landed with a *kraak* on top of the "For Sale" board. It steadied itself for a moment or two and then, head on one side, looked directly at Nan. She froze until it finally spread its wings, took off, floated above the roof of the farmhouse and perched on some guttering. Then it swivelled its head and looked down at her again, white eyes unblinking.

"What are you telling me to do, Mr Crow?" she whispered. "Shall I look inside?"

Nan had been about fourteen when she had visited this house with her mother during the one, blissful, time they had come on holiday without her father. She had never, ever forgotten it.

"I need to call on Annie Hughes at *Coed Uchaf*," Eira had told her daughter that day. "We were such good friends once, but I broke her heart."

Nan was astonished. For her mother to talk about such personal things was incredible, but she knew not to look shocked, or ask too many questions.

"She lives by the old burial chamber, so we'll take a trip there tomorrow and go and visit her afterwards."

"Does Dad know this lady, from when you two met at Valley?"

Eira looked out of the window for several seconds before she spoke. "Yes, he knew Annie back then, which is why I can never go and visit her when he's with us."

That day changed Nan's life. From then onwards, she transposed her idea of the perfect home onto the old farmhouse, imagining herself with her own happy family sitting around the scrubbed pine table to eat freshly baked scones and drink homemade lemonade. She always remembered the kitchen as being full of dogs, flowers, tapestries, bright cushions, and there had been a shelf displaying a sheep's skull, a circlet of mermaid's purse and a necklace of barnacle shells on string. The whole room had emanated such *warmth,* such *comfort* to a sullen teen, who had needed both so deeply. If, today, she pushed open the wooden gate and had a quick peek, who would mind? She had a *connection* with the place, after all. But as she lifted the latch on the gate, the crow scrabbled, and clumps of moss rained down on her, as if in warning.

"No, I won't be scared off. I'm going to have a look," she said, walking up to the house.

Heart racing, she looked in through the kitchen window first. The glass was rimed with salt, and she had to lick her finger and clear a small peephole to see inside at all. As her eyes adjusted to the gloom inside the house, she felt her breath catch in her throat. A huge wooden table still stood in the centre of the room, with eight chairs around it, just as she remembered. On one wall, she could just make out a shadowy alcove with something large and black in the centre of it. As more details swam into view, Nan realised it was a hulking old range, waiting to be fed with fuel again to warm the whole house and its family. She saw herself, her younger self, sitting on the floor in there, warm and happy... and cuddling a dog. So many years ago, and yet so vivid a memory.

Hanging above the range, Nan glimpsed an old wooden clothes airer, its long rails festooned with cobwebs. She breathed on the glass and cleared a larger circle in the grime. A single picture, a sampler perhaps, hung on the wall behind the largest of the dining chairs, a beautiful old Welsh oak "stick chair" like the one she had seen in Dewi's house. She could visualise the head of the household, Annie's farmer husband Tomos, sitting there as he carved the Sunday roast, discussing what crops to plant, when to harvest them and how the lambs were faring, just as Dewi did. Farming talk was more than pleasantries: it was their lifeblood. In front of the chair, a dusty plate, cup and cutlery were laid out on the table, but the room had no life and no warmth today; it exuded neglect and despair.

"It's been waiting for me, all this time. I can feel it," she murmured.

When she looked through the window on the other side of the front door, the room was bare, the only sign of its past life were the sad outlines of armchairs and a sofa in the thick dust on the floor. A hideous glass lampshade hung from the ceiling and a brown stain spread over most of the back wall. If it was not rescued soon, the farmhouse would deteriorate more and more with each rainy, damp day and each battering winter storm, until it joined the other abandoned buildings that dotted the island, their roof joists jutting into the air like fleshless ribs. She felt her eyes fill with tears at the thought of it.

Walking around the side and to the back of the house, Nan watched as, like a cinematic reel, foam-rimmed breakers crashed onto the beach and ripples of light darted on and off the water. There had once been a wonderful garden here, she could tell. Wind-battered bamboo teepees told of runner beans, a slimed greenhouse of tomatoes and trays of seedlings, and soft ridges in the earth of rows of Anglesey new potatoes. This garden deserved to be planted, as the house deserved to be loved, and she longed to do both with all her heart. Sitting down on a worn slate bench next to the back wall of the farmhouse, she breathed in the glorious scene beneath her for a long time, until she spotted a bank of clouds rolling ominously towards the headland. Rain.

The whole sky darkened in minutes. Nan knew she should go back and help Robin pack up, get the girls dressed and off the beach before the weather broke, but she hesitated, wanting to stay next to the farmhouse with a longing so acute it was painful. As she headed back across the headland to rejoin them, a clear image began to form in her mind. The vision of herself living on Anglesey had glowed like a bright coal in the blackest days of her childhood. As she grew up, other choices, other longings, had overlaid it and blunted her purpose: being loved, fitting in, trying to forge a career, getting married, having babies, buying houses – but it was still there, quietly glowing. Each year they were back on the island she had fed her husband snippets of the life they could have here as her longing to stay grew, and each year, she could feel him losing faith with the way they were living in Cambridge but never admitting it to her in case she saw it as weakness. He dreamt of childless, carefree holidays to the Far East, the Seychelles, but their salaries vanished in the mortgage, the energy bill, the childminder and council tax.

That day, as she strode over the clifftop, the wind whipping her hair around her face and into her mouth, Nan saw the way out for both of them: they should move here and live in that farmhouse. She would make it happen.

FOUR

The farm had been on the market for four months, with no real interest, Nan was told in the local shop when she asked as casually as she could. That meant they could probably offer lower than the asking price, which would be a big plus in Robin's eyes and would mean she could have some time off work to settle the twins in. That evening, she would put her plan to her husband, but first, she rang Uncle Dewi to run it past him and glean his advice. His reaction surprised her.

"*Cariad*/Darling, I would love you to live up here, but *Coed Uchaf,* well, it has history for our family, and for your mother in particular," he said. "Does it have to be *that* house?"

Nan bridled. Vague stories of old grievances were not what she needed. "I don't know why Mum and I went to see her friend Annie all those years ago, or what history they have, but it won't put me off buying the most perfect house in the world. It's my *fate*."

Dewi sighed. "I can't argue with fate, can I? What happened is ancient history now, but I'm not sure how your mother will react if you live in that house, that's all I'm saying. She'll probably refuse to visit you, for one."

Nan snorted. "She never visits us anyway, and will be dead against our moving up here, I know – I just don't know *why*."

A pause. "There's a lot you don't know, but if Eira won't tell you, it's not my place to. You must do what's best for you and yours, Nansi, and only you know what that is."

* * *

When Robin arrived back from a very lengthy, trip to the supermarket to buy "treats", Nan made sure he was comfy on the sofa and on his third glass of wine before she made her opening gambit.

"Here are the details of that beautiful old farmhouse we passed today, the one that's for sale. Look at the asking price. Incredible, isn't it? And there's no chain either." She showed him the best photo of *Coed Uchaf,* with a blue sky behind it and the least evidence of the leaky roof or rotting window frames.

"I see a lovely house, Nan," he replied. "But it's on *Anglesey*."

"I know, I know, but do you realise that, if we bought it, we wouldn't need any kind of mortgage to do it up, once we sold Portugal Street? There would be so much room for the twins to grow into, and the beach is two minutes away," she added, hardly pausing for breath. "They'd have an idyllic childhood, and I could do some freelance editing or even Airbnb to help with money, but of course, with *no mortgage,* as I said..."

Robin looked at her directly for the first time. "Hang on a minute. You're serious this time, aren't you?"

"Yes. I really am."

"But what about my job? I've sacrificed a lot for my bloody career, you know."

"I know, but you could keep it and work at home one week, in the office the next."

"Ah, you've got it all planned, I see. Not sure what James

will say about that. What about you? Do you intend to give up on your career completely?"

"Yes, at first, to settle the girls. Then I can work remotely, I'm sure."

"Jeez, you really have thought about it. We'll still need money, you know, mortgage or no mortgage..." His furrowed brow showed Nan that he was engaging with the idea, however.

"Of course, but we'll need a lot less of it up here. Lots of people do this kind of thing, and it would be a much less stressful life for you – better for your health." Nan felt adrenalin surging through her body as her plan gained traction with her husband.

"Well, I suppose it would be feasible if you were at home all the time for the twins. Take the pressure off me in the parenting department, free me up a bit to... *relax* a bit more."

Nan hesitated. What exactly was he asking her to agree to? Eventually, she said, "I know you don't find it easy now the twins aren't as cute and... *malleable* as they were as toddlers, but I love this age and would have time to *enjoy* them more."

She had long since accepted that Robin was an unenthusiastic father. He had not wanted children, but they had come anyway. As the girls grew, he cuddled them less, saying it felt "awkward", which Nan assumed was because he had received so little affection himself as a child. Instead, he told them how the moon affects the tides or why ducks didn't get cold feet. His instinct was to say "No", or to discipline, restrain, refuse. It saddened Nan, but as she had met his parents, she understood. But was he asking for more freedom from his own children? The alarm bells were so loud in her head that she worried they were audible.

That night, as she watched him calculating, drawing up an Excel spreadsheet and weighing up all the options, she knew that she was relying on how exhausted he was, how desperate for a way out of the financial obligations that stretched ahead of them for decades. She was offering him an alternative path from a heart attack, even if she was dragging him along it. For over an hour, she watched as Robin studied the details of each room in the farmhouse, the outhouse, the garden, in complete silence. Then he asked her some tough questions, demanding she answered with one hundred per cent honesty.

Is this really what she wants them to do? *Yes, it really is.*

Would she be OK with him working away a lot of the time? *Yes, she would.*

Would she take responsibility for organising the move? *Absolutely.*

Would she mind being a single parent all week? *Nope. Brownies' honour.*

Would she rein in her natural extravagance in the renovations? *One hundred per cent, yes.*

Will she give him complete financial control? *I always have.*

Wouldn't she miss her friends? *Not much. I'll make new ones.*

Will she really be happy? *Yes, I will.*

Finally, can they sell up and come back if it doesn't work out?

Nan kissed him instead of answering that one. "Trust me, it will," she said softly.

"No harm in taking a look, I suppose. I do like spending time up here now that we have our own base each time, and you let me come and go a bit more..."

"You would always be free to come and go as you please," Nan said, crossing her fingers behind her back. This was a massive concession on her part; she had already wondered why he had been two and a half hours at the supermarket, but assumed he was talking to James about work as well. And she had not dared ask. Once they were here and blissfully happy, he wouldn't want to be anywhere else.

"No strings attached if we go and look at the place?" Robin said.

"None at all," Nan replied.

Within five minutes, she had booked a viewing for 10am the next day.

* * *

She would never forget the surreal experience of being shown around a house she already fully intended to buy. Accompanying her was an unenthusiastic estate agent from South Wales called Ffion, whose sales pitch included such choice enticements as:

"This bathroom needs a total update."

"The kitchen needs gutting, mind."

"One bloke almost got as far as a second viewing. We never heard back..."

Nan ignored her, moving from room to room as if in a trance. She refused to be downhearted when she spotted damp, mouse droppings, leaking taps or even the ragged little circle of blue sky visible in the fourth bedroom, where some tiles had blown off the roof and let the rain in. They would have money to repair all this, and this was her one chance. *Coed Uchaf* was a house that needed to be loved again, and she was going to love it.

"Can you tell me what happened to the people who lived here, the Hughes family?" Nan asked. She could almost picture the old sheepdog stretched out on the floor, and her sitting beside it. "I came here once years ago. My mum knew the mother, Annie, from school days, I think. Have they moved off the island or downsized?" she asked.

Ffion looked at her watch. Was this really part of her role? "Well, the eldest boy died years back – leukaemia, I think – he was a teenager. Then Mr Hughes and his other son, Idris, tried to keep the farm going, but then there was some story about the wife playing away and things going badly wrong. I don't know the details, to be honest, but after that, things went downhill here, and in the end, cancer got the dad, I heard. That's it, in a nutshell. Sad, but life goes on." She looked at her watch again.

Nan was almost as shocked by the matter-of-fact tone of Ffion's voice as she was by the facts themselves. A deep memory stirred, of her mother on the phone in the hallway at home one evening, whispering in Welsh as tears rolled down her cheeks. She must have been comforting her old friend through one of these terrible tragedies. Why didn't she get on the next train to see her? "And Annie Hughes? Where is she now?"

"In a home, I believe. The shock of it all, I suppose. Her legs packed up. The place was a wreck by then, though, and the land – well, like you see it today, really. That's why most of it is being sold off as a job lot to other farmers. Nobody wants the house, though, or the acre around it. They think it's, well, cursed."

"I can see why people might think that," Nan said. "It was such a happy place when I was last here, but I can almost *feel* the family's sadness today."

"Not somewhere you want to hang about, really..." the agent said pointedly.

"Will the money from the sale of the house go to Annie, for her care?" Nan asked.

"Yes, not that she'll know much about it. She's got no close family left now. A cousin is arranging the sale, but her husband's will made sure it all goes to Annie."

Nan turned to look at the old range and remembered Annie's kind face, and the musical undulations of her conversation with Eira that afternoon, weaving between English and Welsh. Why had they both been crying? And why had her mother kept saying "*Sori*/Sorry"?

"Right, I think that's it," Ffion said breezily. "To be honest, if you're interested, put in an offer and we'll accept it. That's what I've been instructed by this cousin. He just wants shot of it."

"OK, thanks," Nan replied.

"Can't see, myself, why anyone would want to live here," Ffion said with a shiver.

"I want to," Nan whispered. "I've always wanted to."

That evening, after more hours of discussion, some raised voices and a few tears, Robin agreed to email a fair offer for *Coed Uchaf* before they went to bed. At 9.45am the next morning, Ffion rang Robin back. Nan watched his face closely as he talked to her, but his reaction, when it came, was not what she had expected.

First, he placed his phone carefully down on the table. Then he took a dramatically deep breath and pressed his fingertips together to create a steeple. Nan wanted to laugh, as his manner reminded her of a corporate man with a comb-over in a TV soap. She waited, for what felt like *hours*, and just as she felt as if she was about to explode if he didn't tell her what Ffion had said, he did:

"Offer accepted. It's a green light."

Nan leapt out of her chair and shrieked, "Amazing! Oh my God, that's wonderful!"

Robin frowned. "Nan, be quiet and sit down. Look, I know this is what you've always wanted, but please be rational now. We need to establish some ground rules here, some parameters, before we go one step further."

Nan stared at him in disbelief. "OK, if you say so, boss."

"That would be funny if this wasn't so serious. Remember all the things you promised: you're willing for me to be away, happy to manage the kids on your own, willing to let me do my own thing when I'm here, not going to blow millions on the refurbishment? This won't work if you didn't mean those things."

"I promised those things, Robin," she said. "And I meant them."

"I just hope it really will make you happy. That's a *fundamental* part of this venture – you know that, don't you? That has to be the cornerstone of this undertaking."

Nan pushed down a surge of panic, as the reality of guaranteeing she would be happy punched her in the gut. Her history on that front was not good, and he knew that. When he had found her, she was lost, awash with alcohol and in the midst of a massive nervous breakdown in her final year at Cambridge. Robin had never asked her *why* she was in such a terrible state or judged her tears or drunken rages; he had just "rescued her" as he always put it.

Nan sighed. This was supposed to be a joyful occasion, but he was spoiling it. Sex would loosen him up, she knew, but when she started to snuggle in to kiss his neck, he drew back.

"Not now, Nan. We need to talk about this as adults. Not something you find either easy or enjoyable, I know."

"Sure," Nan said, stung. How she hated that patronising tone, and how often he used it.

"Once we've parked this issue tonight, we can give the girls their holiday," he said.

"*Park* it? Have you swallowed some MBA business manual? Aren't you *excited*?"

He looked at her for several, uncomfortable, seconds. "To be frank, I don't know how I feel," he replied.

"Robin, this is my dream come true. Can't you see that? Let's be joyful and hopeful and glad, please. It's time to actually do it and make the leap."

"I need to get my head around the implications without lots of emoting from you, Nan."

"But this is a wonderful opportunity, a once in a..."

"Sssssssssssssssh, please. I need to think without any of your nonsense now."

Nan drew back, sudden tears in her eyes. He sounded so very like her father.

"Sorry to be sharp, but I need you to promise me two things before we all get carried away," he said. "First, that you won't tell the kids, or anyone else yet. Second, that we do this my way, or not at all. That's the only way sensible choices are going to be made."

"Yes, fine," she said. She would have agreed to a disembowelment at that moment.

"Great. So, we have a deal. Let's shake on it."

"Robin, you are not at work, and this is not a business transaction," Nan said.

"Shake, please, or the deal's off. This is a huge thing you're asking me to do. I need to know we have an understanding."

Nan shook his hand, but her excitement had vanished. She hardly tasted the lukewarm Cava he opened to toast their future, and she turned away when he reached for her in bed.

FIVE

CAMBRIDGE

At 9am on June 22nd, Nan handed over the keys of their family home in Cambridge to an estate agent called Dean, and by half past, Robin was inching their hybrid Volvo Estate out through the hellish Cambridge traffic and out towards the A14, heading North. The rain of the previous day had vanished. Today, it was June again – hot, bright-skied and sunny. The back seat of the car was crammed with house plants, sleeping bags (after a cold and uncomfortable night on the living room floor), a kettle, a pint of long-life milk and a ginger cake from Mrs Darbyshire next door. The twins' goldfish Rosie and Jim sloshed about in their tank in the passenger well and Fang hissed and spat from her basket in the back seat, clearly furious at the prospect of returning to live on Anglesey after a pleasant year in suburbia. By the time they reached Birmingham, she had both weed and pooed.

"Right, our ETA is about 2.30pm if we take the M6 Toll and only stop for a quick bathroom break at Shrewsbury. We should still get to the house before long the lorry arrives. Then it's all systems go – you've got the 'to-do' list, haven't you?" Robin said, without pausing for an answer. "Ideally, I would want to see Andy and the lads heading back to Cambridge this evening, or we'll have to pay for another day of their time. That's what the quote said anyway, and that's what I'm aiming for."

"Wilko and out, sir," Nan said with a wink. Robin was stressed, and in "management mode". She was quite sure that Andy and his crew would be far too exhausted to do that, but she said nothing. Today had to be a "be very nice to Robin" day, or he might implode.

But it was not until they had passed Birmingham and saw signs to the M54 and North Wales that Nan felt the knot of tension in her own stomach begin, very slowly, to loosen. Pulling a clipboard from beside Fang's cage, she looked at the long list of what needed doing when they arrived. Turning the page, she found Robin's "list of potential problems" and sighed. He had been right in worrying that the survey would expose expensive issues with the house: it needed a new roof, total rewiring and a new damp course. Much of their furniture would have to be stored under plastic sheeting in the outbuildings while they had the first phase of the work done – the roof and some re-rendering. Living there whilst this was being done was not going to be easy, she knew.

As they sped up the A55 past caravan sites, rolling green fields and wide, empty beaches, Nan felt herself relaxing, muscle by muscle. She opened her window to breathe in the sea air.

"Can you close that please?" Robin said straight away. "It's so noisy."

When they were passing Llandudno, Nan suddenly sat bolt upright.

"We have to pick up the puppy next week! How could I have forgotten that?" Nan had found a Welsh collie pup in Caernarfon and reserved her; she would be ready to leave the farm and her mother the following week.

"*I* hadn't forgotten, I just blocked it out," Robin said. "Utterly stupid idea, as I told you, but it's done now. You should never have promised the girls a dog straight away, but there's no way you can put it off until the building work's done, which would have been the sensible option. They are so excited about it. I think it's the only reason they agreed to move."

"Hmm, well, you didn't tell me until it was too late that you wouldn't be around most of this summer," Nan said. "I didn't know I would be training it on my own, as well as dealing with everything else."

"Look, I can't just flit off to North Wales when there are big deadlines," he said. "James said that it will take time for the 'working at home' routine to bed in. Reasonable enough, in my view."

"But not in mine. No wonder Francesca left him," she muttered.

James Naughton was Robin's manager, a lonely, small-minded divorcé who had cajoled her husband into returning to work less than a week after the twins were born and refused to give his employees a fair bonus each year as it was a "disincentive". He had also arranged a 7am "power breakfast" for the two of them every morning the week the twins had chickenpox and nobody in the Green household was getting any sleep. Nan decided that it had been Robin's fault, but looking back now, had he, in reality, had any choice?

"Look, Nan," he said. "I don't *want* to be away from my family, but that was the deal. I'll be there when I can be. End of."

Nan nodded guiltily. She had not given much thought to whether Robin would actually *miss* them. If she was honest, neither had she given much thought to the actual practicalities of these early weeks. How on earth was she going to cook meals without a working kitchen, settle the twins in, instruct builders and house-train a lively puppy, largely on her own? She only knew Uncle Dewi on the island, after all. He said he was happy they were arriving but told her straight away that he was busy on the farm all day. There was no obvious way of her or the twins meeting any other children until school in two months' time. As they neared Anglesey in their stinky, messy car, every doubt Nan had ever felt was shouting in her head, each voice vying to be the loudest. Signs to Llanfairfechan and Tal-y-bont whizzed past, and she felt her breathing begin to quicken. They were getting close now. Turning away, she stared rigidly out of the window so that Robin wouldn't see her chalk-white face and recognise the telltale signs of a panic attack. Things got even worse as they neared Britannia Bridge, leaving the mainland behind them. Vivid scenes of potential disaster ricocheted around inside her brain: if she couldn't pull this adventure off, she would have ruined her marriage, her husband's career and her family's life. Robin would blame her, and then leave her, which would mean single parenthood, debt, miserable kids... and all of it her doing, her fault, the price of another failed ticket to happiness. Just as she was beginning to hyperventilate, Robin said:

"A bakery. Thank God. I'm starving."

By the time they left the one-stop service station half an hour later – crammed with sugar, fat and carbs – the crisis had passed.

"Well, I have to say, the view from where I'm sitting is pretty damn amazing," Robin said, smiling at her as they cruised through miles of countryside ablaze with colour and life.

When Nan smiled back, everything suddenly felt utterly wonderful. She fizzed with hope, and her imagination romped from one idyllic scene from their new life to the next. They could make this work, as a team, as a partnership, and Robin had *agreed* to it, she reminded herself. She had encouraged, cajoled, persuaded, but not coerced him; they had made the decision together, they had come to an understanding. That was how adult relationships worked, how marriage should work, a world away from the bullying and cowed obedience she had witnessed as a child. She had never felt happier.

As Robin turned onto the tiny coastal road that led to their new home, Nan clapped her hands with joy. He was going to love it here, whenever he could be here, and this was where she was finally going to become the woman she had always intended to be. Nothing, past or future, could stop her now.

PART 2

MIXED BLESSINGS

SIX

"Can you ring Andy and check where they are, please?" Robin said, as they neared *Coed Uchaf*. "I can't see that they'll have overtaken us, but just to be sure."

The removal lorry had not taken the M6 Toll and was only just passing Oswestry, at least two hours behind them, so it would be impossible for the men to unload everything and get back to Cambridge that night. They would sleep in the removal van, which had basic bunks, Andy messaged, but Robin tutted in annoyance.

"They should stick to the terms of the contract, which was to aim for a one-day move."

"Robin, it's too far, and in the grand scheme of this whole thing, paying them a few hundred quid extra really won't matter."

They stopped to collect the keys to *Coed Uchaf*, and Nan sat clutching them as if they were a lifebuoy as a final flicker of panic surged through her that this dream would pop like a bubble and vanish. As they neared the edge of the land, the sea glittered like a million tiny diamonds and a stiff onshore breeze sent each wave to its spectacularly foamy crash on the rocks.

Nan dared to open the car window and filled her lungs with the slightly salty air, gulping it down like manna. It was as pure as she remembered, each breath a gift, filling her with hope and energy for what lay ahead. When, at last, she saw their new home on the horizon, everything felt different from the three or four times she had come to the island since their offer was accepted; to meet builders, take measurements or to meet head-teachers. This time, when Robin indicated to turn into the drive, she started to cry.

"We're actually here," she murmured. "This is really happening."

"All a bit much for you, is it?" he said, laying a hand on her knee. "Pretty natural, I'd say."

"It is a bit, yes," she said. "I just can't believe that we live *here* now."

Robin winced. "Don't remind me. It does seem unreal, but yup, it would appear we own a dilapidated six-bedroomed farm-house, an acre of scrubby farmland, a leaking roof, a lot of damp, dry rot and some eye-wateringly massive bills no doubt lie ahead."

"Yay! Isn't it wonderful?" Nan said. "Thank you, so much for doing this for me." She leant over to kiss him and felt tension, like a low hum of electricity, in his body. So, he was excited too.

"Let's see if you're still thanking me in a few weeks' time," he said, opening the car door.

"We'll have our moments, I know, but just *look* at it, Robin..."

And he did. He stood quite still and took in the beach below and the headland, stretching ahead as far as the eye could see. "Yeah. It's stunning," he said. "I don't think I can believe we've really done this either. Perhaps we should have done it years ago. Oh God, I hope it works out, Nan. I do want it to, you know..."

Nan took his arm and held it tightly. "I know, love. Let's take a bit of time to breathe it in before Andy arrives and all hell breaks loose, shall we? Jeez, I'm so excited – my hands are trembling just holding the keys!"

"Well, I for one need to know they work before I can relax," Robin said. "Give them to me – let's find out."

Reluctantly, Nan let him take them, but as soon as she saw the key turn and the door slowly swing open to see the hallway bathed in shafts of sunshine, a smile spread across her face and was mirrored on his. They were home.

* * *

The first hour or so at *Coed Uchaf* shone like a perfectly cut gem in Nan's memory. She had organised a house clearance after they had exchanged, and professional cleaners had whizzed through with a mop and hoover. This was "a complete waste of time and money", Robin had told her, given the building work they had planned, but for Nan, at least it meant that the spider's webs and mouse droppings would be gone. She had also ordered two electric cooking rings and asked for the old fridge to be cleaned and left for them to use until the reconditioned Aga and Smeg fridge freezer arrived. Those were the two luxuries she allowed herself; their fitted kitchen was to be a basic IKEA one. Robin busied himself checking light bulbs and meter readings and Nan went from room to room opening every window to let the fresh sea breeze fill her house. Within a few seconds, a downstairs door slammed, as the "breezes" were now more like "gusts".

"Nan, close the windows! They're pretty old, the glass in them will shatter if you're not careful," Robin shouted. "And I think we've still got a mouse problem too. Droppings everywhere, despite your expensive cleaners."

"Then we'll get another cat! All farms have lots of cats and the girls will love it!"

"Hmm, I'm not sure Fang, or the puppy arriving next week, will love it. A smelly menagerie is the last thing we need."

"You sound like my father, Robin Green," Nan snapped. "Do cheer up." Nope, she really couldn't be doing with a Moanathon today.

Once her husband had worked his way through his "Arrival Checklist", and Nan had made them both a cup of tea and cut him a very thick slice of ginger cake, he relaxed a little. The removal lorry was still an hour away, so they both sat on the bench that overlooked the bay, where Nan had sat many months earlier and effectively made her decision to move here. How much had changed in the interim!

"Just look at that view," she said, not for the first time.

Robin's phone pinged with a text message.

"Better go and ring James," he said, jumping up.

"Weird. He doesn't usually text you. Far too slow. Can't he leave you alone, even today?"

But Robin had already gone inside.

Nan sighed and took in the view alone. Sheltered on three sides, the waves were calming now, less dramatic, and she watched them rush towards the shore, break in a creamy froth and peel back again, mesmerised by the constant rhythm. A group of oyster-catchers had gathered, peeping in excitement as they jabbed at the seaweed on the rocks. Nan sipped her tea slowly. When Robin finally returned, they both sat in silence, watching and listening.

"Beats hot pavements, sirens and exhaust fumes, doesn't it?" she said eventually.

"It sure does," Robin replied. "The tea tastes nicer too."

"I know. No more limescale grit in the kettle."

They grinned at each other like children, and Nan almost melted with happiness.

"The kids are going to love it here, Robin," she said softly. "Just look at that."

He hesitated. "It's great, but they've left a lot behind, remember. I hope the life they're coming to is a happy one. That's all I've wanted, you know, in this whole crazy process. I just want us all to be happy, fulfil our dreams I guess, in our own different ways."

Something in the tone of his voice made Nan turn to him, and she saw tears in his eyes.

"You were never really allowed to do that, love, were you?" she said.

Robin cleared his throat. "Well, after Simon died, I had to be twice as good, in a way – to fulfil my parents' expectations for both of us. Financial management is not what I would have wanted to do, given the choice, as you know."

Nan squeezed his hand. "Perhaps here, in time, you'll find what it is you really want to do, and what *your* dreams are. You've given me mine, and I'm so grateful."

"I want the twins to have a chance at a happier childhood than I had, and I want more for myself too, I must confess."

"It must have been incredibly hard for you to agree to do something so, well, *out there*, as letting us all move here," she murmured. "I am grateful, love."

"I know."

"Do you think Simon would be happy for us too?" she said in a whisper.

Robin made a strange, gulping noise. "I don't want to talk about him now," he said, twisting away from her. "For God's sake, can't you understand that not all of us want to bare our souls every ten minutes, Nan? I do things my way, and it works for me, OK?"

"But *does* it, Robin – work for you, I mean? I wish I had known Simon, I guess, as he's always been the part of you that's missing."

"Nan, please, this is not the time. I'm exhausted, and we're going to quarrel. I don't want to, not today."

Nan opened her mouth to ask him to trust her, to tell her his feelings, his regrets, but he was looking down the road. Their removal lorry was trundling towards them, spewing a cloud of black diesel fumes. It looked incongruous, so *urban,* against this picture-perfect backdrop. Nan almost wanted it to drive straight past and leave them in peace. Did they really need all that *stuff* anyway? Perhaps they could go to local auctions, and pick up some second-hand things instead? Robin could do something with them. He had done some painting in the past, he'd told her, and loved it, so perhaps he could find that creative part of him again, up here?

"Here they come," Robin said. "In their own sweet time, of course, as it's me that's paying."

"I'll get the kettle on, OK?" she said. She kissed the top of his head, but as she did so, and her lips met warm skin, she realised for the first time that his hair was thinning. He had hidden it well. As he frantically waved his arms to direct the huge lorry as it manoeuvred into the farmyard, she watched and saw, yes, there was a definite bald patch on his crown, and he had lost weight – his expensive corduroy "casual" trousers were hanging off him. It had been a stressful time, for both of them. They had never been apart from the twins for so long, and both girls were monosyllabic when they rang them to talk about the move. Glancing down at her dress, Nan realised that they both looked out of place here, as if they were wearing the clothes of someone on holiday from a far more affluent life somewhere else. They would have to change in so many ways to truly belong here.

Inside the house, she made a huge pot of tea and found her clipboard and the rough list of "what to put where" she had made in Cambridge. A huge longing for a glass of wine came over her, but she pushed it down, silently thanking Robin for organising the supermarket delivery with some wine for 6pm, not earlier. When she went outside into the sunshine carrying six mugs and the rest of the ginger cake, she was immediately asked "where all the boxes of 'fragiles' were going". Moving-in had officially begun.

In this house, in this life, things were going to be different, Nan told herself. She would walk along clifftops with their dog, learn how to bake, make their home a bright, comfortable but primarily *welcoming* place. Here, she would be fearless as she had never dared to be. A searing memory of her childhood home in West London sprang to her mind, and she shivered. Eric Brennan, her father, had liked things to be quiet (unless he was the one making the noise). If anyone closed a door in the house and it banged, he hissed in fury. If Eira and Nan laughed at the television, he switched it off. School friends were never allowed to come to the house to play in case they "created" and Eira knew better than to invite the few friends she had made to coffee. Bringing in an outsider risked Eric's everyday nastiness being witnessed, so they remained a sad, sealed unit. If mother and daughter chatted, or shared the trivia of the day, Eric lowered his newspaper and put his finger to his lips with a long, menacing "Ssssssssh". Silence always followed.

There was one thing Nan was absolutely certain of in her new home:

"I'm going to make as much noise as I like."

SEVEN

In the week before the twins arrived at *Coed Uchaf*, mornings began with a new kind of alarm call: the cry of seabirds, the lulling of waves on sand and, sometimes, the distant chug of a tractor, rather than the cold, electronic beeping of a phone. "Getting dressed" involved Robin and Nan pulling on the sweatpants and T-shirts that they had discarded on the floor the night before rather than ironing shirts or polishing shoes. "Breakfast" was a big mug of tea and two slices of toast eaten standing up as they pored over their list of jobs for the day. Robin was happier than Nan had ever seen him, and James was not mentioned. He hummed as he made bookshelves, sanded banisters and freed up sash windows so that they moved smoothly. One evening, she found him in the outhouse, painting in beautiful lettering on an old roof slate:

A fabulous family lives here.

"You're full of great ideas, you really are. I know you loved painting when you were younger, but I've never seen your passion in action, as it were."

Robin laughed, a sound laced with bitterness. "My parents drummed any passion out of me in case I 'wasted my very expensive education'," he said. "And painting doesn't buy Agas, Nan."

"No, I know, love, but it should," Nan replied.

* * *

During that first week in the house, they rarely saw another soul. The postman, Mike, left their mail on the doorstep as there was no doorbell and the mailbox was rusted shut – there was no fear of packages being stolen here. Lunch was a cheese and chutney sandwich (until the chutney ran out, which left just cheese) or chips from Rhosneigr chippie if they were really flagging. Dinner was either a frozen pizza and a bag of salad or pasta and a jar of sauce eaten on the slate bench outside as the sun set, as the weather remained unfeasibly glorious. There was wine every night, probably too much, but they were "kid-free and had earned it", Robin had said with a resounding cheer when opening the second bottle. It felt good to be there alone together all day, and each day ended with them making, slightly fuzzy, love in a curtainless bedroom filled with the smell of the sea. Nan was in paradise.

Halfway through the week, Uncle Dewi joined them for supper in The Oystercatcher, a glorious pub nestled amidst the tumbling dunes and marram grass behind the beach at Rhosneigr. He had no mobile phone, which meant arrangements had been tricky. Nan was surprised he'd agreed to come, as his day began early and his usual bedtime was 8pm, but he seemed genuinely excited to mark the beginning of a new era for all of them. Nan put on a dress, Robin a new, white Ralph Lauren polo shirt and Dewi arrived in a crease-free shirt and some jeans that were still blue (which meant they were probably less than five years old). He had obviously showered, and his soft, grey curls framed his angular face. They met in the car park, where his old friend Mervyn dropped him off.

"You look so *smart,* Uncle Dewi! Like a young Harrison Ford," Nan exclaimed.

"Is Rhian looking after you properly now that I'm topping up her paltry wages?" Robin said.

There was a short silence while this hung in the air like a bad smell. Nan shot a look at her husband; she had known nothing of this gesture at all and, clearly, neither had Dewi.

"Robin, if that's what you're doing, I thank you for it. She does a lot more for me now, yes, for sure," Dewi replied hesitantly. He was clearly shocked, and even if her husband did not notice the proud old man frowning, Nan did.

"Glad to hear it," blustered Robin. "And you look like a silver fox!"

Dewi shook his head, embarrassed. "I have no idea what you just said, but thought I'd make an effort. This is a pretty important thing for me too, you all coming here to live, you know. *Dw'i wrth y modd*/I'm delighted," he said, gradually recovering his poise. "I just hope and pray it's the right path for you to follow. I'm not sure about that yet, *deud y gwir*/to be honest, but I wish you both all the luck in the world."

Nan took his arm and led him inside and to their table, a beaming smile on her face.

As they ate their way through platters of local seafood, licking the buttery juices from their fingers, Dewi slowly relaxed, undoing the top button of his shirt and greeting the staff with bluff goodwill; other diners, he ignored completely. Glasses of wine became bottles, which then became toasts with glasses of fizz, followed by brandies with pudding. By 11pm, Dewi was flushed scarlet, Nan was pleasantly mellow and Robin was complaining that the staff "clearly want to go home". When he went to the bathroom, Dewi leant across the table.

"Nan, *cariad*/love, my taxi's due in a few minutes, but I

want to tell you something. This is what you've always wanted, I know, but I think you've got your work cut out persuading Robin to love it as much you do, once the honeymoon period is over."

"I know, but this first week has been bliss, Uncle Dewi," she replied, hiccupping. "I'm glad to be here and I think Robin's happy too."

Dewi did not look convinced. "There'll be hard times, you know. That's life. You'll need to keep reminding yourself why you came. It'll be a bigger reason than wanting a big house by the sea, you know."

"I know. It was a longing I couldn't quieten," she said. "Something I've wanted since my childhood, when we came to visit you and Aunty Manon."

"You loved the farm and the life we had then, I remember. Not so easy now that Manon and Wyn have gone, but I wouldn't be anywhere else." He paused. "Eira's not happy with the house you chose to buy, as you know, but it's done now."

Nan had put off telling her mother of her plan to move to the island until the very last moment. When she did, Eira was far from enthusiastic, but what preoccupied her the most was the fact that they were buying *Coed Uchaf*.

"Why must you buy *that* house?" she had said. "It stirs up such bad memories. You know that. Surely you remember, when we visited Annie together, how upsetting it was for me?"

"Yes, I do remember, Mum, but if you won't tell me why, I will never understand. I had to go with my instinct... to buy that house and bring my family here."

Nan looked at Dewi sadly and shook her head. "I just wish someone would tell me the truth."

"The place has *history* for your mother, Nan," he said darkly. "That's all I can tell you."

"History nobody will tell me about," Nan replied, swigging the last of her brandy.

"I'm sorry, Nan, but that's the way it has to be," the old man replied. "Look, there's one more thing I need to say to you before Robin comes back." He leant across the table, so close that Nan could see the bristles in his nostrils. "He can't just have come because it makes financial sense. There must be more to it than that. What's in it for *him*?"

Nan felt a wriggle of unease in her belly. That had crossed her mind, too, in the small hours, but she had pushed it away and agreed to his terms.

"Dewi, we came to an understanding, OK? It'll work out fine, I'm sure. And remember, he's paying for Rhian to look after you out of the kindness of his heart, so try to like him, will you? For my sake."

Tapping the side of his nose with one finger, Dewi drank the last drops of his whisky. "He gets what he wants, does Robin Green. I'm just not sure what it is he wants out of this."

"A happy wife?" Nan snapped. "Let's check if your taxi's here. It's time we went home."

* * *

On the day they were to fetch the twins, things felt different from the moment Nan opened her eyes. Their "second honey-moon" week was over, rain was thundering on the leaky roof and the bedroom was dark and smelt of damp. She got up slowly, her body aching; they had been up until 1am putting the twins' bunk beds together and Nan's fingers were peppered with splinters. The girls' new bedroom was huge, with a sash window overlooking the sea, and it looked pretty welcoming by the time they had finished, with plumped cushions and cheap-and-cheerful IKEA bedding.

"God, I hope they like what we've done," she said.

"It's fine, Nan, and you'll be decorating like a madwoman soon enough," Robin said. He looked tired, and glum, as if he also felt that something very special had come to an end. "Hopefully, the girls will be more preoccupied with the puppy you've promised them than whether the soft furnishings match."

"Yeah, of course."

But this draughty room with its threadbare carpet was still a very far cry from the twins' warm, familiar space in Portugal Street, and both of them knew it.

* * *

The weather was appalling on the drive to the service station near Wolverhampton, where Robin's parents would be handing the girls over. Near-horizontal rain made driving incredibly difficult, and visibility was the worst Nan had ever seen. When they arrived, the twins were sitting at a table in the café looking sulky and Christopher and Prue, exhausted.

"Let me get us all some tea," Nan said. She was nervous, as well as shaken after the drive. Her in-laws were always rather brittle towards her, but today, after she had "so foolishly" uprooted their son and family, she expected their worst.

"The girls are very *busy*, aren't they?" Prue said, when Nan joined them. "You're going to have a tricky time until they start their new school in September. It's such a shame they're going to the local school, not Rydal. I've heard it's excellent."

"We've discussed this, Mum," Robin said. "Rydal is very expensive and a long way from our new home. They'd probably have to board, and I'm not having that."

"It never did you any harm," Christopher said, a comment met by weighted silence.

Robin had repeatedly turned down his father's offer of a loan to pay for private schools for the girls. "A loan from my parents is never interest-free," he'd told Nan.

As the silence dragged, Nan blurted, "I think boarding school is cruel, to be frank."

Prue checked her cuticles. "You're *always* frank, Nancy."

"But doesn't everyone speak *Welsh* up there, where you live now?" Robin's father said, before taking a pinch of snuff with smug satisfaction.

"Many people do, yes, but the girls will soon pick it up, I'm told," Nan said, trying to suppress the toxic shot of fear his question released.

"I think you're being rather over-optimistic, dear," Prue said, and Nan duly felt her cheery mood deflate like a punctured lilo. She knew just how Robin felt. Nothing she had ever done or could ever do would meet with her in-laws' approval, but today, she had dared to hope that simple kindness, plus the gorgeous bunch of scented stocks and garden centre voucher she had given them, would act as an emollient. Over a disgusting lunch of greasy fish and greasier chips, Nan listened to Robin's attempts to persuade his parents of the advantages of the move, but he sounded so weary, so half-hearted, he didn't even convince her, let alone his parents. When she went to sit on the twins' table to sort out a squabble, she could still hear their barbs, designed and guaranteed to cut to the quick:

"*Such an unusual place to move to. Why not somewhere nice like Cornwall?*"

"*At least you've held onto your job if you decide to come back, dear.*"

"*Is there much for* you *up there, compared to Cambridge?*"

And finally, Prue's coup de grâce:

"*I really don't think you'll meet the right kind of people up there.*"

"Mum, for goodness' sake, be *quiet*!" Robin said, squirming.

"Farmers and tradesmen, that's all you'll find, Robin," Christopher said. "When have you ever had any dealings with either of them? We've made sure you didn't, in fact."

"I can't accept that you really want to go and rough it in the hills, Robin," Prue said. "I think it's a fad, like all that drawing and painting you did for a while. Utterly silly."

Nan joined them again at this point to rescue him.

"Nancy, you will come back when you've got over this... *whim,* won't you?"

"Prue, please, the girls are listening," Nan hissed. "And it's not a whim."

Robin pulled out his phone and began scrolling. His approach to any challenge from his parents had always been to hide. Nan retreated to the ladies'. As she splashed cold water on her face and tried to stem her rising panic, she reminded herself that, for Christopher and Prue, having crème fraiche instead of custard with pudding was an act of anarchy, so what did she expect? They would certainly be worried about Robin's job, too, as their sense of achievement was firmly rooted in his.

"They're still arseholes," she muttered, heading back with a defiant smile.

"Right, time to go, I think," she said. "Thanks for everything. Girls, we're off!"

As the cars headed South and North respectively, the twins slumped in the back and put their headphones on. Robin gripped the wheel so tightly his knuckles were a livid white. Seeing his parents always led to emotional fallout.

"I've turned myself inside out over the years trying to please those two, but they *never* give me a break and probably never will. It's not my fault that Simon died, is it?"

Nan looked at him, shocked.

"No, it's not your fault, but your parents have a knack of making you feel bad if it suits them," she said. "At least they won't be coming to stay for a *very* long time, looking at the positives."

"Nan, stop it!" Robin shouted. "I know my parents' shortcomings better than anyone, but don't you realise that lots of people agree with them about what we're doing, what we've done? Everyone I know, in fact!"

Nan gaped at him. "What do you mean?"

"Look, your Cambridge yummy mummies may have told you that all you need is an Aga, a Cath Kidston tea towel and a big house by the sea to guarantee paradise, but I mix with people who make *sensible* decisions and do *sensible* things. I've agreed to this and we're doing it, but on paper, it's a pretty stupid thing to do. You might not get any freelance work, and the working at home arrangement might not work out. Not wanting to pour cold water on your dream, love, but have you actually *considered* that?"

"So that's what everyone else thinks, is it?" Nan said.

He sighed. "Yes, pretty much."

"Can't your parents just be supportive, and wish us well?"

"Like your mother you mean, the veritable Voice of Doom?"

They both had to laugh at this apt moniker, and Robin smiled sheepishly. "I'm sorry, love. You know nothing gets to me like they do when they're on the warpath. They're merciless."

"Then don't let them get to you anymore, Robin," Nan said. "Leave them behind."

"Oh Nansi Green, I only wish I could," he replied.

EIGHT

They reached *Coed Uchaf* just as the sun was starting to set behind the cliffs, a blaze of red, yellow and orange. The weather had obviously improved here during their miserable day on the road. Whorls of starlings swooped and billowed across the sky, preparing to roost for the night. Nan unlocked the farmhouse door and both girls stepped tentatively into the hallway.

"It smells in this house," Ceri said.

"And it's dark and spooky," Elin added.

"I don't like it," Elin said. "When can we go home?"

"This is home now. It's our brand-new home," Nan said.

No response.

"Is our puppy here?" Ceri said.

"Not yet, no. We're picking her up soon, when Daddy goes away to work."

Elin started crying. "I don't like it here without a puppy."

"Nor do I. I miss Zillah," Ceri said.

"I know, sweethearts," Nan said. "It's all so new. Let's get you a drink."

They were her absolute priority now, and they needed to

believe it was going to be fine, but inside, she was close to tears. Pouring their apple juice, a wave of doubt rose up inside her, so powerful it almost took her breath away. What if her carefree children were miserable here? Even worse, what if she had been wrong all these years, and hated it here herself? The deal was that she would be happy, and Robin would be free to come and go as he pleased; he had made this crystal clear. Could she actually pull this off on her own? She couldn't speak Welsh, looked and sounded as if she had beamed in from Venus and she had bought an enormous house with the profits from a very mediocre one down South. It did not bode well in so many ways.

As waves of panic washed over her, she was taken back to the last time she had made a huge move like this, to go up to Cambridge to read Archaeology and Anthropology on a scholarship she had been astounded to be awarded. She had unravelled in months. She'd missed deadlines, seminars, supervisions, meals and even doctor's appointments. Most of her calories were from the beer and wine she drank, without limit, until she could no longer feel anything.

By the end of her second year, she had lost a huge amount of weight and had only just scraped through her exams. Plagued with chronic anxiety, she ripped her cuticles raw during every conversation with her counsellor and did not leave her room for days at a time. Every sudden noise had made her shake, and if someone knocked at the door, she retreated behind the sofa, a place where she had spent many hours as a small child, hiding from her father. By the time Michaelmas term began in October, she was at such a low ebb that, at her tutor's suggestion, she decided to leave Cambridge, she had no other choice. But then she met Robin Green, and he had sorted everything out, helped her recover, *rescued* her. Gradually, with his help, she'd stopped using alcohol as an anaesthetic and only drank socially, normally, which really mattered to him. He told her he was proud of her, that she was a good person, neither of which she had ever been told before – and she believed him. They got married, he got a good job, and they bought a house. She'd found reasonably stress-free work editing archaeological papers and they had *built a life,* hadn't they? Yes, they had done all these things together, Nan and Robin, the dream team. This would work out too. Of course it would, she told herself over and over again. Slowly, her breathing calmed, her panic ebbed.

"And he's still here, with you, right now," she whispered. "Everything will be all right."

She carried a tray of juice and chocolate biscuits to the girls, and joined them on the sofa while Robin brought their luggage in. When they had both finished, she held them tightly, pushing her face into their hair to breathe them in.

Ceri pulled away first. "Ow, you're hurting me."

Elin followed. "What's the matter, Mummy? You look sad."

"I'm fine – just really tired. We've been so busy, sorting everything out..."

"But we're happy that you're both here with us at last!" Robin said, coming in laden with soft toys and suitcases. "Poor old Mum's worked so hard, getting your room ready – why don't we go and see it together?" Both girls jumped up. "Sorry about shouting in the car," he mouthed. "Bit stressed."

"I know. Me too," she mouthed back.

There would be plenty more naysayers and setbacks ahead, so she had to toughen up, she knew, but self-belief was a new habit and self-blame, such an old, familiar one. They would make this work together, as a loving family – something she had never had as a child.

"Right, let's explore our new home, shall we?" she said. "There's so much to show you."

"You go up first, you two. Check out the view from your window," Robin said. "This house is going to be fantastic when we've finished it, I promise you."

"And we keep our promises, don't we?' Nan said, winking. "Including puppies."

Taking each other's hand, they followed their children's excited laughter up the stairs.

NINE

A taxi arrived to take Robin to Bangor station at 5.30am the following Monday for his first working week back in Cambridge. He was ready to leave, Nan knew. He had paced the rooms in *Coed Uchaf* for the past few days, glaring at the endless-seeming rain as if it was a personal slight and snapping at Nan and the girls. He had gone out on his own a couple of afternoons, too, saying he needed "space to breathe", but had seemed even more tense when he returned. So when Nan heard the taxi drive away, and it hit her that she would be completely on her own until Friday evening, she did not panic. Instead, she repeated one of her favourite affirmations before turning over and going straight back to sleep:

"I can do this."

Two hours later, the twins bounced into her room, their excited chatter of one thing only: their new puppy! They had decided to call her Shadow, because Nan had read them Enid Blyton's *Shadow the Sheepdog* so many times, telling them that this book, and that dog, had given her such joy as a child. They had all wept together at the sad bits.

"What time are we getting Shadow?" Elin asked.

"Can we go now, Mummy?" her sister added, eyes alight.

"We'll go at midday, 12 o'clock, OK? First, we'd better get a few things... including lots of newspaper."

"Yes! For all her wees!" the twins chorused, dashing off to get dressed.

Scaffolding already surrounded the house, ready for the roofers to come next week, and more builders were due to start inside. All this would be hard enough, but trying to train a puppy would make it even harder, especially if they couldn't let her outside safely, but Nan had promised the girls a dog. Shadow would be a "new girl" too, a faithful friend through the huge changes that lay ahead for them, cast adrift from all they knew. Perhaps it would reassure them that all the other things Mummy had said about their wonderful new life would come true as well; there had already been disappointments.

The days before Robin left had not been easy, chiefly because he had been so irritable and on edge. Promised fun days on the beach had become wet walks in dripping cagoules and a much-hyped trip to see Uncle Dewi was a disaster as he said the ground was too wet to take the girls for a tractor ride. Fang had also gone AWOL, which led to much wailing. As the twins gobbled breakfast, Nan rang Dewi for some advice about puppies, surprised to find him still at home at 9am. He sounded breathless and tired, which worried her. Why wasn't he out in the fields, or the barn? This kind man had been such an anchor in her troubled childhood, and she needed him to be that now, just as much as she had then. His words were always few, but always golden.

"Don't worry, *cariad*/love. A dog is a gift, one you won't regret giving to your children. And a Welsh collie? The best dogs in the world, full of love and loyalty," he said. "Enjoy every minute... but prepare for puddles!"

The rain had stopped by the time they left, and both girls tilted their faces up at the sky before getting into the car. When

Nan looked up, she saw why: the blanketing grey clouds that had spread across the sky for days were being slowly shunted to one side like a tide of grubby water as they watched. Sunshine spread across the ground like a golden tide, and when it hit *Coed Uchaf*, both girls closed their eyes in silent worship. Foot by foot, the whole, wide bay was illuminated, and the vivid greens, blues and yellows of Anglesey returned like one of the "magic" books Nan painted with a watery brush as a child. It was one of the most beautiful things she had ever seen.

"Can we take Shadow to the beach later, Mummy?" Elin whispered. "It's sunny now."

"Yes, we can, but she can't go on the ground until she's had her last jab next week, so we'll have to carry her today," Nan replied. "Are you excited?"

"This much," Ceri said, flinging her arms as far apart as possible.

"Me too," Nan replied. And she was.

In the car, she put on a Gypsy Kings album, and as 'Volare' filled the car, all three of them sang along at the tops of their voices.

"Daddy would say 'turn that racket off', Mummy," Elin shouted.

"He would indeed," her mother said, turning it up.

* * *

Growing up in a household in which any display of affection was actively discouraged, Nan had yearned for a puppy so much that the pain of repeated disappointment felt like a wound that never healed. At the top of her Christmas list, she had written, every single year, "MY OWN DOG", but her father refused to consider it, even when Eira dared to ask him to, because Nan's disappointment was always so heartbreaking.

So, when Shadow arrived at *Coed Uchaf*, Nan felt another

missing piece of her childhood gently slot into place. The pup's warm little body seemed to *belong* curled-up in the crook of her arm or squeezed into the space between the twins' chubby thighs on the sofa. From the very first day, "taking Shadow out" gave a structure to each day, and saved them when they knew nobody, had no plans and nowhere to go. Yes, there were plenty of puddles and poohs, but nobody cared much, and the twins soon became adept at mopping them up.

"She's done another one!" one of them would cry. "Bring the paper and the spray!"

The young collie loved all of them immediately, unquestioningly, and Nan saw more empathy in her liquid brown eyes than she had ever seen in a person. People coaxed you into trusting them before betraying you, or lulled you into believing you mattered, when you didn't, but there was no deceit with a dog: Shadow knew when one of them was happy and rejoiced with frantic tail-wagging. When they were sad, or needed reassurance, her warm, wet nose offered comfort. She accepted how they were, however they were – and everywhere they went, she went too.

They saw nobody except Dewi (who was too busy to be visited often), Mike the postman (rarely, as they had very little mail) and Tony, the cashier on the till in the friendly little supermarket in Menai Bridge (who usually made the twins' day with a wink and a smile). The roofers, Dafydd and Adrian, started work and crashed and clattered on the roof, but they were far from chatty. Nobody called in as *Coed Uchaf* had no immediate neighbours, and Nan knew nobody to call on. She hesitated to ring her friends in Cambridge; they didn't want to hear that she missed the cheese stall in the market a bit, and a bloody good coffee a lot, but that she did not miss *them*. Each day here had its own rhythm, so different from the city, that they would not understand the trivia that mattered now – sighting a seal, watching a heron fishing at the shoreline or finding a whole white sea urchin shell on the sand. Each day held a gem, a small kernel of beauty, and each day was enough in itself.

Nan started telling the girls a story based on something that had happened in their day before they went to sleep each night, which she hoped would help these memories stick. The events she chose were not playdates, gym classes or face-painting parties, but ones that were of value, parts of their new life. Each story was a blaze of fantasy that reflected the places and events that had punctuated it, which made the girls feel what they had done was worthwhile. One night, when all of them felt especially low and lonely, she made up a story about one of the "giantesses" who, legends say, had created the stone burial mound on the headland near *Coed Uchaf* by dropping rocks from their aprons. It was a tale that had always fascinated the girls, so she knew they would welcome her revisiting it.

"Once upon a time, long, long ago, a giantess lived here, all alone. She had only the birds for company and longed for a friend to share her joys and sorrows with."

"We don't have any friends here either, Mum, do we?" Ceri said quietly.

"No, but you will, love... Listen."

"Each morning, the giantess walked along clifftops and strode across the beaches, but she saw nobody and nobody saw her. When she reached the burial chamber, she saw the way the stones had been dragged to the very top of the hill and put one on top of the other so that everyone could see them. The giantess looked around her, then began to collect rocks from the hill and from the shore as she walked alone each day. She laid them one on top of the other, carefully, slowly, never letting one fall."

"What was she building, Mum?" Elin asked, eyes wide.

"Wait and see."

"After many days, the giantess looked at her work, a wide, strong tower of rocks almost as tall as her. It had rock 'feet', drift-

wood 'arms' and a huge rock 'head'. She draped strands of seaweed over it to make hair, and wrapped sacking all around the body. Then she found some white pebbles for eyes, some shells for ears and a smooth red stone for a mouth. Finally, the giantess stood back and looked at what she had made."

"Can you guess what it was, girls?"

"A friend! She'd made herself a *friend*!!" both twins chorused.

"Yes, she had a friend who was always strong and true, like a real friend should be – and just like all the friends you're going to make."

Both girls snuggled into her.

"Oh, and of course... *she lived happily ever after*."

* * *

At the very end of each day, when the twins were asleep, came the time Nan pulled towards. If it was dry, she sat outside on the slate bench listening to the seabirds, with a glass of chilled white wine and Shadow at her feet. If it was wet, she sat next to the Aga, and warmed her feet on its constant warmth. This was the only time during the day when she took Dewi's advice and asked herself why she had come here, and her answer came a little more into focus every day before vanishing again in the daily struggle. Breathing in time with the beat of each wave on the shore, she reminded herself that she had come to this place to find the Nan she had been when she was here before, and so wanted to be again. A woman with hopes and dreams. A woman who believed in herself.

TEN

For weeks, life happened largely without Robin, and without Daddy. Coming home late on a Friday to go back on Sunday evening was "just not feasible" after a week or two, he told Nan. The trains were so unreliable and expensive, and James wanted him on hand. He rang each evening at around 9pm, long after the twins were asleep, and she looked forward to hearing his voice, but as soon as she did, her resentment flared. Their conversations always began with news of his stressful day and how hard he was working. Then he told her about the thriving Cambridge folk scene a friend had introduced him to and how much he loved it. Nan could sometimes hear music billowing out around him, people laughing and the clink of glasses.

"Someone from work, is he, this folky friend?" Nan asked, trying to sound interested.

"Just someone I met, out and about," Robin said quickly. "I never liked 'folk people' before. Everyone seemed so *hairy*, but it's great, energising – especially the Celtic stuff."

"You could listen to plenty of that at home, Robin," she muttered.

Far from missing his family, he seemed to be actively

enjoying himself, whereas Nan had not seen a living soul all day. As the weeks passed, the nightly phone call became an exercise in mutual blame. Things reached a head one Wednesday evening.

"So, how was *your* day?" Robin asked, after a detailed monologue about his.

"OK, the usual stuff. We made chocolate crispie cakes, walked Shadow. Still no sign of Fang. All the other kids are still in school up here, so the girls are a bit lonely."

"They'll be fine. Is the roof nearly done?"

"Yes, I think so. I don't talk to the men much, but they seem to be working hard."

"Good. It's costing enough. Did you ring the other builders, and check their start date?"

"Next week, probably, but they couldn't commit."

"Typical. Well, when I'm back, I can put a bomb under them."

"And when will that be? It'd be nice to have an extra pair of hands around with the kids."

"I know, but I do have to work, Nan. You aren't earning a penny, remember?"

"Yes, I know, Robin. That's what we agreed."

"How are the girls... *really*, I mean?"

"Oh, they have their moments, squabble quite a lot, but getting a dog was definitely a good move."

"That's lucky then." A pause. "You sound shattered."

"I am. It's a long day on your own." More silence where sympathy could have been.

"You said you'd be OK with it, Nan, remember? Oh, work are going to pay all my rental expenses, did I tell you?"

"Great. You'll be able to eat out even more."

A sigh. A tut-tut.

"Look, Nan, I hear the passive aggression, but I'm needed here. This is my career."

Nan could not control herself any longer. "Has James moved the goalposts then? This is not what he agreed, or what we agreed, Robin."

"Nan, you knew it would be tricky, and it's early days. Can't you just enjoy *being there*? It's all you've wanted for years, or so you told me!"

Tears suddenly started rolling down her cheeks. She was thankful they were silent.

"Sorry, yes, yes, I am, it's just I feel a bit, you know, a bit overwhelmed," she said. "I thought I might ask Rhian to come over and clean for me once a week when the twins start school. It's such a big house, and it would mean I could get out a bit more, meet people."

"Oh, I think she's left the island," Robin said. "Yeah, I'm sure somebody told me that. I've stopped paying her anyway..."

Nan was shocked. "Really? Dewi didn't tell me. That's a shame – her leaving, I mean. I remember her telling me that her sister had broken their mother's heart by leaving the island a few years ago, poor woman. Where did she go, do you know?"

"Nan, how on earth would I know and why on earth would I care?" Robin said. "She was a teenager who cleaned, badly, for your uncle and clearly needed to get away."

"Calm down, mate," Nan replied. "I just think she's so young to have left home on her own, that's all. Imagine if it was one of ours?"

"Of course, but she's not, so why are we talking about her?" he snapped. "You can find someone else to clean for you, and I'm more worried about the fact that you're clearly not coping. I know the signs, Nan. Perhaps you need some *help* again – professional help."

"Don't put that pressure on me, Robin. I think I'm lonely, that's all."

He sighed. "We'll talk more when I'm back, OK? Right, I'm home now. Sleep tight."

Nan heard him put a key in a door and hang up. Filling her wine glass to the brim, she replayed their conversation. Robin had just called his Airbnb place *"home"*. And he sounded so much happier, lighter of mood and dismissive of how she felt. Something else swam under the surface of their conversation too, and a ripple of unease stirred inside her. Feeling as if she could hardly breathe, she inhaled so sharply that Shadow looked up, her brown eyes full of concern, and Nan felt the first waves of panic. She had been out of its grip for a few weeks, and dared to hope she had left it behind, but soon her heart began to pound and her fingertips started to tingle and numb. Pulling Shadow clumsily onto her lap she clutched the little dog as if her life depended on it; because at that moment, it did.

Slow, deep breathing was the best way to dispel panic, she knew, but it already had a grip on her, so she squeezed Shadow so tightly that she yelped in pain. Slow minutes dragged as, eyes closed, her focus stayed on each breath until, at last, she felt her heart rate begin to calm and became aware of the gentle pulse of the sea. A shrill cry rang out – a seagull, soaring high on warm thermals, joyous and free in the dying light. Opening her eyes one at a time, she took one more deep breath... and knew it had gone. She drained her wine glass in one.

"Oh hell," she said. "But what did I expect, Shadow? I only told him the bad stuff, not that I sit here and watch the sun set over the sea every evening, or that the girls found a big shrimp in the rock pools and named it 'Daddy Shrimp'?" The little dog licked her hand.

She watched as the last glow of the sun vanished below the horizon and the swallows looped around the farmhouse eaves. The main, unspoken condition of their deal had been that she was happy, at all times.

"I broke the code," she murmured, stroking Shadow's soft head. "I should know better than anyone, never, ever to do that."

ELEVEN

Just as Nan was beginning to think they were condemned to social isolation forever, the slightly surreal kaleidoscope of her life on the island shifted, and a new pattern formed.

It began on a Saturday morning in late July, a month after their arrival on Anglesey. Hot sun blazed through Nan's bedroom window, and there was the unmistakeable sweet-sour tang of wet seaweed in the air. It was going to be a perfect summer's day and yet something was different, something *sounded* different. The twins were still in bed, playing and giggling as they had never been able to do in Cambridge, when even Saturday mornings were not free time as they had a gym session to go to. After weeks without any contact with other children, they had got used to these easy, aimless mornings, but the low hum that Nan could hear today was not their usual chatter – it was something else. When she went downstairs and pulled up the kitchen blind, she stopped and stared: there were at least a dozen cars in the car park below the house and several encampments of windbreaks and picnic blankets already on the beach. The twins had not been to school for so long she barely knew what day of the week it was anymore, but she realised that the schools must have broken up for the summer. These families were here *on holiday,* as *they* used to be in their previous life.

She listened carefully. Hearing voices, *other* voices, with far from local accents, sent an initial flutter of alarm through her body: these people were invading what had been almost solely their space for so long. But within a minute, relief washed over her; she and the girls were no longer living in a lonely slipstream, they had finally rejoined the annual rhythm of other children.

"Thank goodness!" she said, calling upstairs. "Girls – other kids are on holiday now too!"

She punched the air in celebration. If there were other children here, perhaps she could persuade them to play with Ceri and Elin. Nan knew that they were resigned to being on their own all day every day, but they were far from happy. Their quarrels were more frequent and their tendency to miss what they had left behind, more heartbreaking. They refused to talk about the "new school" they would join in a few weeks' time, no matter how many encouraging tales she told them, and learning some very simple Welsh words on the online course Nan had bought in Cambridge was no longer a fun thing to do together. No, they only wanted to ring their beloved childminder, Zillah, (who did not know what to say to them); old nursery friends (who had moved on to new pals already) or, occasionally, Daddy, (who couldn't take their calls at work). Nan's heart ached that they were so confused about what had been done to them.

"Why can't we talk to Daddy?" Ceri said, when she reached Robin's voicemail yet again.

"He never rings until we're asleep."

"And why isn't he here?" Elin added. "He's s'posed to be."

"He's in Cambridge, for work," Nan would answer.

"So does he still live *there*?"

"If he does, he's lucky. Not like us, living here," Ceri muttered.

"I wish we still lived in Cambridge."

"I wish Daddy was here now. He would sort things out."

"He'll be back as soon as he's finished some important work."

"More important than us?" Elin asked, which brought a huge lump to Nan's throat.

"Has Fang gone back to our old house? I know cats do that sometimes."

"I wish we could."

"Me too. I hate it here."

And so it went on. Nan had decided not to respond after a certain point. She could not undo what had been done, so there was no point in pretending otherwise. Worryingly, she found that her children's distress guttered and died far quicker than hers did, and knew that, if nothing changed soon, she would have to see a GP. Even the thought made her stomach clench as if she had been punched. Would she never be able to leave her anxiety behind – slough it off like an outgrown skin – not even here?

"Can we get another cat?" Elin asked.

"We do need one... but Dad isn't keen on pets, girls."

"But they catch mice and there are mice in this house! Can we get one? *Please.*"

"We'll see," Nan replied.

"That means 'no'," Elin whispered.

"It means I'm not going to make you a promise I can't keep," Nan said with a sad smile.

* * *

She took the girls down onto the beach several times in the first week of the school holidays, setting up camp in the softer sand below the headland. She encouraged, cajoled and all-but bribed them with ice cream, but they refused to approach any of the other children... and she knew why. Many were playing in the shallows (often with their dads) or digging sandcastles with siblings or friends whilst their mums sunbathed and read celebrity gossip magazines behind their windbreakers. There were several groups of local, Welsh-speaking mums among the tourists, taking turns to mind their school-age children in the sea while the others entertained the babies and toddlers and distributed food. She noticed one young man who always sat on his own on a rock at the edge of the beach as his daughter shuttled between him and the local kids, but nobody acknowledged him. Nan saw her girls catch this child's eye, cautiously, quietly, as another outsider, and inch a little nearer, but she was always dragged away to play or paddle with the others before they could speak to her.

When the weather changed, as it did in the blink of an eye on the island, the beach was not an option. One gloomy, wet afternoon, the twins quarrelled for hours on end and Nan wept that the happy, outgoing children she had brought from Cambridge seemed so cowed after weeks of isolation. When she heard Ceri yell at her sister:

"I bet Daddy doesn't come home anymore because of *you!*" she decided to act.

First, she rang Robin's office saying it was "urgent", which alerted the receptionist and forced him to take the call. Then she told him that his daughters were missing him so much that they were miserable, which softened him (and distanced the issue from her seeming "weakness"). Then she added that the builders had *promised* to start the kitchen next Monday, but that he needed be here to nudge as "only he could", or they might take longer than necessary. This was enough to get him to agree to ask James for some leave; he would ring her with a decision within an hour. In the interim, Nan rang Dewi.

"Dewi, I need you to make sure Aled and Gethin *do* start next Monday because I've told Robin he has to come home to supervise," she blurted. "It sounds daft, I know, but..."

"He won't come home, otherwise? Novelty worn off already?"

"It's difficult, Dewi. For both of us." A pause. "Will you help?"

"*Wrth gwrs*/Of course. Leave it with me. Aled and Gethin will start on Monday. You have my word."

She blew a kiss into the phone and hung up. Within five minutes, Robin rang back.

"James has agreed, as you say it's so vital that I'm there," he said. "But I can't be pulling stunts like this every time you have a wobble, Nan. I know that's at the root of this."

Nan stopped herself from telling him to jog on and called upstairs to the girls.

"Guess what? Daddy's coming home on Friday!"

"Oh. How many sleeps is it until Friday?" Elin said.

"Only two. Isn't that amazing?" Nan replied.

Ceri put her book down and looked at her mother. "But will he bring Zillah with him?"

"No, love, not this time."

A pause. "Then I don't really care," Ceri said.

But on Friday evening, when a taxi pulled up outside *Coed Uchaf*, the twins ran out to greet their daddy, and he swept them up as they squealed with delight. Nan stood in the doorway, hands on hips, trying not to feel aggrieved that Robin's prolonged, neglectful absence was so quickly forgiven by his children. She would not be as malleable, no way. She was still very pissed off *indeed*. And yet when he put the twins down and she saw his expectant face, she ran into his arms just as gleefully as they had.

* * *

Getting a builder who would commit to the job proved incredibly difficult. When, after about ten polite and not-so-polite refusals, Robin had agreed to ask Dewi for advice. He had recommended Aled Pritchard and his son Gethin, but there was a huge drawback, he said.

"Best on the island they are. Skilled craftsmen. They're not so good on *timing*, though," he said. "He was late for his own wedding, Aled – thought it was the following week and had to be hauled out of the pub. He got dressed in the car."

So Nan had little faith in them turning up, whether Dewi had prodded them or not, and she knew she would pay for it if she'd hauled Robin back from Cambridge for nothing. When she heard their ancient-looking van creaking into the farmyard at 7.30am on Monday morning, she leapt out of bed in delight. Robin let them in, wearing only his dressing gown, but when she suggested making everyone a cup of tea in *her* dressing gown, he was horrified.

"Nan, please," he hissed.

"Robin, I don't think Mike the postie's ever seen me dressed, but he doesn't bat an eyelid!"

She deftly dodged the slipper he threw at her and pulled on her clothes, grinning.

To Nan's enormous relief, Robin and Aled soon established what her husband called "an intuitive working relationship". This translated into Aled effectively bombarding Robin with incomprehensible information about "RSJs", "lime mortar" and "sheep's wool insulation" which her husband had to pretend to understand, lest he lose face, but actually had to google later. This all served to convince Robin that Aled "really knew his stuff", which meant that he and his lovely son were given free rein and the family could actually have a holiday together in their new home.

Each day now began early, as Aled and Gethin always arrived by 8am, so she planned a full day's activities for them all. They walked along beaches peppered with shells and starfish and used their well-worn *Usborne Spotter's Guide* to identify the contents of a myriad different rock pools. The twins were happy to have *their* daddy next to them in the shallows, or playing catch, all four of them, like all the other families, but they still stayed away from the other children as if they were of a different species, which worried Nan enormously.

* * *

For the rest of her life, Nan would look back on one sunny afternoon, a time when her life changed direction completely, without her even realising it. It was the first time she'd really *noticed* Harri, and it was Robin who had made it come about.

"Seen that chap over there on his tod?" Robin said, squinting at her as he had forgotten his Ray-Bans. "He hasn't moved an inch from that rock for hours. If he hadn't got that little girl with him, I'd be a bit worried about whether he's a bit, you know, *dodgy.*"

Nan glanced over at the man, sitting right at the edge of the beach, as he always did.

"Yes, I see him. He's been here most fine days since term ended. His daughter must be in nursery with the others, I guess, so he comes along for her to play with them, but the other mums don't speak to him," Nan said. "He doesn't look dodgy to me – just sad."

"Must be a story there. Loners like that usually have a past, don't they? Gorgeous blonde curls his little girl has, though."

"I know what you mean. Pretty little thing, and she seems very popular too, but her dad looks... *lost,* though he must live locally as he's always around."

"I'd say he looks decidedly weird."

"You really are your mother's son, judging everyone before you even give them a chance."

But when Robin went to paddle with the twins, she looked at the man again, more closely. He was probably only around her age, she decided, but his face told of hardships, and his skin of being outside in the sun, wind and rain more than inside, in comfort. Yes, to Robin, in his smart chinos, leather deck shoes and pink shirt, this man's ponytail, lumberjack shirt and cut-off jean shorts probably would look "weird", but she sensed an aura of such deep sorrow around him that it was almost palpable.

"I know how you feel, lonely man," she murmured. "Perhaps I can help."

When Robin called her to look at the castle that he and the twins had built, Nan saw the man get up to leave, hand in hand with his daughter. She waved shyly, but although she was sure he had seen her, he walked off the beach with his daughter without acknowledging her. Nan was surprised by how much this hurt her feelings.

TWELVE

That time with Robin at home with them all was the happiest Nan could remember for a very long time. He seemed totally present and didn't vanish for mysterious afternoons or skulk in corners on his phone. As each, relaxed, day passed, Nan felt her anxiety level ebb as she allowed herself to accept that she was not the one solely responsible for her children's happiness. She began to hope that Robin shared her relief, her joy at their little family being together again. He seemed to be relishing spending time in the beautiful part of the country they now lived in...

"Are you glad to be here, love?" she asked him one evening, as they watched the sun set below *Coed Uchaf* together. "It's fabulous to be sharing this with you."

Her husband hesitated, then frowned slightly. "Yes, I am glad to have been able to bring you here, to give you this, Nan. I only hope it makes you happy."

"Well, that's not the answer I was hoping for," she spluttered. "Sounds pretty lukewarm on the commitment stakes too. Crikey!"

Robin took her hand and looked at her kindly. "Nan, listen, we've been through a lot together, and doing this was a huge leap of faith on my part – and I did it mainly for you." His voice was soft but edged with resolve. "I'm just not as sure as you are, because, perhaps, your dream will never be my dream. But I'm trying my best to make it work. That's all I can do."

She nodded but said nothing and they watched the sun disappear in companionable silence.

* * *

One gloriously sunny day towards the end of Robin's time at home, they drove into Snowdonia, walked up into the mountains and round Lake Ogwen. The girls gamely picked their way over the rockier parts of the path and revelled in dipping their toes in the icy water before running away shrieking when Nan warned them of monsters in the depths. They picnicked on a grassy ridge, eating their sandwiches with a breathtaking view towards Anglesey. To Nan's surprise, Robin had drunk several glasses of red by the time they had finished eating, but as it only seemed to make him mellow, she said nothing, telling herself that he was on holiday, and had a very stressful job. He started to explain the formation of the magnificent glacial valley in front of them as she cleared away, and soon the twins were rapt. This was how he showed his love for them, she knew, and it moved her.

"Can you imagine a mountain of ice moving very, very slowly downhill in front of us, pushing everything out of its way, even trees and big boulders?"

Both girls looked ahead, and then shook their heads.

"Try imagining a massive white tongue made of ice, as wide as this scooped-out valley in front of you. As it pushed its way to the sea, it carved this valley out of solid rock."

Both girls stared at him, eyes wide.

"The ice went right down the middle!" Ceri added.

"I can see where it went!" Elin cried, "The big ice tongue!"

"Amazing, isn't it?" Nan said.

The girls nodded and scampered off with Shadow tugging on the lead. Robin snuggled up to her on the picnic blanket, but she edged away a little. This was not the time or the place for *that.* He was trying too hard, and it felt forced, silly.

"This is what you wanted, isn't it?" he said, nuzzling into her neck, with winey breath.

"Days like this are what I imagined, yes," she said.

"I think it's all going pretty well so far, this great dream of yours," Robin said. She could hear his breathing quickening, and his hands were on the move.

"Robin, behave," she said, slapping one of them gently. "But I'm glad you feel the whole move thing was a good idea today. Perhaps we can share the dream, after all?"

"Well, it has its downsides. The commute's a bit long, and I do miss the girls, you know."

"I know, but now you're here, it's fabulous. They are so glad you're home." She sighed and picked some crumbs off her trousers. "It's not all roses for me either. Guess I didn't factor in how lonely it is being a single parent most of the time. I feel like that sad guy on the beach sometimes – makes me want to tear my hair out. It would be much better if you were here more, like now. Is there no way you can swing it?"

She knew immediately that she had made a grave mistake.

"And that is *exactly* what I was worried about," he snapped. "That you'd be lonely, miss your friends and put pressure on me to be here all the time. I *told* you all this before we came, but you said you'd be fine with me being away if I had to be, remember?"

Nan cursed herself. She had to remember to go slowly, gently, in persuading him to do anything.

"I'm sorry, Robin. Let's just enjoy today. We're all here together now, and I think it just made me feel, well, super-emotional," she said, grabbing his hand.

"I have to go back to Cambridge soon, Nan. You know that."

She put her finger on his lips to silence him.

"I know. I'm sorry, love," she said. "I'm fine really. It's early days, after all."

Cramming a whole biscuit into his mouth, he chewed angrily. "Try to think how I feel, when you say these things, please," he said.

Didn't he never feel lonely or have doubts? Nan wondered. He would never admit it or talk about his worries or problems if he did, he never had, and it seemed clear she was not really permitted to either.

"Let's forget it. I'll have a beautiful new kitchen soon and two kids to get ready to start school and then I'll meet new friends."

He nodded. They were back on safe ground. "Agreed."

She leant over to kiss him. "I just miss you so much and wish you were here more."

When he did not reply, she wished with all her heart he'd said that he missed her too.

* * *

The twins grieved for Robin when he left to return to work in Cambridge, and, finally, for the life they had lost. They refused to talk to him when he made the effort to ring from his office before their bedtime. They stopped asking to speak to Zillah, or their other little friends. Nan knew that they understood that this new reality was permanent. They were not going back to their old home, Portugal Street, with Daddy, they were staying here on Anglesey with Mummy and it was *horrible.* Nan rang Dewi and begged him to come for supper one evening to cheer them up, as she could no longer bear their misery alone. He agreed, with only momentary hesitation.

"It'll be... difficult, coming to that house again, but I'll be there," he said. "It has history for our family, as I've told you."

"Yes, but you'll never tell me what that history is!"

"Some secrets are best left unshared, Nansi," the old man replied.

"Oh, I am so tired of hearing that!" she snapped, mumbling a guilty "sorry" when his silence told her that he was hurt.

* * *

But when he arrived, he was as garrulous as ever, and everyone's spirits lifted the moment he came through the door with gifts of blackcurrants from the farm garden and a dozen smooth, brown eggs. Ceri and Elin scrambled up onto the old man's knee as Nan had done as a child and kissed his bristly cheeks or let him blow raspberries on theirs. The kitchen was still a work in progress, but the Aga made it wonderfully cosy.

"You kept the old range as well as installing an Aga?" Dewi asked.

"It doesn't work anymore, but I couldn't bring myself to scrap it – it's such a beautiful thing, and the room's big enough. I'll find someone who can restore its outside at least," Nan replied. "I remember sitting near it when Mum and I came, when it was blasting out warmth and comfort..."

"I remember," the old farmer said. "I knew Tomos, who farmed this land, as you know. *Duw*/God, he worked hard, but he was never the same once he lost his boys."

"I know," Nan said, suddenly alert. Was she finally going to find out more about her mother and her old friend Annie, and why they had lost touch for so long?

"Ah, this place was a farm to be proud of when things were good for them."

"Mum was good friends with his wife, but something went

wrong, didn't it?" Nan said tentatively. "What happened between them, Dewi? I really need to know."

The old man slurped his tea. "I'll say only this. They fell out over a man that wasn't worth falling out over. If you want to know more, ask Eira."

"Perhaps I will, if she ever comes to visit," Nan replied more sharply than she had intended. "She says she can't stay with us. Well, she *won't*."

"I've told you before: a long, bitter history and plenty of tragedy to season it. You'll find out when the time's right, but it's not my business, so I'm minding my own." He smiled at her, his eyes lost in the spidering lines around them. He looked tired, and old... his cheekbones were now so prominent that it was clear he had lost a lot of weight.

"You are annoying when you go all mysterious on me, Dewi," she said, laughing.

She had gone to a lot of trouble to source locally sourced food for their supper, as she knew Dewi had little time for "the food barons" as he called the supermarkets. They ate shepherd's pie with minced lamb from the fantastic butcher in Menai Bridge, drank lemonade from the farm shop in Brynsiencyn and finished their meal with a delicious gold-leaf topped cake from Melin Llynon, the wonderful bakery Nan had discovered on the other side of the island. He grunted at the frozen peas she served, but she told him that the farm shop had run out of vegetables by the time she got to it.

"One sad cabbage was the only thing left, and it had seen better days," she said.

"They need to plant more, and rotate their crops," Dewi said. "Everyone needs veg."

After supper, the old man regaled the girls with tales about the naughty things he and their grandmother had got up to at their age and they laughed uproariously at the picture of them both running home naked from the beach when their clothes had been taken by an unexpectedly high tide. Once every mouthful of "the amazing golden cake" was gone, they ran happily outside to throw a ball for Shadow.

"Thank you so much for coming today. The girls haven't laughed like that for ages. You made *Coed Uchaf* feel like a real *home*."

Dewi shuffled in his seat. "It always was a home, Nansi. Tomos and Annie Hughes' home and, at one time, their two boys' home too." He got up slowly and headed for the bathroom.

Nan suddenly felt the prick of tears. Did he think she had done a bad thing, moving here? Did he see her as another greedy incomer, exploiting the relative poverty of North Wales to buy properties for a fraction of what they cost in the South East? She was glad of a few minutes alone before Dewi returned, as she felt wrong-footed, somehow. She had to understand what he'd said, know what he meant. The only way was to ask him directly, something she always tended to avoid if it was avoidable, a lesson learnt from childhood. But she did it anyway.

"Dewi, do you think Tomos would be glad that I watched him plough his fields when I was a little girl, and that being on Anglesey was the happiest time of my life?" she began, trying to hold back her tears. "Would he be happy to know that I've waited since then to make this house my home, do you think – because that's the truth?"

The old man laid one of his calloused hands on top of hers. "I think he would, yes. And neither Tomos nor I would want you to feel guilty about being here. Annie and Eira have their own tangle to unravel and what happened to this family was... well, there are no words, but he would be happy that you love the place as he did."

Nan smiled. "Would he be happy that a new family lives here, do you think?"

"He would, because you will love it and your girls will love it," he replied. "Not sure about Robin, to tell you the truth. I'm still not convinced, but I'm still hoping."

"It's hard for him, being between two worlds at the moment," Nan said.

"That's his choice," the old man said. "But for you, it's different. This island is in your blood. Your mum was born here, and she was Annie's friend, so it's like closing a circle, your living in *Coed Uchaf*."

"I wish Mum could only pluck up the courage to go and see her, Dewi. I know they quarrelled, but that day, when we came here, they seemed to have put it behind them. I can't stop thinking about it."

The old man sighed deeply. "The tentacles of the past reach a long, long way, Nan, and things you think are finished, often aren't," he replied, leaning close enough to her that she could smell the farm on his old clothes and in his hair. "You'll learn that in time."

"I guess so, but I feel there is unfinished business between Mum and this house, and I hate that," Nan said, feeling her eyes fill with tears.

"Try not to worry about battles that were never yours. You are one of us and you belong here in this house because you love it, so don't you ever doubt that," he replied. "You will fill the place with memories, and with the laughter of children. That can only be good."

Nan finally let the tears trickle down her face. "Thank you," she managed to say.

"Not sure what Tomos would think about the colour you've painted this kitchen, though," Dewi said, chuckling. "Looks like porridge."

THIRTEEN

The builders, Aled and Gethin Pritchard, soon became honorary members of the Green family as they sawed, screwed, cemented and hammered Nan's new kitchen into being. The twins, desperate for company, adored them immediately, and by the end of one working day, it was mutual. In the few hours they'd waited for the slate worktop to be delivered, Aled built a simple double rope swing for the girls, sanded silky-smooth "in case of splinters in your bums", and hung it from the large sycamore in the garden of *Coed Uchaf*. The girls loved kicking their heels to and fro for hours every day, watching the holiday-makers on the beach below as they flew above them. Gethin stayed late one evening and restored the range to its black and polished glory because "it deserved it". On their last day, they arrived with two beautiful wooden pencil boxes, with the girls' names carved into the lids "ready for school", but Nan saw a flicker of fear on both their faces. They were dreading it.

Although her daughters would soon be starting at the local primary in Rhosneigr, she had done nothing whatsoever in preparation, as neither child had wanted to think, let alone talk about it. Cambridge friends had plastered Facebook with their kids in pristine uniforms, beaming gappy smiles of excitement. Now, it had to be faced. Bribing hers with the promise of a McDonalds, she took them to Bangor to buy school shoes and uniforms.

"Will our ooniform be like Harriet's?" Ceri asked in the car. "She has a hat."

"No, sweetie. Harriet's going to a very expensive school in Cambridge. Do you remember which school you and Elin are going to?"

Ceri shook her head. "I only remember it has a stupid name that I can't even say."

"But you'll be learning Welsh soon, so you'll be able to say the name easily."

"I don't want to learn Welsh!" Elin said. "The words sounded stupid when we tried them on the laptop, and I can talk English already."

"You'll be fine," Nan replied. "Remember how much fun it was, learning those lovely-sounding words? And I met your new headteacher, who's *so* nice."

As they drove, Nan remembered sitting in a warm school office sipping tea as she was told about the education policy that would see her daughters taught almost solely in Welsh. It had sounded amazing, a real gift, as learning a second language was good for the brain. The teachers could always resort to English if needs be she had told herself. She'd gone home and immediately ordered a "*Teach yourself Welsh*" online course and they all had a happy evening or two sitting around their dining table in Portugal Street laughing at the cartoon heads saying words crammed with consonants and strange spitting sounds. Ceri loved the fact that "*hâf braf*" meant "lovely sunny summer" and Elin cackled at "*sglodion*", for "chips". Nan suddenly recalled odd words from childhood holidays on Anglesey – Uncle Dewi's expletives and Aunty Manon's soft words of kindness – she also remembered how musical this ancient language was, how it ebbed and flowed in a ceaseless blend of sound.

"I wanted to go to school with Toby and Eliza," Ceri said.

"Me too," Elin said.

"We'll see them both when we go back to Cambridge for a visit, OK?" Nan said, glad that she was driving and did not have to see their little faces.

"But *when*?" Elin asked. She was near tears.

"I wish we could go today," Ceri whispered.

"Before too long, I promise, girls. It's all going to be fine."

But at that moment, Nan wanted nothing more than to drive over Britannia Bridge and keep going until they were home, *really* home, in Cambridge. Her thoughts raced with terrifying speed. Perhaps they could rent a house there, the girls could start school with their friends, she could admit to Robin that she had been wrong and that this had all been a terrible mistake? Putting on Stephen Fry reading Harry Potter was the only thing that calmed the twins down and gave her time to quieten her thoughts. She was here, and this was where she needed to be, she told herself. Her children would be happy here too. And they would start by getting new school shoes.

* * *

The woman serving in the shoe shop had vivid bright red hair and such huge fake eyelashes that the twins stared at her open-mouthed.

"School shoes, is it?" the woman said. "There's not much choice left now, sorry. Are yours very fussy? We've had some real brats in this week, to be honest with you."

Before Nan could answer, she saw the tip of a child's ponytail emerge from behind the "Sale" rack, followed by the lonely father from the beach. He was wearing the same checked shirt and cut-off jeans as he had the first time she had seen him, but, close-up, she could see how lean and wiry he was. He reminded her of a greyhound at the starting gates, tense and ready to run. "They look nice," he was saying, as his little girl stomped forward in a very sturdy pair of black lace-up shoes. "And they'll last a while."

"I really wanted the unicorn ones, though, Dad," the child said mournfully.

"They've all sold out, Mim, and you need to get them today, ready for school."

Ceri and Elin had spotted them both and were watching, agog, their eyes glued to the girl's shoes. Ceri brought her mouth right up to Nan's ear, and whispered:

"Can she do up laces, do you think?"

Nan smiled. "Why don't you ask her, love?"

Ceri looked unsure, and looked at her twin, before quietly asking:

"Can you do up laces?"

The little girl looked at her, a proud smile on her lips.

"Yes. My dad taught me. Your mum can teach you if you ask her," she said.

"Uh-oh," her father said with a small smile. "Sorry about that."

Nan mouthed "never mind", floored at how deep his voice was, a really low bass rumble. It had a strength and depth she had not expected from such a slight man.

"I think we're up for the challenge, aren't we, girls?" she replied.

Twenty minutes later, all three girls had the same black school shoes and were shyly chatting by the till.

"You go to Cable Bay a lot, don't you?" Nan asked the man as she swiped her card. "I've, I mean we've seen you there with the other... parents." She suspected she was blushing, which made her blush even more. This man unsettled her somehow. Perhaps he did the same to everyone.

"Yes, it's a nice beach, Trecastell."

Nan recognised the Welsh name for the bay and decided on the spot to use it more. "So, is your daughter going to Rhosneigr school too?"

"Yes. She starts next week."

Nan waited for him to say more, but he didn't, which helped her calm down a bit, and removed the urge to gabble at him. He was a man who didn't waste words, she could tell. Once he'd paid, with cash she noticed, they left the shop together. Were they going to the uniform shop next, she wondered, but didn't ask in case she appeared desperate for company (which, of course, she was)?

"See you at school, girls," the man said, as he walked away. "With those laces perfectly done up." For a moment, Nan saw a flash of boyish merriment in his eyes before sadness returned, like a darkening cloud.

"Yes, we'll see you there," Nan replied.

As soon as they had parted, Ceri turned to Nan and said, "Mum, that girl said her name was 'Mim'. Is that really a name at all?"

"I don't know, love. It might be a Welsh one I don't know. It's pretty though, isn't it – Mim?"

The twins nodded in unison. A few seconds later, Elin asked, "Mum, can we practise tying our laces when we get home?"

"Because we need to practise a LOT," added Ceri.

* * *

Buying their school shoes, miniscule grey skirts and blue "Ysgol Rhosneigr" sweatshirts marked a change in the girls. Nan heard them playing "school" games in their room, and talking about teachers and classrooms, but one huge fear remained, for all three of them, their lack of Welsh.

"But we can't speak hardly any Welsh words, Mummy," they said again and again.

"And we don't want to. Aren't we *allowed* to speak English?"

"Yes, you are allowed, but the teachers want to help you learn Welsh," she replied confidently, though she couldn't help but wonder how it would work in reality. Surely not knowing a single word of Welsh would leave the girls horribly isolated, too shy to use English? If so, how would they know what to do at break time, where the toilets were, where to go for lunch, for instance? Would anyone else talk to them if they weren't fluent Welsh speakers, born and bred on the island? She lost sleep, worrying about this, but knew there was nothing she could do to change it now.

Robin came home for the weekend before their first day at school, and the twins proudly showed him their new uniforms. James had insisted he was back for a meeting on Monday, and Nan was furious. She had hoped they could both drop them off together.

"At least go and wish them luck again before you go," Nan said, at 5am on the day Robin had to leave. "They're worried."

"They're still asleep, Nan."

"I know, but do it anyway, please. You'll wish you had when you're on the train."

"Look, I wish I could stay longer, but James is counting on me to, you know, to..." his words dwindled and died, and Nan did not rescue him. James had no kids, end of story. "I'll come out of the meeting and ring at 4pm and hear all about it then."

"They'll be out at 2pm this week, actually." She stopped, her face crumpling. "Oh, Robin, they could be starting school with their friends in Cambridge and because of *me*, they're..."

Robin sat down on the bed. "Look, it's done now, and you have to believe it will be OK. They'll fight their own battles, just as we did."

"They have to from now on, because I can't be there to do it for them."

"No, you can't, just as nobody was there for you. I have to go. I'll miss the train, though it will probably be bloody cancelled anyway."

Two hours later, the girls got into their new uniforms in virtual silence and ate only a few mouthfuls of toast for breakfast. At the school gate, they clung to the back of Nan's legs, and for a few panicky minutes, she actually considered taking them home and investigating homeschooling. Then she remembered some advice Dewi had given her.

"They need to meet other children. It's not natural that they only have you and each other, Nansi. They need to start their life here properly, and then you can."

Holding both their hands tightly, Nan took them a little nearer the door before kissing them both quickly, letting go and stepping away.

"Have a really lovely day, girls," she said, her eyes already brimming. "I'll see you a bit later, and you can tell me all about it. Bye, sweeties."

As she was about to go, she saw another little girl look at her girls, move a little nearer and say in a very strong North Welsh accent.

"You're twins, aren't you? I wish I was a twin. I'm Hâf and I'm five."

"*Hâf!* Hey, your name means 'summer'," Ceri cried, "like on the laptop, Mummy!"

The little girl nodded. "*Ia*/Yes. So, what are you called?"

"I'm Ceri and this is Elin."

"Wow! My sister's called Elin and my cousin is called Ceri."

All three girls beamed at each other, and Nan felt a rush of joy as she watched them go through the doors and into school together. Only a few mothers loitered in the yard, with buggies and babies on hips, chatting. Nobody spoke to Nan, but as she walked back to the car, one woman smiled at her as her little boy scampered away.

"Find it hard to hand yours over today?" she said, pulling a cigarette from the packet in the pocket of her denim jacket and lighting it deftly.

"It was hard, yes," Nan replied. "But they needed to start." At that moment, her craving to smoke was stronger than it had been in years. "You? Was your son happy to start school?"

"I think so. Well, *I* was happy for him to start school," the woman replied. "*Gwenno dw'i.*"

This was a Welsh phrase, and a social code she recognised. It meant "I'm Gwenno."

"*Nan dw'i*/I'm Nan," she replied immediately. "I've got twin girls, Ceri and Elin."

"Twins! That's a plateful. I've only got Guto, and he's more than enough for me," the woman replied, adding, in a thick cloud of smoke, "He had a massive tantrum all the way here because he was so excited. I needed this smoke, I tell you."

She laughed, a huge laugh that revealed acres of teeth and tonsils. Nan noticed the silver piercing in the centre of her tongue and had a terrible urge to ask her if it hurt, or if food got stuck in it. There was also a tattoo on her neck, and she wanted to go nearer to read the words clearly but knew she shouldn't.

"Cigarette?" Gwenno said, offering Nan the packet.

"No thanks. Tempted, but I gave up a while ago."

"I gave up giving up a while ago. Life's too short not to shorten it, eh?" Another huge laugh.

"Too right," Nan replied, grinning. "Now you're talking my language."

"Well, I'm actually talking yours, if you think about it. Feels weird, to be speaking English, actually."

"Thanks for doing so, though, Gwenno. I wasn't sure how

today would go... whether anyone would talk to me at all, to be honest."

"People take a while up here," she said. "So, do you work?"

Nan hesitated. If she told Gwenno that she had read Archaeology and Anthropology at Cambridge and edited archaeological papers for a living, this might be their first and last conversation. "Oh, I do this and that. I'm concentrating on getting the kids settled at the moment," was all she could muster.

"*Digon teg*/Fair enough. That sounds like hard work in itself."

"How about you? What work do you do?" Nan asked.

"Oh, this and that, but mainly that," Gwenno replied with a wink. "Anything I can find, *deud y gwir*/tell you the truth. I hate it but needs must."

They walked out of the playground together, two very different women, but with an immediate connection that both of them sensed.

"Well, I'd best be off. Have a good day," Nan said.

"Yup. See you later, after another glorious day in Paradise..."

Now it was Nan's turn to laugh out loud, and it felt so, so good.

PART 3

GREEN SHOOTS

FOURTEEN

Nan always said that school was the twins' saviour, because once they had started going there, everything got better.

"It was like one of those oil tankers that takes about a week to turn around," Nan told Ella and her husband Tarquin – an unpublished poet who always wore purple for reasons nobody could deduce – when they called in en route from Cambridge to Dublin that October. "From that day, I could see they were heading in a different direction."

"I bet it was because you started emitting positive energy," Ella said.

"No. I think it was because they made some mates," Nan replied with a grin.

For the twins, school opened up a new world of friendships and experiences. The first few days were strange, as most of the other kids had at least some Welsh, but they told Nan how kind Gwenno's son Guto had been when they couldn't understand a task from the teacher or a comment from a pupil, and how he had alerted the other kids to their difficulty.

"He's told everyone to be nice to us, so they are," Ceri said.

"It's because his mum looks tough," Elin added. "*She* told him to look after us or she'd make them pay."

"That's good of her," Nan said, not sure if it actually was.

"Guto is a brilliant singer, Mum. He sang in the lesson today," Ceri said. "He's won prizes in a... er... big, like, er, competition thing."

"An *Ay-steth-fod*," Elin added proudly.

"And he's teaching us Welsh songs so we can win prizes too."

Within a week or two, Nan heard her daughters using the odd word of Welsh in their games or to each other. Neither seemed to mind using Welsh all day and switching back into English at home. It was just the way it was, and they accepted it. Although she was delighted to see her daughters happy, Nan felt a wriggle of jealousy. Where were *her* new friends going to come from? Loneliness gnawed at her a little more each day.

"I told you they'd be fine, Nan," Robin said, when he Face-timed them one evening. "I think you probably stressed them out, transferring your separation anxiety onto them."

"Thanks for the cod-psychology," she replied. "Good to know that was my fault as well."

"I don't mean that. I just feel you need to loosen up a bit, get out more."

"When I've worked out where to go, I will."

"I'll brainstorm some ideas and email you. Girls, say something to me in Welsh."

"*Sut wyt ti, Dad?*" his daughters chorused as one.

"Not a clue what you said, but it sounds amazing," he said. "And you like school, do you?"

"We like *amser cinio* best," Ceri said.

"What on earth does that mean?"

"Lunchtime!" Elin replied. "Everybody knows that!"

"Maybe you should learn Welsh too. Mum learnt a bit, and we're teaching her more."

"I don't need it, do I? I live here, where people speak *English,* thank goodness."

Nan was too shocked to respond.

* * *

For her, the twins starting school was a very mixed blessing. The summer had been incredibly hard in many ways, and she had felt terrible pangs of regret, but at least she had had the girls for company. Now she was alone all day. She tried opening a conversation with the other mothers at the school gate, but everyone seemed to be from the area, surrounded by family and needed to leave the playground pretty quickly to work, go shopping, or "get on with things". Most of them had been to the same school as kids, so had known each other all their lives. Some mothers even stayed in their cars after the first few days, Nan noticed, and their children ran into school before they zoomed off. She wondered where they were going, and what the long day held for them. One of them looked approachable, probably because she wore a top Nan recognised as one a friend from Cambridge had worn, which triggered a powerful wave of nostalgia for the familiar.

"What the hell is happening to me?" she muttered. "I'm pining for what I deliberately and very happily left behind!"

With a sinking heart, she realised that nobody here seemed to need a new friend, they had plenty already. Gwenno did not seem to pick Guto up every day anymore, and when she was there, she seemed preoccupied, standing on the periphery of the other mums and waving a quick "hello" as she left. Nan gradually realised that her pool of "potential mates" was Gwenno and perhaps the lonely father from the shoe shop, but he always stood alone in the playground, and never returned her tentative smiles with any real warmth. She noticed he sometimes talked to Gwenno when the other mums had left and only then did she see him look animated or his shoulders relaxed. Were they having an affair? she wondered. Part of her was jealous at the thought that they could be doing something so exciting.

When another whole school week passed without any progress at all, Nan's optimism dwindled a little more. This was such a different world to the one she had left behind and the people here were self-contained and reserved. Whenever she opened her mouth, she was painfully aware of her accent; she started to wear sweatpants and old jumpers to avoid standing out for the clothes she wore. Nothing seemed to bridge the invisible gulf between herself and the other women, and it was hard, very hard, when she walked away without having exchanged a word with anyone day after day.

To make things worse, Nan went back to an empty house. James was still unwilling to let Robin work at home on alternate weeks, and Robin seemed entirely happy with the arrangement, perhaps because a promotion had been mentioned. Dewi was supportive, but he was busy all day every day, and Nan had the twins in the evening. She recognised the returns of her crippling anxiety as a second-time mother recognises a contraction and knows *exactly* what lies ahead. Medication was always an option, but she remembered more bad experiences than good ones until the dosage was exactly right, and she was solely responsible for the kids all week, so could not afford days in bed. One wet Wednesday morning, instead of ringing the GP, she decided to do what Eira had always told her to do when she was really stymied: make a list of her options:

1. *Join a gym (expensive, far away and not very sociable)*
2. *Sign up for an evening class (in the evenings, when I can't go anywhere)*
3. *Get freelance copy-editing work (on your own, at home... noooooooooo)*

4. *Visit all archaeological sites on the island (great, but it would only fill one day)*
5. *Decorate the rest of the house (hard work, at home, but would make me feel good)*

She quickly realised that five was the only realistic choice. She had always intended to decorate the rest of *Coed Uchaf* herself rather than pay the professionals who had done the kitchen. She loved the satisfaction of decorating, the speed of transformation that was possible, but she had imagined doing so between idyllic walks along beaches and meeting new friends whom she would invite back for simple lunches.

"Fat chance of that," she said, putting a big tick next to number five.

The next morning, horizontal rain meant a long walk with Shadow was off the cards, so she was in the local DIY shop by 9am. An hour and a half later, and £245.25 lighter, the car was satisfyingly crammed with cans of paint, sandpaper, a steam wallpaper-stripper and an assortment of fillers, masking tapes and paintbrushes as she pootled home slowly along the coast road. The rain had eased a little by then, and she glimpsed pockets of vivid blue peeking from between the banked grey clouds out over the horizon.

"That sky looks like I feel right now," she said aloud. "Focus on the blue bits, Nan."

She had already decided to start with the living room, currently home to miscellaneous chairs and two IKEA sofas. With big sash windows that overlooked the bay, she wanted to make it the light, bright room she had envisaged when she had first revisited the house all those months earlier. The wallpaper was already hanging off the wall in gruesome skin-like strips, which meant getting the rest of it off was a doddle with her new stripper. In fact, the main problem proved to be Shadow, who insisted on dragging the long shards of dusty old wallpaper behind her like a grubby train as she raced between rooms. By 3pm, when Nan had to fetch the twins, the room was almost completely paper-free and ready for sanding down, preparing and starting to paint.

"Where's the TV gone?" Ceri wailed, when she saw the chaos.

"It's horrible in here now," Elin added.

"Ta-da!" Nan said, pulling the dust sheet off it with a dramatic flourish. "And it's pizza for dinner, as I'm much too tired to cook anything else."

All was immediately forgiven.

* * *

Dropping the girls at school the next morning, she felt as if she had a purpose once more. She walked Shadow along the beach as the windsurfers sliced up and down on the water, their bright sails vivid in the sunshine. There was a stiff breeze, and as she lifted her face to the sun, Nan could taste the salty smack of the sea on her tongue. Rounding the corner of the bay, she saw the Neolithic burial chamber in the distance, and remembered the day when Dewi managed to borrow the key to so she could finally go inside. The place had always felt special to her as a child, and its mellifluous Welsh name, "*Barclodiad y Gawres*", "The giantesses' apron", and the legend of its formation had always made her tingle with excitement. When Eira had unlocked the metal gates that day, Nan had pushed to the front, but in the dim light, her eyes had struggled to make out anything at all. A ripe, earthy smell filled the space, and the air felt cold and damp, but gradually, several huge shapes loomed out of the darkness as if coming towards them. Nan had shivered. They were massive slabs of rock, hauled by handmade ropes and sheer will to this remote hill, then arranged as was felt fitting. Nan had walked further inside and ran her index finger over the swirling spirals carved into some of them, symbols with such meaning for whoever had made them, but impenetrable to her. This had been such a holy place thousands of years ago, and it still felt like one – a tiny cathedral, inspiring as much wonder as she had felt in St Paul's in London on a school trip. When they emerged into the grey skies of the bay that February morning, Nan had smiled, a smile that warmed her from within. It had been worth waiting to come here again... as most wonderful things in life were usually worth waiting for, she told herself as she turned to go home and start painting.

When she first saw the man walking towards her, she felt a lurch of resentment. This was *her* headland, *her* precious burial chamber – how dare he invade it? He was effortlessly hauling a huge piece of driftwood behind him with ropes, as his dog skittered from side to side, yapping at it. As he got nearer, she recognised the dad from school. Within a minute or two, they faced each other on the cliff path, two lonely people just feet apart.

"Hi," she said, and coughed. Her voice was so unused to conversation that it sounded strangely creaky. "That is one big bit of driftwood."

The man smiled shyly. "I know. Part of a tree trunk. Beautiful, isn't it?"

Nan smiled back. It *was* beautiful, smoothed and honed by wind and waves and bleached almost white. "What are you going to do with it?"

"Not sure yet. Something that does it justice, I hope."

Just as Nan was about to say, "I'm Nan Green", he walked straight past her and off into the distance, the branch leaving a deep groove in the sandy path behind him.

"*Hwyl*/Bye," she called after him.

And he turned and waved at her.

FIFTEEN

Nan replayed this minute-long meeting all the way home – how the man had smiled, how he had put his head on one side like a quizzical bird, the fact that this time he had actually waved at *her*. What was his story? Robin was probably right, that he had a long and complicated one, full of broken hearts and broken promises. Perhaps if she ever actually got to know Gwenno, she could ask her, but until then, she could only guess, and imagine.

Back at home, she let her clothes fall to the floor in a messy halo around her feet, pulled on an old onesie and opened the first can of paint, a thick, chalky blue that promised to "reflect natural light". As each wall changed colour, Nan was so happy that she skipped lunch to keep going. It was a beautiful afternoon, and by the time she had finished, the room danced with so *much* natural light that it felt as if the sea and the sky outside the room had been invited inside. It was simply stunning.

"It looks so big now!" Ceri said, as she scampered in after school. "And it's echoey."

Nan laughed. "Yeah. I like it. I don't want to put those massive old sofas back in here."

"We could get big beanbags, like in school! We put them in the cupboard after circle time, so we could do that," Ceri said.

"We'll see," Nan said, imagining Robin's face if he had to sit on a beanbag. "I could get some for you two, I suppose."

"And one for you, so we can all snuggle," Elin said.

"OK," Nan replied with a twinge of sadness. Had they already got used to their sub-family of three? In some ways, this proved that she was managing to hold things together, but it had never been the plan, to move here *without* her husband. Had her children glimpsed a truth she chose not to acknowledge herself – that he was never really going to join them?

"Mummy, can we?"

"What, sorry? Oh, yes, beanbags. Sure, let's order some right now," she replied, glad of an excuse to shut down her thoughts.

* * *

Every day for two weeks, Nan heaved ladders, dustsheets and paint cans out of one finished room, straight into the next. It thrilled her to see the house come to life, as if she had waved a magic wand over it. She bought throws, cushions, rugs, bedding, blinds and lamps online and looked forward to a bit of banter with Derek the DPD delivery driver who delivered them all to her. *Coed Uchaf* soon sparkled with whites, blues and creams, offset by vivid shots of colour, exposed slabs of slate and varnished wooden window frames. The day before Robin was due home for the first time in three weeks, she spent £30 on three huge bunches of gorgeous Stargazer lilies because they reminded her of a blissful afternoon at the Hockney gallery in Saltaire: the dazzling mix of light, colour and texture she had seen there had inspired her vision for this house, she now realised. When her husband walked in, he looked genuinely impressed.

"It's amazing, it really is, to see what you've done in a few weeks," he said, as she gave him a tour. "And on your own too. The lilies are great, but there are rather a lot of them. And we need our sofas back, for goodness' sake. We can't afford new ones."

She frowned. "Try to stick with the positives, please, Robin."

"... but the lilies smell fabulous. Wow, you've really got rid of all the gloom, but kept the warmth of the old place. Good job."

"That's more like it. Hard work, but worth it," she replied.

"You always did like decorating, I remember, and it must have been good to have a project. I'm sure it's all cost a small fortune, but at least you've saved us having to pay professionals again."

He was pleased with her, Nan knew, but there was a thread of reservation woven into his praise. She just managed to stop herself from asking him why. Their phone call relationship was taking its toll; it was becoming more and more difficult to actually *be* with each other these days.

"Getting it done before you start work was a good idea too. Have you contacted anyone about that, by the way? You said you'd check out some freelance copy-editing."

Nan felt as if he'd thumped her in the belly. Her bum didn't hit a chair from 7am until 10pm every night of the week (something Robin wouldn't know, of course, as he wasn't here). The last thing she wanted to do was chase up boring freelance work only a few months after their arrival. It would isolate her even more too. Why didn't he see that? Why was he making her feel inadequate only seconds after commenting on how well she'd done?

"Have you any idea how much work it is to run a house like this, Robin?" she seethed. "And my priority is to settle the girls."

"I agree, but you've done the house now and the girls are settled," he said.

Nan slammed her coffee cup down and heard it crack alarmingly. "No, I haven't contacted anyone about work yet, if you really want to know," she snapped. "I find I'm already pretty busy, Robin, bringing up your kids. Somebody has to."

Robin blanched and Nan saw she had struck a nerve. "I know and it must be tough on you, and I know I'm not here as much as we hoped, but you will think about doing some work, won't you? Otherwise, the whole thing rests on me, and my approval rating with James."

Nan paused and took a deep breath. "I know, love, and I *will*, but not yet, OK?" she replied. "We've got a big lump sum in the bank from the sale of Portugal Street, and I really don't want to rush into something I'll regret. I'm busy with the house, I really am."

"Fine. It's up to you. I'm sick of point-scoring, Nan."

He picked up his phone. This conversation was finished.

After putting the twins to bed, Nan went to get a bottle of wine in an attempt to make peace. When she returned, Robin had hauled both sofas back into the living room and was sitting down, wearing reading glasses. Sure, they were trendy, designer frames, but how did the man with 20/20 vision suddenly need *glasses*? He *definitely* had a bald patch too – and a fast-growing one. Would he soon be taking up pipe-smoking, or snuff-taking, like his unbearable father? Was the future Robin to be seen in cable-knit cardigans and nautical neckerchiefs? Shuddering, she made both their glasses large ones.

* * *

The evening could only end one way: sex. It was still the quickest way to get Robin to relax, and to agree to things, Nan knew. She also knew that neither of them really felt like doing it but do it they did. It was a perfunctory, disappointing affair.

"I need to get someone in to help me make some kind of secret door between the two back bedrooms so that the girls can have adjoining rooms. Remember we talked about it in Cambridge?" she said in bed afterwards.

"I remember, but is it really necessary? Can't they carry on sharing?"

"They can, but we promised them their own rooms here, Robin," she replied. "What's the problem?"

"Nothing, but please let's keep the costs down. Running two households is expensive. I've just checked our bank balance."

"Hang on. I thought James paid for your Airbnb?" she asked.

"You don't have any idea about money, Nan," he said quickly. "Work don't pay for my food, for instance, or drinks. I have to eat out a lot, with clients, as I've told you."

"Tough gig," she said. "Must be awful."

"Sarcasm is the lowest form of wit, as my father always says."

"Funny that, as he uses it often enough."

"Please don't insult my parents. They have been nothing but kind to you."

"You are *joking*, I assume?" she said, but one look at his face told her otherwise.

"They've put up with a lot, Nan, and so have I. You are not the daughter-in-law they expected, you know. They've never said it, not out loud, but I think I've disappointed them."

Nan listened as her husband thumped his pillow and settled down to sleep. Who *was* this man who had chosen her to spend his life with, and why had he done so if she fell short of his family's expectations? She remembered the first time he'd approached her in college, asking for change for the vending machine, when his ease of manner and unassailable public-school surety had completely flummoxed her. He'd asked where she lived, and she had told him (which she knew was not wise). Then he'd laughed when she told him there was no way he could visit her because her room was a health hazard. There was something faintly vulnerable about him, even then, beneath a veneer of confident formality, and it was a combination Nan recognised from her childhood. She sensed that he needed to be loved just as much as she did.

The possibility that her husband was now going to become a pompous snob like his father was truly terrifying, but the thought that he might become *her* father was even more so. Nan's main memory of her father Eric was his red-rimmed eyes behind his glasses as he squinted to read his newspaper in the funereal light of the living room. He had terrible eyesight, a shortcoming that had been responsible for him being rejected from the army. Instead, he was whisked out of an apprenticeship in car maintenance at the age of seventeen and sent to RAF Valley on Anglesey to help maintain the Hawker Hurricanes of 615 Squadron. In a pub near the base, he had met Eira, who went to a dance there every Saturday night with her friend Annie Hughes. He had quickly married her and brought her to London, where he spent over forty years waiting for a son and working as a car mechanic – a job he hated, and a life he hated even more. Nothing seemed to have worked out well for any of them, Nan thought as she lay in the darkness.

As she tried to ignore her husband's snoring and fall asleep, she heard her father's voice saying something forever seared in her memory:

"My life has been a series of disappointments, and you're one of them, Nansi."

SIXTEEN

Nan and Robin bickered all that weekend. Predictably, as they drank more and more wine to try and relax, they ended up on the familiar battleground of her saying how cold his parents were, and him saying what an inadequate grandmother her mother was. It was exhausting.

"Most grandmothers would be champing at the bit to look after twin girls, but yours hasn't stayed with us more than three times since we married. She hasn't even engaged with the fact that we've all come to live in her birthplace yet, has she?" Robin said one particularly awful evening. "And she's said she won't stay in this house because of some ancient feud."

"And your mother refuses to come here until we can recommend a good five-star hotel within ten minutes' drive, which we can't, as there aren't any."

But Robin was not giving in. "I just feel that, as your mother, Eira should be here, showing you and her granddaughters some support... but then she's hardly been hands-on '*Nain*' from the off, has she? Birthday and Christmas gifts and the odd postcard of a London bus has been about her limit. She never even came to see us when we lived an hour's train ride away."

Nan couldn't deny this, and her mother's reluctance to visit them in Cambridge had upset her a great deal and she had never understood the reason for it until, shortly after Eric's death, she had decided to confront her one evening. What she learnt in that conversation explained everything, but she had never shared its contents with Robin.

"Dad hurt you, Mum. I heard it all, you know," she had whispered to her mother. "Why didn't you just leave him?"

"If it wasn't me, it would have been you."

Nan hesitated. Did Eira really not know that it *had* been her anyway?

"But why didn't we both leave, you and me?" she asked.

"Where could we go? Things were different then."

"We could have lived with Uncle Dewi."

"Your father would have dragged me back, shamed me in front of my family. They had warned me not to marry him, you see. Didn't trust him."

"But he did terrible things, Mum. He was cruel... to both of us," Nan said.

"I know, Nan, and I'm really sorry. I feel guilty about it every time I see your little girls, and I remember you at that age." She looked directly into her daughter's eyes.

Nan said nothing. Had Eira really not known what her husband was doing to her when she was barely older than her twins? She couldn't bring herself to broach that subject, not now. It would be the most difficult question she would ever ask, and the most painful, for both of them, so she did not ask it.

"I wasn't brave, like you. I felt I had to stay with him, to be punished," Eira said. "And I was, for most of my adult life."

But Nan could never explain that these were the reasons behind her mother's distant, almost selfish, behaviour to Robin, or tell him her shameful secret.

"My mother had decades of not being able to make her own

choices, Robin," she said calmly. "You don't know what we had to put up with – not all of it. I've never told you."

He nodded but said nothing. He was too drunk to register what she had said.

"I've decided to ask her again to come up and visit us. She may say 'no' and if she does, we both accept that. Understood?"

But Robin was fast asleep, the dregs of his wine dribbling onto his cream chinos.

* * *

As October half-term drew nearer, Nan began to worry about how they would all cope without the structure of school. She couldn't carry on doing things around the house when the girls were around, and it couldn't be like the summer, with no routine, absent friends and sulky kids, with the added bonus of unpredictable weather. It was time for her to arrange some play-dates, but the twins' best friend Hâf was going to Disneyland Paris, and they were a little reluctant to invite Guto over ("He's a *boy*, Mum") which left only Mim, the shoe-laces girl... which meant approaching her father.

"Her dad never has friends over to her house. I don't think he lets her go to other houses either, but can we ask if she can come here, Mum, *please*?" Ceri pleaded.

"He must have his reasons for that, but sure, I'll ask," Nan replied. "Oh, did you ask her about her name, girls?"

"Yes. She said her real name is Mimi, but she and her dad both hate it," Ceri replied. "I like Mim better anyway. Mimi sounds like a dog's name."

Nan laughed, and immediately wondered why he had let his child be given a name he hated, but she said nothing. It was yet another strand of mystery surrounding him.

"Her dad could come to our house too. Mim says he likes

old things, history stuff, like you do," Elin said. "You could chat about things."

"And he doesn't have any friends either," Ceri added brightly.

"I see," Nan said. "We should get on jolly well then, shouldn't we?"

She knew she had to pounce at pick-up time on the final Friday, as it was threatening rain which always dispersed the parents as quickly as a crow amongst pigeons. Her heart was pounding as she walked towards Mim's father, despite her best efforts to be relaxed. When a startled look crossed his face, she felt relieved that he was just as unsure about social interaction as she was. Slowly, a cautious half-smile replaced it.

"Hello," he said.

"Hi, I'm sorry to bother you, but I wondered if Mim might like to come and play with my two one day during half-term?" she said. No reply came, so she gabbled on. "No worries at all if you've got plans, and I know that most people *do* have plans, but we don't, of course." Again, silence. "It's just a thought, I mean the girls get on really well..."

She waited, as the man scuffed his string-laced boot on the tarmac like a cornered schoolboy. It was almost painfully endearing.

"I think she would like to, yes," he said eventually. "Thanks for asking."

"So, er, shall I take your number and text you?" she said, feeling as if she was asking for casual sex in the back of a car. "I'm Nan Green, by the way." She held out her hand.

Very slowly, like a wary animal, he took it and held it for a few seconds. Nan had never felt such a lithe but strong hand in her life. Whatever his work was, he worked with his hands, but he was not a labourer. He had a craftsman's hand.

"I'm Harri," he said, letting her hand drop awkwardly. "Oh, sorry, not very good at people stuff these days. Lack of practice."

"I know what you mean," Nan said, blushing unexpectedly. The sheer resonance of that voice was amazing: he *had* to be a singer.

"Nobody else talks to you either, do they?" Harri said. "I think we'd better start our own clique. But we might persuade Gwenno to break away from the Witches and join us."

Nan laughed, but then, totally without warning, she felt her eyes brimming with tears. She wiped them away with her sleeve, mortified. "Oh Lord, sorry."

"Hey, I'm sorry if I upset you. Don't worry. You're new, that's all," he said, moving a little nearer. "We take time to trust people who are new and... different. It's nothing personal."

"Thanks. Sorry about the tears. Doesn't take much to set me off these days."

"Me neither, to be honest with you, so your secret's safe with me," he said. "Now, let me see if I can do this..."

While he fiddled with his phone, his brow furrowed in irritation. She looked at him more closely. His shoulder-length brown hair had a few greys, and was loose, tumbling around his shoulders. The tanned skin of his face was so deeply lined around the eyes that it looked as if he was permanently squinting into the sun, and yet, somehow, he still looked young. He wore the same clothes he had worn every time she had seen him, and his jawline was softened by thick, auburn-tinged stubble. Nan wondered – just for a second – about his personal hygiene. All in all, after a luxurious minute of close study, Nan decided that he was incredibly good-looking.

"Right. Give me your number," he said. "I think I can just about add it on this 'brick' now."

He held up his mobile, which was the exact same ancient Nokia Nan had used before Robin insisted she upgrade to an iPhone.

She laughed out loud. "Ha, I had a phone just like that and I loved it!"

His tongue between his teeth, she watched him painstakingly add her number. "I keep things simple. I usually still write things down, to be honest, but there's no paper here."

"So, what's your surname for me to add you to my elite list of contacts, Harri?"

"Parry," he said, adding a second later, "Harri Parry. Awful, isn't it?"

"No, not awful. I think it's sort of... *musical*," she replied. "I hate my name too – Nansi. That's why I call myself Nan."

He looked at her, his brown eyes calm and reassuring. "I think Nansi is a fine name. You should use it. I expect you were given the Welsh version of it for a good reason."

Nan was spellbound. He used few words, but each one meant something. The way he said her name, the softness of his island accent, made her catch her breath.

"So, what day would suit you best, Harri, to get the girls together? We live just by Cable – er, *Trecastell,* actually. A farmhouse called *Coed Uchaf*. Do you know it?"

Harri's eyes widened quickly, then narrowed again. "Er... yes, I do."

"Are you OK?" she said. "You've gone very pale."

He fumbled, putting his phone in his pocket. "Yes, fine. It's just that, well, my mam went to school with Annie Hughes, who lived there. I knew their son too. Small world – or it is up here anyway." He started inching away from her, though the kids had yet to come out of school. Something had spooked him, Nan could tell.

"Wow! So did my mum! Which means that your mum, Annie and my mum all met as kids in this very same school. That's great, and what an incredible coincidence!" she exclaimed, hoping she had managed to sound more at ease than she felt.

"Yup," he muttered, looking down at the ground. "Life is full of surprises – some nice, some nasty."

They both turned to look at the school door, where the children were starting to trickle out.

The twins came first and capered around Nan excitedly. "So, can Mim come and play? Have you asked him yet, Mummy?"

"Yes, I have, and hopefully, next week," she said. "I'll text you, Harri Parry. Good to talk to you."

"Yes. *Hwyl*/Cheers, Nansi Green," he said.

Nan looked back from her car and saw him kneeling in the midst of the noisy gaggle of mothers, buggies and children, zipping up Mim's coat. He put his arms around her and squeezed her tightly, her mop of tight blonde curls mingling with his darker brown mane – it reminded her of molten dark and white chocolate. Then they walked away without a backward glance.

"We can build a den in our room," Elin said. "Mim's really good at making things."

"Her dad's even better," Ceri added. "He built her a house in a *tree*."

"He gets really sad, Mim said. Sometimes, he drinks wine like you do," Elin said.

Nan blushed. "Right. Does Mim's mum drink wine too?"

"Dunno. Mim just says 'she's gone and she's never coming back'."

"Oh... I see. That's a shame," Nan said, her thoughts racing.

"And people say that's why nobody's ever been to play at Mim's house. She told us."

"People say all sorts of things about other people," Nan replied. "We haven't had anyone round to play either. So, tell me, what kind of things does he make, her dad?"

"I don't know, but she said he uses things he finds, like, shells and wood," Elin said. "Mim said he made her a *real mermaid's palace* one day, in their kitchen."

"How wonderful," said Nan. "And no, I can't make one for you two."

* * *

Harri brought Mim over on the Tuesday of half-term. They had walked, as their car "wasn't in the mood to go anywhere", which was a very long way for such little legs, Nan thought. As soon as the twins opened the front door, all three girls shot upstairs to the girls' bedroom, leaving Harri standing on the doorstep. He looked almost paralysed and was so pale that even his lips were drained of colour, and there were moons of shadow beneath his eyes. Nan began to worry that she seemed to be having a very negative effect on him.

"Come in, please," Nan said. "You look like you need a *panad*/cuppa. Or a brandy."

When he hesitated, a wary look on his face, she added:

"We can sit outside if you prefer," she said. "Bit windy, but fine with me."

He took a deep breath. "No. Let's go in."

But he still hung back, leaning against the doorframe of the kitchen with his mouth slightly open and his feet rooted to the spot. Nan knew that he was having what looked very like the beginnings of a panic attack; she knew the signs too well. But what was triggering it? "Harri, come in and sit down," she said gently.

He felt his way to a chair and sat quite still as Shadow circled him, her tail whipping, nose up for approval. As his breathing calmed, he raised a flattened palm and the dog immediately crouched low, her slim body flat to the floor, only coming up again when he laid his arm by his side. It struck Nan as the most elegant of dances.

"You know about collies then. She's worried about you," Nan said.

"Yes. Such sensitive creatures, they are. They feel our feelings, I believe. I'm OK now, thanks. Sorry about that. It's just, well, I haven't been here for so many years." He looked around him slowly and cleared his throat. "It's amazing, what you've done. I remember this room as a bit gloomy. And always smoky. Does the range still work?"

"No, sadly, but it's just been restored to look as beautiful as it ever did. I have an Aga."

"And you actually cook on it, do you? You'd be amazed at the number of people who move up here and just have them for decoration," Harri said.

Nan winced. Did he see her as one of the "people who move up here". "I have to cook with it," she said. "I don't have another oven."

"*Da iawn*/Good. You'll need it in this house in the winter, believe me." He smiled, a real smile, one that lit up his face like the sun emerging from behind a cloud. Nan felt as if she had passed some kind of test.

Walking over to the old range, he patted it affectionately. "Gethin did this up, didn't he? Such a good job. I knew he and his dad had done some work for you. We used to come here as boys, you know, to see... to visit the Hughes family."

"Everybody really does know everyone up here, don't they?" Nan said. "Mum did warn me about that!"

"Oh yes. Your sins are never forgotten, or forgiven," he murmured, and the words lingered in the air. Nan saw a shadow pass over his face before he spoke again. "Right, enough of me being maudlin. Can I have a tour, please?"

"Sure, but don't judge my decorating skills too harshly," she said. "I did all the painting myself. If the bugs don't move fast enough, they get glossed!"

"*Digon teg*/Fair enough," he said. "I promise I won't look too closely."

Nan laughed. "Judging by the racket coming from the girls' room, we'd better start there."

Harri followed her slowly, almost reverently, from room to room. Nan saw him stroke newly painted walls and touch stripped wooden window frames and found herself aching with hope that this meant he approved of what she had done. When they reached the twins' room, the three girls had used their bedding, some towels and a clothes airer to make a ramshackle den that took up the whole of the floor space.

"I think you need some refreshments in there," she said. "I'll go and get some."

"Dad, you come in too!" Mim shouted. Harri crawled under the duvets and vanished.

"This is one great den, girls," he said. "Bit cramped, but very comfy," he said.

Nan returned a few minutes later, with a bowl of popcorn and three cartons of fruit juice, and overheard Ceri saying, "Mummy said we could have a room each in Wales."

Then Elin added, "She promised to make a secret door from my room to Elin's room, but it hasn't happened."

"I'm sure she'll keep her word," Harri said. "Look at everything else she's done."

"But can you help her do it?" Ceri said. "Our daddy's never here."

"And Mim says you're good at making things. *Please,*" Elin begged.

If Harri replied, Nan didn't hear it, as the girls shot out in search of the snacks. When he emerged, smiling sheepishly, she slapped her hand to her forehead in mock despair, mouthing "*sorry*". She hardly knew this man, for goodness' sake, and he wasn't a builder or someone who did odd jobs. He was more than that, he *made* things.

When they went downstairs and she began to prepare home-made pizza for the girls' tea, Harri sat at the kitchen table sketching on Ceri's drawing pad. He had decided not to eat with them but was happy to stay until Mim was ready to go home he said, and Nan noticed that he rarely took his eyes off his daughter. When she started rubbing her eyes wearily, he gently prompted a "thank you for having me" and got up ready to leave.

"Would you like a lift?" Nan asked. "It's a long walk back."

"No, thanks. It's a lovely evening. We had a great time, didn't we, Mim?"

"This is the first time I have been to someone else's house to play," the little girl said. "It was ace."

Outside, the twins sat on the double swing kicking their legs as father and daughter set off across the beach, hand in hand. It was only later that Nan found what Harri had been drawing as the kids ate – an intricately detailed picture of a small doorway between the two bedrooms upstairs, with suggestions for materials and rough measurements. Beneath it, he had written:

"Hope this helps you keep your promise. Gethin could do it for you. Diolch/Thanks for today. Harri & Mim"

Folding the paper very carefully, she hid it away in a drawer.

SEVENTEEN

Eira eventually agreed to come to Anglesey for the end of half-term week, but she still refused to stay at *Coed Uchaf.* This dashed Nan's hopes of her mother looking after the girls while she went shopping, to the garden centre or to the gym in Bangor, but she knew that her mother was pretty selfish in defence of her hard-won freedom. But Nan decided, once again, to try to get her to talk about the history behind her feelings about the farmhouse. Part of her sensed that, if Eira could only release that pressure, that long-held secret, she would feel much more at ease, and accept the house as her daughter's new home. She decided to ring her and talk about it head-on.

"Mum, look, we're just looking forward to you being nearby for a few days. I know you feel uneasy about staying here – I assume that's because the last time you were here, you met your old friend again and it was all very emotional."

"Yes, that's an issue, I must say, but it's also that Dewi gets so lonely, and I can clean the place up a bit and cook for him if I stay there. I grew up on the farm with him, remember, and it's wonderful to go back, especially now I'm free of your father."

"But the farm's pretty basic these days, Mum. We've got a

beautiful spare room and the girls would love to spend some time with you."

"I love your girls, you know I do, but I do find them *tiring* after a while."

"Yes, they can be tiring, I know, but they are your only grandchildren, Mum."

Nan heard the passive aggression in her own voice too late to soften its effect on Eira.

"No, I'll stay at Dewi's, thanks, and that's final. I'll come over on the bus, but I wouldn't want to get in your way, or Robin's, of course, if he comes home next weekend."

"He won't be home when you're here, but I do know... how he can be, sometimes, and I'm sorry about it, Mum."

Of *course*. Her mother was worried that she would have to see Robin, who would wince at her fat, fluid-filled ankles, point out how dry her Welsh cakes were and purse his lips if she wanted to watch "mindless soaps" in the evenings, as she always did.

"Yes, well, he's got a very good job and you love him," Eira said. "I've told you what my family thought of *your* father."

"You have, many times," Nan replied. "But did *you* love *him*, Mum?"

Nan heard her mother exhale slowly. "How many times have you asked me that, girl? Yes, I think I did. At first, anyway. He made me feel special, even called me his 'hot-house orchid'. Sounds stupid, looking back on it now." She paused. "Do you know, I really thought he'd chosen me out of all the other girls. As if."

"At least you got me out of it, Mum," Nan said, feeling her mother's negativity beginning to weigh down on her.

"Something to be very thankful for, yes," Eira replied. "And I am... thankful, I mean."

"I know. But if you stay at Dewi's, promise me you'll come over to see us. I won't hassle you, but you will, won't you?"

"Yes, yes, I will. But it won't be easy for me to come to that house again, as you know."

"Mum, *why*? Your meeting with Annie was so long ago now, I just don't understand..."

"No, you don't. Got to go now. Someone's at the door. See you soon. Bye."

And she hung up.

* * *

At 11am on the second day of her mother's visit to the island, there was a knock on the front door of *Coed Uchaf*. When Nan opened it, Eira was standing there in her best coat with her mother's prized pearl brooch on the lapel. She looked as white as a sheet, and Nan began to wonder if everyone who visited her home entered it in a severe state of shock.

"I took the bus. Lovely ride, it was. Feel a bit queasy now, though," she said.

Hugging her tightly, Nan got the same response she had in girlhood – loose-hanging arms, a quick peck on the cheek. She even smelt the same, of Elizabeth Arden's *Blue Grass*, but at least there was something comforting in that.

"Hi Mum! Come in!" she cried excitedly, taking her mother's hand. "Right, hold on to me, close your eyes, and I'll lead the way." She led Eira into the kitchen first. "*Please* don't go on about how much it all cost. Right, open your eyes!"

There was a long, long silence, as her mother slowly looked around the room, her eyes filling with tears as she lingered on particular details. "It's... amazing, Nan," she said eventually. "And the range – oh, look at the old range!" Her voice broke, and she pulled a handkerchief from one of her sleeves and dabbed her eyes.

"I fell in love with this house the day we both called on Annie all those years ago... and now here I am, living in it."

Eira sighed. "That was a long time ago, and I haven't set foot in this house since then. That was the day she forgave me, and I forgave myself."

"But forgave you for *what*, Mum?" Nan urged, sensing a slight chink in her mother's reserve. "You've never told me, and I so wish you would."

"Yes, Dewi told me you'd been nagging him about all that," Eira replied. There were more tears in her eyes now, which was rare enough for Nan to know not to push her too hard, too soon. "I just don't know if I can bear to talk about it yet."

"OK, that's fine, but why didn't you come and see Annie when you and I visited each year?" Nan asked gently. "Then things wouldn't have festered between you for so long." Her mother looked at the floor. "Was it Dad? Did he say you couldn't?" Silence. Nan pressed her advantage. "Why was he so *mean*?"

"He just was," Eira replied, fiddling with her coat buttons.

"But you kept in touch, right? I'm sure I remember hearing you speaking Welsh and crying one time on the phone. Was that when Annie told you her son had died?"

Eira nodded. "Poor Arwel – he was so young, with his whole life ahead of him. She begged me to come up for the funeral, but your father said he would never have me back if I did, and then what would have happened to you?" she said.

"Dad *forbade* you to go?" Nan said. "Even to the funeral of a child?"

"Things happened between your father and Annie, Nan, things he should have been ashamed of, but they are *her* secrets now. We have to accept that your father didn't like tears, or people showing any emotion. He was always so full of 'death is a part of life' – until it was his turn, of course," she said bitterly. "He said I couldn't even speak to Annie on the phone after that, as she was 'emotionally blackmailing me'. What kind of *friend* was I? A terrible one, and that's all there is to say about it."

Nan said nothing, but she desperately needed to know more. She sensed that this sorrow had underpinned her childhood, her life; the burden of it should be shared now. "Mum, you said Annie knew Dad from Valley, where you met him. Was he horrible to her too? Did she know what he was really like, I mean?"

Eira paused. "I could never tell her what he made our life like... until that day, when we visited here," she said. "I think Dewi told her how miserable I seemed when we came back to visit, but I never even confided in him how bad it really was... for both of us."

"I wish you had, Mum. It might have stopped him," Nan said. Again, they were circling around the awful, unspoken truth of her teenage years. "Was Dewi friends with Annie then? He seems fond of her."

"Every farming family up here is a friend, Nan. I wondered if they might, well, get together when they were both left alone. No point being alone, is there, unless you want to be?"

"Do *you* want to be, Mum?" Nan asked, studying her mother's face closely. She had always hoped her mother would find a companion at least, but did she want to?

"After a lifetime with your father, 'alone' is just fine," Eira replied.

Nan poured her mother a cup of tea and watched her blow on it twice, close her eyes and sip blissfully, just as she had always done.

"Lovely *panad*/cuppa," she murmured.

"Mum, I'm sorry to ask you about these things, but do you know about Annie's other son, Idris, dying as well? I don't know any details."

Eira put her cup and saucer down. "Yes. Dewi told me. He was only twenty-one, and the girl he'd married broke his heart. There was talk of his widow having a baby, but Dewi told me that nobody was sure who the father was. She left the island, not surprisingly, and Idris died not long afterwards. It broke his mother's heart I hear, as if it wasn't broken already after Arwel."

"But you still didn't ring Annie, even after that? What about after her husband Tomos died?" Nan asked.

"No, I didn't, and I know it was awful, Nan. Dewi has told me so ever since. But that's why I can't go and see her again, can't you see? I had my reasons, though, believe me."

Nan raised her eyebrows. "Then please tell me them. I'm struggling here."

A pause, fraught with unsaid words. "No. For the last time, I can't, or rather, I won't. Too much water has gone under the bridge and no good would come of it."

"She was your *friend*, Mum. I think..."

"And I think it's none of your business," Eira snapped. "Who told you all this anyway? The local gossip, no doubt."

"Mum, no..."

"Enough! Nansi, I wish with all my heart that Tomos was out in those fields, and you weren't sitting in my friend's kitchen, but there it is. I can't change it, and nor can you."

Nan flinched. Eira had not used that cutting tone with her for years. There was something raw beneath the surface, a splinter buried so deep that even nudging it caused her mother great pain.

At that moment, Ceri and Elin rushed into the room and raced around the kitchen with Shadow, shrieking, before dashing outside again. It was a brief ceasefire, but it gave Nan enough time for Eira's bitter words to sink in and for her to muster a response.

"Isn't it good that we bought this house, for a fair price, when nobody else wanted it, Mum? Annie will get good care for the rest of her life because we did."

"Nansi, I think you're coming here was a huge mistake, and I've told you that from the start. This is not a magical land where everything works out perfectly. It's real life, where things can be hard and people, unforgiving. I blame Robin more than you. He's a fool in some ways, but he should have known better, even if you didn't."

There was long, long silence as Nan felt guilt, hurt and finally anger flood through her body. Outside, her daughters' laughter rang out as they played tag in the garden.

"Please don't take your misery and regrets out on me. You should have been a better friend to Annie and you know it."

"You have no idea how your father would have punished me."

"Oh yes I have, Mum," Nan whispered.

Eira said nothing, but smoothed her skirt, a sign she was getting ready to leave. "That's as may be, but sometimes, the past is best left well alone. It's a waste of time bringing it all up again."

"So the years of therapy I had were a waste of time, were they, and the way I felt about myself when I met Robin? Should it all be swept under the convenient carpet of 'the past'?"

"Right, I'm going now. It was a mistake coming here today, as I knew it would be. There's a bus in fifteen minutes." She got up and walked towards the door.

Nan followed. "Mum, we need to talk about these things, for both our sakes. Please don't let us part on a quarrel again."

Eira spun round. "We will always quarrel if you never let me *forget*!" she hissed. "I'm free of him now, and so are you, don't you see that? Let it all stay in the past and live your life."

Nan grabbed both her mother's hands. "Mum, that's just what I'm trying to do, and I don't mean to hurt you, but you must remember that the past made me who I am, with all my faults and needs and stupid mistakes. It happened to me, and it happened to *you* too."

Tying her headscarf tightly under her chin, Eira said, "Well, I can't feel guilty about that, not anymore. I just can't."

"We can't change many things, but you could visit Annie

again now, in the care home. I think it would help you feel better."

Her mother turned away, buttoning up her coat.

"I'll drive you there myself, Mum."

"I'll see," Eira said. Which Nan knew, as her children knew, meant "no".

EIGHTEEN

Anglesey is renowned for its winter storms. Nan had heard all about them as a little girl, when she had sat on Dewi's knee, wide-eyed at his tales of roof-slates being blown into the sea like dandelion seeds and ancient trees being ripped from the ground like carrots. Despite years of vivid imaginings, she had yet to experience one of these storms, but this year, everything was different; she was not joining the slow-snaking traffic heading South on the A55 on a summer Sunday evening. She was staying here.

In many ways, Nan was looking forward to the wild winter weather she had heard so much about. She had come to start anew, to slough off the past, however painful, and what better way of doing it than to stand in the eye of a storm and let it rage around her? The day Eira left to return home, Nan and the twins drove her to Bangor station and as they waited on the platform for the (delayed) train from Holyhead, they felt a new, icy bite in the wind. Her mother lifted her nose and sniffed, like an animal.

"A big storm's on the way," Eira said darkly. "I can feel it."

"Look, the trees are all bendy," Ceri said. Nan followed her gaze and saw that the entire wood covering the hill behind the station was buckling and swaying.

"They are, aren't they?" she replied, feeling a tingle of excitement.

"It's like the seaweed swooshing in the sea," Elin said.

"You take care in that big old house," her mother said, hugging both her granddaughters before allowing herself to be hugged by her daughter.

"That house has been through a good many storms, Mum. We'll be fine. See you at Christmas, perhaps?" Nan asked.

"Perhaps. No promises, mind."

By the time they had waved Eira off, popped into the supermarket and set off for home, the wind was even stronger. Nan gripped the steering wheel tightly as she drove across the suspension bridge, trying not to think that this strip of stone and ironwork was all that kept them from the churning sea below. Gusts like the thump of a fist buffeted the right-hand side of the car, making the twins shriek with a mixture of fear and glee. The two flags on the Anglesey side whipped and slapped against their poles, and leaves whirled across the car windscreen like dervishes.

They finally reached *Coed Uchaf* after a white-knuckle drive of almost an hour. The road had been strewn with small branches, wheelie bins and even a trampoline which had upped anchor from someone's garden. The hawthorn tree by the farmyard gate that Nan had always loved for its gloriously curved shape was now not the only tree leaning away from the wind blasting off the sea. *Every* tree seemed to be gripping the ground as the rising gale tore at their branches and screamed around the house. The girls' swing was tightly wound around a sycamore's branches, as if it had decided it needed to hold on to something solid. Nan opened her car door and heard the hinges thwack as they reached their widest point in a second. Bracing herself, she heaved open the back door and an empty crisp packet was sucked out of the car, flying past her face and into the sky. She closed the driver's door and tried to shout at the girls to keep their heads down and run towards the house, but they couldn't hear her. As they struggled to stand up, their little faces scrunched against the blast, Nan grabbed one of each of their hands and they staggered to the doorstep where she managed to get the front door open. She shoved them all through it before bolting it top and bottom and leaning back against it, panting. She couldn't risk returning to close the rear car door. It would have to take its chances in the wind.

But once they were inside, the noise was almost as bad as it was outside. The sash windows in the kitchen – optimistically left open for "fresh air" – groaned and rattled in their rotten frames. Several doors upstairs slammed with such force that both twins screamed in terror. Shadow was crouched in her basket by the Aga, shaking pitifully.

"She's scared," Elin said, getting into the basket with her. "So am I."

Nan and Ceri looked out over the bay below the house. It was almost unrecognisable. Huge breakers crashed against the cliffs and filled the air with reams of laced spray, and the surface of the sea was peaked with frothing white tips like meringue.

"Mummy, is it snowing?" Ceri cried, as a fierce gust sent gobbets of sea foam up from the rocks below where they hit the windows before they dissolved and vanished.

"No, it's seawater whipped up by the wind, love."

Within minutes, the rime of salt on the glass was so thick that it was hard to see out at all and the light in the house became almost ghostly, just as if heavy snow had fallen outside. The noise was merciless and both girls were terrified as objects flew past the windows – a bin lid, a plastic sheet, an embattled crow.

"Mummy, are you scared, like Elin and Shadow?" Ceri asked.

Without hesitation, Nan replied, "No, I'm not. Remember what I said to Granny. This big old house has seen a lot of storms in its time and it's still standing strong." Inside, however, she recognised the first flutterings of panic, as this was pretty terrifying and she was alone.

"But what if this is a *super big* storm?"

"Oh, don't worry. Uncle Dewi told me they have big storms like this every year." She heard the quaver in her voice, but hoped with all her heart that her kids could not.

Suddenly, they heard a terrible groan, shattering glass and a thud on the ceiling so powerful that they were all showered with plaster dust. Almost immediately, the air in the house dropped by several degrees and an icy wind raced down the stairs, scouring through each room in turn. Crockery rattled on the shelves and the huge paper lampshade above their heads jerked and twisted like a man on the gallows. Ceri tried to join Elin and Shadow in the dog basket and when there was no room, she began to cry.

"Right, I need you both to stay here while I go and see what's happened upstairs," she said. "Why don't we make you and Shadow a camp under the table. That way you can all snuggle up together while I sort it out? Share this packet of biscuits out between the three of you."

"*All* of them?" Elin asked. "The whole *packet*?"

Nan crouched down, winked and whispered, "Don't tell Dad, but yes. All of them."

When she went into the living room to get cushions and throws for their "camp", the curtains were flapping almost horizontally from the windows like a surrealist film. Whatever had shattered upstairs had let this incredible storm inside her house, and she had to deal with it, there was no one else. Creeping up the wide oak staircase, Nan felt as if she were going into battle, her weaponry a dustpan and brush and a pair of Marigolds, but she had never felt stronger. When she reached the top stair, she saw it – an oak sapling had been uprooted and the topmost branch had crashed through the sash window on the landing. The beautiful crown of a tree lay on her new sisal carpet, its leaves flapping impotently, glittering with thousands of slivers of glass. The window was completely destroyed.

Her phone vibrated in her back pocket. The screen said "*Harri, Mim's Dad*". Nan only hesitated for a second, but just long enough to register the slight lurch in her belly that seeing his name triggered.

"Hello, Harri," she shouted.

"Nan, just wondering if you're OK over there," Harri yelled back. In the background, she could hear incredible bangings and clatterings, as if everything in his home was being violently shaken all at once. "It's bad, this one, and set to get worse. Are you all right? I assume your husband's away?"

"A tree's come through one of the upstairs windows," she replied. "I don't know what to do, to be honest, Harri. And yes, Robin's away."

"A tree? You'll need to put a tarpaulin over the window before the rain starts, Nan. It'll soak through your floorboards and do some serious damage if you don't."

"Oh. I don't know if we have one," she said, feeling her sense of invincibility begin to seep away. This was not fun anymore, and she was not an Avenger.

"*Be?*/What? I can't hear you!"

"I said I don't know if we have one, a tarpaulin, I mean," she shouted. "I'd could have a look in the outhouses, or ring Robin..."

As soon as she said the words, she knew this was not an option. Her husband was hundreds of miles away, and she knew exactly what his reaction would be. An unhelpful blend of:

"I knew something like this would happen," and *"I can't do a thing about it from here, can I? Ring Dewi – he'll help if he can."*

"Mummy, are you all right?" Ceri was standing at the bottom of the stairs, her brow creased in concern. She looked small and pale and scared.

"Yes, yes, I am," she shouted. "Don't worry... but we've got a tree in our house!"

"Nan? Are you still there?" Harri shouted. "I'm coming over, with a chainsaw and a tarp."

"Harri, you can't. It's too dangerous out there."

"Nan, listen to me. Stay downstairs, don't go near any more windows, and we'll be there in about fifteen minutes," Harri shouted. "Hopefully, we can beat the rain."

He hung up before Nan could protest.

* * *

Harri and Mim arrived in their battered 4x4 about ten minutes later. When Nan unbolted and opened the front door, she felt the full force of the storm hit her body and had to cling onto the frame just to stay upright. Harri carried Mim in first, depositing her under the kitchen table with the twins and Shadow. Then, shoulders hunched, he zigzagged to nudge her open car door closed with one buttock, before heading off to get a huge chainsaw. Then he battled out once more to haul a massive, black tarpaulin into the hallway. He and Nan then struggled, together, to close and bolt the front door behind him.

"*Iesu*/Jesus, it's a wild one," Harri said, struggling to catch his breath.

"My uncle did warn me, about the storms, I mean, but well, I never expected it to be this... *extreme,*" Nan replied almost apologetically.

"We have real weather up here, you see," he said with a cheeky wink.

"I'm tempted to offer you a chunky chocolate bar," she said.

He grinned and a spark flickered in his eyes that Nan had

not seen before. She had made him feel happy and it made her feel *amazing*.

"Right, let's get up and at that tree."

As the wind whipped his hair around his face and leaves flailed around his hands and arms, Harri braced himself on the frame of the shattered window. Then the roar of the chainsaw mingled with the shriek of the wind as he sliced through the thickest part of the branch, letting it fall to the floor with a defeated *thunk*.

"Help me push the rest out a bit," he said to Nan. "Just a few inches will do."

They grunted and shoved the trunk of the sawn-off sapling until it was just outside the window so that Harri could try to cover what had once been the window with the tarpaulin. Nan helped him loop ropes around the banisters, the curtain pole and door handles to secure this flimsy barrier between the inside and the outside. Then they wrestled with the huge sheet of canvas as the wind tore it out of their hands again and again, sending it billowing out of the window before sucking it back inside. Gradually, they managed to tame and fasten it, but not before Nan noticed that the almighty din was beginning to lessen, and there was a change in the atmosphere both in the house and outside it. The sky was almost black, and the sea was coated with an inky slick rather than the frantic white peaks of earlier. Almost instantaneously, the wind dropped dramatically and there was an uncanny silence before they heard rain thundering on the roof above them.

"We were just in time," Harri said. "That quiet always happens before the rain starts. It's like the sky is holding its breath."

"The whole house would have been soaked through," Nan replied. "I'm so grateful, Harri."

"*Dim problem o gwbl*/No problem at all," he said with a sincere but exhausted smile. "I'll have a *panad*/cuppa first, please, and then deal with the branch – saw it into smaller pieces for you. It'll make good logs for the winter when it's dry and seasoned. I can find you someone to fix the window in the next few days, or if you're willing, I can do a quote for you and do it myself when they all tell you they're 'too busy'."

"That would be great, thanks," Nan said. "Because I know they all will."

It all felt natural, easy, talking to this man. He had earned a cup of tea, so he asked for one. He knew how to sort out the branch, so he would do it. He understood how things worked up here, and seemed to accept them, both good and bad. She wondered, again why Harri was bringing up his daughter alone, without her mother, and always left standing on the edge of the playground by a group of people he had probably grown up with. Was he excluded for some reason or had he chosen to stay apart? She suspected the former, but how could such a kind man have done something to deserve that?

"So, what will your husband have to say about all this?" Harri said.

Nan hesitated. Robin would have plenty to say about how much they should pay for the repair and even more about why she had left a window wide open as it was "an open invitation to burglars", but she couldn't tell Harri that. She could feel him looking at her, waiting for an answer to his question with his head on one side, as she had seen him hold it before, but his gaze felt comforting, like a gentle breeze on her cheek, not accusatory. He did not stare or criticise or judge or tut-tut – he simply waited and understood.

"He'll be absolutely livid," she said. "A new sash window will cost a fortune."

"But the weather is beyond your control – just so you know, Nan," he said. "It's not your fault this storm happened."

"But I left the window open. That was stupid of me."

"It was fine weather this morning, remember?" Harri said.

"That won't cut it with Robin," she muttered.

"I bet he'll say that he'd have done a better job of fixing it up than we did."

She bridled then. "Hey, that's a bit rude, Harri. You've never even met him."

"Sorry. But, well, Gethin told me he does that kind of thing, your husband."

She sighed. "I know. And Gethin has a point," she said. "Robin won't be happy, whatever I do. He likes to be in control, as you've obviously heard."

"Well, a) he can't control the elements, and b) he's not here."

"You're right," she replied. "He can't and he isn't."

In Cambridge, Nan was used to people whose words danced around their meaning: there was something almost thrilling about someone who actually said what they meant.

"I happened to think you dealt with your first crisis pretty well," Harri said.

"Did I?" Nan said, feeling herself blush. "Yes, with your help, I suppose I did."

"It won't be the last one – just so you know."

She laughed. "Thanks for that. You remind me of my mother, talking like that! The Voice of Doom Robin calls her. At least I've notched one victory under my belt."

They went downstairs to join the three girls, who were still *cwtching*/snuggling with Shadow under the table. Harri immediately crawled underneath to join them and encouraged them all to sing a folk song they had learnt in school while Nan filled the kettle. She could barely see the headland or the burial mound out of the window, as the rain was a solid sheet of falling water. A few brave seagulls scudded across the sky, letting themselves be taken wherever the wind took them. How wonderful, she thought, to be utterly free and accepting of what life brought, be it rain, wind or sunshine.

"What a day," she said later, as they sipped their tea and

munched toast. "It seems a lifetime ago that we took Mum to the station."

"Welcome to Wales," Harri said. "Things can change in an instant here."

"For better, or for worse?" Nan asked.

"Better be ready for both," Harri replied with another, even cheekier, wink.

NINETEEN

On the first day of school after the October half-term, Harri and Mim were not in the playground. Nan, Ceri and Elin were bitterly disappointed, as they had bought them a voucher for the new pizza place in Menai Bridge to thank them for their help during the storm.

"Why aren't they here?" Ceri said. "Half-term's over now."

"Has Mim gone to live somewhere else, like we did?" Elin added, panicking.

"No, love. I don't think they've done that," Nan replied, surprised at how much she hoped she was right. Then she saw Gwenno out of the corner of her eye; they hadn't spoken for several weeks, and Nan had given up hope of a friendship. It felt a bit needy to ask her, but she needed to know where Harri was.

"Hi, Gwenno. Have a good half-term?" she asked.

"It was OK. Shame about the weather being wet, wet and more wet," Gwenno replied. "Sunny today; typical."

"That storm was something else," Nan said, clearing her throat. "We were just wondering where Harri and Mim were. Are they away, do you know, or ill? Sorry to be nosey..."

"It's not nosey to notice he's not here; he'd be glad someone has. He's taken Mim down to see her mother," Gwenno replied. "It's rare she wants to see Mim, so he takes her out of school when he's summoned. I think he should tell her to get stuffed, but he always puts his daughter first."

"I see," Nan said, though she didn't. "I know his partner doesn't live with them. Where *does* she live, do you know?"

"As far away from here as she could get for £50, is what I say. And good riddance."

"Oh. Right." A dozen questions bubbled up in Nan's mind, but part of her didn't want to know the answers. Did this woman still have a hold over Harri, if he went running to her when she clicked her fingers? And what did it matter to her if she did?

"Is young Mr Parry a good friend of yours then?" Gwenno said with a grin.

Nan blushed. *Was* he? "Well, our kids are friends, and he helped me when my window broke in that storm. So, yes, I guess he is a good friend."

"Great. He needs more of those, believe me," Gwenno said, heading towards the car park alongside Nan. She lit a cigarette and exhaled slowly. Then fixing Nan with her kohl-rimmed eyes, she said, "Just take care with that one: that's all I'll say. He's a lovely lad, but he's... *damaged*. Yes, that's the right word. Sad things have happened to him. He needs gentle handling, and kindness."

"*What* things, Gwenno?" Nan blurted. "Why is he on his own, when he's so... nice?"

There was a long pause. "You need to talk to him about that. I say it's wrong that he's still punished for it, but it doesn't make me popular round here. It's his past, not mine."

Nan nodded. "We all have one, don't we – a past, I mean?" she said.

"With good bits and bad bits, usually," Gwenno replied

with a sad smile. "Mainly bad, in my case, to be honest. Cigarette?" She offered Nan the packet.

"Oh no thanks. I'm sticking with giving up."

"Oh yeah. I forgot. Good for you. I'm just a puny weakling, see – zero willpower."

"I still really miss it," Nan added. "Smoking the odd one, I mean. Robin, my husband, hates it so much that I reckon he'd know if I had one, even from Cambridge!"

"Guto's dad was like that," Gwenno said. "Ruled the roost big time, and I just let him. Stupid was my middle name back then, and I gave up on so many dreams, waiting for him to love me. Not anymore, though. I stick up for my friends, and I stick up for myself."

Nan nodded in understanding. This was not what she had expected from their conversation, but she was learning that, on the island, people rarely were how she expected them to be. Appearances gave no reliable clues either. Gwenno may seem tough, but she was clearly sensitive, caring and easily hurt, and Nan had never met anyone like her.

"Where we moved from, everybody talked about everybody all the time, but they pretended not to."

"Nobody pretends here – they just do it. You'll find others who'll tell you all about Harri if you ask them, but not me. Take him as you find him, I say. He's been a good mate to me."

"And we all need them," Nan said softly.

Gwenno took a last, deep drag and stubbed her cigarette out on the ground.

"It must be hard for you, moving up here. Your husband works away, doesn't he?"

"Yes, back in Cambridge, where we moved from," Nan said, adding quickly, "But I wanted to come here."

"Sure. It's a beautiful place," Gwenno said. "But it's pretty tough, doing it all on your own. I should know. But with twins, I can't imagine!"

Nan forced a smile. She could easily become gossip fodder herself if she gave too much away to this woman she barely knew. She had to be careful. "Robin's home fairly regularly, and he's going to work from home a lot more once things settle down. I'm lucky, really."

"Not the same as having five days a week off-duty, though, is it?" Gwenno said. "You'll just have to hope his colleagues aren't too fit!"

Nan turned away, completely wrong-footed. Was this what people were saying behind her back, that Robin was playing the field? She felt a hand on her elbow.

"God, I'm so sorry. That joke was way out of order. It wasn't much of a joke, really. Just rude. I am a complete *twmffat*/idiot, you'll realise, as we get to know each other better."

Nan smiled. "It was a bit near the knuckle, yeah, but it's OK," Nan said. "I know it must seem pretty unusual, what we've done, but I have to trust him. His work is there, and I want to live here and that's the way it is. For now, anyway."

"Great, that's great," Gwenno said, kicking at some moss with her faded Converse.

"I really didn't mean to offend, but I seem to manage to do it, all the time. If it's working for you, that's fine and it's none of my business anyway."

"We try our best! But what about you?"

"Short story, really. Partner left when Guto was nearly two. He's got two more kids now, with different women, and he left them both and now lives somewhere in Kent, last I heard. I had this done to remind me of him."

As she pulled down the neck of her jumper with a triumphant smile on her face, Nan saw the words at the centre of Gwenno's tattoo, curved around a grinning skull: Get lost Jack.

"Oh Lord," Nan said. "That's brave of you!"

"No, just daft. Guto absolutely hates it, poor lad, but I can't afford to have it removed." Her smile vanished. "I find it hard to trust any man, now, because of one bad one. Does that make any sense?"

"Complete sense. You're not the only one," Nan murmured.

"I just hope Guto's nothing like his father," Gwenno said. "He's a good lad, isn't he?"

Nan saw sudden tears glint in her eyes. "He certainly *is*. Gentle, and very kind. My girls love him – and his singing."

"He never stops bloody singing! Look, we could walk our dogs together one time if you like. Guto says you've got a young collie and Reg loves a naughty playmate."

"That would be fantastic. Shadow's not too bad these days – touch wood!"

"Then Reg can lead her astray. Put your number into my phone."

"I'll really look forward to it, Gwenno," Nan said, thrilled. "Thanks."

"Me too, but I must say I'm a bit busy at the moment, with work."

"Well, you know where to find me," Nan said swiftly, to hide her disappointment.

"I do. Right, got to walk him and get to work. My hours get slashed right back now the season's finished. Then I have to take whatever I can get – cleaning jobs, usually."

"Where are you working at the moment?"

"In the café at the Sea Zoo. I hate it, and the early shifts mean I can't be here for Guto, but I have to pay the rent." She lit another cigarette. "There were so many things I thought I'd do with my life, you know, when I was at school. Did you?"

"God yes. I was going to be an archaeologist."

"Wow, like digging up Tutankhamen?" Gwenno replied. "Love all that."

Nan smiled, delighted to have another stereotype blasted out of the water. "So, what were your dreams?" Nan asked.

"Promise you won't laugh if I tell you," Gwenno said, expertly blowing smoke out of the side of her mouth and away from Nan. "It'll probably surprise you, looking at me."

"Promise I won't laugh."

"I wanted to grow things – fruit and veg, mainly. Yeah, I wanted to plant seeds, care for the seedlings, watch them thrive and then harvest things I had grown. I haven't even got a window box where we're living now, and it frustrates me so much."

"That's a great dream, and it doesn't surprise me. Remember that you're doing a lot of nurturing for Guto right now..."

"Shame I won't be able to eat him when he's ripe, though," Gwenno said with a howl of laughter. "Right, gotta go. Ta ra, Nan." Grinding her cigarette end into the ground, she strode off.

"Bye! Have a good day, and thanks so much for the walk invite!" Nan called.

But Gwenno was already in the car and did not look back. Nan saw a Cocker spaniel through the slobber-smeared back windscreen of the tiny car as it pulled off, creaking and bouncing over the potholes in the road and leaving behind a cloud of stinking exhaust. Getting to know that woman better was going to be fascinating.

"I might even take you up on that smoke," she muttered.

TWENTY

The journey between Cambridge and Anglesey became such a huge issue that Robin, tired of cancelled or delayed trains, bought a second car – a soft-topped Mazda sportscar, which Nan quickly dubbed his "midlife crisis car". But even this did not solve the problem of the distance between them. The next time he was due home in early November, torrential rain, gale force winds and patches of treacherous black ice on the roads made driving conditions so appalling that he called Nan from a service station near Wrexham at around 8pm.

"I left the office at 3pm and I'm still two hours away. It's like there's a line dividing this country into weather you can cope with and weather that makes life impossible, and you cross it at Birmingham. I'm going to have to stay in a Travelodge and come up tomorrow. Sorry."

"Sounds safer," Nan said, though he didn't *sound* "sorry" at all. "The girls will be disappointed, though. They've stayed up specially."

"Blame the Welsh weather, not me, Nan," he replied, hanging up.

"I hope you say that when you see the window upstairs,"

Nan said aloud. The quotes for a replacement window were astronomical, and she was really not looking forward to telling him.

With a heavy heart, she went to tell the twins the news. Robin's prolonged absences had begun to take their toll, and she had seen their sadness when other Dads came to concerts or parents' evenings or helped build the new bike shed in one corner of the playground.

"He never rings us, and now he isn't even coming home when he said he would," Ceri said. "People think we don't *have* a dad, like Guto."

"He likes being in Cambridge better," Elin added.

"Does he have a new family there now?" Ceri said. "A better one than us?"

Nan made soothing noises, but she remembered Gwenno's words, and the worm of doubt they'd awakened. *Was* Robin hiding something, or someone, from her? They never said anything loving to each other anymore and their now pretty sporadic conversations tended to focus on the girls. Robin had been here so rarely of late that, in her lowest times, Nan wondered if she had been in fact "posted" here with the girls to let him live the childless life he'd always wanted. He *could* be having an affair for all she knew, she had no real way of checking, and he made no sexual demands on her anymore. Such thoughts made for a very restless night.

When Robin finally turned up at 1pm the next day, Nan was clearing away the carnage after the twins had "helped" her make pancake batter and squeeze lemons ready for the celebratory brunch he had missed by being late. But when she heard his key turn in the lock and the click of his brogues on the tiled floor, the enormous relief that she was no longer on her own, solely in charge of everything washed over her like a tidal wave and she began to cry.

"Nan, what on earth's the matter?" he said. "Stop this. I'm

home now." He peeled her off his chest and stood back to look at her, his face taut with impatience. "God, you look terrible. Are you all right? Why don't you go and have a little nap? I'll sort the girls out."

"Sorry, yes, I'll be fine now. It's just been tough, you know. It's nearly three weeks since you were last here, but no, I don't want to go to bed and miss all the fun..."

The twins burst into the room like a mini tornado, hair flying and arms flailing. Nan ducked out of the way as they both crashed into their father, hands pawing at his body as if they were drowning. He knelt down to let them clamber all over him.

"I think they've missed you," she said, trying to ignore the twinge of jealousy she felt. After a storm of kisses and hugs lasting several minutes, Robin stood up, resting both his hands on his daughters' heads proprietorially. He was beaming.

"Well, that was worth waiting for! OK, you two, let me have a few minutes with Mummy. I think it's time you got dressed." Pursing his lips, he looked at Nan with mock disapproval. "Once you are, we'll go and do something nice today and let her have a bit of a rest."

"Oh, I don't need to rest," Nan said. "I'll be fine now the cavalry has arrived, finally."

"Finally, yes, thanks to the weather, Nan. This place is at the end of the known universe, remember. You look very tired."

"I am tired, but I want to do something nice too," Nan said. "We've been looking forward to doing things all together, haven't we, girls?"

The girls nodded, but after a playfully stern look from their father, went upstairs to get dressed, as instructed.

"Not sure you're up to doing anything very much, Nan," Robin replied. "Look at this mess, for starters. I'll deal with it, but I think you'd feel better if you just chilled out here today."

Nan hesitated. There was something steely in Robin's words, as if he had already made up his mind to leave her behind. She was struggling to get a grip on the conversation. "I'm fine. Not sure why I got so tearful. Hormones, I guess."

"Well, I hope you're not pregnant!"

Nan stared at him, her mouth open. "As if."

"We all know that hormones have often been one of the reasons why you're completely irrational in the past, don't we?" Robin said, taking off his immaculate-looking coat and hanging it on the back of a chair carefully. "One among many reasons, that is."

"Thanks for that," Nan replied. There was now a tangible edginess in the air, as if someone was dragging their nails down a blackboard. Robin seemed *different*, somehow – harder, more distant. "Is that coat new? Looks pricey..."

"It was, but not as pricey as an Aga, Nan. I got it a few weeks ago. It's not brand-new."

"Well, I guess I haven't seen you for weeks, so I haven't seen your coat," Nan snapped. Would he ever stop reminding her of the cost of the Aga?

"My having to earn a living must be terribly inconvenient."

Nan turned away from him, stroking Shadow to calm herself down. The little dog had completely ignored Robin – probably because she hardly knew him.

"Ah, I'd forgotten about your dog. That's why it smells in here," Robin said, wrinkling his nose. "Guess I'm not used to it."

"Shadow, you mean? Our family's dog? Remember us, your family?" Nan said.

"You're clearly overwrought, Nan, so let me take over now. I've made plans for today and we're going to have some fun. I can see you're *struggling* again. You've got that desperate look. I recognise it from when we first met and you were in such a state. Remember?"

Nan slammed her hand down on the table. Of course she remembered! And how very convenient to shift the blame onto her, as if having hit the booze and suffered from depression in the past was a crime that could never be atoned for.

"Is it irrational to feel emotional when the husband who's been away for weeks comes home and is horrible to me?" she hissed, her heart pounding. "I think not. You've stopped ringing the kids too. Too busy 'having some fun'?"

Robin folded his arms. "I told you. I had meetings lots of evenings and couldn't ring them. They don't seem too bothered, judging by that welcome. It's you that has the problem."

How Nan hated these snipes: she had no weaponry against them. It reminded her of her childhood, where Eric was the master of the cutting put-down. As she felt her breath begin to quicken, her palms to film with sweat, she knew that she needed to make it stop now, even if that meant taking the blame. It was the only survival tactic left to her.

"This isn't what we planned, Robin," she said. "That's all I'm trying to say."

"Nan, we've been here so many times. I have to work, and you were the one who wanted to move here, remember. I did worry that this arrangement would all be too much for you."

"Look, it *is* tough sometimes, tougher than I could ever have imagined, but things will be a lot easier for me when you work at home more, as James agreed you could," she replied.

Robin sipped his coffee and then shook his head.

"Nan, why would I push for that, when I'm greeted with this?" he said. "Go and have a lie-down, for all our sakes. I'll do the clearing up."

"I beg your pardon?"

He glared at her. "Just do it, Nan, please. Now."

She froze. She had heard that tone of voice before, and it was pitiless. Going upstairs, she closed her bedroom door and waited for it to end, as she had always done. She had a lock on her bedroom door now, as she had never been allowed at home, so she used it. That would show him.

* * *

She heard the girls excitedly getting dressed and waited for them to knock on the door to come into her room. Surely, they would want her to come out for the day: they knew how much she had been looking forward to Daddy being around more. Why didn't they insist she let them in, burst through the door and bounce onto bed, faces glowing with anticipation of a day out as a family? When she heard Robin coming up the stairs, she understood why.

"Sssssssssssh, girls. Mummy's having a little sleep. She's really tired because she's looked after you all this time while Daddy's been working," he said. She waited, breath held, until he saw the window that had been destroyed in the storm. "Oh my God! What a mess, and what a botch job this is!" Nan heard him tug at the plastic tarpaulin she and Harri had struggled to fix over the gaping window. "Another big bill coming my way I assume," he muttered, right outside the bedroom.

Nan curled up tight, arms hugged around her knees.

"Is Mummy not coming to the Sea Zoo with us?" Ceri asked.

"No. She's worn out, sweetheart."

"But we helped her make the pancake battery," Elin added.

"I know you did, and we'll make pancakes later with your world-class *batter*, shall we? Let's have lunch out, as a treat. We'll leave Mummy to have some peace and quiet and look after Shadow. Dogs can't come to sea zoos and pizza places, can they?" Robin said.

"No, they can't," the girls chorused.

"Right, let's go. Shout 'bye' to Mummy, and I'll see you downstairs," he said.

He was letting them say goodbye, was he? How gracious of him. Nan guessed he wouldn't risk upsetting the girls... and neither would she. When she unlocked her door and they crept in to say goodbye in person, she made sure the smile on her face was warm and happy. Spoiling their day would not make her feel any better or change the growing toxicity of her marriage.

"Are you too tired to come, Mummy? But I really want you to," Ceri said.

"You might feel better when you see the fish at the Sea Zoo," Elin added. "Please come."

Nan felt a huge lump in her throat. How she would love to see the joy on their faces as they watched the seahorses dance and counted the lobsters in the tanks. This was really hard, but she had to avoid a huge row. She yawned and rubbed her eyes: the twins would recognise that as a sign of "tiredness" from Disney movies. "I think I'll have an easy day at home with Shadow. We'll have a lovely time together, just me and her."

"Girls! Hurry *up!*" Robin yelled from the bottom of the stairs.

The twins gave their mother a quick hug, and scampered downstairs.

She could feel tears coming now, bitter, resentful tears. If she had protested, she would have been punished, a dread that had threaded through her childhood. Why was her husband angry with her for daring to express how she felt? As tears dripped down her cheeks, this misery felt horribly, horribly familiar.

"Bye. Have a good rest and feel better," she heard him call, but his tone was far from caring; he was giving her an order.

TWENTY-ONE

November can be a ruthless month on Anglesey. Arctic winds sneak through every gap in every window frame and whistle under every door. The sky is drab and grey and the sea like liquid metal, whipped into a white-tipped fury when storms blast the island. Nan knew that she had two options once Robin and her children had left for their day out: to hunker down and endure her solitary day or to seek company to soften the blow. She rang Dewi, who surprised her by answering the phone.

"Hello. *Dewi Jones yma*/Dewi Jones here."

Warmth flooded through Nan's body at the sound of his voice, his familiar name.

"Dewi, you're there! You never answer the phone in the middle of the day!"

"O, Nan. Hello *cariad*/love. Yes, I'm in bed, actually. Not feeling tip-top today. Pain in my back."

Nan's thoughts raced. Dewi had always been invincible in her eyes, and her mother had told her that he was more tired lately, but the fact that he had admitted to being even slightly under par unsettled her. She could not burden him with her marriage problems now.

"Oh you poor thing. Have you got enough painkillers?" she said. "I could drive over? Or do you need me to ring someone, Dewi? Have you been in touch with the doctor, if the pain's really bad?"

"Calm down, calm down, I'll survive," Dewi said. "Is something wrong there? You sound very, well, *paniglyd* is the best word I can find for it. You'd say 'stressed', I suppose."

"But the Welsh word is much nicer, isn't it? No, I'm fine, really," she lied.

"Yes! You really do need to learn our beautiful language properly, Nan," he said, and laughed, a rich, low sound that made her long to lay her head on his chest as she had done as a child and hear his voice "rumble".

"I assume it's nothing serious as you're managing to laugh at me, but yes, you're right, and I *am* going to learn it," she said. "I need to, to help the girls."

"And for yourself. It's part of belonging, I think." Movement, rustling. "Ouch, sitting up really hurts."

"Are you all right, Dewi? I can be there in under an hour..." she said, "I'm worried about you."

"I'll be OK, *cariad*/love," Dewi replied. She heard him pause and sigh deeply. "So you're on your own again? I thought Robin was coming home this weekend?" he said.

"He's... er... taken the girls out to the Sea Zoo today," Nan replied. "To give me a break."

There was a silence, which Nan could not bear for long. "I'm going to have a lovely easy day here with Shadow. I just wanted to, well, hear your voice, really..."

"Nan, tell me the truth now. Are you all right? You spend too much time alone as it is."

A longer silence. "Yes, of course I am. You take care of you, and I'll take care of me – OK?" she said, hoping he had not heard her voice wavering. "I'll leave you in peace. Get lots of rest. Love you."

But as soon as Dewi had hung up, Nan felt a numbing gloom start in her toes and move up through her body like an unwelcome anaesthetic. It was a darkness she recognised. If she stayed here, she knew she would sink down into it; she could not let that happen. It was threatening rain, and she could see the branches of the tree behind the house flailing in the wind. She grabbed her favourite old leather jacket and the dog lead and within minutes, was striding across the headland with Shadow running happily ahead. It was wild, but she needed it to be today. Perhaps, if it rained, that would scour away her doubts and help her see a clear way forward.

"I can't let him spoil this place," she told herself, as she stomped along the gorse-lined path. "I don't need him here all the time to be happy. I can be happy anyway."

By the time she passed the burial chamber, the gusts coming off the water were so strong that they hit her in the chest like a body blow. The black sky threatened a huge downpour, and yet on the horizon, Nan saw a shaft of sunshine cut through the clouds and light up a thin strip of water far out at sea. She walked nearer the cliff edge and stopped, bracing her body into the wind, to marvel at it for a few minutes. "This is what I came for," she said aloud, spreading her arms as a bird spreads its wings. When the wind took her jacket and it billowed out on either side of her slim frame, she felt its full force buffet her so hard she could hardly breathe. If she let herself fall now, gently, down into the churning sea below her, all the struggling would all be over.

"Help me be happy!" she shrieked at the sky. "Help me be *me*!"

There was a shout behind her, loud, guttural enough to reach her above the wind.

"What the hell are you doing?"

Nan turned, her body relaxed, as her feet went from under her and the wind took her staggering back across the grass. She flailed back towards the cliff edge, reeling like a drunkard, until she felt somebody pulling her arm very hard, hurting it, in fact. It was Harri, who dragged her towards his body and held her tightly to him as they both lurched back towards the path in a strange dance until they were in the entrance to the burial chamber. They stood there panting for a few seconds in the lee of the wind, Shadow circling them in alarm, barking. When Harri finally released his grip on Nan, she was smiling, but he was clearly furious.

"That was amazing," she said. "It felt as if I was, well, channelling the elements!"

"It looked as if you were about to die! Don't you know how *dangerous* it can be up here in weather like this?" Harri shouted.

"I don't think I care today. In fact, I *know* I don't," Nan shouted back at him like a petulant teen. "Nobody would miss me anyway."

Harri looked at her, an angry frown etched on his face. "I don't know what's going on in your head but think of your girls. They would be lost without you, and you would miss out on so many things in their lives. We can't take risks like that, ever, do you understand? Our actions have consequences because we have *kids*."

Nan looked at his face and saw pain in his eyes. Whatever had happened to this kind and gentle man to have shaken his soul like this? She suddenly felt very silly indeed.

"I'm sorry, Harri. And I put you at risk too."

He nodded. "You did. And I have Mim to think of, so it's not cool, not cool at all. Tell me that you'll never do something like that again. Promise me."

"I promise," Nan murmured, now terribly aware of the risk she had just taken.

"Why are you out here alone in this weather anyway? Isn't your husband home this weekend?"

"He is, but he doesn't want to be with me," she said, putting her head in her hands. "Oh, what can I do to make it right, Harri? It's all such a bloody mess!"

"I see," he replied. "Do you want me to walk you home, so you can talk to him?"

Nan shook her head. "Nobody's there. They all went out and left me. I can't face spending the whole day all on my own," she said. Giving in to the self-pity she had tried to keep at bay, she started to sob.

"Right, OK, we'll walk to mine. It's not that far. Mim's at my mum's for a few hours. We could even have a drink. I think I need one."

"A drink. Now that's an offer I won't refuse," Nan said.

"Neither's this, if you want to stay upright."

He held his arm out, and she threaded hers through it as, heads down, they began to battle along the beach towards Rhosneigr, the wind blasting into their faces. Nobody knew where she was going, and she hardly knew this man, but trusting him right now seemed like the best decision Nan had made in a very long time.

* * *

Harri's home was typical of the tiny, one-storey, squat Anglesey cottages that dotted the island. Set slightly back from the beach, with knobbled whitewashed walls and a vivid blue door, it had a beautifully carved wooden gate and a path made of shells that crunched under their feet as they ran to escape the rain. Sheltered from the worst of the gales, it entranced Nan from the moment she saw it.

"Oh, it's gorgeous, Harri," she said.

"It has its charms," he said, peeling off his coat and then taking hers, before hanging them both in front of the wood burning stove that glowed in the middle of the room. "A bit gloomy, compared to *Coed Uchaf* these days, but it's home. Tea first, or straight to booze?"

"A *panad*/cuppa, please," Nan replied. "It's a bit early for alcohol. That's probably the limit of my Welsh conversational skills, just so you know."

Harri laughed. "No worries, but we'll have to do something about that," he said. "Sorry, will you excuse me a minute? I need to do something quickly."

Nan sank gladly into the deep old armchair by the stove, Shadow at her feet, damp and exhausted, as the kettle slowly began to murmur on the hob. She was delighted to have a few moments to look around the room, and her eyes darted about eagerly. It was a treasure trove of the unexpected. At one end, was the kitchen – a small space, lined with an eclectic mix of handmade wooden cupboards all painted different, weathered, colours and topped with vivid ceramic tiles the exact blue of an Anglesey summer sky. One wall was completely covered with paintings of the sea – some large, some tiny, but all framed with beautiful pieces of smooth, bleached driftwood. Several layers of fishing nets were draped across the two, tiny casement windows, which gave the room its slightly gloomy air and surprised Nan. Why would he want to shut out such a glorious view? Surely privacy was not an issue here. It was so small, dark and warm that Nan felt as if she was sitting inside a peach stone. A pile of poetry books teetered under the window, slips of paper in many of the pages. Opening the slim leather-bound one on the top of the pile, she realised that it was the Collected Poems of W.B .Yeats. She turned to find 'The Lake Isle of Innisfree', the poem she had loved above all others as an angst-ridden teen in a claustrophobic London suburb. The final verse had spoken to her then, and did so even more now, releasing a rush of emotion that took her breath away:

I will arise and go now, for always night and day I hear lake
water lapping with low sounds by the shore;
While I stand on the roadway, or on the pavements grey,
I hear it in the deep heart's core.

"Sorry to leave you on your own," Harri said. He turned on a lamp and lit a row of tiny night lights on the windowsill. The effect was magical. "Ah, you like Yeats' poetry?"

"I do indeed. I hope you don't mind my opening your book."

"Not at all. Books are for sharing."

"This is such a gorgeous place, Harri. Have you and Mim always lived here?"

"Yes. She was born in front of this wood burner, actually. Bit cramped, with the birthing pool in here, as you can imagine, but it was amazing. She just slipped out, like a little fish."

"How wonderful," Nan said. "My birthing experience was a bit different with the twins – emergency section and all that. I didn't even get to listen to my whale music." They both laughed. Now had to be the time to ask about Mim's mother, but Nan knew she had to do it carefully. "Your partner must have been a lot braver than me to do it without drugs. What was her name, if you don't mind my asking?"

"And if I do – mind you're asking, I mean?" he said.

Nan blushed, wrong-footed. "I'm sorry. I shouldn't..."

"Don't worry. I knew you'd ask about her in the end."

She watched him scoop loose tea into a teapot and take two delicate, mismatched bone china teacups down from the wooden shelves on the wall. His every movement was slow and careful; he moved with an almost liquid surety Nan had only ever seen in practical, capable people. He was not a man to drop things. Handing her a cup of lightly fragranced tea, he sat down opposite her, and she waited for him to begin.

"Her name was Catrin. We were in school together. She

broke several hearts in the village, including mine. Then she left. End of story."

"I'm so sorry, Harri." A pause. "Why didn't she take Mim with her?"

Harri put his cup down on the floor and rubbed his hand across his stubbly chin. "Because in the end she hated her and hated me even more."

Nan was shocked. Before she could think what to say, a sudden noise from one corner of the room made her start. It was followed by a manic, metallic gnawing sound. "What on earth? Have you got *rats?*"

"Ha! No, not rats. It's Yeats, my hamster. Mim's hamster really, which she very kindly let me name."

There was a silence, and Nan sensed that she had to let the conversation go where it wanted to, that there was no rush to find out this man's secrets, or for her to reveal hers. In this room, it felt as if there was never much of a rush to do anything.

"What do you do for a living, Harri?" she asked.

"Mainly tinkering with things, making stuff from what I find – carpentry is the posh term: glorified woodwork is the truth," he replied.

"Ah, of course, yes. You're brilliant at making things – that's what Mim's told my two. I can see she's right, looking around." Her eyes explored the room again, taking in the bark-edged handmade shelves, the smooth wooden benches either side of the table. Everything was made with such respect for the raw materials they were crafted from: the knots in the wood were celebrated, polished up and joins between the pieces of everything he had made, velvet smooth. She spotted a bowl brimming with nuggets of frosted sea glass.

"Oh, I love sea glass!" she exclaimed. "It tells such a tale of where it's been and what it's witnessed, don't you think?"

Harri smiled. "Yes, I do. I love things and places that have a *story*," he said.

"Oh, me too," Nan replied. "I studied archaeology at Uni simply because of that, actually."

A pause. "I'm sure you must miss it – all of it, I mean. The beautiful buildings in Cambridge, having all that history around you..."

"Sometimes, I miss some things, but I wouldn't go back, even if I could," Nan said. She laughed. "I really just said that, didn't I? I must be settling down here then."

Harri beamed at her, his face lit up with a genuine happiness she had not seen before. "Well, I'm more delighted than I can say to hear that."

Logs crackled in the wood burner in the short silence that followed, sending sparks crashing against the glass door. The air of anticipation in the room was almost overwhelming. There were many more questions, and they were tiptoeing nearer them.

"Tell me, Harri, *why* did Catrin hate you?" Nan risked eventually. "And I can't imagine how she could hate her baby. Didn't you try and stop her leaving?"

Harri stood up, rubbing his calloused hands together. "It's complicated, Nansi. And painful. Mim will be back soon, with my mum, so I'd rather not get into it right now."

"I'm sorry. I don't need to know your business."

"And I don't need to know yours," Harri said. "It's simpler that way, for both of us."

"But I *do* want you to know that I'll talk to Robin this evening. We've always sorted things out before. We're from such different backgrounds, you see. It's hard."

"Yep, life is hard, but marriage must be harder. I wouldn't know."

"Yes, it is, at times," she said quietly. "But for all his faults, Robin let me come here."

"But now you need to be *happy* here, with or without him,"

Harri said. "Because you're not, are you? You were standing on the edge of a cliff an hour ago."

"I was just enjoying the wind, honestly," Nan said. "I'm fine – just a bit lonely, I suppose."

"I know how that feels."

Nan paused, unsure what to say next, or how to say it. Eventually, she opted for "breezy".

"Right, I'd better get home in case they've come back. Thanks for all your kindness, Harri. The weather looks better now."

"Well, it's stopped pouring, if that's what you mean," Harri said. "Can I just show you something before you go?"

When she nodded, he led her into a tiny lean-to workshop adjoining the cottage. On a workbench in the centre of the cluttered space, Nan saw a huge piece of bleached driftwood, intricately carved into the shape of a seagull on a slab of rock. It was perfectly poised, wings wide, as if only waiting for a gentle breeze to lift it into the air. She could almost feel its free spirit about to fly away and be released from within the wood. On the floor, she saw the dustsheet he had obviously just removed for this, her special viewing. For several seconds, the only sound was the beating of the waves on the shore below the cottage, and their breathing.

"Oh my goodness, this is that piece of driftwood I saw you hauling home from the clifftop that day, isn't it?" Nan said quietly. "It's beautiful, Harri. But how did you know what to make with it?" She looked at him.

Holding her gaze, he replied, "I guess I saw something in it that nobody else had seen."

* * *

When the rain intensified once more, Nan knew that she could not walk home yet. She accepted Harri's offer of a glass of his home-made damson wine. As they settled comfortably back in their chairs, she resisted the urge to rib him about her girls telling her that Mim's dad "drinks wine, like you", in case it offended. She knew more than most how sensitive a subject it could be. They were both sipping in contented silence when the door opened and an older woman stood in the doorway, holding Mim's hand. A freezing draught made the flames in the wood burner gutter and die.

"Mrs Green!" Mim cried happily. "Have you brought Elin and Ceri to play?"

"Hi, Mim. No, not today," Nan said, getting up. "They've gone out with their daddy."

"How convenient," the woman muttered.

"Mam, please," Harri growled. "Close the door and come inside. It's pouring out there. This is Nansi, a friend from school, who got soaked in the rain and came in to dry off."

"And she's *my* friends' mam as well. They're *twins*, *Nain*/Gran," Mim said.

"I'm so sorry to intrude, Mrs, er..." Nan murmured. "And do call me Nan."

"Beti. Harri's mam. *Bore da*/Hello."

Nan held her hand out and Beti reluctantly shook it for a second or two before dropping it.

"Harri doesn't have many visitors, you see. You took me by surprise," she said, her eyes as wary as any wild animal's. "Aren't you the one that's moved into *Coed Uchaf*?"

"Yes, I am," Nan said nervously. "Do you know the house then?"

"Yes. Poor Annie would have hated to see her farm as it is now, with all the land sold off," Beti said brusquely. "It's sad to see her now, but her mind's still as sharp as a tack."

"You've never told me you visit her, Mam," Harri said quietly.

"I go from time to time, yes. She was my friend

before... Well, she never recovered from the loss of her boys, really." She shook her head sorrowfully. "And now, her home's ruined too. A farm should stay a farm, where things grow or are nurtured, in my view."

Nan flinched as if Beti had pressed a tender bruise.

"Nan's mam was a friend of Annie's as well," Harri said. "She went to school with you both as well and Nan visited the farm every year when she was a girl."

Beti's eyes widened. She edged towards Nan, her chin only a few inches from her face. "Your mam's from here, is she? What was her name?"

"Eira Jones. Her twin brother is Dewi, who was like a second father to me. We came to Anglesey every year. That's why I wanted to bring up my children here, because I..."

"Eira Jones," Beti cut in. She wasn't listening anymore. "Oh, she was a lovely girl. Could have had anyone, but she married a man who made her go to London. She always wanted to stay here, poor girl. Yes, you've got the look of her – I can see it, now I know who you are, Nansi."

"There you go, Mam. She belongs here as well, wouldn't you say?" Harri said.

"I would," Beti said. "And I think Annie would be happy to know that Eira's girl is in her house."

"That means more than I can say, Beti," Nan said, her voice almost a whisper. "Mum wasn't sure she would be, you see."

"Well, there's a reason for that," she began, but stopped.

Beti sat down, and Harri poured her a small glass of wine and busied himself putting biscuits on a plate. Within a minute or two, his mother had visibly relaxed.

"I didn't mean to be rude, Nansi. It's just that I find it hard to trust people, you see, what with everything that happened to Harri..."

"Mam, *stopia*/stop!" Harri snapped. "This is not the time or the place."

Beti took Nan's hand and squeezed it hard. "He's a strange boy. It's a mystery to me why he thinks he's to blame for anything. He's a good boy, he is – a kind soul, my Harri."

"I know, Beti. And I'm so glad to have met him."

Beti smiled. "Eira Jones's girl has come home, has she? Well, well. You tell your mam she needs to come home now as well, *reit*/right?"

Nan smiled, warmed with damson wine, and with joy. "Yes, Beti. I'll tell her."

TWENTY-TWO

When Nan got home, she was soaked, cold, tired and windblown, but brimming with energy. In Gwenno and Harri, she felt sure she had the beginnings of two new friends. She just had to bide her time, be patient; she needed them far more than they needed her. After a long, hot bath, she began preparing the family's favourite pasta bake, making sure she topped it with lashings of cheese that the twins would love when it crisped and browned in the oven. She resisted the urge to finish the half-bottle of wine that glared at her across the kitchen because she wanted a clear head for the conversation she needed to have with Robin. But it was almost 8pm when Nan heard his car skid into the yard, followed by the unmistakeable sound of her husband bellowing at their children. Shadow vanished under the table and stayed there; she was not used to shouting.

"After all the money I've spent on you two today! Your behaviour is simply unacceptable. Elin! Ceri! Stay here until I've finished speaking to you!"

Within seconds, there was a desperate banging on the front door and Nan rushed to open it. Elin almost fell inside, with Ceri close behind her. They looked tired and drawn, and there were large pink half-moons under their eyes. Both had obviously been crying and they were looking over their shoulders at the car, and their fast-advancing father.

"Daddy's always cross," Elin said tearfully.

"He shouts all the time," Ceri added. "I wish he didn't come home at all."

"Let me get you both a hot chocolate to take up to bed with you. Sit in the lounge, and I'll be back in a second, OK?" Nan said.

"That other lady didn't like us, did she?" Elin whispered to her sister.

"But we didn't like her either, did we? She looked like Barbie," Ceri whispered back.

"OK, sweethearts," Nan said, her thoughts racing as she hurried out of the room to get their drinks. When she returned, trying to disguise her shock, the girls were almost asleep. "You look tired and I'm sure Daddy is too. You can tell me all about what you did in the morning. It must have been such a busy day." Nan could hear the sugary, unnatural tone in her own voice, but it was all she could manage right now.

The girls followed her up the stairs, heads hung low. When they went into their room to undress, Nan looked back to see Robin, his arms full of coats, fluffy dolphin toys and Pizza Hut hats, manoeuvring himself inside the front door before dropping the lot on the floor and slamming the door. He looked even more shattered than the twins, but, unlike them, he looked angry, not sad.

"That was one tough day," he said. "Give me a hand with all this, will you?"

Nan hesitated, her instinct was to help, but he had to know that he had hurt her this morning and that she was angry too.

"The girls are absolutely exhausted, Robin. I'll get them to bed and then I'll come and help you. I assume you've eaten. I had made a pasta bake, but it will keep."

"We had the full works in Pizza Hut, but the ungrateful little brats seem to have forgotten that."

"You're a bit *overwrought*, I think. Go and relax. I'll be down soon," she said. It felt good to use the word he had often used about her, about him.

"Oh, right. Fine," he replied. "I need a very large drink."

Nan felt she couldn't quiz the twins about the "other lady" tonight, however much she wanted to. Someone they had just got into conversation with, probably. She had enough to worry about without obsessing about there being another woman. Whatever had happened, it was obvious things had not ended well, but when she went downstairs to join Robin, braced to tell him what exactly she thought of his unkindness, she saw a bottle of red warming on the range and heard the familiar, soothing sounds of Miles Davis. Her husband was lounging in the kitchen, tickling a sleepy Shadow with his toes, a huge glass of wine already by his side.

"Come and sit down, love. Sorry I was grumpy when we got in," he said, patting the seat next to him. "I'm not used to having the girls all day, you see."

"No. You're not," Nan replied. "Tiring, isn't it?"

She sat down, but at the other end of the sofa. He had obviously realised that he had gone too far, but if this was his idea of saying sorry, it was not enough, and she would wait a while before believing he meant it. He was not getting off that lightly this time.

"Do you feel better after a day chilling in your gorgeous home?" He poured her a glass of wine, and handed it to her with a slow, lazy-eyed smile. She took a very large gulp.

"Yes, and no."

"Enigmatic. Tell me more, oh wise one."

"Robin, you're not funny. I really needed some company today," she said, realising the sheer unfamiliarity of saying exactly what she meant. "And you punished me for that need by leaving me here on my own. You know you did, and it was really unkind."

Her husband put his glass down and made a steeple with his fingertips, which never boded well. He looked exactly like his father, Nan decided. A lecture was coming.

"Listen to me. I have had a knackering week at work, a difficult, long drive back and I could see the moment I walked in the door that you were... *on edge.* I know you better than anyone, remember." He laid a hand gently on her thigh, and she noticed that his hands were butter-soft and his nails neatly cut and buffed; surely he had not had a *manicure*? The Robin she knew would laugh out loud at the idea of a man doing that. Her nails, in contrast, were so ribbed and cracked she wanted to curl her fingers up and hide them.

"But why were you horrible to me? We were all looking forward to you coming home," she said, hearing the first waver in her voice. Damn, her feelings were breaking through already. Always a weakness, in his eyes.

"I didn't mean to be horrible. I was stressed, and we all show stress in different ways, don't we?" he replied. His face, his words, expressed sympathy, but his eyes did not.

"Of course, but if you know me so well, you should have known that the last thing I needed was to be left on my own. Days are long when you spend them alone – you have no idea what that's like," she said, feeling her voice wobble again and her courage ebb. It was happening – the emotional tide that always overwhelmed her and lost her every battle.

Robin leant in. "No, I have to be in work all day, but this is what you wanted, Nan, and I gave it to you. I don't think I should be punished for that, do you? You were... *low* when I arrived, and I decided it was best for me and the twins if we left you here to recover. Sometimes, you can snap out of it, can't you? I thought I was doing you a favour, honestly – giving you a chance to get past it."

Nan floundered as she tried to find words to make him understand that it hadn't felt like that to her. None came, so he kept talking.

"Oh, we met someone you know at the Sea Zoo. She was working in the café and the girls recognised her. *Gitto's* mum, was it?" He scowled as if the name was distasteful.

"Ah, that's Gwenno, Guto's mum," Nan said guardedly. "Did you say who you were?"

"She saw the girls with me. I'm sure she'll report back, tell you she saw us quarrelling in the queue." His boyish pout told Nan that the experience had been hugely stressful for him. Sympathy came there none. She could imagine Gwenno taking one look at Robin and knowing exactly who he was.

"She looked pretty scary, to be frank. A hideous tattoo on her neck. Not the kind of person whose word you could trust, I'd say, and I hope she's not typical of parents at the school or we'll have to think again about where the twins go."

Nan spluttered. "Don't be rude, Robin. What do you mean you don't think I should *believe* her? You don't know anything about Gwenno. She's great."

"I can only go on what I saw, Nan," he spluttered. "*Get lost Jack* is hardly nice, is it?"

"Don't judge people you don't know. You can't, not up here, and I think that's good."

There was a long silence, inadequately filled by Miles Davis.

Robin gulped his wine, and his cheeks began to glow. "OK, let's calm down and try again, shall we? So, tell me, what did you do today?"

Nan hesitated. Part of her still wanted to ask him about the identity of the woman who the twins had said "looked like Barbie", but she decided not to. An angry, defensive Robin was a dangerous beast. "Well, I went for a walk, and I met Harri who mended the window with me and I went to his house for a drink," she stated as baldly as she could. "He lives in a gorgeous cottage right next to the beach. I met his mother, too, and she went to school with Mum and knew Annie Hughes."

"You went to his *house*?" Robin said, spitting each word out like olive stones.

"Yes. He was so kind to me when, well, I was on the headland and it was incredibly windy and I was very near the edge and he..." Nan stopped. She had seen her husband's face and a shot of fear went through her.

"I can picture the scene perfectly well. Harri was the knight in shining armour again, was he, showing up your inadequate husband? No doubt you told him how I had *abandoned* you today, just like I left you all to the mercy of the storm."

"Robin, stop it please," Nan said. "He just happened to be there..."

"When I couldn't be? Again. How very convenient."

He refilled his glass. Nan waited for hers to be topped up, but when it wasn't, she found she was completely unable to lean across him and grab the bottle herself.

"Look, it was no big deal. We walked to his place and had a chat," she said, adding, "He knows the situation... with your work I mean. That you're away a lot."

"I bet he does," Robin snapped. "It's a cliché, you know – down-at-heel locals preying on the wives of absent breadwinners."

"Robin! That's even more incredibly rude than you were about Gwenno! If Harri hadn't helped me today, I don't know what could have happened. It was wild out there."

"I'm sure he meant well, but you're very gullible, Nan. And vulnerable too."

Nan felt as if she was desperately paddling to stay afloat. "I'm probably too trusting, yes, but I'm not a fool. I have to try to make a life here when you're away. Surely you can see that?"

Robin grunted. "I suppose so, yes, but I didn't think you'd

be spending your time with women like that Gwenno. There's something not right about her, in my view."

Nan felt a flare of anger. "Gwenno has a lot more to her than you realise, and Harri is kind, he likes poets I like, loves history and our kids adore each other. He's a craftsman too, working with wood – his work is amazing."

Robin wrinkled his nose. "Oh, took you to see his etchings, did he? Another bloody *artisan*, I suppose. You need to be careful. You know nothing about this Harry chap."

"I know enough," Nan said, adding quietly, "But there's a lot I don't know, yes."

"Is he *trustworthy*?"

"Yes, I'm sure he is. I can suss people out pretty well, you know."

"You barely know him."

"Not yet," she said. "Friendships take time, and I have to start somewhere. I need friends, Robin – you know that."

Her husband closed his eyes and leant back on the sofa, his anger suddenly spent. Nan noticed that there were more than a few white hairs at his temples now, and he looked so *tired*. For a second or two, she pitied him and the path through life he had been forced to take, but she could not let him stifle her new life before it had even begun.

* * *

As they lay in bed later, she could not fall asleep. Instead, she stared at the ceiling, listening to the oystercatchers peeping and the wind rattling the loose cowl on the roof as questions fired in her brain like a volley of shots. Had they come to any kind of real understanding after all the bitter things they had said to each other recently? How did he somehow take away her power to express her feelings? How would they ever build a life here if he was judgemental about everyone? Did she actually want to stay with a man who made being her real self so hard, who no longer even seemed to love her?

As she heard her husband breathing in the easy, regular rhythm of deep sleep, Nan was not sure she did. She had clung to this man as a lifebuoy when chaos raged around her. He'd scooped her up when she was at her lowest ebb, shamed and vulnerable, but had he ever made her feel that he really valued her, for herself?

Why am I still with him? she thought.

The answer came, like a clear voice slicing through the darkness; she whispered it aloud.

"Because he's all I deserve."

PART 4

TWO PATHS

TWENTY-THREE

Winter's grip on the island advanced slowly, incrementally at first, until there was no escaping it. On some days, occasional slivers of blue still lit up the sky above the sea and the wind could be forgivingly mild, but the horizon between sea and sky had all but vanished, and everything was rinsed with a dull, leaden greyness.

Coed Uchaf was a lively, noisy home when the twins were in it, but an atmosphere of gloom pervaded each day when they were not. All the rooms were freshly decorated, but to Nan, every one of them spelt out her loneliness a little more. Nan often walked Shadow without seeing a single soul. At pick-up, parents scurried away from the mercilessly exposed playground and even Harri only waved briefly as he skedaddled to shelter. Gwenno had taken a second job cleaning at the hospital for the winter months, so her mother now dropped Guto at school. Nan asked how she was, and her worries were confirmed.

"She's chasing her tail. Worn out, she is. *Bechod*/It's a shame. All she wants to be is outside, always has. Breaks my heart to see her struggling."

Frustrated, and lonelier than ever, Nan wondered how she

could ever really belong here when nobody had time to become her friend.

But there were positives. The girls were happy and settled in school, and she heard them speaking more and more Welsh to each other. Her heart even warmed to hear them squabble in a language they had known nothing about only months earlier. When they started to get irritated that she didn't understand them, she returned to the online Welsh course she'd tried before they left Cambridge, but she found that the words and sounds slipped away like water down a drain.

"Why can't I just *learn* it, like the girls do?" she said to Robin, as they Facetimed after one disastrous lesson.

His face looked impatient. "It's a waste of time. I've told you that before."

"But Dewi and Harri told me I need to keep going, and practise."

"Are their circumstances like *yours*, Nan? No. You're English, and you grew up in England with a Welsh mother who never spoke Welsh. Just give it up. It's a dead language and I wish our girls didn't have to waste their time learning it, let alone you. Right, got to go."

"But I need *something* to focus on," she said, aware of the whine that had entered her voice. But he had already hung up.

The next day, Nan decided it was time to do something to avoid drowning in self-pity. First, she organised for the door to be made between the girls' rooms by a builder that Gethin recommended. Harri's amazing drawing was the blueprint (though she didn't tell her husband that). He had also agreed to design and carve some wooden panels to frame the door, each one depicting something from the seas around them – a starfish, a mackerel, a leaping porpoise. It would be truly stunning.

Once that was organised, Nan decided she would try to get as fit as she possibly could, forcing herself to walk Shadow for miles each day, whatever the weather. This made her feel good, and soon her skin took a hearty glow and her calves had new, shapely muscles, but she was still painfully lonely as she usually saw nobody. Every so often, she visited Dewi, but he had no time during the day, when she had many long hours to fill. She felt herself diminishing a little more each day and, within weeks, stopped the long walks. Shadow was soon as restless and agitated as she was.

The onset of winter had always been hard for Nan, but here, where the darkness was enveloping without the orange glow of street lights or the distant hum of traffic, it was even harder. Each morning, after dropping off the girls at school and the briefest of walks with the dog, Nan started going back to bed and staying there until lunchtime. Nobody would notice, and nobody would care.

Whenever she spoke to Robin, she tried to lay a trail of clues for him to follow, seeding tiny snippets of the truth about her unhappiness between layers of upbeat commentary on what the girls were doing, but he did not pick up on any of her hints... or chose not to. One afternoon, she rang him at work because she could not bear another single minute alone.

"I just wondered when you might be home again."

"Why, Nan?"

"I... well... I need to see you."

"You need to see *people*, Nan, not just me." A pause; a sigh. "Did you follow up my suggestion of doing a class if you still feel that you can't work yet?"

She heard him tapping on his keyboard.

"No. I don't know what I would study, really."

"Well, are you eating properly?"

"No, not really," Nan mumbled. "I never feel hungry."

She had eaten two biscuits and an apple in the past twenty-four hours and lost nearly a stone in the past month. Her face looked saggy and old in the mirror and the girls had noticed how thin her wrists were.

"Go this afternoon and do a big shop. That will make you feel better."

He was dumbing down to her again, making her feel small and childish. She hated it but felt completely powerless to stop it. She had no control over anything anymore.

"You could always ring your old Cambridge friends for a chat," Robin said. "What was it I used to call them – oh yes, 'The Titterati'. You all sat around talking about The Meaning of Life, while breastfeeding for Britain." He dissolved into giggles.

"You know I hated it when you called them that," Nan replied.

"Nan, where's your sense of humour gone? I can see you're struggling, but staying at home brooding is probably making it all worse. It always did in the past, remember?"

Her chest tightened as the familiar feeling of stupidity took a stronger hold. The next stage was panic which she couldn't let happen... so she cried instead.

"I know, and I'm really sorry," she said. "I thought it wouldn't happen here, but I don't think I really knew what it meant, leaving everything behind. It's so very different from the way I'd imagined it, with us all here together and yes, I am struggling."

"Oh God, not again," Robin hissed, his mouth pressed right to his phone. "It's a bit late for all this, Nan. We sold our nice house in Cambridge, you resigned from your job and we've royally burnt our boats. We had an *understanding*: your part of the deal was that you were happy and would let me live my life as I want to, as I need to."

Nan screwed her eyes tight shut. What did he mean by that? What was he actually *saying* – that they were effectively separated now? "I know. Yes. I'm sorry. I'll go to the doctor."

"Yes, please do that." A pause, another sigh. "I'll talk to James again about working from home a bit more, but he's not keen, and as I am the only source of income we have, *one* of us has to keep a grip on reality."

Voices called across the office. "Robin, mate – coming for a pint?"

"You have to go – I can hear them calling you. Sorry."

"Nan, why don't you book a make-over or have a new hair cut or something? I don't know what else to say."

Nan snorted, a stream of snot shooting from her nose as thick, gulping sobs took her words away. "There's nothing you *can* say, I know. It's all my fault."

"Nan, everyone can hear you crying. It's embarrassing."

She flinched, hearing distant cheery voices and a door slamming; they had gone to the pub without him.

"Nan, I've done all I can and I'm getting sick of this. I can't wave a magic wand and make you happy. Go to see the doctor and I'll call you tonight. Bye."

Pouring herself a large glass of red, Nan knew that from now on, she was on her own.

* * *

When Robin dutifully called that evening, she told him that she felt better, had eaten a big dinner and made a doctor's appointment for the following morning (none of which were true).

"That's great. Onwards and upwards, girl," was his response. The call was brief.

The next time Robin came home, he avoided any mention of how low Nan had been. He didn't hug her, let alone initiate sex, and spent a lot of the weekend murmuring into his phone as work demanded "so much time and energy". Although the girls greeted him warmly, once he had heard the Welsh twang in their speech and told them to "speak properly", they avoided him. None of them was sad to see him leave on that Sunday evening.

In fact, for the first time, Nan was actively *glad*. Yes, it was incredibly tough, but at least she knew what to feel, how to behave, when she relied only on herself. Robin was right, she needed *people,* but the only ones she knew here were Dewi (who was busy), Harri (who was avoiding her for some reason) and Gwenno (who was frantic). But she knew that she had to talk to someone soon, or go under. The girls needed her, so she had to try harder. She texted Gwenno before her pride had time to protest.

> Hi there. Hope you're OK. Your mum tells me life is pretty busy. Wondered if you fancied that dog walk some time. Shadow still needs leading astray... Nan

Within minutes, a reply arrived.

> Great. Meet in the school car park tomorrow. Left other job as the boss was a cow. Probably a stupid move, but I don't care! G

When her phone rang, Nan was still absorbing this message and was almost too paralysed to pick up. Had Gwenno reconsidered? Was she cancelling already?

"Hi. Quicker to call than text. Meant to say to bring food and your swimming stuff."

"Swimming? But it's *November*, Gwenno," Nan said.

"Yup. The best swimming season of all," she said, in a tone that brooked no argument.

TWENTY-FOUR

When she looked back years later, a handful of days in Nan's life stood out, like gems. The day she knew that she really was Gwenno's friend was one of them. After all the lonely weeks of dark, wet weather, the sky that day was clear, sparkling with crisp sunshine. The seabirds woke Nan early, as they, too, seemed to be full of excitement at the possibility of a better day. She showered quickly, dressed in at least four layers and went downstairs, where she made a stack of sandwiches, fruit cake and a flask of very sugary tea and crammed them into a Disney backpack with her swimming costume and a towel. The very thought of going into the icy sea horrified her. She had yet to invest in expensive, unused "outdoor gear" that Robin had bought for himself, let alone a wetsuit. She always walked in wellies and a tatty old waterproof from a charity shop in Bangor. Humming tunelessly, she buttered toast and poured juice for breakfast, and the twins sensed her lighter mood the moment they came downstairs into the kitchen.

"Mum, you look happy today," Elin said.

"Yes, I'm going for a walk with Gwenno today, Guto's mum."

"She *looks* scary, but she's nice really. Guto says they still haven't got any money, so he won't be getting anything for Christmas."

"That's sad. I know she's been working really hard, doing two jobs..." Nan said. She realised, as she often did, how very, very lucky she was, despite everything.

"Is Guto's mum your friend now?"

"I hope so. I think so, yes."

"Then Guto can have some of my presents," Elin said.

"And mine," added Ceri.

Nan smiled at them. "That's so kind, girls. We'll sort something for Guto, I promise."

"But you still like Mim's dad, don't you? Is he still your friend too?" Elin said. "Mim said you met her grandmother, and she was..."

"...a bit grumpy," Ceri added. "Like our Nainy Eira. She's always grumpy."

Nan smiled wryly. "Yes, she was at first, just like Nainy, but she was all right in the end. And I haven't spoken to Mim's dad in a while."

"Mim told us he's been sad, like you," Elin said. "He hates the winter."

"Really? Does he?" Nan exclaimed. Was this yet *another* thing they had in common? "I was thinking of inviting everyone round for Sunday lunch one day soon. It might cheer us all up a bit, winter or no winter. What do you think?"

The chorus of whoops gave her the answer she was hoping for.

* * *

Gwenno was waiting in her car at the school car park, her dog Reg charging from side to side of the boot yipping with delight.

Nan had no idea where they were going but was determined not to ask questions and go with the flow.

"We'll go in my car, OK?" Gwenno said. "There's nothing that can happen to it that hasn't already happened, and yours is much too shiny."

"Shall I have Shadow by my feet, in case the two dogs don't get on?" Nan asked.

"No. Chuck her in the boot with Reg. They'll either eat each other or bond for life."

Nan opened the boot slowly and Shadow jumped in to join Reg who, after a quick attempt at mounting her, wagged his tail. "'Bonding for life' it is then."

"Now it's your turn. Do you really trust me enough to get into this filthy car and come with me, Mrs Green?" Gwenno said, a mischievous twinkle in her eye. "I know it's not easy for you to live dangerously. I've met your husband, remember?"

Nan laughed out loud, a sound that filled the air and came from deep within her – and one she had not heard for a very long time.

* * *

They drove on roads Nan had never been down in all her years of visiting the island – tiny, grassy lanes which took them inland, away from the coastline she knew. Hedgerows exploded with clouds of twittering sparrows as they drove past, and the wintry sun was just warm enough to make the dewy leaves steam gently. They chatted about kids, the weather and their favourite soaps, only venturing into less comfortable territory once, when Gwenno confessed to being worried about how she was going to make ends meet with a zero hours contract.

"Guess I'll be able to pick up more hospitality work towards Christmas, but it's soul-destroying. I need to be outside. I really need it."

"Yeah, your mum told me. I wish I could help," Nan said weakly.

"You are helping, by being here. I feel I can be myself with you, so I hope it's OK to be honest and say I'm not finding things easy at the moment."

Nan laid her hand on Gwenno's arm. "You're speaking to the world expert, here."

There was a short silence, while both women realised the implications of their words. This felt like friendship: openness, empathy and kindness. And it felt fabulous.

"I'm glad you said you were free today. I don't really know many people – well, any people, as yet. Harri's probably told you that things... er... got on top of me a bit recently."

Gwenno looked at her gravely. "He told me about a close shave on the clifftop, yes. Harri and I tell each other stuff like that. We've both had some tough times, and shared things."

Nan nodded. "It's good that you can. You're lucky to be such good friends."

"We only have each other, really, as you've probably noticed." She crunched up a gear. "I saw your husband at the Sea Zoo the other day, did he tell you? He looked, well, *strained* is the best English word I can think of."

"Yes. He said he'd seen you," Nan replied. "Sorry if he was offish. He said it had been a trying day, in lots of ways."

Gwenno said nothing more but looked as if she wanted to. Instead, she lit a cigarette, opening her window so that the car filled with a chilly blast.

"Nan, tell me, does your husband know how bad you were feeling that day?" she said eventually.

This was tricky ground. "Yes, and no. I've been there before, you see – on the edge, in more ways than one."

"So have I, and so has Harri," she said softly. "We're on your side, *cariad*/love. Just sayin'."

In the back of the car, Reg started to whine. "Getting excited, Reg?" Gwenno said. "We're nearly there."

"Robin says he's tired of trying to save me, you see," Nan blurted. "He says I'm *needy*."

"We all have needs, Nan. Doesn't make us needy."

"Yes, you're so right," she murmured. "Why have I never seen it that way before?"

Smiling, they drove on towards the sea in comfortable silence.

When Gwenno turned down a gentle hill towards a small harbour, a cloud of slick-feathered starlings gathered, swooped, parted and then re-gathered out over the water in front of them. They seemed to sense each exact tiny movement of their neighbours and fly in sheer celebration. It was a breathtaking sight.

"A murmuration," Gwenno said, pulling up so that they could watch them. "I love that word, don't you?"

"Yes, I do. Look at them. Aren't they amazing? How do they know how to follow each other so closely, so carefully, and never crash?"

"Small brains, big hearts, I say. I think they're doing it for you, a dance, if you like. An airborne haka!" Gwenno guffawed at her own joke, then coughed with a smoker's zeal. "Cigarette, or have you still given up enjoying yourself?"

"I think I might be on my way back to the dark side, but not at the moment, ta."

They parked outside a row of deserted holiday cottages and Shadow and Reg bounded ahead up the footpath, over and around the cliff. When both women got out of the car, Nan was relieved to see her new companion tug on a flimsy old mac fastened at the top with a safety pin and some very knackered-looking walking boots. She also noticed that the car was riddled with rust and hoped it would survive the drive back without bits falling off. How would Gwenno be able to get to any job if she couldn't afford to repair it, though? Buses on the island were infrequent, expensive and unreliable.

"Right, follow me," Gwenno said.

"Where are we going?" Nan asked, with a sudden flicker of doubt. She barely knew this woman and had absolutely no idea where they were or where they were going... Trusting anyone was hard for her to do.

"You'll see," Gwenno replied. "You worry too much."

"Habit of a lifetime," Nan replied with a grin.

"Let you off. Look at all these lovely little houses, empty for months of the year while Guto and I have to live in a damp shit-hole where mice have a party in my kitchen every night."

"You don't agree with people having second homes?" Nan said, treading very gingerly and painfully aware of her own huge house.

"No, I don't. They should rent a caravan, or even one of these fancy lodges, but don't buy the island's houses. They should be people's *homes*. And as for all the gardens going to waste, that breaks my heart even more."

"Shame *you* can't grow things in them, isn't it, as they're unused?" Nan said. "Your dream was to grow things, wasn't it? I remember."

"Well remembered. I did, actually, once, cheeky mare that I am. I planted some seed potatoes in a bit of earth at the back of this huge house that nobody ever used. Planned to sell them, make a bit of cash, but someone reported me, and I got a police caution and a fine. But who was the real criminal? The bloke from Surrey with more money than brains."

Nan, who had heard this argument many times, could not help but agree.

* * *

The path followed the edge of the land so closely that they could soon hear the churning water crash on the rocks below and feel the spray mist their faces. Despite all the recent rain, the track of baked mud and grass was fairly dry and made for easy walking, but it was narrow, so they walked in a line, in silence. There was no need for words anyway, they both felt completely at ease, and had plenty of time ahead to talk. Today was mainly about not feeling alone anymore.

After about an hour, they rounded the headland and a glorious, open bay greeted them, framed by thickets of wind-blown hawthorn. There was an old wrought-iron bench on the edge of the cliff, which offered the most spectacular view out to sea.

"Perfect spot for a *panad*/cuppa. Wish I'd brought a flask," Gwenno said.

Nan patted her backpack, smiling. "Well, you're in luck, because I *did!* Hope you take sugar, though, because this tea is seriously sweet!"

The two women drank tea and ate Nan's fruit cake (with both dogs sitting, drooling, in front of them) and listened to the distant, mournful cry of a curlew and the beat of the waves below them. When the clouds were parted by a soundless wind, far out at sea, the sun lit up the horizon and it shimmered like a ribbon of molten gold.

"This is what I came to the island to find, this peace," Nan said. "But somehow peace has become 'disappointment' and 'loneliness'."

"Change the way you look at the island then. See it for what it is. A lump of rock surrounded by the sea. The island will nurture you, help you thrive and grow strong, like a plant I guess, but you have to plant the seeds of change yourself," Gwenno said earnestly. "Oh, and have you gathered that I really love talking about growing things?"

Nan laughed again, happy to be spending time with this

strong woman she had only just begun to know. "Have you? Found peace, I mean?"

"It's a work in progress," Gwenno said. "I have my moments, my regrets, especially when I think about all the things I wanted to do, or how I let Guto's dad treat me."

"Jack, of '*Get lost*' fame?"

"That's the one. How did you guess? Oh, I did love him, but he made me feel so bad about myself," Gwenno said. "I've learnt to put on my game face, you know, keep everyone at arm's length."

"But not Harri?"

"Harri I can be honest with. He understands how it feels to need real love but to be offered something less and told to put up with it."

Nan wanted to say, "So do I," but resisted; saying nothing about her past was still her go-to tactic, and Robin's warning not to trust this woman had not gone completely unheard. Instead, she asked, "What happened to Harri? Why is he bringing up Mim alone?"

Gwenno hesitated. "I still think it's best that he tells you, when he's ready – and he will, believe me. *He trusts you.*"

"I know how it feels too, to need love but not receive it. My father never gave me a moment's love in my whole life. He bullied me, silenced me, *hurt* me..." her voice cracked.

"You don't need to say more. We all have things it's hard to talk about," Gwenno said, laying her rough, reddened hand over Nan's. "But I understand. And I know how hard it was for you to tell me that."

Nan smiled, her heart full of thanks. "Perhaps I'm a work in progress too."

"Of course, you are! We all are, and at least you're *making* progress."

"Thanks for that. I'd started to think I was going backwards, not forward, but perhaps Robin actually did me a favour, telling me he'd had enough of me being a misery guts, spurring me on to do something about how low I was feeling – like contact *you*!"

Gwenno winced. "Well, he can have one brownie point for that, but perhaps you've had enough of *him*. He sounds a bit unkind to me, and I don't think you need him half as much as he thinks you do, Nan."

Nan was quiet. Hearing someone she hardly knew judge her husband that harshly was not easy to listen to, even if it was true. She decided to say nothing, but she would think about Gwenno's words for hours after they had parted.

Eventually, they packed up their picnic things and set off again along the coastal path. Ten minutes later, Nan glimpsed a brick chimney and a cluster of half-ruined buildings right down on the shore of a stunning pebbled bay ahead. Lit with weak winter sunshine, the bricks glowed a rich orange.

"That's where we're heading. Porth Wen, the old Victorian brickworks and the clearest water you'll see in your entire life," Gwenno said.

"That's where we're swimming, is it? It's a bit of a sad ruin, isn't it?"

"Takes one to find one, girl," Gwenno said, slapping Nan's back so hard she collapsed, coughing. "You up for a dip? It will be chilly, I know, but you won't regret it, I promise you."

"Do I really have a choice, Gwenno?"

"Nope."

"Then bring it on."

But by the time they had scrambled down the rocky footpath to the brickworks, the sun was noticeably lower in the sky and the air much cooler. As Gwenno and the dogs set off down to the water's edge, Nan felt her bravado begin to crumble and the first signs of panic spread through her body. This was the Nan she knew, the one that she despised. She was not like Gwenno who strode out, tattoo and piercings blazing as if heading into battle with the world. Nan's instinct was to run, to hide. How could today possibly be any different, when she had never been brave enough to face her fears before?

"Come on. It's now or never," Gwenno shouted back to her, pulling her clothes off roughly as her teeth chattered. "I know exactly what you're thinking, that we're mad, but I really want you to do this – I want *you* to know you can do it. A few seconds in – that's all I ask."

In a frantic flail, and struggling to hold a towel around her, Nan pulled off all her layers and, shaking violently, heaved herself into her swimsuit. It hung off her in folds, as she was now so skinny. "This is bonkers. We don't even have wetsuits," she bleated.

"You need to feel the water on your skin for it to work its magic. We'll put wetsuits on for the rest of the winter, OK, but it's got to be skin today!" She strode down towards the water. "Come on, after me! Splash yourself all over before you go under, though, and take it nice and slowly."

Gwenno turned and ran into the water, shrieking, splashing, until she was in up to her thighs, her flesh scarlet with the cold. Then, in one smooth movement, she threw herself under the curl of the next wave and was gone.

Nan stood on the shore, heart pounding and palms sweating despite the cold. Voices ricocheted inside her head: Eira would tell her that "she would catch her death"; Robin would point out that wild swimming in winter causes a high percentage of cardiac arrests in the uninitiated. But she also heard her twins cheering her on, and it was their voices that gave her the courage she needed. With a light, sure step, she marched down to the water and just kept on going, whipping up the water around her so that it splashed all over her body as she went. She shrieked. It was absolutely freezing – cold enough that her feet and legs were numb in seconds. This was crazy, perhaps even dangerous, but she needed to go beyond doubt and blame and regret. Before she had time to stop herself, she took a huge breath, dived beneath a wave and the sea closed over her head. The sound of the water was deafening, her jaw ached and her skin was raw and stinging... and yet it felt like an embrace.

Two or three hurried breast strokes were enough, then they were up, gasping, sprinting back onto the pebbles, eyes wide and laughing hysterically. Nan felt as if she had been electrified, as her entire body zinged and tingled with exhilaration, and with pride. They both struggled to dry themselves, stumbling, hopping as they heaved all their layers of clothes over their still-wet bodies in a desperate rush to be warmer.

"You see? You did it! You can do *anything*. And this little island can give you all you're looking for, if you let it," Gwenno said, as she shivered.

Nan pulled her blue-tinged lips into a smile. This was the coldest she had ever felt. And the most alive.

TWENTY-FIVE

The two women met and swam together several times a week throughout November and into early December. Very quickly, Nan started to crave the shock of the cold water and the exhilaration she felt after she had surrendered to it. Firm friends now, they grew to trust each other completely, not batting an eyelid when the wind took their towels and exposed their shivering, less-than-perfect bodies, not judging if one wanted to stay in longer than the other or just couldn't go in any deeper than their pubic bones. They shared secrets, laughed uncontrollably and shed many tears. The differences between them were huge, but Nan had never felt happier in another woman's company. Gwenno described how hand-to-mouth her existence had now become with her unpredictable working hours and meagre benefits, and the everyday sacrifices she was having to make to ensure that her little boy was well-cared for. When Christmas came up, Nan did not say that the twins had told her that there would be no gifts for Guto, but she longed to help her in a way that her proud friend would feel able to accept.

Their meetings became the highlights of Nan's week, and she enjoyed them far more than the rare weekends Robin came home. She even wondered if she was in love with Gwenno at one point but decided that she was just overjoyed at having found a good, true friend at last. There were things they did not say, but both of them sensed a shared wound in the other, a barely healed scar: they did not need to say it, to know it. After they had talked, swum and laughed together, Nan's thoughts returned again and again to how she could help Gwenno without seeming patronising, or feeling she was pitying her.

The solution came to her as she stood at the kitchen sink one gloomy winter afternoon and she cursed herself for not having seen it before. It was staring her in the face, literally: the long-abandoned kitchen garden at *Coed Uchaf*. Gwenno could grow things in it! It was a large plot, with room for lots of planting, some grimy cold frames for cucumbers and courgettes, a greenhouse for tomato crops (once the glass was replaced) and a row of unkempt espaliered fruit trees – or whatever she fancied growing, really. It needed to be cared for as it was an eyesore, and Nan had seen several fat-tailed rats lurking in the brambles. Best of all, this garden had always supplied whoever lived in the farmhouse with fresh produce, Dewi had told her, so it could feed their two families and perhaps even supply local people. The farm would be a proper, working farm again! Cambridge had plenty of pricey organic vegetable box schemes for (largely) middle-class people who wanted to eat sustainably. Perhaps it would work here, too, with Welsh families who valued locally grown but reasonably priced food? She remembered Dewi's words vividly:

"Oh, you never went to Tomos and Annie's place without coming home with a boxful of veg," the old man had said. "Wouldn't take a penny for it, though. They said it was a gift from the land they loved, not from them."

Resisting the urge to ring Gwenno immediately and tell her what she had decided, she went to her laptop and drew up a plan of action, so that the proposal was a rough business suggestion rather than sympathy. Her Excel spreadsheet included what rate of pay she could offer (not much, but it would be on a par with the jobs her friend had been doing), how much she could spend on repairing the greenhouse, seeds, saplings and seedlings (also not much) and how much control she wanted to have over the project (even less). She would have to gloss over the costs for Robin but knew she could persuade him that it was "adding value to their property", a subject very close to his heart.

Their next swim was arranged for a wild, windy day in December, and it was the coldest it had ever been, so Nan and Gwenno undressed on the beach without exchanging more than a few words. This was endurance, today, a real test, and they knew it would not be easy, but they did not allow themselves to hesitate, or to doubt that they could do it. As they yanked up their shortie wetsuits, Nan noticed that Gwenno had lost weight, probably because she had confided that she gave the majority of whatever food she had to Guto (who had a very big appetite for such a very small boy). Nan decided that she had to put her plan to her friend today when they were drinking their usual hot, sweet tea in the car. If she waited much longer, the frosts of deep winter would have made digging the ground impossible.

"Right, let's do this," Gwenno said, striding towards the steel-grey sea. "It looks sooooo cold. We must be bonkers."

"Wait for me," Nan called. "We need to hold hands to go in at all today."

"Great plan. Then neither of us can bottle it."

"No bottling allowed."

And so, holding hands, they walked resolutely into the icy water together, without pause, squeals suppressed, until it reached their waists. Then Gwenno turned to Nan, smiled, squeezed her hand hard and let it go, before diving into the water and disappearing. Nan did the same, and both of them surfaced together a few seconds later, their skin a vivid pink, shrieking at the sky like banshees.

* * *

Later, when they sat in Gwenno's smelly, steamed-up car (which Nan had dubbed "The Crate"), Nan broached her plan. Doing so in a respectful, sensitive way was the part that worried her most. She began tentatively.

"Gwenno, I had an idea the other day."

"Really. I had one of them in 1992. Overrated, in my view."

A throaty peal of laughter.

"Haha. Listen, please. I have a proposal to put to you."

"Hope you've got me a *very* big ring then."

More laughter.

"Stop it! This is serious. I'm really trying here..."

"OK, but if it's anything to do with skinny-dipping on Christmas Day, count me out. That's where I draw the line."

Nan giggled so uncontrollably that she needed several minutes to control herself again.

"Right, now listen and don't talk until I've finished?"

Gwenno saluted and mimed zipping her mouth shut.

"Look, there's a fabulous old kitchen garden behind *Coed Uchaf*. The estate agent's details said it was at least half an acre, but I think it's more. The soil must be good under all the weeds, as Dewi told me Tomos and Annie grew loads of fruit and veg there." Nan paused and glanced at Gwenno. She was absolutely still. "Well, I thought we could do the same. Dewi would give us manure to pep the soil up a bit and he has loads of tools I know he'd lend us. There's a greenhouse which needs some TLC, some cold frames, a potting shed. You could plant whatever you wanted to, and we'd pay you a fair hourly rate, regular hours and supply the seeds and stuff. Robin isn't here, and I'm no gardener, so you're the boss, but I'd help you whenever you needed a second pair of hands. How does that sound?"

Nan paused again for a reaction, but when her friend said nothing, she went on. "It's wild now, I know, and there are rats, so we need to sort it out, but you'd be doing us a favour, honestly. I thought perhaps we could even start a veg box scheme in the village if it goes well. It's such a trek to a supermarket from here and our stuff would be organic and local. I thought we could ask people what they'd like us to grow rather than the endless schemes in Cambridge where you got a misshapen squash, some grotty spuds and a small chilli, none of which you could actually cook with. I just think..."

Gwenno grabbed her hand. "I think it would be wonderful," she whispered, and burst into tears.

"Great! So do I!" Nan said, relieved. "I'm sure we can make it work, together."

"And you'd *pay* me?"

"Yes, but it won't be much more than you're on now," Nan said. "But it's got to be better than what you're doing, and you must always get Guto to school first."

Gwenno wiped her nose on her sleeve and beamed at her friend, tears still glinting in her eyes. "It sounds like my dream come true, Nan," she said, before adding with a wink, "But I'm the boss, and don't you forget it!"

* * *

Over the next week, the two women spent many hours hammering out the details of their joint venture. First, Gwenno needed to be reassured that she was not being treated as a "charity case", but that they were establishing what could be a viable business. Giving up any chance of shifts at the Sea Zoo was a risky strategy if not. Then Nan had to persuade Robin that it would be an investment and that they owed it to the money they had ploughed into the house thus far to finish the job, and to do the garden as well. He didn't seem at all interested, but the mention of rats got his attention. Eventually, he decreed that as long as costs were kept low, he gave his consent.

Once broad details, and an initial planting scheme had been sorted, Gwenno arrived at the house each morning after the school run and set to work. She knew that, until the end of January, her main task would be clearing the ground, digging the soil over and enriching it ready for planting in the spring, and she worked with such zeal that Nan often had to remind her to stop for a *panad*/cuppa. Within a week, Gwenno had cut back the matted brambles and exposed an even bigger expanse of earth for growing than either of them had imagined. Harri had been keeping his distance, which had hurt Nan's feelings, however much she understood his reluctance to become embroiled in her domestic strife. When she asked him to help them both now, he did not hesitate. With his help, Gwenno erected a polytunnel and slotted new panes of glass into the greenhouse and the cold frames. Trays of vivid green Winter Gem and Lamb's Lettuce seedlings would go out there when they were ready. Broad beans went into the most sheltered area of the garden, in the lee of the stone wall and well away from the blasting wind from the sea.

"We'll use every square inch, I promise you," she told Nan. "I've drawn up a detailed plan of what I want to plant where. I'll need somewhere warm inside the house to put some more seed trays, but I'll transfer them to the greenhouse as soon as I can. Any possibilities?"

And so all the trendy pots, sculptures and miscellaneous knick-knacks that Nan had brought from Cambridge and displayed on the house's many windowsills were boxed-up and replaced by row after row of seed trays. Some of this extraneous *stuff* was taken to a charity shop in Bangor in desperate need of some sellable stock, and some of the nicer things were listed on eBay, with proceeds going into their great project. Nan felt immediately lighter of heart.

"Why did I ever think I needed all that crap anyway?" she said.

"Because everyone you knew had lots of it too. That's a way of life you've left behind – crap-gathering," Gwenno replied.

Ceri and Elin were desperate to be involved, so Gwenno enlisted them to check on the seed trays every morning before school, and report back to her in the playground before she arrived at *Coed Uchaf*.

"Remember to turn the trays every day," she instructed them earnestly. "They'll always grow towards the light, so you need to confuse them a bit."

She involved Guto too, poring over seed catalogues with him to choose which varieties of vegetables to plant when the earth warmed in the spring. He tended to go for ones that looked exotic, like Purple Sprouting Broccoli or Romanesco, but that was fine with her. She showed him her planting planner, criss-crossed with tiny potato rows, wigwams for runner beans and cloches for more delicate crops – it was a work of art in itself. Nan found it wonderful to have her friend here so much of the time, and enjoyed making them a hot lunch each day, as the weather was bitter. Shadow was ecstatic to have Reg as a daily playmate and Harri popped in if he was passing and was usually dragooned into repairing a tool or lifting something heavy. If he brought Mim over, all four children sat at the kitchen table and made lists of what plants and seeds were thriving, and which ones needed their TLC. By mid-December, each day had such an easy, familiar routine that nobody could remember when life had ever been any different. They were a team, and it was sheer bliss, for all of them.

One afternoon towards the end of the school term, Gwenno popped in to use the bathroom before they had a slab of cake and a coffee and left a series of very muddy boot prints between the back door and the loo. At first, Nan was irritated, but she stopped herself.

"How stupid of me to choose white floor tiles when we live on a farm," she muttered.

And in that moment, she realised what she had said: *Coed Uchaf* really was a working farm again, things were growing all around the house (and inside it too) and the land was working for the people who lived there. She hoped with all her heart that Annie and Tomos Hughes would have approved.

TWENTY-SIX

As the Green family's first Christmas on Anglesey drew nearer, the twins' school went into festive overdrive. The girls brought home Welsh carol sheets, templates for Welsh Christmas cards, baubles with Welsh dragons on them and a letter outlining the school's ambitious plans for celebrating. It was clear that a "*Nadolig Llawen*/Happy Christmas" was a very big deal on the island, and Nan was determined to play a part in it. She went to the planning meeting but sat at the back of the room with Gwenno and Harri, for the first half an hour of minute-reading and general school business. Once the mulled wine kicked in, however, she volunteered to bake one hundred mince pies, run the raffle, organise the face-painting stall, judge a Christmas card competition and put together a playlist for the end-of-term *Disco 'dolig*/Christmas disco. A ripple of kindly laughter went around the hall when volunteers to lead the "wintry walk" along the beach were requested and Harri yanked her hand down.

"Better let some of the others get a look-in," he hissed. "Share the saintliness, please."

"I just feel I ought to, you know, *help*."

"You are helping. And stop feeling *guilty* about everything."

"I don't, thank you very much," she replied tartly. "I just want to do my bit."

But he was right: she did feel guilty about many things. Again and again, she felt the prickling of guilt whenever she had to go straight to the second part of each school letter, the English translation. She was mortified whenever the head-teacher Huw Williams spoke to her, because he had such a strong North Welsh accent that she often had very little idea what he had actually said.

"What if he's telling me that his mother's just died, and I'm grinning like a loon?" she said to Robin when he rang one evening.

Her husband dismissed her worries, but promptly googled the headteacher, saw he'd trained in Bangor and never taught anywhere but on the island and decided he was just "another small-town yokel" they didn't need to worry about. But Nan remembered his small acts of kindness, such as congratulating the twins on their "wonderful Welsh names" and telling her how kind they had both been when a boy was being bullied in the playground.

"Mr Williams is a good man, Robin," she said.

"But with such *a narrow perspective*. What that place needs is a cold blast of reality and to get over their obsession with being *Welsh*."

Nan said nothing but was glad when the conversation ended. Later that night, she returned to it in her thoughts. For her, being Welsh, feeling Welsh, was much more than jingoism or pride. It was a love of history, of country, of song, of story-telling and of family. It was a feeling in the soul and a loyalty to the land that she had encountered nowhere else, but recognised as a small child, when she had first come here. It was not exclusive – if you understood it, felt it, valued it, then there was a chance that you could share it. Her mother had had it in her blood (even though she had never been allowed to speak the language of her girlhood in Eric's house) and she had given it imperceptibly to her daughter. Nan was determined to pass it on to both of hers.

"I am going to master this bloody language if it kills me," she said. When she signed up for a weekly Welsh class starting in Bangor after Christmas, Robin, predictably, objected.

"Look, it's a dying language spoken by a few people in a twenty miles radius and some sheep. We didn't know how *zealous* everyone was about it, did we, when we moved the twins up there, poor things?" A strategic pause. "Well, *I* certainly didn't, Nan."

Something fundamental had shifted in their relationship, she knew. Like ice that thaws, then freezes and widens a fissure, Nan sensed that the distance between her and her husband grew wider every time they spoke. He seemed harder, somehow, and far from loving. To her, it almost felt as if, because she was on the island, as she had wanted to be for so long, he no longer felt responsible for her happiness.

"I don't think people are zealous. It's part of who they are, that's all."

"But it's not part of *you*, is it?" he said. "Do something useful instead, like find some work. I'm still reeling from the cost of all the building work, Nan. I'd say that learning Welsh is the least of your priorities."

"Robin, feeling that we belong here remains my priority at the moment, and I think it *is* a part of me, actually. Anyway, we should still have plenty of cash in the bank – unless you've been spending it all, of course. I certainly haven't."

Silence.

* * *

Despite the uneasy truce that prevailed between them, Nan was determined that the first Christmas in their new home would be special. Eira was coming, but insisted on staying with Dewi, who was still "under the weather", which was unusual for him. They would both come to *Coed Uchaf* for Christmas Day, however, so Nan was desperate that there would be no shouting or plates of turkey dinner thrown at the wall in *her* household, as there had been in her childhood home. Robin had not mentioned his plans, but he had plenty of annual leave left. Fortified with a glass of wine, she decided to tackle the issue, and rang him.

"Christmas is a big thing up here. Do you think you can get here by Wednesday the seventeenth?" she asked him. "The girls are both angels in the school play that night, which is pretty ironic, haha."

"Hmm, that's a bit early for me to stop work. It's my Christmas do in the Randolph on the Tuesday, and I may not be up to driving the next day."

Nan wanted to remind him that drinking too much at the party was a choice, not a necessity. Surely Robin would arrive at that realisation himself?

"So you won't be home until the week of Christmas itself?" she said. "Look, you can work up here for the last few days..."

"It's a nuisance, I know, but James has pencilled me in for several festive social events with clients. It's an important time of year workwise."

Nan sighed. "It's an important time of year for your children too. Will you be free to join us for Christmas Day, do you think?" she asked. "Mum and Dewi are coming over."

"Of course I will, Nan. I'm just being realistic," he said. "You do so like to *dramatise* everything. It's very wearing."

"I'm sure it must be, but I'm just checking, as we really don't see much of you these days."

"Actually, I get the feeling that's the way you like it, Nan."

"Of course I don't bloody like it," she hissed into the phone, in case the twins overheard, "but I've got no choice but to get on with it, have I? You're hardly ever here, and you know it. I did not sentence myself to solitary confinement for the rest of my days, however much James likes to keep you at his side 24/7. At least I have some friends up here now, thank goodness."

"Who, Gwenno and Harri?" Robin replied, distaste almost palpable in his tone. "I still think you've sunk pretty low, with those two. Remember that Gwenno is actually an *employee* now, which should change your relationship somewhat and might be a good thing."

"She's my friend, first and foremost – and always will be."

"That's as may be, but I do think Mummy had a valid point, worrying about the kind of people you're meeting up there. I think I'll take the opportunity to get to know your new friends this Christmas."

"Great idea. I think they've got the impression you're a pompous git, so it will be great if you convince them you're not." She hung up, wondering exactly when her husband became such a complete arsehole.

* * *

Later, when she had calmed down, she found herself wondering if this the way it was always going to be between them. It had been far from the conversation she had planned, but she always felt powerless to take control where Robin was concerned. Beneath the snide insults, this was more than a game, a silly spat – this was serious now. They had to try to salvage their marriage before it was too late. If her husband wasn't mature enough to do it, she would have to be. She rang him back.

"Right, let's stop point-scoring, shall we? We're better than this. Spend some time at home this Christmas, please. We need you to. Come to the play and then work at home for a few days.

You'll be able to chat to Gwenno and Harri, get to know them. You've got the wrong impression of them both, just as they have of you. We have to try to do this better."

Silence, then a low grumble of agreement. "Things are certainly not going well."

"You're right there. We're all going to the pub after the play, too, which should be fun. Harri's mum said she'll mind all the kids at hers for an hour or so."

"Have you actually *met* Harri's mother?" came the crisp reply. "Is she reliable?"

Nan tried to stay calm. She would not let him provoke her again.

"Yes, I told you. Her name is Beti and she was at school with Mum. Remember?"

"I'm not convinced that's much of a recommendation... and no, I don't remember."

"I told you that I met her when I went to Harri's cottage for a drink that time, after I... after he..." She stuttered to a halt.

"Oh yes. How could I forget your going to a total stranger's house after he saved you from leaping off a clifftop. Who could compete with those heroics?" he goaded.

Furious, Nan stood up and bellowed into the phone with a voice she had only used once before, in childbirth, "STOP it, Robin! Why are you being so utterly *childish*?"

Once the words were out, she started to tremble, waiting for his reaction to her daring to vent at him for once. Only when it came, several seconds later, did she dare to exhale.

"I can be a tad childish, I know," he said. A pause, before he added, "And now, I'm also deaf."

Nan laughed, and he laughed with her. This was a flash of the man she loved... or had loved – the one who had a sense of humour!

"Look, if you don't drink too much at your Christmas do,

you'll be fine to join us. The girls would be happy if we had some proper time together again," she said, "and so would I."

She waited for his response, but instead heard a voice in the background, a woman's voice.

"Takeaway's here, Rob."

"Got to go. My takeaway is here. Love to the girls... and you." He hung up.

Nan sat back in her chair and felt as if a million spiders were crawling all over her body. Who was the woman with him? She had called him "Rob", something he had always, always hated. And Robin had never allowed them to order food in, insisting that his meals were cooked from scratch. Worst of all, there was something familiar about the voice she had heard, but she just could not place it. Perhaps she was a colleague, over to eat with him as they worked? As possibilities whirled, sensations she recognised began to return: her breath quickened, her palms became sweaty. She tried her affirmations, her deep breathing; she even went to the kitchen drawer and found a rubber band to put on her wrist and "ping". When none of these techniques helped, she remembered something her friend Ella had once told her: if you visualise something good, it will happen and the panicky feelings will fade and then vanish. As Ella's theories went, it was less wacky than usual.

"Now's the time to test it out, Ella."

And so she saw her husband – handsome, confident and home for a long Christmas break with his family. She saw *Coed Uchaf* decorated to perfection, with twinkling lights and two huge trees, spectacularly vindicating her decision to make it their home. The twins buzzed with excitement – about the show, about Christmas and were thrilled with the little homecoming gifts Robin had brought them from the quirky shops in Cambridge. As their children played on the rug, and Shadow snuggled between them, she and Robin snuggled up on the sofa before the blazing wood burning stove, basking in the happy home they had created. Then she visualised them at the show, beaming as the girls mumbled through the play, haloes askew and words forgotten. When Welsh carols filled the school hall with music and the lilt of the language, Robin smiled at her as he finally realised just how beautiful it could sound. Finally, Nan saw the people she had begun to get to know on the island at the pub around a table, smiling, friendly and keen to get to know her elusive "other half". Robin would buy a round (which would go down well) and after a few pints, he would relax and be the best version of himself and they would see why she loved him. They would have a wonderfully happy Christmas all together and everything would be well again.

Second by second, Nan's panic ebbed away because she could see it all so clearly and it was exactly what she had dreamt of. All she had to do was believe it could actually happen.

TWENTY-SEVEN

The night of the school Christmas play was decidedly wet. The hall was packed with more than a hundred gently steaming people who had been drenched by torrential rain just as they'd arrived. Grizzling toddlers squirmed in their buggies and grannies wiped their rain-smeared glasses with their cardigans and then squinted at the stage. Nan, who had been in the hall for an hour or so chatting, drinking coffee, moving chairs and folding raffle tickets, was oblivious to all this because Robin had not yet arrived.

"He's on the way, though, right?" Gwenno called from the stage, where she was frantically spreading straw over the ground in the "stable".

"I don't know. I haven't heard anything since yesterday, before he went to the work Christmas party. He isn't picking up calls or messages, so he must be driving."

"You know what they say about *those* parties." She winked.

"Haha, very funny," Nan said drily.

She had already revisited her suspicions about another woman since the last phone call with her husband, but decided to shut them down, for her own sanity. The woman in his flat had probably been his landlady, telling him his takeaway had arrived at the front door, and it had been silly of her to jump to other conclusions. He was working much too hard to have time for an affair anyway!

"He said he'd do his utmost to be here, and I promised him that we are going to have the best Christmas *ever*."

"Well, he'd better put his foot down, as the shepherds are tea-towelled up and ready to rock," Gwenno said, scurrying off to check on the kings' crowns.

"I will actually kill you if you don't make it in time, Robin Green," Nan muttered.

Ten minutes later, Mr Williams stood at the front of the hall and introduced the play, switching between Welsh and English so deftly that nobody felt excluded. It would be "a fitting celebration of our wonderful school and all the amazing children in it", he said, as everyone in the hall cheered and clapped.

"He makes even English words sound beautiful, doesn't he?" Harri whispered in Nan's ear. "And that takes serious skill! Believe me – I've tried!"

She smiled, grateful that he'd quietly come to sit in the seat she'd kept for Robin, to spare her embarrassment. It had taken courage to do so. She was sure it would have been noted that her husband was not there and that Harri Parry had sat in his seat instead. As the first children came onto the stage, she felt her mobile vibrate: she ignored it. Within seconds, she was glowing with pride as she saw the twins shuffle into view, tinsel haloes and kitchen foil wings in place.

After the nativity scene and some simple Welsh carols that brought tears to every eye in the room, the children sat in rows on the stage, and looked at Mr Williams expectantly. This was clearly the part of the evening they were most excited about.

"*Reit, pawb*/Right, everyone," he said, smiling at the glowing faces beneath him. "Now I'd like to hear all your

Christmas wishes, but I want none of them to involve a present, remember? Nia, let's start with you."

"I wish for the slide in the playground to be mended," a small voice said.

"That would be great, wouldn't it? Let's hope someone from the council's in the audience!" Mr Williams said, winking at the adults. "Right, Tecwyn, what would *you* wish for?"

"If I'm not allowed to wish for a dog, can I wish that my mum gets one so that I can share it?" a tiny, freckle-faced shepherd said.

Everyone erupted in laughter and there was a muffled "no chance" from the back.

"I think we can allow that wish, Tecwyn," Mr Williams said. "But it's bending the rules a bit. Ceri Green, what would you wish for?"

Nan watched her daughter blush, turn to her sister and nod.

"Me and my sister wish for our mum to be happy because sometimes she's lonely because my dad's never here," she said.

The silence in the hall was punctuated only by a few gasps, a couple of "awws" and a muttered "*Bechod*/Shame". Nan felt all the blood drain from her face.

"I think that's the best wish we've had yet," the headteacher said. "And such a kind thing to wish for. Everyone gets lonely, especially when they come somewhere new. Mrs Green, where are you?" He scanned the audience, looking for Nan. "I hear you make up stories. We love hearing stories. Will you come in and tell us some after Christmas?"

Nan nodded. "Of course," she said, just managing to stem her tears.

"Then both your girls' wishes will have come true!" Mr Williams said. "*Da iawn*/Good."

* * *

"I hope you're still coming to the pub," Gwenno said, as they stacked the chairs up after the show. "I think you deserve a drink after that. Thank God Guto just asked for more singing in school, or I'd be a nervous wreck."

Harri joined them. "And me. Mim wished to paint some pebbles in art, which was pretty random, but fine with me as long as she doesn't expect me to provide world peace!"

"It nearly finished me off, what my girls said, to be honest," Nan said. "I'm sort of glad Robin wasn't here to hear it, but I am hopping mad he missed the play."

"I'm sure he got held up in traffic or something..." Gwenno said.

Nan showed her friend her phone, with Robin's text: '*Left late. Something came up. Sorry.*'

"Look, it happens, Nan," Gwenno said. "It's a really long drive from Cambridge..."

"You've changed your tune on my darling husband," Nan said. "Luckily, the twins don't seem to be as upset as I am. Yes, let's go to the pub. And I'm going to take you up on that offer of a cigarette before he arrives, if it still stands."

"It certainly does," Gwenno replied. "Go you!"

* * *

When Robin eventually arrived at the pub, it was almost 10pm. Nan was three large glasses of white wine and a sneaky cigarette down and feeling very pleasantly chilled. She cheered when he came towards their table. She would tell him off for missing the play later. Right now, she was having the most fun she'd had for ages.

"Robin! At last!" she cried, raising her glass to him.

"Hey, the Great Exec returns!" Gwenno said. "What are you drinking, sir?"

"Nothing for me, thank you. I drove straight here," Robin

said. "The traffic was absolutely appalling and the weather after Birmingham, even worse."

Nan's heart sank. He was in a very bad mood. He looked shattered, and now he would be sober, grumpy and anxious to leave as soon as possible.

"Sorry I'm late," Robin said. "And really sorry to miss the kids' play."

"Heavy night last night at the work do?" Gwenno said. Only Nan saw the twitch around her husband's eyes, betraying his irritation at what he would have seen as rudeness.

"Yes, actually. And lots to do in the office before I could get away."

"Soda water it is then," Gwenno said. "Need a top-up, Nan? Or another smoke?"

Nan's face fell. What Gwenno thought was hilarious Robin certainly would not.

"I think she's fine on both fronts, thank you," Robin said.

As Gwenno went to the bar, Robin made no attempt to introduce himself to anyone sitting around the table. He checked his phone, which told his wife that he felt uncomfortable, but told the others that he couldn't be bothered to talk to them. When he accepted a glass of soda water from Gwenno with a very insincere smile on his face, Nan mouthed, "Please be nice." His raised eyebrows told her he had understood.

"So, hello all. The children are with Harri's mother, I hear. But which one of you gents is Harri?" Robin said, looking and sounding like a well-meaning aunt.

"Me," Harri said, holding out his hand with a smile. Robin shook it with such extreme public-school vigour that Harri winced in pain.

Nan looked at her knees. Why did he have to make everything a contest, a show of machismo? Harri was a gentle man who had been kind to her, there was nothing to prove here. Robin sat down on a stool, tweaking up both tweed trouser legs beforehand as he had been taught as a pupil at boarding school, to prevent creases. It was such a telling gesture, an indicator of class that would not be lost on Harri or Gwenno. Picking up the pub menu, she saw her husband's contempt at the limited choices in the twitch in his lip.

"Robin, haven't you eaten? The kitchen here closed at 9pm," she said.

"Ah. No, I didn't stop to eat, as I was late, but I don't think I could stomach chips right now and they seem to be staple fare. I'll get some crisps. Are they allowed to sell crisps after 9pm on a Wednesday night on Anglesey? Or nuts?" He looked around him dramatically. "Looks like this place is *full* of nuts, actually."

Smiling at his own wit (and utterly unaware of the reaction around the table), he excused himself and strolled to the bar. As everyone lifted and sipped their drinks in silent unison, Nan could only imagine what they were all thinking. Surely her husband was not being this crass intentionally? He was behaving as if he had landed from another planet! Sure, he was always a little awkward in the company of people so different from his normal milieu – brusque, tactless, even a bit rude – but tonight, everything he wore, said and did howled "I am wealthy" and "I am better than you". Her eyes filled with tears because she should never have hoped that he could belong here. Quietly, she asked Gwenno to get her another large glass of wine; numbing herself was the best option left, she decided.

As it kicked in, she tried to open a conversation about what amazing work Gwenno was doing in their garden, but Robin did not seem interested. She warned him that every windowsill in the house was covered with seed trays and watering cans – no response. His only concern, he said, was that "the outlay was minimal" and Nan could tell that her friend was now offended. She tried again.

"So, Gwenno plans to start a veg box scheme in the village

in the spring, love. People we've spoken to seem very keen to have locally grown produce," she said.

"Great. Good plan," he replied. "Sorry, got to make a call." And he vanished.

"I can only apologise, Gwenno," Nan said to her friend, who shrugged dismissively.

Things were no easier when Robin returned. For an acutely painful half hour, he asked everyone a polite question about themselves and then took no notice of their responses. Visibly bored, he then got into close conversation with Siân Williams, a notorious gossip, and her mouth was close enough to his ear for Nan to blush when she saw people staring at them with knowing smirks. All the progress she had made here, so slowly, so painfully, could be reversed in a single evening by what her husband was doing now. In a small place like this, every move was noted. Draining her glass, she signalled to him that it was time for them to leave.

"Yes, good idea, looking at the state of you," he snapped.

She turned to Harri and Gwenno to say goodbye, but Robin had already taken her arm and yanked her towards the door, leaving her friends staring, open-mouthed. When they got out into the car park, all the wine she had drunk hit her like a sledgehammer and she staggered and fell heavily, banging her head on the side of Robin's car and sliding to the ground. She rubbed her head, her bottom lip quivering.

"Ouch. That really hurt. And my arm is sore too, where you grabbed me."

"For Christ's sake, Nan," Robin said, pulling her up. "Is this what you get up to with your new friends? What on earth has happened to you? It's a Wednesday night and you've just been to a school play, for goodness' sake! And you've been smoking – you *stink!* You'll be getting a bloody tattoo next!"

"I needed you to be there tonight. I am VERY ANGRY with you!" she shouted, swaying.

"Are you now? I am sorry to have missed the silly play, but it couldn't be helped."

"Why couldn't it? What was more important than us? James Naughton's latest money-making scheme?" she slurred, pointing a wobbly finger at him. "I want to know what was so vital that you had to miss our kids' play, Robin. I *deserve* to know."

She looked at him directly for the first time that evening and, drunk as she was, she saw something different in his stubble-shaded face. She had seen it before, in her father's eyes whenever she had disappointed or annoyed him. It was not hate, but neither was it love.

"You don't deserve anything in that state. Let's go and get the girls," he said.

Hot tears started pouring down her face as if she had flicked a switch to release them. "You blame me, don't you? I know you do. For all of this, this... *mess*. Yes, always blame Nan, it's always Nan's fault, isn't it?" she gabbled. "Stupid, silly Nan."

"Stop it! You're drunk and I'm exhausted, and you look a bloody wreck. I'm here for Christmas, aren't I, in this godforsaken place, just as you asked me to be?" He thrust a bottle of water in her face. "Drink some of this before the girls see you. And get into the bloody car." He pushed her head down and shoved her into the passenger seat.

Suddenly, Gwenno was standing in the open doorway of the pub, her eyes fixed on Robin.

"Don't you treat my friend like that," she growled. "You're hurting her, you bully."

Nan would never forget the look of complete astonishment on her husband's face. He ran his hand through his hair nervously, guiltily.

"I... didn't mean to be rough. I'm just tired, and embarrassed," he said, his voice low and defensive. "You really don't understand how difficult Nan can be, Gwenno, when she..."

"I understand that she's one of the bravest women I know, Robin. And one of the kindest. If you hurt her again, in any way at all, you'll be hearing from me. That's all I want to say. *Nos da, Nan*/Good night, Nan."

Nan started to whimper as Gwenno walked back into the pub. This was awful, and she had been so happy earlier. Robin got into the car and slammed the door.

"Robin... please... she was just looking out for me... and Gwenno is, well, she doesn't mince her words."

He looked deeply shocked. "Stop talking please. I've had enough words for one night."

They drove to Harri's cottage to fetch the twins in silence.

TWENTY-EIGHT

Every time Nan tried to lift her head from the pillow the following day, it sent agonising ripples of pain into almost every part of her body. At around 11am, she finally managed to open her eyes without wanting to puke, and the first thing she saw was the mixing bowl that Robin had put on the floor next to the bed. In an instant, she was back in her dingy room in college in Cambridge, where he had found her in a similar state on so many mornings, many years ago. Nothing had changed, not really, she was still a liability. She closed her eyes and lay without moving a muscle for what seemed like an eternity.

Eventually, very slowly, she levered herself upright. So far, so good. Perhaps she hadn't been *that* bad last night? It was Christmas and a pub, after all. Perhaps the girls hadn't realised anything was wrong? Perhaps they could all get on with having the lovely first Christmas in Wales that she had planned and Robin would behave as if last night hadn't happened? A quick glance at her phone told her otherwise.

> I've taken the girls to the school and gone to work in the university library. I haven't walked your dog. This is not what we agreed and cannot continue. You were a disgrace. R

There was also a text from Gwenno and one from Harri, but she could not bring herself to open them. For now, her marriage was her priority. After several cups of sugary tea, three slices of toast and Marmite and some paracetamol, Nan felt physically capable of texting Robin back, but when she tried, no words seemed to express what she wanted to say. Clearly, he expected her to begin with an apology, but for what? For drinking too much? Yes, fair enough. For falling over? OK, that was pretty silly. For daring to be angry with him? No, she would not apologise for that. He had let her down, embarrassed her and he owed *her* an apology – hell, he owed the twins one too, for missing their play. His behaviour had been even more atrocious than hers, but in different ways. Thinking back, the thing that hurt most was the look on her friends' faces as Robin had dragged her out of the pub – a look that asked her why on earth she was with this man at all.

Shadow was whining, desperate for a walk. Last night's clothes were on the floor next to the bed, so she pulled them on quickly and almost retched at the faint smell of smoke they still retained. Putting her hand in the top pocket of her shirt, she found a cigarette, a secret gift from Gwenno – now squashed and probably unsmokeable – but kind enough to release the tears she needed to cry. She read her friend's text:

> Hope you're OK and found my small contribution to the 'Let's Save Nan' campaign. I won't come to work today in case Robin tries to kill me with a trowel. In touch soon. XX

She replied immediately:

Robin has gone out, but I'm OK. I found your little gift. Diolch/Thanks. XX

By the time Robin and the girls returned home late that afternoon, Nan felt almost human again. She had cooked a chicken dinner and begun decorating the house for Christmas, picking swathes of ivy and some berry-laden holly and winding them through the banisters with some red fairy lights.

"It looks like a winter wonderland!" Elin said, clapping her hands in glee.

"I think it looks more like Santa's Grotto, but what do I know?" added Robin with a smile that gave nothing away.

He came towards her, and she felt her breath quicken. Was he still angry, or had he forgiven her? His face was unreadable as he put his hands on her shoulders and looked into her eyes. "Enough bloodletting, Nan. I've been doing some thinking today and let's say no more about last night. I can't believe what happened, actually – what's happened to us. It's Christmas in a few days. Let's enjoy it and talk things through properly after it."

Something had changed, something as subtle as the tone of his voice, the firmness of his touch. She no longer felt anger in his touch, but resolve. But what had he decided?

"I'm sorry too," she said. "I was upset when you were late and I drank too much and I wanted my friends to like you, to see the *real* you, and it..."

He put a finger on her lips. "Stop, Nan. I understand, really, but we do need to agree that things will be different from now on. That kind of episode has to be a one-off."

"*Episode*? But..."

"No buts. From now on, no more histrionics. You really let yourself down. It was embarrassing for your friends and even more embarrassing for me."

Nan felt the first stab of anger. "Gwenno came out and

yelled at *you,* remember? You hardly covered yourself in glory. And I don't know what Harri made of it all, but I..."

"Well, *I* know," Robin cut in. "I saw him in the playground this morning, and he avoided me. That says 'embarrassment' in my book. Men don't tend to like women who drink. I certainly don't, as I made clear when I first met you."

Nan gasped. "That's really sexist, Robin! We were all having a great time until you came and made me feel awful. Perhaps Harri didn't see you..."

"Perhaps, but I feel that you need to think who you want to keep on your side, Nan – people like that, or me, your husband. I'm certainly not up for more evenings like last night."

Now she was very angry indeed. "Look, I can't conjure up people that meet your stupid standards! I really like Gwenno and Harri and so would you if your head emerged from up your own arse for five minutes."

"Charming. I don't think we are ever going to fit in with that circle, Nan, honestly. They're even worse than the Titterati and they were bad enough."

Nan stared at him. "Robin, when did you become quite so narrow-minded – a characteristic you say you hate in good, kind people like Huw Williams."

"That's a question of professional standards, not like or dislike. He's a head teacher which means he needs a wide worldview." He took off his coat wearily, a top of the range Barbour she had not seen before.

"Robin, what the hell is wrong with you? I feel I don't know you anymore."

"I think the problem is *you*, not me. These past months have given me time to think about our relationship."

"Me too," she spat. "We don't really have one, do we, unless you count your rare conjugal 'visits' which are actually more confrontational than conjugal these days?"

Robin shook his head. "You really want to do this now, do

you? I have a lot of work to do for James before Christmas, and I really need to focus on that."

"I sometimes think you should be married to James, as it sure doesn't feel as if you're married to me anymore," she said, slamming her mug down.

He exhaled dramatically. "Right, let me spell it out. We're struggling financially, which you said wouldn't happen; you're still miserable a lot of the time, which you also said wouldn't happen. We don't agree on how the girls should be educated, and I don't think I will ever be able to live here all the time. There, now you know. Basically, I can't sustain this charade for much longer and it's not fair of you to ask me to."

Nan gulped, like a landed fish. When she could breathe again, she felt as if she had been punched, very hard, in the belly.

"The 'charade' being our marriage?" she said. "Robin, are you actually telling me you'll *leave* me if I don't pretend to be happy when I'm not? Or stop spending when I'm not spending? What could I be buying, for goodness' sake? I've done all the decorating myself and there aren't many tempting shops up here!"

"I have expenses to meet too, of course, but..." Robin said, rubbing his chin in his "thoughtful" mode. "Perhaps I put it too *baldly*, but things need to change, Nan."

"I need to change, you mean."

"I can't be doing with the *neediness* anymore. I have my own worries, my own priorities, my own *life*, Nan."

Hot anger pulsed through her. She remembered Gwenno's words: "We all have needs, Nan, but that doesn't make us needy." This was not a marriage, or even a partnership: it was an arrangement that no longer suited him, and she was going to have to be very, very careful what she did next. She took a long, slow in-breath before speaking again.

"Robin, can you tell me, out of interest, *how* are we in financial trouble?" she said. "If I'm not spending lots of money, then you must be."

He smoothed his hand over his hair and Nan noticed that the few white hairs she had seen on his temples were now an unfeasible auburn. His phone buzzed.

"I won't take this now, don't worry," he said with a smug look at her. "Suffice to say, we need to be more careful with money after Christmas," he said.

"And all the other stuff you just dropped on me? What about that? We really need to talk, Robin."

"We will talk, and we will work through this, but for now, let me do what I need to do workwise and then let's enjoy Christmas, as a family, for the girls' sake. I know you've looked forward to it, and we need to do this in a mature, sensible way."

His phone buzzed again, and Nan saw his hands fluttering towards it. "James, I assume?" she said. She felt as if she was underwater, and everything swimming around her.

He ignored her. "Drink, or are you still too delicate for booze?"

"I'll go and get you one, but it's water for me today," she said.

"Great, fine, good idea. I'll lay a fire."

But when she looked back into the room, he was texting furiously.

A wave of sheer exhaustion hit her so hard that she had to sit down at the kitchen table. For several minutes, she stared blankly at the polka dot oilcloth as if it contained the secrets of the universe. How did they have money troubles? It didn't make any sense. She looked around the room she had always wanted to be the heart of their new home. There was the cream Aga, the slate work top, the Belfast sink she had imagined as she sat in Cambridge, planning it all. There was even a dog snoozing beside it, another of her lifelong dreams. Everything was perfect and yet she felt only despair.

"I need to trust you if we are going to salvage anything from this trainwreck of a marriage, Robin," she murmured. "And I don't."

* * *

Stacking the dishwasher after an awkward supper, she could hear Robin and the twins playing on the games console. He had drunk more than a bottle of wine and was getting louder and louder.

"Ceri, stop cheating!" he boomed. "I will not play with a cheat."

"She isn't cheating, Dad," Elin said. "Ceri won. You did that bit wrong."

"I most certainly did not, madam."

"Ah the lesser spotted competitive male," Nan muttered, pouring herself a very small brandy. At last, she read the text from Harri she had been putting off all day. Had Robin been right, did he now think of her as a seedy lush? Her heart was pounding as she read:

> Last night wasn't your fault: it was a shame, but the shame was his. You are a strong and beautiful woman, Nansi, and I think the world of you. H

She allowed his words to wash over her. They made her feel as if what had happened was silly, but not unforgivable. She was not a "disgrace", "stupid, silly Nan" and nor was she a little girl, hiding from a sin that wasn't hers to atone for.

"You are a strong and beautiful woman," she whispered, rolling the words on her tongue like a sugary treat. "Yes, Harri, I am."

TWENTY-NINE

When Nan's phone pinged with a text from Gwenno at 7am the following morning, she was half-awake, and could already hear Robin tapping on his laptop in the spare room, where he had slept.

Meet me at Tyn Tywyn car park at 9.30.

Are we swimming?

Nan replied, slightly miffed at being given an order, but she knew Gwenno preferred the direct approach.

No. We're talking.

OK. See you then.

As she showered, dressed and cooked eggy-bread for the girls' breakfast, a niggling anxiety about what her friend wanted them to talk about lurked in the pit of her stomach. This did not bode well.

* * *

The day was wild, as many days were on the island in December. The sea had been whipped into white-topped peaks by the wind, and flecks of foam blew up from the shoreline and landed on the silvery marram grass like pearls on a thread. Nan dropped the girls off for the last day of term, drove to the car park and stayed in the car listening to the radio while she waited for Gwenno. She was rarely late, which unnerved her. When she saw her friend's car lurching across the car park, the expression on her face did not allay Nan's anxiety. She got out of the car and Shadow cannoned off into the dunes.

"Hiya. Not brought Reg? I was hoping you'd come back to work in the garden today," she said. "I'm sorry, Robin was such a complete prat at the pub."

Gwenno walked, then stopped about a metre in front of her, turned around and stood with her legs a hips-width apart. This reminded Nan of a showdown in a Western, and she almost expected her friend to draw a gun. Gwenno looked so hard and *mean* that for a split second, Nan wondered how on earth she could call this woman a friend. She was seriously intimidating.

"I walked Reg first today because I need to concentrate," Gwenno said. "And we're discussing something more important than the garden, which is hard for me to even *say, deud y gwir*/to tell the truth, because that garden is bloody important to me. Nan, my friend, today we are talking about *men.*"

Nan laughed. "Oh Lord. I'm not much of an expert on them."

"I saw that plain as day the other night, but I think it's time for me to stop biting my tongue and not saying stuff. I need to tell you what happened to me, so that it won't happen to you." She paused. "Let's walk a bit. I know exactly where it will be a bit more sheltered."

As the two women climbed up the sandy ridge that led to the beach, Nan noticed the banks of marram grass were flattened on the dunes like a rippling carpet, and she could hear the sea roaring long before she saw it. Once on the beach, an onshore wind blasted into their faces, such a cold, scouring blast that she was sure it could strip the skin from her face if it wanted to. How on earth were they going to be able to talk about anything, or even hear each other, in conditions like this? She looked at Gwenno, hands over her ears, but her friend strode off towards a sheltered nook in the lee of the dunes. There, the grasses were still upright, forming a delicate screen to protect them from the wind. The noise dropped the moment they sat down, and they watched the sea churn and crash for a few moments as if it was a film, playing for them alone.

"I know we could have met somewhere more, well, civilised, but I find being close to the elements makes me feel braver. Probably sounds weird, but that's why I swim, why I love the freezing water and the wind that almost slices through me, it's so cruel and cold. I need it, to feel strong again," Gwenno said.

Nan nodded but said nothing. She had felt the power of the wind and waves too.

"I've never told you much about how it was with Guto's Dad, Jack, but when I saw how Robin treated you at the pub, I knew I had to, Nan. You need to believe the worst of him."

"But that was out of character for him, honestly. He's never hurt me like that before..." Nan blurted. "He's not violent, honestly. He just gets frustrated with me..."

"That's what I used to say, until the bruises became ones I couldn't hide, and the trips to A and E so frequent that my GP started asking questions," Gwenno said darkly. "I want you to be completely honest with me now. Do you think he still loves you?"

Nan hesitated but knew the answer in her heart straight away. "No. I feel as if I am in his way, as if he wants to take another path without me. He was my rescuer, you see, in the past, but I think he wants to cut me loose now."

"Then let him. You don't need rescuing anymore, Nan,"

Gwenno said. "You're here, where you were meant to be, and you have other people who care about you. I didn't have that – Harri was going through his own hell when I was with Jack."

"Why did you let any man treat you like that, though? I just can't imagine the Gwenno I know doing that."

"I was not the woman you know then, Nan. I met Jack at a party when I was twenty-two, got pregnant and that was it on the 'living the dream' front. Jack was proud of his 'super sperm', as he called it, that he wouldn't hear of an abortion. I should have realised then that what I wanted was right at the bloody bottom of his list of priorities, much as I love my boy, of course." She paused, and somehow managed to light a cigarette, despite the driving wind. "So, I moved into his bedsit in Llangefni, we milked the benefits system, and I pretended I didn't know he was dealing drugs when people called at all hours of the night. When Guto arrived, things got worse, fast. Jack often needed to sleep all day, but the baby cried so he couldn't. The money for booze and drugs was much less now that we needed to buy nappies and formula milk with it. Thank God he hit me, and not my baby, but I became his punch bag. And I took it. Day after day, week after week, month after month."

"But why, Gwenno?" Nan asked, shaking her head.

"Because I felt I didn't deserve any better. I learnt to accept the crumbs of affection I was offered and block out the way he made me feel – as if I was worthless, someone who needed to be helped through life as I couldn't get through it without him. Does this ring any bells, Nan?"

Nan nodded wordlessly.

"I don't mean to bully you, but I want you to think about this, whether he hits you or not. How much do you value yourself and your own capacity for living your life as well as you possibly can? That's what you need to consider." She looked into Nan's eyes and did not look away. "I waited too long to walk away, but I managed to in the end, with Mam's help, and I dearly hope you will too, when the time comes. I don't think Robin deserves you. I really don't."

Nan put her hands over her face and breathed deeply. This whole conversation felt surreal and uncomfortable, and she wanted it to stop. This was not happening to her, even if it had happened to Gwenno. No, she was wrong, but there was only one way to make her friend see that, by telling her the secret she had shared with no one, ever.

"But there's something you don't know about me, Gwenno," she said softly. "Robin saved me from something far, far worse than the silly squabbles we're having now, when he met and married me, and I can never forget that. My father... he... abused me, in every way imaginable, and I was a wreck for years afterwards. Robin doesn't know the full extent of... what went on at home but he helped me find a way through it and build a life. He had to be firm with me sometimes, and I guess he feels he still does, but he saved me, Gwenno. I don't think I would still be here if it wasn't for Robin Green." A pause. "And remember, he let me come here..."

"I hear that, and it's right to be grateful for all those things, but we're talking about *now,* not then. He isn't there for you now, or not enough anyway. You don't need him as scaffolding anymore, a safety net in case you mess up. You can build your own life now – you're doing it, every single day. And I think he is too, away from you."

Nan looked at her. "What do you mean by that? Do you think he's being unfaithful?"

"Look, it's not my place to accuse without definite proof. If you feel you can mend things between you, *digon teg*/fair enough – try to – but I do think you need to think long and hard about what he's willing to give you, and whether that's enough. You, my friend, are what matters to me, Nan – not him."

A pause, filled by seagulls' cries as they looped above them, hoping for scraps.

"Something's changed, for sure," Nan said. "I can't work out what, but I can feel he's already drifted too far out for me to reel him back in. And, in a way, I don't even want to."

"Well, at least you've realised that. I think you deserve more, Nan – so much more. You deserve to be truly loved."

"And so do you," Nan replied, her eyes full of tears. "We both do."

They hugged each other tight and long, and neither of them noticed the wind drop, or the wintry sunshine begin to set the sea alight with flickers of silver. When they let each other go, both women knew that theirs was a bond forged in pain, and unbreakable. It would last for the rest of their life.

When they eventually returned to more familiar conversational ground – the kids, and, of course, the garden, Gwenno had news. She had approached some of the local pubs and restaurants, several of which were interested in veg boxes the following spring, she said. They felt that being able to use produce grown on the island would also be a big draw for the tourists who arrived from March onwards. Any dish on their menus with the words "organic", "pesticide-free" or "locally sourced" in the description was bound to sell well. Even the village shop had agreed to trial some of their produce.

"I think we're going to need another polytunnel, Nan, because it looks like we're going to be very busy indeed after Christmas," Gwenno said.

"We?" Nan replied.

"Yeah. I think it would do you good to get out there with me, or at least help me box up and deliver stuff during busy times. I can't meet all these orders on my own."

"We'll be real business partners then?" Nan said.

"That all sounds a bit like we're on *The Apprentice*, but yes, we will." She paused and lit another cigarette. "But I'm still the boss, remember that at all times, please."

When Nan saluted, both women dissolved into giggles.

THIRTY

Nan endured Christmas that year. *Coed Uchaf* was resplendent, the food, plentiful and the girls delighted with all their gifts, but there was no joy at the heart of the house. Instead, there was a ceasefire.

Eira and Dewi came to eat on Christmas Day, as promised, but Nan could see that her mother was once again besieged with memories as soon as she walked through the door, and conversation was stilted and awkward. Robin made a complete mess of carving the turkey which dented his ego and sent him into a terminal sulk; the roast potatoes were hard in the middle and the pigs in blankets were charred. Nan realised that this was the first big meal she had ever cooked in the Aga, which explained what a disaster it proved. To add to the tension that was palpable in the house, she was deeply shocked to see how unwell Dewi looked. She listened in horror as Eira told them all details of the battery of tests he had endured, oblivious to Robin's tutting and the twins' widening eyes.

"I'm so sorry, Dewi. I didn't know. I should have come over to see you more."

"You're busy, so I didn't tell you. You have worries of your own," the old man replied.

"*Is* she, and *does* she?" Robin said. "What worries might those be?" It was early evening and he had started on the Prosecco at noon. "She assured me that we would all live a life of rustic bliss when we came here. One hundred per cent guaranteed, wasn't it, love?" His add-on smile, intended to imply he was "only joking", failed to convince anyone.

"None of us know how things are going to work out, Robin," Eira said.

Robin blinked at her blearily and span round in his chair to yell at the twins on the sofa.

"Can you both be *quiet!* I'm sick of listening to those bloody things." He pointed at their new Nintendo Switches that had been pinging, beeping and whooshing all evening. "Put them away or I'll throw them away."

"Go and play somewhere else, girls," Nan said. "Daddy's very tired."

"Daddy's very horrible, you mean," Ceri whispered.

"Robin, you need to know that Nan's found it tough here, with you away," Dewi said firmly. "A big change from Cambridge, however much she wanted to come. And you both made the decision, I recall. You signed the papers, sold the house, banked the money."

Robin looked at Dewi, struggling to focus. "Yes, I did, but we had an understanding, an *agreement,*" he said, slapping the table with the palm of his hand. "Nan being miserable and needing me here all the time was *not a part of that!*"

There was a long, long silence.

"Perhaps if you were here a bit *more,* it would help," Eira said. "She's doing her best and it can be hard to live here however much you love it. That was why I've never come back."

Nan smiled at her mother. That wasn't wholly true, but it had taken courage to say it.

Robin scowled. "I do what I need to do to keep this family afloat, Eira. Bit late for you to offer your two pennyworth and motherly support, isn't it?"

"Robin, please," Nan hissed. "Let's all go and watch some TV, shall we?"

Robin did not see the look Dewi and his sister exchanged as they trooped into the living room, but Nan did, and felt ashamed of her husband in more ways than one.

* * *

"Things are really not good between you and Robin, are they?" Eira whispered, as they both washed up the mountain of dirty pans while Dewi snoozed and Robin drank whisky. "He seems, well *flin* is the Welsh word for it – 'annoyed' – with you, especially."

"I actually know what that word means, Mum, but I do wish you'd taught me more Welsh when I was little and learning a new language was easy."

"Nan, things were different then. Everyone was discouraged from speaking it."

"Not in London, they weren't!"

"Your father let me call you Nansi, the Welsh spelling of Nancy, the name he chose, but that was it. 'No Welsh in my house, ever', he used to say. 'A stupid language spoken by stupid people'. It was one of his many ways of getting at me."

"I remember," Nan said. "But why did you always do what he told you to?"

"Perhaps because she might not still be here, if she hadn't," Dewi said.

He stood in the doorway, his face clouded with anger. "Don't judge your mother too harshly. She did the best she could, for herself and for you. Your father was a horrible man."

Nan felt his eyes on her – kind, always kind, but seeing right to the heart of things. "I know," she said.

Eira stifled a sob. "You knew, what he... did, Dewi? Even though I never told you?"

"Anyone would have known, Eira. I wanted to protect you both, but you wouldn't leave him and there was no prising him out of his dingy little castle."

"I'll never understand why we didn't just *leave*."

"I could ask you the same thing, Nan," Dewi said. "Robin is mean, and is making you very unhappy, it seems to me. Why don't you 'just leave' him. What's really stopping you?"

His words crackled in the air between them, like static.

"I don't know," she said eventually.

Eira shook her head. "Well, neither did I, but I do now. Don't repeat my mistake, love. Everyone deserves to be loved."

Nan remembered Gwenno saying something very similar, something equally well-meant. Again, the prospect of coping alone reared up before her, stark and terrifying.

"Eira, I need to go. I'm tired," Dewi said. "I'll say goodbye to the girls. Robin's too far gone to care."

"I can see how unhappy you are," Eira said, folding the wet tea towel neatly as she spoke. "It's hard to walk away from these men, I know. Especially when there's money and children involved, but there are always choices."

Nan nodded. "I need to think. I need to decide. I don't know what's gone wrong, but I don't think it's fixable anymore."

Eira moved closer and put a hand on Nan's arm, which alerted her to something not right. Such warm gestures from her mother were very rare indeed.

"I'm sorry to add to your troubles, but I haven't had a chance to tell you today. It's bad news I'm afraid. Dewi's got prostate cancer. It's advanced, as of course he ignored the symptoms. It won't be long, the doctors say."

Nan froze, as she realised that one of her worst nightmares had just come true. "Oh my God. Is he in pain?"

"He has strong painkillers, and they'll use radiotherapy to control it. He didn't want you to know at all, as he knew how things were here, but *I* want you to know."

Nan began to cry. "Mum, I wanted the girls to love him as much as I do, to feel as if the farm was their second home, but we hardly ever see him and now he's going to die. Nothing's worked out the way I meant it to. Nothing. It's all a disaster, Mum, and it's all my fault." She fell into her mother's arms, sobbing.

"*Cariad*/Darling, it's not. Robin's punishing you because he's not happy in himself, in who he really is. Once I understood *why* Eric was cruel, I knew it wasn't anything we'd done."

"Why, Mum? Tell me why he did those things to both of us?"

Eira sighed. "Because they had been done to him," she replied.

"Of course," Nan said quietly. "I think I knew, really. He always cried... afterwards, I mean."

Eira flinched. "He did after he'd hit me too."

"But why is Robin so angry with me? I haven't tried to control him, put him down and made him feel as if he would really rather I wasn't myself. He does all that to me."

"I don't know how men's minds work, or what demons he's wrestling with, but I did wonder if there was someone else, in Cambridge?" Eira said, watching Nan closely. "Perhaps he's found someone who suits him better and if he has, might that actually be good thing, and set you free?"

This suggestion lit the blue touchpaper on all the suspicions Nan had held for so long, and they exploded in her head like a firework. *Was* her husband in love with someone else? Was that why he'd dyed his hair, manicured his nails, bought new clothes, no longer wanted to sleep with her? Was it not stress or a midlife crisis or overwork but the inevitable end of their marriage because he now loved someone else? The possibility did not hurt as much as it should have done.

"I don't know, but I need to know for sure," she said.

"Yes, you do. If you find out what's going on, you'll know what to do for you and the girls," Eira said. "First things first: money. Do you have your own bank account?"

"No, I don't," Nan replied. "Robin's in charge of finances – he always has been. I mean, his career is financial management, after all, and he said I'd be rubbish at them when we got married."

"Perhaps you were then, but not now. You manage this huge house and your new business, remember," Eira said. "I can't tell you how relieved I felt when I was in charge of my own money again."

"I remember, Mum. I thought you were heartless when you started decorating and shopping when Dad was dying, but I get it now," Nan said.

"And you're not alone, as I was. You have *friends*, Dewi tells me."

"Yes, I do. Ones that *really* don't like Robin!" she replied with a tearful smile.

"He's not an easy man to like, I'm afraid."

"No, not now – perhaps he never was, but I did think he loved me at least."

Eira's brow furrowed. "Perhaps he did, yes, but remember us, 'Eric and Eira, a match made in heaven'? Things change, but you do need to find out *how,* and *why*."

Dewi returned, looking exhausted. Looking at him, Nan felt a sob rise in her throat. How could she not have noticed how thin he was, how desperately ill he looked?

"Time to go, Eira. Right now. I need my pills."

"You're a brave girl," her mother whispered in her ear as

they hugged goodbye. "I promise I will help you and so will Dewi, while he can."

* * *

By 10pm, Christmas Day was well and truly over, and Robin's rasping snores filled the living room. Tiptoeing around, Nan turned off all the lights and covered him with a blanket. His phone, lying on his chest, blinked: he had three new voicemail messages. Nan hesitated, her hands hovering over the buttons below the glowing screen. If she listened to any of them, he would know that she had done so. If she didn't, she would have to find out what was going on in other, perhaps more devious, ways. Robin snorted, the phone clattered to the floor and the screen went black. She left it there and crept upstairs to bed.

* * *

He returned to Cambridge two days later. He had refused to discuss anything when Nan urged him to "talk properly", as he had said they would do after Christmas. He seemed preoccupied, spending a lot of his time huddled in the living room, texting. The mood in *Coed Uchaf* was so strained that everyone breathed a sigh of relief when they heard him drive off far faster than he should have done.

"I don't like Daddy anymore," Ceri said, as both girls coloured at the kitchen table later.

"He doesn't like *us* anymore," Elin added. "I think it's better when he's not here."

"He doesn't want to be here with us anyway," Ceri said. "He was only happy with that other lady, the one with the curly hair that came to the Sea Zoo with us."

Nan had not yet quizzed them about this. Now, she knew she had to.

"Who was this lady, girls? Was she a friend of Daddy's?" she said.

"She met us at the Zoo and didn't come in our car at all, but Daddy knew her. He didn't tell us her name. I didn't like her because she made us hurry past the wave tank in case she got wet," Ceri said.

"Because she had very fancy clothes on," Elin added.

Nan knew she could not ask her poor kids any more questions now, but their comments stung her into action. This could not go on, she had to make a plan and for that, she needed help. She invited Gwenno, Harri and their kids for tea that evening. While all the kids gleefully kneaded and pummelled pizza dough, her friends offered advice – very freely indeed.

"I really think you need to go to Cambridge before the girls go back to school. See for yourself what he's up to," Gwenno urged, wiping her grease-filmed lips after her sixth slice of pizza. "You have a right to know."

"And you should probably get the login details for your joint account, so you can see where the money's really going," Harri added. "Talk to the bank, on your own."

"Can I actually *do* that? It feels deceitful, like spying," Nan said.

"You still trust him, do you?" Harri replied. "I don't think I would."

Nan shook her head slowly. "No, I don't. I can't. But I'm scared, Harri. Once I unpick one stitch, the whole thing might unravel."

He took one of her hands and pressed it between his, and she felt a comforting warmth spread through her body. "That's already happening, but you're still alive and kicking."

"You do need to know what you're dealing with, Nan," Gwenno said. "I wish I'd known what Guto's dad was really up to a whole lot earlier. Things would have been so different."

"Just different, or better?" Nan asked.

"Over," Gwenno replied.

* * *

The following morning, Nan told the ecstatic twins that they were going to go back to Cambridge for a few days to stay with Zillah, their childminder. She would stay with her friend Ella, which would give her the freedom to do what she needed to, knowing that the girls were happily watching wall-to-wall Disney movies. Shadow was despatched to Harri's.

Packing the twins' bags for the trip and tucking their Welsh school reading books between socks and pyjamas, Nan thought back over the months since they had come to the island. She was finding out more about herself, and what mattered to her, each day, but the process was difficult, and costly. Outside the window, the wind-scoured trees and the grey sky, heavy with rain, made the ease and sunshine of the summer seem a lifetime ago. Those were the days when she had assumed, unquestioningly, that life would be better here once they had all settled down. She had to go back to Cambridge, from where she had dragged them, if only to remind herself that it was, or that it still could be – even if she was here alone.

PART 5

DISCOVERIES

THIRTY-ONE

Cambridge, like many cities, is overlaid with an almost palpable drabness in the week between Christmas and the New Year. The festive lights and window displays seem tawdry, and hordes of pale, skint, overindulged shoppers shuffle around overheated shops looking for something that will give the whole ghastly festival some meaning. Driving along Jesus Lane, Nan was relieved not to be flooded with an intense wave of nostalgia for the life she had turned her back on. Instead, she found that she pitied those still left living it, as the traffic inched its way between endless sets of traffic lights.

She settled the twins at Zillah's and drove out to the Science Park to wait outside Robin's office. Would he actually be leaving when most people did, at 5.30pm, or staying at his desk until 9pm, as he had told her he so often had to do? She felt decidedly seedy hiding in the doorway of the office block opposite Naughton Consultancy as Robin's co-workers trickled out, but this was how it had to be if she was to find out the truth. Jodie, his secretary, came first and the familiarity of her gait made Nan catch her breath. She had known these people so well. Jodie was going home to her Spanish husband Diego, who worked for the council, and their Siamese cat, Yoko. It seemed so utterly surreal that the daily routine had gone on in this place all these months without her, just as it had when she had been a part of it, waiting for *her* husband to come home. The irony hit hard.

At 5.45pm, she saw him. It was dark, but light enough in the glow of the street lighting to see that he had had a haircut since returning to the city two days earlier. He was wearing his new Barbour and the rich crimson silk scarf his mother had sent him for Christmas, and which had looked ludicrously, luxuriously impractical when he had opened it in *Coed Uchaf*. Here, in this world, it was perfect.

He turned right and started walking quickly towards his sporty little car in the office car park. She noted the easy, confident stride of the public schoolboy who had "rescued" her when she had nowhere else to turn, a confidence bred of a sense of entitlement, which she had seen in so many of her fellow students but had never shared. He made a call, and as he spoke, his face was open, smiling, and she could almost hear the familiar rise and fall of his voice. He looked light of heart, free of worry and utterly sure of his place in the world.

She crawled behind him back into town. The darkness would stop him recognising their car, as he certainly wouldn't be expecting to see it, and she had a good idea where he was heading. A heavy drizzle began to fall; they inched past the brightly lit shops and cafés until he parked in Park Street car park, round the corner from their old home. She parked at the other end of the ground floor, next to a huge 4X4 that hid her Volvo, and waited for him to get out before doing so herself. When he paused to text, she just had time to duck down and hide, feeling a frisson of excitement at her newfound spying skills.

Robin stopped outside the grandiose Pizza Express in Jesus Lane, where he checked his phone again before going inside. Slightly shocked, Nan stood behind a bus shelter and felt her heart begin to race. He was meeting someone here. Her mouth filled with hot, sour saliva as the reason she was here, in this city that was no longer her home, became real for the first time. She had come to find out about Robin's other life, the one without her and the girls, but she had an incredible urge to turn and run away.

"What the hell am I doing?" she whispered.

What good would it do to find out that her marriage was over? Her mother and her two new friends had all had their own relationship tragedies, so why was she even considering actively *choosing* to join them? Grabbing the metal bus stop, she bent double and dry-retched, but when her breathing slowed again, and the waves of panic ebbed, she remembered. She was almost sure that her husband was inside that restaurant waiting to meet the woman with whom he had a secret life, and if it was true, nothing could ever be the same again, whether she wanted it to be or not. She had to know: the choice was no longer hers to make.

Her phone pinged. A text, from Gwenno.

Are you OK? Sending love and strength. X

"Right on cue, my friend," Nan murmured. "I need you to be there for me now."

A taxi pulled up outside the restaurant and first one, then another, long slim leg uncurled from inside its dark interior. It was raining heavily now, and Nan watched as a young woman held her handbag over blonde curls and tottered into Pizza Express on red heels. Her face was out of view, but Nan did not need to see it to know she was beautiful, and young. Tears streamed down her cheeks as she dialled Gwenno's number. Her friend picked up immediately.

"He's in a restaurant, and a stunning woman's just gone in

that I'm sure is going to meet him. What should I do? Go in and confront him, like in some awful B movie?"

"If you crash in there make a scene and you're *wrong,* he'll crucify you. Watch and wait."

"I can't believe this is happening. All I know is that this Robin Green isn't the man I married."

"No, but perhaps you just needed to see who he is *now, cariad*/love."

"Her legs go on for miles," Nan said. "Bet *she* doesn't have broken veins and cellulite."

"Neither did you, at her age. Get something hot to drink while you wait and call me later," Gwenno replied. "I'm very proud of you, Nansi. I wish I'd been half as brave with Jack."

Nan hung up. That word again, the one her mother had used: "*brave*". But she felt less courageous now than when she had pressed herself against the bathroom door while her father hammered on it, or when waves of pain had crashed over her body in childbirth. Then she had been brave indeed, but now, she felt weak and pitiful. Robin had promised to "take care of her" all those years ago, and she had let him do so, whatever the cost to herself. If he planned to jettison her, who would take care of her now?

* * *

At 8pm an Uber stopped outside the restaurant and, seconds later, Robin came out and got into it. Nan watched, shivering, cradling a long-cold coffee cup. A part of her still hoped for some kind of miracle, to spare her having to deal with the outcome she most feared: that the father of her children was being unfaithful. Perhaps she had been wrong, and Robin had eaten dinner on his own and was now heading back to the lonely Airbnb she'd heard so much about? Minutes passed and the car didn't move. She fantasised about crossing the street and climbing into the back seat alongside him. He would be surprised, shocked even, but then he would hug her, and they would go to his room together and make love...

... but then she saw the young woman. Tilting her face upwards, she shook her glorious hair before joining him in the Uber. Nan stared: there was something about the way the lantern above the door lit up her cheeks, the line of her nose – this was someone she had met, in another place, another life perhaps. The wisps of memory refused to cohere into *who* or *where*.

Soaked and miserable, she felt her phone buzz in her pocket – Gwenno, wanting an update. She let it ring out. The only person she wanted to speak to now was her husband. Scrolling through her contacts, she found the Airbnb address he had given her months ago:

6 Park Parade

"That can't be right. It's just around the corner. Why did they get a taxi?" she murmured. "This is silly. I'm going to ring him and ask him the truth."

To her surprise, he picked up the phone after only a few rings.

"Hi, Nan. Everything all right there?"

All the muscles around her mouth froze momentarily. He sounded cheerful, normal. She realised that, having called him, she had absolutely no idea what she was going to say.

"Are you on your own?" she blurted.

Silence. "Why do you ask?"

"Are you, Robin?"

"I'm with a... colleague, actually. We're sharing a cab as I've had a few drinks."

Nan hesitated. This was feasible, but where was he taking a cab with her when he could have walked to his lodgings? As the shock of everything she'd witnessed began to erode her reserve, she nearly told him that she was in Cambridge, that she had spent her evening trailing him, but managed not to.

"Where does your colleague live then?" she said.

"Grantchester, since you ask."

"Ooh, that's out of your way."

"Er, I guess so, but it's only polite to see her home," Robin replied, his voice taut. "Why are you asking me weird questions?"

"Just bored, I guess. And then you're heading back to your room in Park Parade, yes?"

A silence, short but long enough. "Yes. She wanted me to see her to her door as she's been having hassle with a neighbour, if you really need to monitor all my movements," Robin replied, adding, in a lower tone, "Have you been drinking? You promised you wouldn't do this."

"Robin, I need to know if..."

"Nan, this is not acceptable. We'll speak tomorrow."

Nan shouted, "Don't you dare hang up on me again!"

But he already had.

She stared at the blank phone screen before yelling. "I HATE YOU!"

"Do you *mind*?" said a whiskered elderly lady.

"Not at all," Nan snarled.

THIRTY-TWO

"So you don't really know if he was telling the truth or not?" Gwenno said, when she called Nan early the next morning.

"No, but I'm eighty per cent sure he was lying, and he was going wherever she was for the night. She hadn't come straight from their office in that outfit, that's for sure!"

"You're going to the bank this morning, aren't you, to find out where the money's going? I was really worried when you didn't pick up last night."

"I wish I had. You might have talked some sense into me, and stopped me from ringing him," Nan said. "This was not how I planned things at all."

"Planning something's not the same as having to actually do it. You're coping brilliantly and not many people have to spy on their husbands."

"That doesn't make me feel any better about doing it, Gwenno," Nan replied.

"I know. Sorry, but needs must. After the bank, you need to go to his Airbnb place and check it out. Knowing is better than guessing in the long run: you know it is."

"Yes, I do," Nan replied sadly.

* * *

An hour later, she was sitting opposite Jason, manager at the Market Square bank where she and Robin had opened their first joint account within a week of getting married. Nan could see that his mouth was moving, saying something that his eyes made clear was important, but she could not take in his words. When the sound of the man's voice stopped, she was aware he was expecting her to respond. She had no idea how.

"Mrs Green? Are you OK? It's a lot to take in, I know, if you've never, well, been involved in such things up to this point in time."

Nan blinked at him. "Yes, yes, it is." A pause. "Sorry, what was it you said again?"

"I'm looking at the transactions in your account now, and it would seem that your financial situation is, well, a little precarious."

"You mean we don't have any money?" Nan blurted. "I have no idea about our finances, you see. Not a clue. Robin's always sorted them, but that has to change, it seems."

"Mrs Green, it's complex, but it would seem that... er... someone has committed to some regular outgoings beyond your means, and this has left the account a little depleted."

"I don't understand. When we moved to Anglesey, we got rid of our mortgage and Robin earns well, or I think he does. I'm beginning to doubt everything now."

"I see. Well, there are regular payments to an accommodation agency here in Cambridge from your joint current account and some other, larger transactions."

"Look, can you just tell me what he's spent it on, in as few words as possible, please?"

"I can't, no, Mrs Green. I feel at this stage that it would be best if you and your husband discussed the matter," Jason said.

"But can't I see our account for myself?"

Jason wriggled in his seat. "Yes, that's permissible within the regulations."

Then he got up, rather too eagerly. "I'll leave you in peace to do, er, what you need to do. Would you like a coffee, tea, a glass of water?"

Nan shook her head. She was reminded of a Dickens character as Jason scuttled out of the office as fast as he could politely do so. Their balance was clear – £895 overdrawn – and she began to scroll back through the transactions on their joint account. It was their daily life, in miniature. The supermarket, the pharmacy and the pet shop were all her, running their home on Anglesey. Naughton Consultancy, Robin's salary, paid in only yesterday. The amount stunned her. Heart thumping, she scrolled through the payments for meals out at Cambridge restaurants she knew were expensive. This was his life here, and a very nice one it was too.

"You were really slumming it in Pizza Express, Robin, weren't you?" she muttered.

When she went further back, to the beginning of the month, she found a payment of £2,250 to '*Jacobson and Findlay*', a letting agency on the Chesterton Road on 3rd January.

"But work is paying for your accommodation, Robin. What's *this* rent for?"

At the beginning of the December, she found an identical payment – same date, name and amount. And the same on November, October, and September 3rd.

As she inched through the list of transactions; £1,500 to '*Sable Photographic Agency Ltd*'. In September, £925 to '*Ella Intimate Couture*' in August. The smart new coat she had admired had cost him £350 from *Moss Bros*, she discovered, and he also seemed to have treated himself to some new handmade shoes from *Ducker & Son* on King's Parade at £590. By the time she saw £1,450 to '*Venetian Hideaways*', she was struggling to breathe. No wonder they had no money! Robin had a life she knew nothing about, with a woman who enjoyed the good life, it was clear.

When the numbers finally stopped swimming in front of her eyes, Nan realised that it was all here – their life, stretching back over almost all the time she had been on Anglesey alone, organising builders, dealing with trees crashing through windows, walking dogs, bringing up two children single-handedly. In July, she saw what must have been another of the large transactions that Jason had mentioned – a money transfer to *Healthwoman Clinic* for £3,700, followed by a second of £1,750 to '*Hampstead Spa*' a week later. What health procedure was that money for and why would a woman need a trip to a very costly spa to recover from it? She felt her gorge rise at the most obvious possibility just as Jason opened the door, looked at her face and sat down.

"I can see that this is very difficult, Mrs Green," he said. "It's not possible for me, or the bank, to rectify it, but I can say without hesitation that your account cannot sustain the current level of outlay. You have your house in Wales as collateral, of course, but..."

"Of course," Nan said firmly. She fixed her eyes on his and knew exactly what was implied: if the debts continued to escalate, or Robin made other huge payments, the bank could make them sell *Coed Uchaf*. She had to think fast. "I know this is embarrassing, but can I separate at least some of our finances in some way, without my husband knowing?"

The young man looked at his desk and rolled a pencil backwards and forwards. "I feel that you need to have a discussion with Mr Green, first of all. Once you've decided how to proceed, then the bank will help you however we can, going forward. You do have a large arranged overdraft on your account."

Now was the time to do something she had done so seldom

in her life: ask for help. "Can you help me set up my own account now, Jason?" she said. "I'm frightened. I don't know what's he doing behind my back."

Nan held her breath. It was time for Jason to step up.

"Yes, you could set up your own personal account, as of today, and, er, do what you feel necessary thereafter, Mrs Green," he said. "What you and your husband decide to do about your joint finances going forward, I will leave up to you."

Twenty minutes later, Nan felt her coat being draped around her shoulders and her bag handed to her, but she remembered nothing about walking out of the bank or down a King's Parade heaving with tourists. She went into a tea shop and sat, staring into space, for almost an hour. Eventually, she drank her cold tea and rang her mother.

"Mum. It's me. He's having an affair."

An intake of breath. "*Arglwydd mawr*/Dear Lord. I knew it! Why are men all the same?"

Nan felt something shift inside her, a cog smoothly linking with another. "Did Dad have an affair too? Bloody hell! All those 'meetings', the times he needed 'peace and quiet' and sent us off to Dewi's? He had another woman, didn't he?"

Eira sighed. "Yes, he did. Maureen O'Reilly she was called. Only eighteen when it started, the poor girl. You were about fourteen or fifteen, I think."

Another cog slipped into place. "So that was why he didn't...?"

"Yes. He left us both alone once he had Maureen."

There was a silence, before Eira went on:

"It sounds awful, but it was my ticket to freedom, to be honest. And he left me well-provided for, out of guilt, I suppose. Maureen emigrated to New South Wales with a plumber while you were at Cambridge. He never bothered with me after that, and you were safe, thank goodness."

"It all makes sense now."

"Is she *young*, this woman?" Eira asked shyly.

"Yes, Mum, from what I could tell. And Robin's spent thousands on her. We might even lose the house," she said. "He'll never let me divorce him and risk all this coming out. He'd lose his job. James wouldn't think much of it, and even less of him fiddling his expenses with the rent. What the hell am I going to do, Mum?"

"You're going to take control, that's what. Don't let that man take away your home, the home you've wanted for so long. He doesn't deserve it, or you."

"But he'll twist everything, make me believe it was my fault, that I made him so miserable he had to do this. That's what he's so good at, Mum," she said, her voice getting louder as emotion took over. "He's a weasel, and he can change in a second. It's like trying to pin jelly to a wall, trying to pin him down. You've never seen him in action, how *nasty* he can be..." Eyes glared at her from behind tiered cake stands.

"No, I haven't, but I believe you, and it's you I care about. This is not your fault, remember, however he makes you feel. You need to find the courage to beat him at his own game. I know you have that courage, Nansi."

"But he has to win every game, every time," Nan said, her voice a whisper.

"Not this time. You need to get yourself a job. You need your own bank account, with your own money going into it."

"That's exactly what the bank manager advised, and I've done it. £1,000 a month is going into an account for me and the girls, just to make sure we're not left high and dry. If Robin asks, I'll tell him it's a savings account for the girls, which I suppose it is." She paused, and a wave of exhaustion hit her. "Thanks for being there for me, Mum."

"I should always have been there for you," Eira replied softly.

"Yes, perhaps," Nan replied. "But Dad hit you. And I think you thought if he did that to you, he wouldn't hurt me as often."

"I did. But I never knew about... the other things he did to you, not until he was dying, and morphine freed his secret. He was ashamed. I hope, somehow, that you can forgive both of us," she said, her voice so low, it was almost a whisper.

A fly buzzed lazily against the windowpane. Nan watched its exhausted struggle for release for a few moments, before opening the top of the window. So her mother had not known the worst of what had happened to her until her father's death, but she knew now, and they were actually talking about it. This was a moment she had waited for for years, and now it was here, it changed everything.

"Nan, are you still there?"

"Yes. I'm here," she whispered. "It wasn't my fault, was it? What Dad did, I mean."

A gasp, a snuffling sound.

"Mum?"

"No, *cariad*/darling. It was never your fault. How could it be?"

Nan hesitated. "He told me it was. And I believed him."

"I wish I could hug you now," her mother said.

"Thanks. So do I," Nan said, knowing full well how hard her mother always found it to hug anyone. This was such painful territory, for both of them, it was like walking on glass splinters.

"I want to tell you that I am proud of you, Nansi Brennan. You remind me of my mother."

"Ha, you always told me she was a tough old bird!"

"She was, she had to be. Life was hard on the island in those days, but she was pure gold. Strong and loyal and kind. I see such a lot of her in you."

When the fly finally flew out of the open window to freedom, Nan felt something release in her, too, like the snipping of a tether that had always bound her body tight.

* * *

When she had collected herself, she went to 6 Park Parade, where Robin had told her he had been lodging all these months. The houses were much bigger than their old home around the corner, with sash windows and wrought-iron railings entwined with age-old wisteria that Nan was sure would be magnificent in the summer. They all overlooked the expanse of Jesus Green, which she had walked every inch of in the past. An elderly woman opened the door and smiled. Nan struggled to smile back at her.

"Hello. Can I help you, dear?"

"Hello, yes. I'm... looking for Robin Green. I believe he rents a room in your house."

The woman's smile faded. "He stayed here once or twice, in the summer."

Nan heard herself say, "Oh, I see."

The woman folded her arms, braced for a chat. "It's a bit of a nuisance, actually. His office pay for the room every month, so I can't let it to anyone else, but I let it for a bit of company, someone to chat to, but Mr Green's never *here*. He still parks his car in the car park round the corner most of the time, though. I've seen it there. Bit odd, as he doesn't sleep here."

"Yes, it is, isn't it?" Nan stammered. Tears were not far away.

"It's easy money, but I'd rather have someone to talk to," the woman went on, oblivious to Nan's increasing distress. "Do you know him, Mr Green? There's a few of his things here – an old coat, books, shoes and some photos of a family. Not that I was prying." She looked at Nan, her gaze more searching now. "Come to think of it, you look a bit..."

"Thanks so much... er, sorry I don't know your name," Nan said. "I'm sure I'll find him."

"Mrs Nowak. That's my name. And yours is?"

Nan walked away quickly, without looking back or feeling guilty. Striding down Sidney Street into a biting wind and trying very, very hard not to cry in public yet again, her phone rang. It was Gwenno, wanting news, but Nan did not pick up. There was a time for telling everyone what she had discovered, but first she had to find the courage to deal with it herself.

THIRTY-THREE

Nan and the girls spent the Friday of New Year's Eve in the garden at *Coed Uchaf* with Harri, Mim, Gwenno and Guto. Wrapped in sleeping bags and blankets, they ate the ferocious chilli Harri had cooked and toasted marshmallows over the firepit as a few shadowy gulls circled them hopefully. It was freezing, but it was the best New Year's Eve Nan could ever remember. When the girls went inside to watch TV at about 8pm, she drained her glass and told her friends all about Jason, the glamorous, long-legged girl and the house Robin was renting with her, his new woman and her replacement. They stood up as one, waddled over in their sleeping bags and wrapped their arms around her.

"Glad you've told us at last. I had my suspicions, I'll be honest, but at least you know the truth now. She's spot on, your mam, telling you to go and find out the truth," Gwenno said. "Any idea who this woman is?"

"No, but she's young and beautiful, which is enough," Nan replied.

"You're young and beautiful too," Harri said. Nan smiled

and looked at him gratefully, but his face was troubled, and he looked uncomfortable. Something was on his mind.

"I think the idea of you getting a job out of the house is a good one, actually, right now. I can manage most of the veg stuff for the moment. You need to spread your wings a little."

"That won't be easy, as there's so little up here workwise. Let's get on the laptop and see what vacancies there are."

"What, right now?" Nan bleated. "Oh, let's not spoil tonight with too much reality, please! Let me contact my freelance links in Cambridge first."

"Do you want to go back to writing articles about archaeological 'digs'?" Gwenno said. "We do enough real digging here, don't we?"

"Not really, but it's all I know. I need to try, for my self-esteem... and the cash."

"We're going to make our fortune with our veg boxes, you mark my words. Especially when we get the second polytunnel up and running."

"I know. Just until we do make our millions, OK?" Nan said, punching her friend's arm.

* * *

But in Nan's absence, her Cambridge contacts had moved on, or been promoted, and none of her enquiries bore fruit. She wasn't sorry, but she was increasingly worried. The three friends convened again a few evenings later and hunkered over Nan's laptop drinking wine and looking for a local job for her, which proved even more disheartening. There were the usual "security roles", "care workers", "waiting on staff" and a "part-time classroom assistant", but none were even a remote fit and all paid appallingly.

"We all know how few professional jobs there are up here unless you work in the hospital or the university," Nan said.

"That's why Robin said he could never see himself working here."

"Hang on," Harri said, grabbing the laptop and typing in the university website address. "I'm sure someone I still know from my student days said there's a part-time vacancy in the Archaeology department for some 'dig supervisor', starting in the New Year. He was going to apply but needs something full-time. Why didn't I think of it before? Look, here it is."

"So you went to Uni, Harri? I didn't know that," Nan said. There was so much she didn't know about this man, and yet it seemed to matter less and less to how she felt about him. How he felt about her remained a mystery.

"I started a History and Fine Art degree, yes, but 'life got in the way', as they say. Right, here's the advert."

Nan scanned the details of the vacancy quickly. She ticked a lot of boxes, but there were a lot more, she didn't. The role involved managing groups of volunteers – largely teens with time on their hands – doing grunt work at local digs.

"Is it worth even trying for?" she said. "It says, 'Welsh speaker preferred' and the closing date's January 5th, pretty soon."

"Let's look at your CV," Harri said. "But we'd better switch from wine to tea or coffee, I think."

"It's time to look forward, not back, *cariad*/love," Gwenno said with a smile.

* * *

When she opened her eyes every morning, Nan waited for grief and panic to hit her, but what she felt more than anything was relief. Threads of sadness, loss and anger were in the mix too, but there was no going back – her friends had finally convinced her of that. As she made breakfast and packed lunches for the twins' first day back at school, two things preyed on her mind above all: that Robin could force them to sell her beloved *Coed Uchaf* if he needed money, and the fact that she still had no idea who he was now sleeping with.

Had he known this girl in Cambridge before they moved? Was the freedom to set up a love nest in the city the thing that had been "in it for him" as Dewi had hinted? The thought that he had never really intended to join them on Anglesey made Nan feel sick. If that was the case, how long had their family been more a lie, than a life?

* * *

She drove straight to Bangor after dropping the girls off and walked Shadow along the pier right to the end, breathing in the stiff, salty breeze that always blew there, however calm the day. Then she walked along to the Archaeology Department of the university to hand in her updated CV and cover letter. The young man behind the reception desk didn't even look up when she stood at the desk, waiting.

"Hi. I've heard that the department is advertising for someone to manage its community volunteers, help oversee their involvement in local digs. The closing date's today, but I hope I'm in time."

No response, as the young man tapped on his keyboard.

"First day back at work after Christmas, is it..." she glanced at his name badge, "Bryn?"

Bryn gave a final tap at the keyboard and took her CV. The flimsy plastic clip that had been holding the pages together pinged open and sheets of paper fluttered onto his desk and the floor behind his chair. As they both scrabbled to pick them up, lay them out and put them back in order, she saw him sneak a crafty look at the top sheet of her CV and his eyebrows arch in surprise.

"Sorry, I should have put it in an envelope," she said

pointedly. It was private, surely. "I really do think it's great to get young people involved in archaeology at grass roots level and opportunities like this are few and far between up... er... ah..."

"Up *here,* were you going to say? Tell me about it," he said, meeting her gaze for the first time. "*Ond 'dach chi'n teimlo'n hyderus yn y Gymraeg?*" he asked with a weak smile.

Nan was struck dumb at first, though she had understood perfectly. "*Ydw*/Yes."

"So, you know that I just asked if you felt confident in speaking Welsh. A lot of our volunteers do, you see..." he added with another arch of an eyebrow.

"*Dw'in dysgu Cymraeg rwan*/I'm learning Welsh now, and I'm starting classes soon," Nan blurted. "But I'm not fluent yet..."

The receptionist sighed. He had clearly heard this phrase a *lot.*

"*Da iawn*/Good. I'll put this in an envelope for you and get it to HR today. We haven't had *too* many applicants for this as it's part-time. You won't hear for a few weeks, but *pob lwc*/good luck."

"*Diolch yn fawr iawn*/Thanks very much. I really need to get a job. *Hwyl*/Bye!" she called, hoping she sounded cheerily confident.

But Bryn was already back on his keyboard.

* * *

For the next few weeks, nothing had really changed, and yet everything felt different. Nan visited Dewi most days, taking soup or a casserole, but she never knew how she was going to find him when she did. On some days, he was out with the livestock, fork in hand, spreading silage with gusto, but on others, the sheep in the fields waited in vain for the sound of his quad bike coming to check on them, his barking dogs riding pillion, and he spent the day in bed, in pain.

Outside, January raged, the sea a churning cauldron whipped by icy winds and the trees around the house shivering in their nakedness. Nan moved from room to room at home like a butterfly unable to settle, waiting for news of the job and numbed by the knowledge of her husband's betrayal as it seeped into her a little more each day.

The person she found she felt easiest with was Harri. When waves of panic began lapping at her heels, it was his face she visualised, his voice she heard, and it calmed her. He never minded when she rang him or called in unexpectedly. They had not even hugged each other, but Nan felt closer to this man than she had ever done to anyone. He was low himself, as he, too, despised January and Mim had been unsettled after the last visit to her mother and blamed him for the huge absence in her life. Nan knew better than to ask questions, but she could see he was suffering. One gloriously clear January day, he announced that he had organised a day out for the two of them – a tour of the main archaeological sites on the island, starting and ending at the school gate.

"After this, you'll know what you're talking about if you get an interview," he said.

"If I get one," she muttered. "Haven't heard a thing from them."

"Things take time, especially after Christmas," Harri said. "Nobody could do a better job than you. We've just got to hope they see how brilliant you are."

She beamed at him. To be praised so fully, without provisos, felt like a sip of nectar.

They criss-crossed Anglesey, from the remains of Prince Llewellyn's court at Llanddwyn, to the prehistoric village at Din Lligwy and the standing stones at Llys Rhosyr and finally, to the spectacular covered burial mound at Bryn Celli Ddu.

"I think this is even more spectacular than the burial chamber near us," Nan whispered. "I can feel the holiness of it, the *sacredness* in every single stone."

Harri smiled. "I come here sometimes when I need to centre myself, if that doesn't sound too silly," he said. "Did you know that on June 21st, the solstice, the inner chamber is pierced by shafts of light from the rising sun and lit up, as bright as day?"

"That's wonderful," Nan said. There was a silence, until she added, "We moved here on June 21st last year. I wish I had been in here, instead of driving up a motorway."

"Next summer solstice, we'll come together," Harri said. "We'll stand in there and feel the sun warming our bones and giving us hope for the future, shall we?"

Nan looked at him. He was so close, as the chamber was cramped. She could smell the coffee he had drunk at their café stop, see where he had missed a patch of his chin shaving that morning. The temptation to kiss him was almost unbearable and she knew in her bones that he felt the same way. She stepped back instead.

"Let's do that," she said quickly. "I think we both deserve some hope."

* * *

January passed slowly, as it always does. Each day, Nan walked the remotest sections of the coastal path, along the north-eastern tip of the island, where pebbled coves nestled between the cliffs and fat seals lounged on seaweedy rocks. She could walk for hours without seeing a soul, so she ranted aloud at the sky. This was what she needed now. Whatever she said, the gulls still wheeled above her, and the waves still hit the shore with their own relentless rhythm. It felt good to say the unsayable out loud before going home and having to be upbeat, make tea and tell bedtime stories.

A text from Robin one morning telling her that they "needed to have that proper chat soon" unnerved her. Had he found out about her spying trip to Cambridge or her day out with Harri? Had he seen the direct debit into her new account? She read his words as she strode across the beach and yelled her response at bewildered seagulls.

"I'm to be jettisoned soon, am I? Me and our beautiful little girls? You got me to trust you, to love you. Now you've spoilt *everything*. How dare you *do* this to us?"

But when the promised "chat" never materialised, Nan wondered if his aim had been to keep her on her toes. She was certainly in no hurry to listen to his excuses or hear his plans for the future. No, she was playing a longer game now – one that put her and the girls first and one that would involve strength and patience.

It was the beginning of February and Nan had not spoken to her husband for a fortnight, when she heard his car pull up outside the house late one evening. She ran to the window, peered out into the darkness and saw him get out. A key turned and the door opened.

"Hello, Robin," she said calmly. "I wasn't expecting you."

"Yes, I know. But we need to talk," he said.

"Right, OK. Come in and I'll get you a drink," Nan replied. "It's a long old drive."

Although she knew that this was probably the beginning of the end, she felt stronger, and readier, for what lay ahead than she had ever done.

THIRTY-FOUR

A whoosh of icy cold filled the hallway, lingering long after Robin had closed and locked the front door behind him. For several seconds, there was an equally chilly silence between them as he peeled off his coat, scarf and gloves and laid them on the hall table. When he finally looked at her, she saw that there were deep hollows beneath his eyes and he had a patchy, pepper-and-salt beard. He looked defeated as he slumped down on the bench by the front door, and when he dropped his head into his hands, Nan saw that he would soon be bald.

"You don't look well, Robin," she said. "Is something wrong?"

He lifted his head and looked at her. The skin around his eyes was flaky, deeply lined, and his lips so dry and cracked that they looked almost white.

"No, not feeling one hundred per cent, to be honest. I'm so tired, Nan. We do need to talk, but not now. I can't do it tonight. Let's declare a truce until I've had some sleep, please."

"OK," Nan said calmly, though she was furious at what felt like a stay of execution. She had to stay in control of her emotions, though, at all costs. Both Harri and Gwenno had drilled that into her.

"Are the girls asleep?"

"Of course, they are. It's really late. You can go into the spare room."

But she saw such a look of sadness in his eyes that she added, "Better to talk when you've had a good night's sleep." But he had already started climbing the stairs.

* * *

Late February can bring unexpected, sunny days on the island with skies as blue as any in July, and the following morning was one of these. Nan took the twins to school, walked Shadow, put a wash on and mopped the kitchen floor while Robin slept, undisturbed. Then she wrote a list of what she wanted them to discuss when he woke up:

- The situation
- Your mistress
- Your spending
- Your reasons for doing this to me/us
- Our future

"That's one hell of an agenda," she said aloud, as she read it through.

Gwenno was in the garden, planting out seedlings in religiously neat rows, with labels handwritten by the twins. Nan gave her a coffee, and a warning.

"Robin's here, and he wants to talk," she said. "I think this is it, the 'big chat' he's been threatening me with, so ignore anything you hear, OK?"

"I can't promise not to dash in there with a pitchfork if I hear you crying or screaming blue murder, Nan. Hold your nerve, don't let him bully you, remember that you're a star and if all else fails, come and get me. I'll tell him exactly what I think of men like him."

"I know you will. That's what I'm worried about!" Nan replied with a wry grin. "I feel quite sorry for him, actually. He looks so rough, and I have so much more in my life than he does."

"Like yours truly, you mean?" Gwenno said, winking.

"Wish me luck," Nan said, as she went back inside.

"Just be yourself. You're a Welsh-woman now, remember," Gwenno shouted after her. "Bloody unbeatable, we are."

* * *

When Robin finally came downstairs, Nan was even more shocked at his appearance than she had been the night before. His face looked creased, his eyes bloodshot, and the ring of hair around his baldness stood up like an unlikely frill. There was none of his customary badinage as he slammed around the kitchen making coffee, but he poured none for her, which was reassuringly typical. When he sat down at the kitchen table, Nan suppressed her urge to fill the awkward silence with accusations. No, she had to wait for him to tell *her*, not to tell him what she already knew, but it was really, really hard not to throw his coffee in his face.

"What's going on, Robin?" she began.

He took a slow gulp of coffee, closed his eyes and kept them shut for several seconds. Nan had always hated his time-buying technique, like his saying, 'Pardon?' when he had heard her perfectly well or wagging a finger in her face until she stopped talking.

"What do *you* think's going on, Nan? I hear you've been playing the sleuth." His tone was like acid, eating through her careful 'agenda' in seconds.

"I don't think that's the issue here," she rallied. "Who's your informant anyway?"

He threw back his head and laughed. "*Informant?* You've been watching too many spy shows! Since you ask, I popped back to Park Parade to pick something up and Mrs Nowak told me someone who looked *exactly* like the woman in my photos had called, asking for me. It had to be you, though running away from old ladies isn't quite your style."

His words stung, but Nan clung to the advice Gwenno and Harri had given her: let him do the talking, stay calm and don't get emotional. Robin carried on, and his voice was relaxed, but his expression told her that he was very angry indeed.

"What exactly did you think you were going to achieve, Nan?" he said. "You've got your dream house, and it's clear you really don't want me here."

She gulped. "I don't now, Robin, but I did when we came. You know that."

"This isn't what I bought into, Nan."

"Stop saying that, will you! The only thing that's changed is that you don't want to be here with us, which is what *I* bought into, Robin," she replied.

"I disagree. Take the friends you've made, for instance. That ghastly woman Gwenno, and Harri – he has history, you know. Perhaps you should have done a bit of digging before you cosied up to him and made me a laughing stock!"

Nan shook her head sadly. "You made yourself that, Robin, not me," she said, but a knot twisted in her stomach. What did he know about Harri that she did not?

Robin poured himself more coffee. "My friends warned me that you had an agenda for moving here. My parents had grave concerns too, as you know, and now I can see they were right. I've been taken for a fool, funding your fantasy."

"What? We talked about it endlessly, Robin. We *agreed*..."

"I'm not saying you intended this to happen, but perhaps it

was in the back of your mind as you drove us all off a cliff edge in search of your dream life. And people are gossiping about you and Harri locally. I can't have that, Nan, I really can't."

At this, Nan lost any semblance of control. "How dare you accuse me of being unfaithful! You're such a hypocrite, Robin Green!"

Robin spluttered, as he was not yet sure how much she knew. Nan decided to put him out of his misery. "Just out of interest, who was the bimbette on your arm coming out of Pizza Express the other night, the one you live with in Grantchester? And how much of our money have you spent on her?"

He hung his head, and his reply, when it came, was coldly brief. "OK. So you know."

"Yes, I know. Who is she, Robin?"

He steepled his fingers and looked at her, his eyes steely, "Rhian Owen."

Nan gasped. "Rhian Owen?" She grabbed the edge of the table to stop herself swaying. Of course! He had had a soft spot for her from their earliest visits to the island, when she had cleaned for Dewi. Why the hell had she not seen that coming?

"She's a wonderful girl and, well, we've, er, had a bit of a silly thing over the years – nothing serious, you know, but chatting and a bit of... canoodling, but we got closer last summer, chiefly because both of us were so unhappy."

"Because *you* were unhappy?" she said. Panic was stirring in her, a familiar beast.

"You're not the only one who feels miserable you know, Nan," Robin replied. "Rhian made me feel I mattered to her. She *respected* me. When she left Anglesey, she found me in Cambridge and things, well, developed. I never meant it to happen, but it did."

"Now I know where you were when you vanished for hours on our holidays up here every year. Running in the wild open spaces – hah! You were sleeping with a teenager in a barn!"

"No, Nan, honestly, it was only flirtation until she came to find me, nothing more," he said, veins pulsing on his temples. "I was at my wit's end last year. I knew we'd made a terrible mistake, selling up and buying this money pit of a house. I was working so bloody hard with you yelling at me to come home and James yelling at me to stay in Cambridge. Hell's bells, I've tried to make you happy. I even gave you the kids you wanted that I really didn't." He stood up and strode over to look out of the window, adding, "But it was never enough, was it?"

"But you love them, don't you, Robin – our girls?" she said, shocked. The room had begun to buckle around her, the walls melting and swaying – signs that she both recognised and dreaded.

"Of course, I do," he replied, "but this isn't the way I wanted my life to pan out. I told you when we met, I'm not a complicated guy. I don't want years of childcare, DIY and rustic boredom and I simply can't cope with all this angst. I vowed after Simon died that I would try to live a happy life, and I wasn't happy anymore... with you."

"You bailed out because you can't cope with adult life. You'd rather spend your time with schoolgirls who don't ask you to take a good hard look at who you really are."

Robin's face told her that she had struck a nerve. "Are you such a good judge of character? Do you actually know about your friend Harri Parry's past?"

"I know that sad things have happened to him..."

"Well, perhaps you need to ask him *what*, Nan. From what I heard, he really isn't someone you should place your trust in."

Nan's final ounce of courage evaporated like a popped bubble. "Tell me what you heard," she hissed. "Tell me, Robin."

"Titbits from a charming lady called Siân Williams in the pub at Christmas, since you ask. The meaty stuff was curtailed by our hasty exit that night, but I think you need to know what kind of person you're getting involved with, Nan."

Anger surged through her. "Involved? Robin, nothing has *happened* between Harri and I, nothing at all. And I will talk to him in my own good time."

Robin leant forward, rested his elbows on his knees and looked into her eyes in a way that reminded Nan of a therapist; it inspired instant distrust.

"I believe you, Nan, but don't judge me too harshly until you've done so. Things haven't been right between us for a long time, you know that and I know that. It's why this whole stupid experiment hasn't worked. We want different things and, basically, Rhian makes me happy."

"And I don't?"

"No, I'm sorry, you don't. Not anymore, and I can never live here with you and the girls," he said. "I want a divorce, and that's why I came back – to talk about that, the custody of the girls and finances, because it all needs to be fair. I only earn so much..."

"I guess living the high life costs a lot, yes, and you've spent thousands of our money already," she replied bitterly. This suddenly felt horribly real.

Robin stood and came towards her. "As things stand, we have no mortgage, and you earn nothing. We sold our most valuable asset, a house in Cambridge." He let this sink in.

"You agreed to what we did, Robin, as Dewi reminded you at Christmas," Nan said.

"Yes, I did and more fool me, but it was a mistake. Let's focus on the future now."

He was now firmly in charge of the conversation, as always.

"I propose that you keep *Coed Uchaf* and the car but leave me enough of my salary to try and buy something small outside Cambridge. We'll get the solicitors to do the sums if we must, but I hope we can sort things out amicably."

Nan looked into his eyes – tired, red-rimmed, but hard. "You've really thought it all through, haven't you? What will the girls and I live on? Aren't I entitled to half your salary at least? I think I'd better get a very *good* solicitor to sort things out."

Robin glared at her. "Look, this place will always cost money, but I can't agree to fund it anymore. If you want to stay here, *you* have to make it work and contribute to the huge cost of running it, it's as simple as that. This is your dream, not mine."

"I've applied for a part-time job at the Uni, actually," Nan blurted.

"Great! It may lead somewhere. It will get you out of the house, meeting people as well. That will help snap you out of the Glooms."

Nan turned away from him, but he had already seen her tears.

"Oh, here we go – the waterworks again. You can't go on hoping everyone else will take control and sort the nasty stuff. I did that for far too long."

He laid a hand over hers, but she pulled it away.

"I never asked you to manage my life, Robin. I just needed to be loved. And I don't need that anymore – not from you anyway."

"That's fine by me, and I'm glad we have made a decision at last," Robin replied. "But promise me you'll ask Harri Parry about his past."

"I will, and he will tell me, but remember that we *all* have a past, Robin, crammed with things we'd really rather forget, but I believe it's best to be open with the people you care about," Nan said. "Perhaps you should try it some time."

"I'm going out. I have things to sort," he said, grabbing his car keys. "And I'll be leaving again tomorrow."

When she heard Robin drive away, she found Gwenno in the greenhouse and collapsed, sobbing, into her arms.

THIRTY-FIVE

For Nan, life was strangely blurred, out of focus, during the time immediately following their decision to divorce. She crept into a corner like a wounded animal, contacting nobody. When Eira began to sound panicky in her voicemails and Harri's missed calls were in double figures, Nan told them, but she ignored their offers of company, she needed to be on her own – perhaps, subconsciously, because she had to get used to it.

The weather was atrocious, relentlessly grey and wet. Gwenno couldn't work in the garden, and even *Coed Uchaf* seemed to hunker down into itself, each room feeling chilly and comfortless however high she put the heating on. Nan spent most of each day reading in a chair next to the Aga with a hot water bottle on her lap. She tried so hard to believe that the future could be one of hope, of better things, that she rang the HR department at the university, hoping, praying, for some good news about her job application.

"I'm really sorry. All applicants should be informed this week that funding for the job has been reallocated. There is a possibility of more funds in the future, and I can keep your details on file if you might still be interested."

"Yes, I would be interested," Nan said dully. "Please let me know if things change."

* * *

Nan hadn't forgotten what Robin had said about Harri. She knew she was going to have to ask him again about his past, but she was finding that actually doing so was incredibly difficult. He was kind, sensitive and the girls adored him. They knew that she was fond of him, too, as she had seen them both watching them chatting and laughing together. A very small voice inside her told her that the twins would probably be delighted if they got closer, but she shut that thought down. He was a good friend, at a time when she had few of them. That was enough.

But as she sat by the fire watching the flames lick up into the soot-blackened stone chimney and tried to pinpoint what she felt about Harri Parry, she knew this was not true. Whenever she heard his voice, or saw him across the playground, her heart leapt as it had never done before, even in the early days with Robin, which had always been clouded with drink and despair. She had no clear idea if this was love, lust or a longing for someone to trust, but she was absolutely certain that to explore her feelings for him now, in the midst of a divorce, was not an option. If this *was* love, it would have to wait.

Within a week, letters started arriving at *Coed Uchaf* from the prestigious Cambridge solicitors Robertson & Lewis. Robin did not contest his adultery, but when he tried to get Nan to agree to a financial settlement she did not understand, she rang Harri for advice as Dewi was now far too poorly to be troubled.

"Hi, sorry not to have been in touch for a while," she said, when he picked up. "We're getting a divorce. I expect Gwenno's told you."

"She did, yes. She also told me that you know he's having an affair with Rhian Owen," he said. He paused. "Nan, before you say anything else, I have a confession to make. I knew about it – someone told me, but I hoped it was gossip, and I couldn't bring myself to tell you. She's as fickle as her sister, it seems. I'm sorry I've not been around to support you, and sad I wasn't honest with you."

Nan felt all the blood drain from her face in seconds. "People knew he was seeing Rhian? It gets worse and worse," she said. "And Robin was worried that people are gossiping about you and me!"

"Are they?" Harri said softly.

"Apparently, yes. Are you... upset to hear that?" she blurted, immediately regretting sounding so needy.

"No, I'm not upset. I am used to hearing much worse gossip than that about myself, Nan," he said slowly. "And as for the divorce, well, I think you deserve to be happy, and you're not. Everyone who... cares about you can see that."

"Thank you," Nan replied. "I don't understand the money stuff, Harri – never have, but now I'm worried Robin will rip me and the girls off," she added.

"I'm hopeless with money too, but I know a man who isn't," Harri said. "Emrys, my mate from school. He's on the autistic spectrum, so expect the unexpected at times, but he's an absolute force of nature in this kind of stuff. You'll need a solicitor to do the formal divorce business, but I can help you there too. My mother has a friend whose daughter, Gwenda Jones, deals in divorce all the time. She's very sharp, very direct, but good at her job."

"You and your network!" Nan replied. "I'm glad of it, though. I want to keep things as local as I can, have as little to do with Robin and his cronies as possible."

"I totally understand that," Harri said. "And thanks for forgiving me, about Rhian."

"Nothing to forgive, you just cared about me being hurt."

* * *

When Emrys arrived at *Coed Uchaf* at teatime one day, Nan was glad Harri had prepared her for meeting him. He'd "come on the 5.12pm bus", he told her the moment she opened the door "which actually turned up at 5.18pm". He was wearing a battered trilby, round, horn-rimmed glasses and a green gaberdine mac that reached almost to his ankles. His smile, however, lit up the room. Harri sat with the girls in the living room as Emrys and Nan pored over the outgoings from the joint account at the kitchen table, steadily munching through a whole packet of ginger biscuits.

"Your husband's really been on spree, hasn't he?" he said. "And he's made no efforts to hide it."

"He knew he didn't need to, as I can't see our account," Nan said. "Or rather, *couldn't.*"

"Here is an estimate of the monthly funds he should need in Cambridge if he is to take on a mortgage to buy himself a modest property."

Nan wriggled in her seat. "Robin's not good at economising, and he's the only breadwinner in this family at the moment. He won't like 'modest' at all."

"Then he should have behaved better," Emrys replied firmly. "He has a family, responsibilities and he is a grown-up. We need to get you a solicitor, and send an immediate response to *his* solicitor, outlining what we regard as a fair settlement of assets, Nansi." Then he shouted, "Harri! Can you ring Gwenda Jones right now please?"

"Perhaps not right now, bud. It's late, and the girls need to go to bed," Harri replied, coming into the kitchen to join them.

Emrys paused, processing this information. "Then I will draft my thoughts tomorrow and send it over to you to forward to Gwenda. I'll cc. you, Nansi. I have email facilities."

"Doesn't he need a notebook, to write stuff down?" Nan said to Harri, after he'd left.

"Photographic memory. He was a real asset in school, I can tell you! Right, better go."

"Thanks a million for all your help," Nan said.

"Happy to help whenever you need me to, Nansi," he said softly. "We all are."

She closed the door after him and leant against it, her hands shaking. Harri had said her name so lovingly, his eyes fixed on hers. Yes, to be accepted and supported by her community felt good, but in that moment, what she longed for more than anything was to know that this man loved her.

* * *

Emrys was as good as his word. The following day, a long email appeared in Nan's inbox. He had calculated her average and expected expenditure, the projected costs of the twins until they came of age (including university loans) with a contingency for holidays and for maintenance on *Coed Uchaf* (having contacted an estate agent for a rough current valuation). His conclusion was bleak, however.

For this settlement to work for both parties, Mr Green will have to manage his expenditure and his expectations with more modesty than demonstrated of late, and Mrs Green will need to seriously consider obtaining further, guaranteed, sources of income.

Nan's heart sank. How could she make up the gap between what Robin needed to live in Cambridge and what she needed here? How could Gwenno's veg box scheme possibly make any real money, and how could she get a job that paid more than minimum wage? Panic rising, she forwarded Emrys' email to Harri. His response was immediate.

I thought this might happen. Will ring Gwenda now. Yep, we need to come up with a plan. Tuesday evening, at yours, 6pm? Sorry can't do sooner.

A *plan*? She smiled as she remembered her friend's chaotic cottage. No, Harri could never make a coherent plan, she was quite sure, but he could probably come up with ideas which would help *her* make one. And if she and Harri were alone together, she might be able, finally, to ask him more about himself. She had promised Robin she would. As she wrote her reply, she felt that she needed to know all his secrets now more than ever.

All good with me. We need to talk about other stuff, too, Harri. You know we do. See you then. N. Xxx

... but she deleted the "Xxx" just before pressing "send".

THIRTY-SIX

Before Tuesday arrived, Dewi's health deteriorated so rapidly that it was clear he was nearing the end. Frustrated at his increasing weakness, the farm he could no longer manage and worn down by pain, he had become angry and ill-tempered. It distressed Nan to see the kind man she had always loved snap and shout at his carers, and she could see that the current situation could not go on. Dewi needed someone familiar, someone who loved him to care for him now; she would have to ask her mother.

"I've got lots on, and I can't bear to watch him go, Nan," she said. "It was bad enough with your father, but with a man I actually *love*..."

"But Dewi needs you," she said. "I know it will be hard, and you probably have plans and commitments, but you need to come. He's your twin brother, a part of you."

"I know, and that's why it will hurt so much to lose him, but I'll be there tomorrow," her mother said with a long sigh.

Nan was far from convinced that her mother was happy in a soulless London suburb, alone between whist games or pensioners' teas. Every time they spoke, Eira prolonged the conversation, asking about the twins' lives, the dog, the island weather... anything to flesh in the details of Nan's new life on the island, and postpone the return of the ticking of the clock as the hours crept by.

"I wish you would just take Beti's advice, and come home, Mum," Nan murmured, once her mother had hung up.

* * *

Hugo Robertson, Robin's solicitor, received Gwenda Jones' initial suggested settlement very coolly, but Gwenda was having none of it. She was more furious than Nan was.

"He wants me to sell the house to punish me for bringing us here," Nan told her.

"But it's your home, and your children's home. He will have to offer more than is on the table at the moment, but I can't give you a cast-iron guarantee that you won't have to downsize, Nan. His lawyer seems reasonable enough, but I suspect that your husband thinks he knows the law better than his lawyer does."

Nan assured her that this was entirely likely.

Very late one Friday evening, just as she was about to go up to bed, Robin rang.

"Hello. I'm ringing to tell you that this settlement thing is a real pig's ear!"

She could hear the boozy venom in his voice. He must be drinking alone as he had let slip that Rhian was "not a fan of alcohol".

"I've worked so hard for so long and yet you get to keep most of what I've worked for. It's a *travesty,*" he spluttered.

"It's a *divorce*, Robin," Nan said in as calm a tone as she could muster. "We have two children who need food and a home."

"But they don't need one with five bloody bedrooms, an Aga and a state-of-the-art wet room, Nan! How am I going to afford to live if you don't release the equity in *Coed Uchaf*? Isss not *fair*," he shrieked. "You've ruined my whole *life*, Nan."

"Many people would argue that you've ruined mine, actually," Nan replied. "I'm now a single parent of twins with no career and no prospect of one, but you're starting a new life with gorgeous young Rhian whom you say makes you happy..."

"She does, yes! Very, but still..." he stopped to slurp, and hiccupped. "Listen, Hugo assures me I have a valid argument for a fair proportion of the value of the house."

"Well, Gwenda's not so sure about that."

"It's the biggest asset we have, so it should be *shared*," he bleated.

"It's our home, not an asset. It's all I have, Robin."

He hiccupped again more violently. "I was under duress when we went there. My parents warned me not to marry you, you know, said I was 'too soft'. I wanted to take care of you, help you get control of your drinking, help you pull free of your depression, but I let you *control* me in the end." He was gabbling now and sounded desperate.

Any germ of sympathy Nan felt for this man and his financial predicament evaporated. There were things she needed to say to him, and right now, she felt brave and strong enough to say them. So she did.

"You've controlled me our whole married life, Robin, kept me on a leash like a *pet*. You decided what I could and couldn't do at home, at work and made sure I and everybody else knew how useless I was. You conned me, making me believe that we would be a family in our new home, when in reality you'd had enough of this little pet and saw an ideal way of pressing 'delete' and getting yourself a new one. You tried to cover your tracks – renting a room, keeping your car parked near it – but it was all a sham. That's why you agreed to sell up and come here, isn't it, Robin – so that you could start again, with someone else to manipulate? Rhian was the ideal candidate, I can see that, she worshipped you."

Nan heard him breathing heavily. She had not finished yet.

"While we're chatting, what do your parents think of who you've replaced me with? I bet they're chuffed to bits with Little Miss Rhian. Do they know how much she's cost you so far or that she wants to be a glamour model, or that she's *aborted your baby*? I found out what happens at that expensive clinic you paid for her to go to, Robin."

Strange, gulping noises came from her phone.

"Where is she tonight? Have you let her go out with her mates? You never let me do that, or if you did, you punished me and mocked them afterwards. Well, I won't take that from you anymore, Robin Green. Dewi is dying and I need to spend what little time he has left letting him know how much I love him. And I have friends, real friends, strong friends, who value me, support me and *love* me. I am not going to be bullied by you ANYMORE. Got that?"

She heard the clatter of the phone being dropped, heavy footsteps and then the unmistakeable sound of vomiting.

"Night night, Robin," she said, and hung up.

THIRTY-SEVEN

It was a cruel irony that, as life was returning to the island a little more with each newborn lamb, blaze of daffodils, or first crop of spring veg from Gwenno's new garden, Dewi's grip on life grew weaker.

Friends helped his only farmhand, Ivor, with the lambing in February, but they all knew that the farm would quickly go bankrupt with nobody in charge and no plan for the future. Nobody felt able to ask Dewi if he had made a will stating his wishes. His son Wyn was never going to return to the island, as he had turned his back on farming years ago and had been to visit his father only a couple of times in his illness, citing his "work schedule", but Nan knew the real reason was that the situation broke his heart.

"This land was Mam and Dad's reason for living – that, and me," he said during one of his visits, "and I let them down." They had talked all evening and had made a sound start on the bottle of Penderyn whisky Wyn had bought for her. "I can't help him now, and I know I've always disappointed him as a son – his *only* son. It's always been such a burden to carry, his *expectations*."

Nan nodded. "I know. I suppose the one good thing about being my father's only *daughte*r is that my father never had any expectations of me in the first place."

Wyn's face was stricken. "I tried to make Dad proud, but farming – it's not me. It was *never* me, Nan."

"He knows that, Wyn, but I expect he doesn't know what to do. Has he written a will, do you know? If he hasn't, the land may all be broken up."

"I really don't know if he has. He's always hated solicitors and I can't ask him in case he thinks I just want the money, but I don't, Nan, I really don't. I don't need it and I probably don't deserve it, as I left him to manage this place alone," his voice cracked, and he paused. "I care about it more than my father will ever realise, but I can never live here. I just can't."

"I know another man who feels like that, and who has lived for years under the weight of his parents' expectations," Nan said with a sad smile. "And this island is not for everyone."

"But you're really sure it's for you, are you, Nan?" Wyn asked.

She hesitated for a few seconds. "Yes, it is. I have never felt I had a 'home', really – in my childhood, when I was a student, but here, I have that at last. Yes, even if I have to lose *Coed Uchaf*, I still want to live on the island – I *need* to."

"Do you really think Robin will force you to sell up? Legally, I think he can't, until the twins are eighteen."

"I know that, but it seems unfair to deprive him of a reasonable home if I'm living in a huge one, just to spite him," she replied.

"I think it seems so unfair that you're going to have to leave your dream home."

Nan looked at her cousin fondly, her happy-go-lucky playmate of so many years ago. It was good to be sitting here with him, despite the sadness that lay ahead for both of them.

"It was my dream home, yes, but I don't like that phrase

anymore, you know," she said. "It's a house, it's not *me*, and I don't think it's my dream either – or not all of it. In fact, Wyn, I think I could even bear to lose it and start again. I'm stronger than I thought I was."

He laughed. "We've all known that for years, girl! You lit up our house when you came each year," he said, "but I must be honest, Nan. I remember hearing Mam and Dad talking about you having... *problems*... with Eric and telling me what a brave girl you were." He took a slug of whisky. "Tell me, did he hurt you and Auntie Eira?"

Nan looked at him, and saw the same kindness in his eyes she had found so comforting as a lonely child. She trusted him enough to answer his question with the truth.

"Yes, he did," she whispered. "I never told Auntie Manon, but I think she guessed. I haven't even told Robin the worst of it. I couldn't. I thought he would blame me, hate me, even. Mum says she never knew... about *that,* either, until Dad was dying and he let it slip. Eric was a very convincing liar."

For a few moments, the only sounds in the room were the crackling and spitting of logs in the wood burner. Wyn reached out for Nan's hand and held it tightly. Then he drained his glass. "Can I tell you something now, Nan, something that might have helped you if I'd said it a long time ago, but, well, life took us in different directions? I'm going to be in your life much more from now on, I *promise*."

"Great, but let's not bare any more of our souls now, Wyn. It's late, and I'm really not up for it."

He shook his head. "I know, Nan, but you need to hear this."

"Wyn, it's OK, really. Too many home truths in one night are bad for your health, you know."

"It will help you, honestly," Wyn said in a tone that made it clear it was no longer a request, but a *fait accompli*. "Listen, my parents only ever really distrusted two people that I know of –

your father Eric, and Robin, your husband. They tried, very hard, to like both of them as they were family, but they never could. Mam said Robin was '*fel llong heb angor*' – 'like a ship without an anchor' and Dad always said, 'She deserves better', and you do, Nan. There, I've said it. My soul is duly bared."

He slumped in his chair, looking as if he had run a marathon.

"Thanks, Wyn. I think that does help me – sort of," Nan said. "And I must introduce you to my friends, Gwenno and Harri, who think exactly the same thing!"

"Things are going to get better for you, Nan. I know it," Wyn said, his eyes moist. "You're a truly amazing woman, you know."

"Thanks, cuz. Dewi is proud of the man you've become as well. I know it. Let's try to talk to him tomorrow, with Mum, about the farm and what he wants to happen... afterwards."

Her cousin nodded. "*Diolch*/Thanks, Nansi."

"And I would be really happy if you were around more, Wyn."

"I've missed having you in my life," he said with a smile.

"Well, I'm back in it now, and I'm not going anywhere," Nan replied.

THIRTY-EIGHT

When Nan went into Dewi's bedroom one bright spring morning a few weeks later, the first thing that sprang to mind was a line of poetry she had studied in school: "*April is the cruellest month*". For her, to watch this invincibly strong man die as the sun shone bright and the hawthorn tree outside his window lit up the sky with its frothy blossom was "cruel" indeed.

Eira was at her brother's bedside, as she had been for several weeks, devotedly caring for him. His head was bent low now, as she held a beaker of water to his lips, but he struggled to sip, even from the straw. When he lay back on his pillow and she stroked his thick, grey curls back off his forehead, Nan was stunned at how alike these twins looked in their old age, something that had never struck her before. Dewi was thinner, of course, but his sister had the same wide nose, the same sharp jawline, and her hair was white and wispy too. The bond between them was palpable, a presence in the room.

Nan sat down, having pulled up a third chair for Wyn, who had come back "for the end", as he put it. It would not be long now, and they all knew that they had to find out Dewi's wishes for his funeral, the farm, and for the days ahead when the pain could worsen. He had refused to discuss going into a hospice, or "that palliative nonsense" as he called it, snapping whenever anyone had tried to mention the possibility. Nan understood: the local hospice, a place of cushioned quiet and imminent death, was so far removed from the way he had lived his life and the man he still was. She knew that he wanted to die in his own bed, as his beloved Manon had done all those years ago.

"Try and take a little more water, Dewi," Eira said. "You have to drink."

"Why?" he replied. "Will it change anything?"

"It might make you feel a bit brighter. Your body still needs water."

"We do need to talk to you, Uncle Dewi, so a drink might be a good idea," Nan said.

"So that I can answer back, you mean?" he replied with a wan smile. "Right, better brace myself for battle then."

Eira dabbed some dribble from his chin, passing the tissue to Wyn to dispose of.

"Good to see you making yourself useful, boy," Dewi said, winking. "And nice to see you two cousins back together. You were the best of friends as children."

Wyn smiled at Nan. "Yes, we were... and we still are, Dad."

"You'll take care of this special girl for me now, won't you? That good for nothing Robin was a bit of disappointment on that front," he said. "On every front really."

Wyn nodded. "*Wrth gwrs*/Of course."

"I'll take care of her too, Dewi," Eira said.

Everyone in the room pretended not to have seen her brother's dismissive shrug.

"Are you divorced yet, *cariad*/love?"

"Not yet. It takes time to... sort things out," Nan replied, trying not to think about the acrimonious message she had received from Robin that morning, blaming her for the "dire conundrum" they were in.

The old man's answer came in a second. "You mean it takes time to persuade him to be fair with the money. He was always a slippery one. Has he got another woman?"

Nan squirmed. "Ah... I... well."

Wyn came to her rescue. "Dad, Nan and Robin will sort everything out between them. We need to sort a few things out with *you*, actually." Clearing his throat, he went on, "First, I have to ask you whether you've made a will."

"A *will*? Of course I've made a will, you daft boy. Made it years ago."

There was a collective, if suppressed, sigh of relief.

"Good, so we know what you want to happen... with the farm, after you're gone," Wyn said, a wobble in his voice. "Because I can't come back and look after it, Dad. I'm sorry."

Nobody spoke, so the steady ticking of Dewi's ancient alarm clock was the only sound in the room. Motes of dust shimmered in a sudden shaft of sunlight, caught on their slow journey from ceiling to floor. It felt as if time was suspended, and father and son were alone in the room.

"I know that, my boy. You must sell it of course, but please sell it to a farmer. That's all I ask," the old man said. "I've talked it over with John Roberts. He's keen and he'll work the land well. His son Glyndwr would work with him and live in the house – they've got another baby on the way, him and his wife, so they could use the space."

Wyn reached for his father's hand. "You really don't mind, Dad, that the farm will leave the family?"

"I mind, yes, but I accept it. The land that must be taken care of, that's what matters to me. I owe it that much." He paused and closed his eyes. "You have taken a different path, but it's your life, Wyn, and you've done well. It's all in my will, how the money from the sale is to be distributed."

Tears were streaming down Wyn's face. He leant over the bed and gently kissed his father's head. "*Diolch*/Thanks, Dad."

"*Arglwydd mawr*/Good Lord, look at you, boy, blubbering away! Your mother and I may have been less than perfect, and the place might have been a bit of a mess when you were growing up, but we took care of the important things, like making our wishes clear for such times as these."

"I only wish Eric had been as gracious as you, Dewi," Eira said softly. "He put himself first right to the very end, as he always did."

"But you must leave all the bitterness you feel about him behind you now, Eira," Dewi said, wagging a skinny finger at his sister. "Sell that house in London, give some of Eric's money to Nan and buy yourself a little place up here. You belong here. You know you do."

Nan thought she saw her mother's tired face brighten with hope at this possibility, but in seconds, it vanished. It was probably so hard for her to imagine ever being happy...

"It would be wonderful, Mum. I've told you that. The twins would love it. *I* would love it," she said.

Eira looked down at her lap, lips pursed. "I'll think about it."

"Good. Glad that's sorted then," Dewi said. He looked exhausted now and his energy was ebbing fast. "Don't you want to know what's happening to the money from the sale of the farm? I can tell you now, if you like and..."

Wyn sat forward quickly. "No, don't, please, Dad. We'll know when it's *right* that we know."

"*Da iawn*/Good. I suppose that's as it should be. But I do wish I could be here to see what comes *next*. I would so like to see you happy here at last, Nansi, my lovely girl."

"I am happy here, Dewi. I've got some great friends. I've actually started a business with one of them, growing veg. And the twins are loving life..." her voice dwindled.

"It's money that's the fly in the ointment, is it? He wants

you to sell *Coed Uchaf,* doesn't he? We'll see about that." The old man snorted and lay back on his pillows, closing his eyes.

When, seconds later, he blurted, "So who are these friends of yours and why haven't I met them?" they all jumped.

Nan laughed. "I suppose I was never sure what you'd make of Gwenno, to be honest, but she's the kindest woman I've ever met. She's even managed to sell our veg to several of the best restaurants and hotels on the island, which is amazing. And Harri Parry, he's had his troubles, but he's such a gentle, constant soul. I hope you meet them both."

"Harri Parry rings a bell, to be honest. The victim of some spiteful tittle-tattle or other, I seem to recall, but I'm too tired to remember it. Truth is often the last thing at the centre of such *sothach*/rubbish. Too many people have been brought down by a wicked tongue around here. If he's one of them, he has my sympathy. Life's too short – I should know, as I'm about to leave it."

"Oh, Dewi, please, now we know your wishes, can we stop talking about you... not being here anymore," Nan said.

Dewi lifted her hand to his lips and kissed it. "It's part of life, is death, but yes, we will." He turned to look at his twin, who was sniffling into her handkerchief. "I have one more problem to sort before I go anywhere. There's something I need you to do, Eira."

"Don't ask me to scatter your ashes over the fields. I couldn't bear it."

Dewi laughed, a thin, rattly sound that soon became a racking cough.

"No, not that. I've left instructions for that, too, in my will. But I want you to go and see Annie Hughes, while there's still a chance you can talk to her."

Eira blanched. "It's been too long, Dewi. I can't. And she's so ill now."

"All the more reason to go then. She will feel better and so will you. She has nothing left, Eira. Her husband and both her boys are gone. Do it, please – for me. Take Nan with you, to tell her that she lives in *Coed Uchaf* and that she loves it. Annie would like to know that. Promise me you will."

Outside, in the farmyard, they heard a sudden explosion of barking as the sheepdogs greeted the nurse who had come to give Dewi another morphine injection.

"I'll take that as a 'yes' then," he said. "Now get out of here, all of you, unless you want to see my bare arse."

THIRTY-NINE

Dewi died on Friday April 29th, with his sister, his son and Nan beside him. He barely spoke another word after their conversation a week earlier and they were sure that telling them his final wishes, his parting thoughts, had drained his last ounce of strength. The palliative care team had recommended he be admitted to St David's Hospice in Llandudno for the end, but Eira had refused to let them take him.

"My brother will die on the island he loved, in the home he loved and that we grew up in together. I'll take care of him here."

And she did.

On the same day Dewi's death was announced in the local paper, Gwenda Jones forwarded an email she'd received from Hugo Robertson, Robin's solicitor, attaching the final draft of the divorce settlement. It confirmed Nan's willingness to sell *Coed Uchaf* "if it proved financially necessary", which Gwenda said she "deeply regretted" but Nan had stuck to her guns and refused to succumb to anger or bitterness. If Dewi's death had shown her anything, it was that a home was far more than just a house, and her husband deserved one too.

"I can't even think about this today," she told Wyn. Neither of them had slept much the previous night, and they were drinking tea and eating toast in the living room as if in a trance. "Let's focus on your dad first."

"I don't think I can focus on anything for a while," Wyn said weakly.

When Ceri and Elin dashed in from the kitchen, arms windmilling, shouting at Nan and Wyn to "come with them right NOW", they did not leap up to follow them.

"Girls, Uncle Wyn and I are really tired today. Can you just play quietly this morning? We have to help Nainy sort some things out for the funeral, and..."

"But, Mummy, you *have* to come. There are *puppies* in Shadow's basket!"

"What?" Nan exclaimed.

Elin grabbed her hand, pulled her up out of her seat and dragged her into the kitchen. In her basket next to the Aga, Shadow was happily feeding three tiny black and white collie pups. Gwenno had already been hauled from the garden and was kneeling by the basket open-mouthed.

"Well, this is unexpected!" Nan said.

"Didn't you have her 'done'?" Wyn said. "Is this an immaculate conception?"

"No, I never got round to it, with everything else that's gone on since we got here," Nan replied, kneeling down next to the basket. "Oh, aren't they *beautiful*? Clever girl, Shadow!"

The twins were jumping up and down, clapping their hands together with uncontainable joy. "Can we keep them, Mum? Can we feed them with bottles, like the lambs?" Elin asked.

"It's because Uncle Dewi died, something has to be born," Ceri added.

"Perhaps it is, sweetheart," Nan replied. "Dewi would love that idea, for sure."

Wyn crouched down and looked at the pups more closely. "They look like pure Welsh collies to me," he said. "Hmmm, remember when you brought Shadow over and left her down in the yard with Dad's dogs while you helped your Mum give him a bed bath...?"

Nan laughed out loud. "Yes, I do! Ooh, the little minx!"

"As you said, Dad would be *wrth ei fodd*/over the moon," Wyn said. "I'd love to have one of them, when they're ready, if that's OK with you, as a lovely memory of him." He stopped, and stared at Shadow, eyes wide. "Oops, she's having another one, I think. Look, girls!"

The twins watched, rapt, as Shadow grunted, wriggled and another puppy slipped into the world, covered with slime and bloody trails. Neither child moved a muscle or took a breath until they saw Shadow lick the pup clean and heard its first high-pitched squeak. Only then did they look up and beam at their mother; it was a moment she would never, ever forget.

"But how on *earth* do we look after puppies?" she asked Wyn.

"We'll google it!" the twins cried, dashing off to do so.

"Shadow will do most of it herself," he said, "but I'd have a vet come and check her over, just in case. They look like a healthy bunch."

"Four puppies! Strong breeding stock, you see, our family," Nan said with a smile.

"But there are going to be puddles and poohs everywhere, so brace yourself," Wyn said.

"I know," Nan groaned. "But perhaps the girls are right, Wyn – new life, after a death. It has to be a good thing – *look* at them. I'm going to enjoy the ride and bugger the mess."

"*Bendegedig*/Brilliant," Wyn replied, applauding.

"Crikey. Whatever next?"

"You're going to be fine, Nansi, *whatever* happens next. I know it."

* * *

The days leading up to the funeral were a whirlwind, each one a mixture of celebration of the past and sadness at a future without Dewi in it. He had left detailed instructions on the hymns and readings he wanted, which had included the dictum that "no money be wasted", so Eira and Nan wrote their own, handwritten, order of service and decorated the tiny chapel in the nearest village with bracts of fresh lilac, twigs and wildflowers from the hedgerows around the farm. He and Manon had married in this church, and it felt achingly appropriate that his life was celebrated here, at the end of it. With Wyn's permission, Nan rang Robin and told him about the funeral arrangements, but she had a twinge of panic that he might come and bring Rhian with him as his new partner and someone who had also known Dewi. She prayed he would do neither.

* * *

The funeral was held on a fine, chilly, blue-skied day in the first week of May. The fields were lush with green shoots and the cherry trees around the chapel laden with the last of their candy-pink blossom. The delicate scent of lilac filled the air and the twigs Nan had picked in bud a few days earlier had exploded into leaf. As people filed in quietly – the men removing their caps, the women wearing their smartest Sunday coats – Wyn stood in the doorway to greet them. Nan watched as he greeted faces from his childhood, still as warm and kindly now as they had been then, in the fields or at the village harvest supper. She hoped he felt welcome here, even if he could not stay, as she would. The island was in his blood, and would always be a part of him, one of the unbreakable links that bound them.

The chapel seemed to glow with shared memories when the

congregation sang "*Ar hyd y nos*" and there was such a quiet reverence that many wept. As they sang, Nan turned to the back of the chapel and suddenly glimpsed her husband trying his best to make his mouth form the Welsh words. He looked tired, beaten and Rhian was not by his side. She sought him out at the funeral tea, but as she walked towards him, she felt no lurch of anxiety in the pit of her stomach, no dread of how he might speak to her or what he might say. She felt only sadness, for what could have been.

"Robin, hi. Thanks for coming," she said. "I didn't think you would."

"I'm not so sure Dewi would thank me, but I'm grateful that you asked, Nan."

He twirled his teacup in its saucer, his usual conversational panache quite gone.

"Are you all right?" Nan asked. "You look... not yourself."

"Nan, you've read the latest version of the settlement from Hugo. How do you think I feel, knowing that I have to make you sell the home you've wanted all your life?"

"But it's what you've pushed for all along," she replied calmly. "It's our biggest asset, remember?"

He pushed his fingers through his now visibly greying hair, a gesture that told Nan he was anxious. "I know I have, but this whole disaster has brought out sides of myself that I hate. It's not something I'm proud of, you know – destroying our family."

She moved a little nearer but stopped herself. She must not comfort him. He had bullied, patronised, controlled and betrayed her. And yet today, strangely, she felt no bitterness at all.

"You would never have been happy here. I hope you find somewhere you *can* be, but I really don't need that big old house to be happy, much as I love it. Me and the girls will be fine somewhere smaller. Have you talked to them yet?"

Robin smiled and nodded. "A bit. They seem so much more

grown-up, even after these few months apart. Elin's so lively and Ceri, well, she's super thoughtful and intuitive. She came and spoke to me in the church when nobody else did, did you see?"

"No, I didn't, but I'm not surprised. She's a kind soul. I'm proud of them and they're happy here, so they won't mind moving house. Well, not much anyway."

Robin winced. "I hear you have puppies. I was going to ask if I could take the twins on holiday for half-term, but I can't compete with puppies! When they're weaned, I guess, in the summer," he said, adding, "I assume you're not intending to keep *all* of them?"

"Just one, so the girls can have a dog each. Wyn wants one too, as the father was one of Dewi's dogs, we think!" she said, grinning. "But I don't see why you can't take the girls on holiday after that. It's shared custody, as much as the distance between us allows. You'll need to get your new place nice for them to visit you." She paused for him to respond, but he said nothing, so she asked the question she had hoped not to have to ask.

"What's Rhian up to? House-hunting, is she?"

Robin looked at the floor and Nan knew, without him saying a word, that Rhian had left him.

"She's going to live in Dubai with an investment banker."

"I'm sorry to hear that, Robin," she murmured. "Really sorry." But when she looked at his sad, needy face, the ground wallowed under her feet, and her breath quickened. Did this mean he wanted them to get back together? Is that why he had come today? She knew, in an instant, that was not what she wanted, even if he did. Steeling herself not to pity him, she said, "Look, I have to go and help Mum with the refreshments now. Next week is set for the final decree, I think, so we'll be in touch soon enough."

"Yes," Robin replied meekly. "Before you go, Nan, I was looking for your friend, Gwenno. Is she here?"

Nan hesitated. "You want to talk to Gwenno? OK, well, I expect she's doing the dishes. The first lot of veg boxes are going really well, by the way, and we have loads more orders. We've got two polytunnels in the garden now, full to bursting."

"That's good to hear. Well done. I'll find her, and congratulate her and apologise too. When the sale of the house goes through, do you think you'll start the business again, somewhere else?"

"Not sure," Nan replied, as she wasn't. "Gwenno will make something happen, though, I know."

"I have no doubt of that," Robin said, before adding shyly, "And Harri? Where's he?"

"Now I'm *really* worried. Why on earth do you want to talk to Harri?" she said.

"Nothing to do with you two having an affair, don't worry. You're far too sensible to do that," Robin said with a sad smile. "I just wanted to, well, apologise to him too, I guess."

"Harri's not here. His mother, Beti, wanted to come so he had to stay with his little girl. I haven't had the chance to ask him about his past yet, before you ask, Dewi's illness intervened, but I have to say I think it's none of your business."

"No, of course it's not. It's just all such a mess, Nan," Robin said, with a catch in his voice.

Instinctively, she rested a hand on his arm. "Yes, it is, but there are good things ahead, better things, for both of us. I'm sure of it, Robin."

"I have to hope you're right."

They both looked over to the other side of the hall, where Eira and Beti were deep in conversation. Nan wondered what they could be discussing so confidentially. She had not told her mother how fond she was of Harri, but hearing Robin dismiss the possibility of her having a relationship with him only made her more aware of how much she wanted one. If Eira asked any questions after her chat with his mother, Nan decided to answer them honestly; there were already too many secrets surrounding Harri Parry. As her mind started generating possibilities as to what they could be, she became aware of a gentle touch on her shoulder.

"You've disappeared into your own little world, Nan, you always did, I suppose. I envied you that," Robin said. "I'll say goodbye to the girls before I leave. Take care, please."

When he kissed Nan on the cheek, she smelt his sweet, spicy aftershave and beneath it, the musk of his sweat. She realised that she no longer yearned for his touch, or his reassurance; he simply reminded her of the past.

FORTY

The day after Dewi's death, Eira moved into *Coed Uchaf* to stay with Nan, as the empty farm made her sad. She took to baking cakes and biscuits in industrial quantities "for the funeral" and then "to keep her mind off things" (which meant frequent trips to the friendly little supermarket in Menai Bridge to replenish supplies). Nan understood that her mother was grieving, but the mess and the cost of her baking habit soon became an issue and tensions in the household mounted to such a degree that it felt as if a storm was imminent. One afternoon, Eira came home to find Nan in the lounge and closed the door behind her, and the storm finally broke.

"Nan, I don't want to pry, but I really need to talk to you about Harri Parry," she said, sitting down on the sofa in a soft cloud of flour, in which she was constantly covered. "I know he's helped you out in the past, when Robin was away, but..."

"But what, Mum?" Nan said, her hackles rising. "He has been an amazing friend to me and the girls. I really don't know what I would have done without him, in fact. I had no support from anywhere else, did I?"

"I know you didn't," Eira said, not meeting her gaze. "And I know you're not happy with me about all that, but this is something else. Look, Nansi, things haven't gone *smoothly* for Harri in the past, with women, I mean." She rubbed her hands together, which produced another floury cloud. "Not that it's all his fault, of course. It's never just one person's fault."

"No, it's not, and you should know that better than anyone, Mum," Nan snapped. She really was not in the mood for this today. "I need to email Gwenda back and clear up all this puppy pooh so can you say whatever it is you want to say so that I can get on, please?"

"Look, I talked to Beti, his mam, at the funeral and, well, she didn't go into details, but she did say Harri's been through some very difficult times and can be... *unpredictable,*" Eira said. "I'd heard gossip, of course, but I take no notice of that up here."

"Aren't we all unpredictable at times?" Nan snapped. "I really don't want to talk about my friend with you, Mum. I know he's had issues and I know I need to talk to him."

"Nansi, listen. Beti's a bit scared of him – of his moods, I think."

Nan paused, feeling the shock of this tingling through her body. Gwenno had reassured her months ago that Harri posed no danger to her, or worse, to the girls, but perhaps there were things even *she* didn't know about his past?

"What do you mean? I know Harri can get very down at times, but so can I," Nan said. "And Beti probably drives him mad. I know she would me."

"Just be careful with him, that's all I'm asking. Until you know the truth."

"Fine. Yes, you're right, I will be. And I am going to talk to him about his past, I promise. While we're here, I wanted to talk to you about the amount of baking you're doing, actually, and how much it's all costing me, Mum..."

Eira got up from her chair and looked at Nan directly.

"I enjoy baking, and the girls enjoy my cakes," she said.

"And don't try to change the subject, please. Just be careful who you love, this time. That's all I ask. I'm off to put some Welsh cakes in. Your Robin *hated* them, didn't he?"

Eira left the room, but the doubts she had sown did not leave with her.

* * *

The reading of Dewi's will was arranged for a fortnight after his funeral. Wyn, Eira and Nan had been asked to attend the office of Thomas Davies, his appointed solicitor in Bangor, but none of them were expecting any surprises. Dewi had made his wishes very clear.

"I don't know why Nan and I have to be here, Wyn," Eira said. "The farm has been left to you, I hope. Nan and I might get some of Mam's trinkets, but I've got better things to do."

"Like bake more cakes," Nan muttered grumpily. "Has John Roberts made a formal offer for the farm yet?" she asked. She was worried. Robin had still not approved the final divorce settlement, saying he wanted to make "final tweaks", and this state of limbo in several areas of her life was exhausting.

"I know his intention is to buy the place, but we have to hear Dad's wishes and then wait for probate first, Thomas Davies says."

"Don't know why we have to pay these solicitors so much either. They don't seem to have any idea of haste, or people wanting to get on with their lives," Eira muttered.

Nan quickly stifled a laugh, as Robin's nickname for her mother popped into her mind: The Voice of Doom.

They sat down, refusing offers of coffee or tea. Then they watched as Mr Davies opened a buff-coloured file and turned the few pages in it very, very slowly before stopping and smoothing the one he had selected with his palm. A waft of mustiness filled the room: fresh air had been excluded from this paper-lined chamber for a long, long time.

"Can you be as quick as possible, Thomas," Eira said, checking her watch. "And remember to speak in English, so that we can all understand you *os gwelwch yn dda*/please."

The elderly man nodded and began to read Dewi's will aloud, translating from the Welsh original as he did so, but with the lilt of his mother tongue colouring every English word he said. When he had finished, Wyn, Eira and Nan sat in stunned silence for at least a minute, as if his voice had hypnotised them.

"So, there you have it," Thomas Davies said, putting his glasses down on his desk. "You look surprised, all of you, but you must have guessed that Dewi would do something unexpected." Nobody spoke. "Are you happy?"

Wyn gasped, slapped his forehead, and beamed at everyone in the room, in turn.

"Happy? I'm *delighted*!" he said. "It is just as I would have wanted it to be."

Nan turned to look at him. She felt weak, as if all the energy had drained from her body. "Really, Wyn? You don't mind that he's left a third of the sale of the farm to Mum and another third to me? I never expected..."

"Nor me! I'm rich in my old age!" Eira cut in, dabbing her eyes. "I could never have dreamt it."

Mr Davies watched them carefully from the other side of his desk.

"Good. Then let us proceed to the next stage of things." He paused, relishing the shock his words triggered. "Yes, there's more to disclose. You probably *won't* be surprised to hear that Mr Jones did have *strong* suggestions as to how some of the money he left you should be used, ladies. They are not legally binding, of course, but I cannot emphasise enough how *fervent* he was in advocating them." He paused, clearly relishing his choice of word. "Are you ready to hear what they are?"

Nan's mind was already buzzing. If she changed the distribution of capital in their settlement, she could buy Robin out, stay in *Coed Uchaf* and he would be able to buy a flat in central Cambridge and live the life he had always wanted to – and, perhaps, a better one. She felt a sharp elbow in her ribs.

"Yes, we're ready, aren't we, Nan?" Eira said, hissing, "I want to go home."

Mr Davies put his glasses on once more and cleared his throat.

"Eira Brennan, your late brother strongly advises you to purchase a house on Anglesey with some of your inheritance. He suggests you 'spend your latter years where you belong', I quote. He also suggests you and Nansi go on some holidays with your granddaughters 'to make up for lost time', to quote further."

Eira nodded and dabbed her eyes.

"Mrs Green," Thomas Davies began.

"Oh, call me Nansi, please," Nan cut in. "I don't feel like Mrs Green anymore, to be honest, even though, technically, I still am – for a few days at least."

"Nansi," the old man said with only a whiff of distaste for such informality. "Your late uncle would like you to stay at your home, *Coed Uchaf*, and trusts that this money will facilitate that."

"It will indeed. Thank you, Uncle Dewi," she said, with an instinctive glance at the ceiling.

"There is a further request from him, however, which you can choose to ignore if you wish, but about which he was most... *enthusiastic*," the old man went on, delighted to have found a wholly appropriate English word again. "He would like you to use any remaining finances to restore the outbuilding at your home and create 'a facility for families in need of the restorative experience of time on the island, as you benefited from your visits here as a child', I quote. He states that you already know which builders to use for this undertaking, should you decide to proceed."

"Yes," Nan said with a gasp. "Aled and Gethin Pritchard, of course. Oh, that's such a wonderful idea. Dewi knew how much coming here meant to me when I was little."

"Excellent," the solicitor said.

Nan had already begun to feel as if she was inside a Victorian novel, but when Mr Davies pulled out his vintage Parker pen, she half expected it to be a quill. Wyn had not said a word during the reading of the second part of will. Now, he spoke.

"But how did Dad want me to spend my inheritance?" he asked. "You haven't said."

The old man replaced the lid on his pen and looked up. "He had no specifications for you, Mr Jones. In fact, your father told me, I quote from memory only, that 'he trusted you to do good things and that you didn't need any advice from him on how to lead your life'."

Wyn gulped. Nan put her hand on his sleeve and squeezed his arm. Her cousin had spent so long feeling he had disappointed his father. To learn that he had not was momentous. He was struggling to hold back tears.

"Thank you, Mr Davies," he said. "I will spend it wisely, and well."

"But have some fun, Wyn, *please,*" Nan added. "Dewi would *definitely* have wanted you to do that."

FORTY-ONE

That year, the rest of May was blissfully hot on the island, with wide, blue skies and hours of glorious sunshine. Nan had precious little time to enjoy it, however, as every inch of the garden had burst into life, and both she and Gwenno had to work long hours to harvest the vegetables, fill the boxes, and deliver them in good time. Their order book was full, with new customer enquiries all the time. Gwenno made sure that once one crop was finished, another was coming on right behind it in the polytunnels. One evening, they were still working outside, and packing boxes, as the light faded; Guto and the twins were kept busy drawing pretty labels for each box before they were loaded into Gwenno's car for delivery early the next day. When they finally sat down with a glass of wine at the kitchen table, Gwenno turned to Nan with tears running down her face.

"What's the matter? You're crying!"

"Yeah, I am. Tears of joy, my friend," Gwenno replied. "You do realise that you have made my dream come true, don't you, Nansi? Look at what we've done! I had no hope left in life, none at all, until you took a chance on me. I will never forget it. Never." She blew her nose noisily on a sheet of kitchen paper.

"Gwenno, you took a chance on me too, remember. You saw past the 'posh' accent, the big house, the snooty husband, and saw the real me, struggling like a spider in a web."

"He wasn't just snooty; he was unbearable. And, like my Jack, a real git."

Nan hesitated. "Yes, you've got a point, but do you know, I feel sorry for him. He has nothing, and I have so much," she said sadly. "And he did let us set up this crazy veg scheme..."

"The one that's doing incredibly well, you mean? Less of the 'crazy', please! You're too kind for your own good, I think. He'll be fine."

"I hope so," Nan replied, refilling their glasses. Both women looked forward to these end of day chats, as both remembered how bitter loneliness and failure had felt.

"Actually, I had an idea," Gwenno said.

"Uh-oh. That could go one way or the other," Nan replied with a grin.

"Haha. Look, when we've got through the summer rush in the garden, why don't we build some kind of garden for the kids at the school? Simple stuff – some raised beds, a trellis, a bird table, perhaps a cold frame if the teachers think they won't kick a football through it. What do you say? Now that you're an heiress, and funds are no longer a problem..."

"Sshh! It's not public knowledge yet, so keep stumm about that, please."

"My lips are as sealed as they'll ever be, which is very sealed indeed. Promise."

Nan sipped her wine slowly. "I say '*syniad da*/good idea'. Let's do it, but we need to plan it, and not overstretch ourselves. I think we'll need Harri on board too and I know he'd like to do something for the school. First, I need to talk to him and get things straight between us."

"You do, I know, but I think he's ready to talk to you about his past now. It's not as bad as he thinks it is, but it's his story to tell," Gwenno said. "You're made for each other, you two, so don't blow it, Nan." A pause, a glance exchanged. "No pressure."

* * *

Harri came over a few days later to build the pups' outside pen, "helped" by three very overexcited little girls. Nan wanted desperately to tell him of Dewi's bequest, but knew she could not, not yet. The legalities ground on, and Robin and his solicitor had to know first. She had made her decision about the settlement, but this state of limbo was so unsettling; she wanted to make plans and to create a future, but the questions she had for Harri circled inside her head like goldfish in a bowl. If he was to be a part of that future, they needed to be honest with each other and keep no secrets.

One morning, he called in for a coffee and to repair a rip in one of the polytunnels after dropping Mim off at school. They sat outside in the sunshine, listening to the oystercatchers peeping on the rocks below. Scores of them were perched in a long line along the water's edge, waiting for low tide, when they knew that the rock pools would be brimming with marooned crabs and tasty, transparent shrimps. Harri sipped his coffee, and Nan watched him with a longing to throw her arms around him that she had never felt as strongly before. But until she knew what had wounded her friend so deeply and turned his community against him, she could never know if she could ever truly love him. It was time to ask.

"I need to ask you what happened with Mim's mother, Harri," she began. "I need to know – you know I do."

There was a long silence before Harri put down his mug and said, "You won't like what you hear, and you won't like me once you've heard it."

"Why do you say that? Gwenno knows, and she still likes you."

Harri sighed. "Gwenno is an exceptional soul in her capacity to forgive. I didn't dare to hope that you might be another one."

"At least give me a chance, Harri," she replied. "It feels like a massive obstacle in our way, something that's stopping us..."

"Saying that we love each other?" he said softly. "Well, I'm going to say it anyway, before I tell you anything else. Nansi, I love you. But do you, can you, love me?"

Shadow nudged against their feet, her nipples pink and raw from feeding her ever-ravenous pups. This gave Nan a reason to look down, to hide her face. How could she answer, what should she say? She had known, and yet not dared to hope, that this day would come, that he would ask this question, but she had never got as far as deciding her answer. Paralysed, she found that she could not give him one at all.

"I see," he said dully. "So, can I ever have any hope that you might love me back?" Harri asked, his voice cracking. "I am not a bad person, Nan. I just made a mistake."

Nan hesitated. "I believe you, and I've made plenty of them, believe me, but I need to know what it was, before I can answer your question."

"Yes, of course you do. To know if you can forgive me," he replied, turning away.

"No. To know if I can love you – truly, honestly and without secrets. That's how I want to love and be loved from now on. No compromises."

Grabbing her hand, he pulled her up. "Right, come with me now," he said. "There's somewhere I need to take you."

"Now? But... I..."

"To really understand me, you need to come."

When they pulled out of the farmyard, Harri's old Land Rover backfired so loudly that a flurry of crows flew up from the roof of the outbuilding like a ragged black cloud. Nan looked back to see them wheeling above her home and wondered if things would ever be so perfect and peaceful again once Harri had told her his secret.

* * *

They drove right across the island, taking tiny roads past farms and smallholdings where the explosion of frantic barking from free-roaming sheepdogs told Nan that they did not see many passers-by. Harri turned the radio up very loud, and drove very fast, so asking him any preliminary questions about what was ahead was impossible, and obviously unwanted. The agonising knot in Nan's stomach was mainly nerves, but she acknowledged that it included a hefty shot of fear too. What had she got herself into with this incredibly enigmatic man?

After about half an hour, they stopped at a gateway overlooking a stunning, horseshoe-shaped bay. Ahead, Nan could see a small, whitewashed building on what looked like an island in the middle of seawater. Its arched window and empty bell tower told her that it was, or had been, a church. Anglesey's coast was dotted with them, sentinels of past faith and endurance in the face of constant, merciless attack from the elements.

"Is this the 'church in the sea'?" she asked, adding. "I've always wanted to come here, but never made it."

"You can only reach it at very low tide, over a rocky causeway, so you have to pick your time carefully," Harri replied. He paused, his slim fingers trembling on the steering wheel. "Idris Hughes and I used to come here fishing together all the time. It was our special place, but we knew its dangers too. If you get caught out by the tide, you're marooned for hours. In rough weather, there's no way of getting a boat out to you."

Nan waited in silence as Harri shifted in his seat, beads of sweat on his forehead, staring at the church in the distance. She touched his fingers to calm them. Their jagged twitching was making her nervous: he was *unpredictable*, Eira had warned her...

"Do you want us to get out? Why did we come here, Harri? It's OK, you can tell me now."

He took a gulping breath, clearly struggling not to break down, and so she waited.

"Idris Hughes, my best friend, Annie and Tomos' son, lost everything because of me, Nan. He left, and then he died, alone, on that island, with none of his family around him, because of me."

Nan felt the skin on her arms fizz as if she had touched an electric cattle fence in the fields. "Oh, Harri, no. That's so sad," were the only platitudes she could muster.

"I betrayed his trust and threw away a lifetime of friendship for... for what? For flattery, vanity or just for sex? I can't remember. All of them, I suppose."

Nan felt a tingling of anticipation all over her body. It was coming soon, the secret she had waited so long to hear.

"What happened, Harri?" she said.

"Can't you guess yet?" he cried. "God, to me it's as if my guilt is written in huge letters all over the sky."

She hesitated. "I think I can, some of it, but I want to *know*, not to guess. Tell me what happened, from the very beginning to the very end."

Harri looked at her, a haunted, desperate look. "I don't know if I can."

"You must. For both our sakes."

He leant back in his seat and closed his eyes. "I know. But you won't love me if I do."

At that moment, another car pulled up to one side of the Land Rover and two small children and a bouncy labradoodle got out as the adults began scrambling in the boot. Soon, they were all heading to the beach, the kids carrying fishing nets and their parents laden with cool bags, windbreakers with towels and picnic blankets draped around their necks. It felt surreal, to be watching them doing such normal things, but it was mesmerising. Nan and Harri watched in silence as they picked a spot, set up camp and banged the windbreaker posts into the sand with a rock. Only when the adults sat in their deckchairs and the kids stripped off and ran excitedly towards the sea did Harri speak again.

"OK, here goes. Idris was a good person, through and through. He was only twenty-one when he started running the farm with Tomos, his dad, and married Catrin Owen, a girl he'd worshipped since school. I remember him proudly telling everyone in the pub one night that they were trying for a baby 'straight away'. He had everything in life, Nan. If anyone needed help on the farm, they went to Idris and Tomos. He was a friend to everyone, especially to me, and he was always aware of how precious he was to his mam and dad after his little brother died so young."

"So awful. And it must have made the three of them even closer," Nan said.

"It did, but I ruined all that when I let his wife get me into bed after some party. She told me she wanted to pay Idris back for saying her sister was prettier than her. She said she was frustrated with him because he couldn't get her pregnant and I was 'more mature' as I was a couple of years older." He paused, his face clouded with misery. "She could never get enough attention, Catrin Owen, nor her flirty little sister either."

"There must have been a reason for that. Probably, a sad one," Nan said, trying to ignore the memory his words, and that surname, stirred.

"We were all very drunk at this party and she said she'd done it before and Idris accepted it, but I knew that was a lie, and I was Idris' *friend*." He put his head in his hands. "There was no excuse."

"But there was a reason, if not an excuse. These things happen," Nan said, the words sounding as hollow as they felt. "I could tell you some tales about the things I've done that I'm not proud of..."

"Slept with your best friend's partner? I bet you've not done *that*," Harri cried. "Yes, these things happen, but they *shouldn't*, and a baby was born without a proper family because we let it happen. It was all so wrong, all of it. Unforgivably wrong."

He pulled a battered wallet from his back pocket and took out a photo, curled at the edges after years of gentle handling.

"Look, here we are at Idris and Catrin's wedding, the year before he died."

Nan saw two young men in suits, pints in hand, red carnations in their buttonholes. Both of them looked so young, so full of expectation of how glorious their life would be. One had a mop of dark hair draped over one side of his face and the other man was beaming from beneath a mop of tight, golden curls. As she looked again, something else stirred in her memory, buried deep.

"Catrin even tried it on with me that day. I put it down to too much champagne, and resisted, but the writing was on the wall. I saw that afterwards," Harri said sadly.

"This was Idris Hughes, Annie's eldest son, who should be farming *Coed Uchaf* if life had gone to plan," Nan murmured, staring at the photograph as if unable to look away.

"Life rarely goes to plan in my experience," Harri said. "Look at me now."

Nan squeezed his hand. There was no glib answer to that, only reassurance that he was not alone in it.

"And Mim's the baby you mentioned, is she?" she asked.

"Yes. Catrin told Idris she was mine. Told him I had given her what he couldn't. That was what broke him in the end, thinking he wasn't a 'proper man', whatever that means. It matters around here, especially in farming. It's all about *breeding*, isn't it?"

"Understood." She hesitated; this was tricky territory. "But do you know if Mim could actually be Idris' baby? Did Catrin ever do a paternity test?"

Harri bridled. "I don't know, and I never asked. When Mim was born, I loved her so much, and it never seemed to matter, especially when Catrin left a few months later. The baby was my responsibility, and mine alone, or that's how it felt. We only had each other. She's been my rock, you know. I owe my life to that little girl."

Nan thought of Robin, of his reluctance to make sacrifices for his own children. How incredibly different these two men were.

"But Catrin decided to come straight to you, and not find out who the father really was?"

"Yes, that's how utterly selfish she was. Idris begged her to stay. He was beside himself, inconsolable, but she'd made her choice. She was bored with him, I think. She said he was '*rhy dda*' for her, 'too good'. And he was. I'd intended to go away, perhaps to Ireland and set up a wood-carving studio, but I had to stay then. She said that life in a cottage by the sea with a carpenter sounded much more exciting than slaving on a farm from dawn till dusk seven days a week." He smiled, a weak, bitter smile. "She hated it, and me, by the time she left."

"Harri, tell me the rest."

"She came to my cottage late one night, stood on the doorstep in the pouring rain and told me the baby – she had called her 'Mimi', like a poodle for goodness' sake – was mine, that she couldn't go bear to home, that she wanted to be with me. I believed her – I even told myself I *loved* her. What else could I do?"

"Nothing. You had to take her in, look after her and the baby," Nan said.

"But when Idris rang, and she told him that we were going to bring up our baby together and that she wanted a divorce, he couldn't take it. He just drove off into the night in the farm pick-up truck. He came here when the tide was out and walked over to the church. Once the tide was in, and he knew nobody could save him in time, he went to the only tree on the island and..." His voice broke. "I felled it the next day and burnt it to ashes."

A breeze had sprung up. Neither of them spoke for a few minutes as they watched a flock of starlings swoop, gather and part again above the beach.

"I won't say I imagine how that must feel because I can't," she said. "It was a tragedy, but you've paid for the consequences dearly."

"We all paid, in different ways. Idris and his poor family, more than anyone. And Catrin hardly knows her own child; she couldn't handle the cold-shoulders, the hissing voices whenever she walked into a shop, and she blamed me for it. She said I'd led her on, preyed on her vulnerability when she was drunk. So yes, I paid, and am still paying, but at least I have Mim. For years, everyone except my mam crossed the street to avoid me. Catrin's parents harassed me, and you know what happened to Rhian, her younger sister."

"She's left Robin and gone to Dubai with some new rich boyfriend now. Did you know?"

"No, I didn't. Poor old Robin. She was always too pretty for her own good, Rhian Owen."

"Harri, can't you see that despite everything that's happened to us, and because of us, we're the lucky ones? We have our kids, and we have each other," Nan said.

"*Are we*, lucky I mean? Mim has grown up without a mother, I'm not sure I'm her real dad, which means my mam may not be her real Nain, and Annie, who *might* be, is in a care home, pining for a family that I helped destroy! I don't feel lucky, Nan. I feel cursed."

His shoulders began to shake, and huge sobs racked his strong body. Closing her eyes, Nan laid a hand on his back and waited as he released what had been building inside him for such a long time. She understood why he blamed himself. He had been stupid, selfish, but he had also been deceived. He had lost his best friend and sacrificed his dreams to raise a child that he did not even know was his own. Surely, any debt he owed was amply repaid?

She opened her eyes. "Is that everything you need to tell me, Harri?" she asked. "If there's more, just say."

He lifted his head and she saw how much he had suffered, and for how long.

"There's one more thing, and I feel guilty even telling you this, but part of me can't bear to know if Mim is or isn't mine. She *feels* like the best part of me, but I should really find out if she's Idris' daughter, for his sake."

"I think you're right. When the time is right, you need to find out," Nan replied. "But it won't make any difference to how much you and Mim love each other."

"But it would mean that Annie Hughes is her Nain," Harri said, shaking his head. "How can I ask Mam to bear that?"

Nan paused. "That's hard, but I think your mother will always have known this day would come. I think she would be able to share Mim with Annie, if that's the way of things."

Harri looked at her and nodded slowly. "I hope you're right."

"I know I am," Nan replied.

"*Diolch yn fawr iawn*/Thanks so much," he said, and took both her hands in his. "Thank you for trusting me enough to come here today. I feel as if a huge weight has been lifted off me, to be honest. I've wanted to tell you all this for so long."

"I'm so glad you felt you could, but I really want you to

believe me when I tell you that yes, you made a mistake, but you were not responsible for Idris' death, Harri. That was his decision alone, and not your fault."

They held hands and watched the waves ebb and flow in silence as, like a metronome, they met the shore, and then left it again, a gentle, constant pulse.

"I've not been here at all for years. We loved it here, as boys."

"And it's still the same, still a special, peaceful place, isn't it?" Nan replied. "You can put the past behind you now. Let the wind and the waves and the tide wash it away."

He smiled and looked into her eyes. "Thank you, *cariad*/darling. But now you have to decide something. I brought you here to answer to a question, remember?"

Nan sighed. "That seems like a lifetime ago! You'd better ask it again."

"Nansi, do you love me, my darling, dearest *pilgrim soul*?"

"Ah, 'When you are old', another of Yeats' best," Nan said.

"*One man loved the pilgrim soul in you, and loved the sorrows of your changing face.*"

"Well, there have been plenty of 'sorrows'," she said, "and our faces will keep changing as the years pass."

"So let us pass them together," Harri said. "Answer me, could you, one day, *love* me?"

There was a silence, long enough for one more wave to hit the shore and ebb again.

"I already do, Harri Parry. I already do."

FORTY-TWO

Summer is the most joyful time on Anglesey, when both sea and sky sparkle and the clifftops are carpeted with pink sea thrift and ring with the cries of fish-full gulls. When the phone rang in *Coed Uchaf* one sunny afternoon, Nan was tempted to let it ring out. She and Harri were hopping around her bedroom like idiots, trying to get dressed in time to pick Mim and the twins up. She answered, "just in case", to find it was Gwenda Jones, her divorce solicitor.

"Ah, hello, Gwenda," Nan said. "I was going to ring you. You must have heard from my Uncle Dewi's solicitor, Thomas Davies, by now. It's all taken so long to sort out."

"No, Nan, I haven't heard from him. But that's not the reason I'm calling. I don't know what changes you wanted to make to the settlement, but if I were you, I'd leave well alone. Hugo Robertson informed me yesterday that Robin has agreed to let you keep the house."

"What?" Nan exclaimed. "Why on earth...?"

"Perhaps it's last-minute jitters, or an attack of conscience, but apparently, he's agreed to take less capital so that you can stay at *Coed Uchaf*. I assumed he discussed it with you."

"No, he hasn't because he knows I'd refuse. Gwenda, I was going to tell him I don't need as much money now. I can buy him out of the house with Uncle Dewi's money when the legal stuff's done... if it ever *is*."

"What are you talking about? *What* money?"

"That's what Thomas Davies is supposed to tell you about. My uncle left me a third of his estate in his will, Gwenda, so I can buy Robin out easily," Nan said.

"What? You actually want to make things easier for your adulterous, nearly ex-husband and change the settlement figures?" Gwenda said. Nan heard her tapping her nails on her desk. "I do have other clients, you know – couples who really hate each other, as divorcing couples usually do..."

"I'm sorry, Gwenda. Actually, can I call you back in a few minutes? Bye." She hung up.

"That will not have gone down well with any solicitor *I've* ever known," Harri said.

"Can't be helped," Nan said. "Can you fetch the kids, please? I've got some stuff to sort."

"Of course," he replied, "but is everything OK? What's all this about buying Robin out and Dewi's money? Have I missed something?"

"In a way, yes. Look, it's complicated, and it's still supposedly confidential – so I can't tell you yet – but it's the right thing to do," she replied.

"What is? Helping Robin out? Why? I don't get it."

"Harri, trust me. I'll tell you everything later, but in the meantime, could you take the girls to McDonald's to give me a bit more time?"

He kissed the top of her head. "McDonald's? We're slipping into far too many naughty habits today, I think."

"Naughty but nice," she said. "Now go and do my bidding!"

* * *

She had to get in touch with Thomas Davies as soon as possible, so that first Gwenda, and then Hugo Robertson, Robin's solicitor, knew what was happening. Mr Davies was the cause of the delay, it seemed.

"Don't let this all fall apart, Mr Davies, please," Nan muttered, dialling his number. "There's too many people's happiness at stake."

Ringing his office was almost as surreal as visiting it, but eventually, his secretary Angharad said that she could speak to him even though he was "having his afternoon tea".

"Mr Davies, it's Nansi here. I really need you to inform Gwenda Jones, my solicitor, that I have come into money from my uncle's estate and can buy my husband out." Silence. "A *lot* depends on it."

A china cup chinked onto a china saucer before Mr Davies said, "I have recently drafted a letter to be typed and posted to Ms Jones at my secretary's earliest convenience, outlining the situation."

"I'm really sorry, but she needs to know as soon as possible. Now, in fact."

"Let me be clear here. You wish to share your recent windfall with Mr Green? Am I correct?" Mr Davies said, incredulity colouring every crisp consonant.

"Yes, I do," Nan replied. A long silence followed.

"Well, well. Life never ceases to surprise, does it?" the old man said, with more kindness in his voice than Nan had expected. "I will do as you ask immediately."

Nan thanked him and looked at her watch. The day was running out.

"When did I become this strong, assertive woman, Shadow?" she said to the little dog, who was wagging her tail in anticipation of an outing. "I'm loving it!"

As she left the front door, she looked at the long outhouse in the farmyard – its windows long rotted away, its roof sagging and pitted with holes. She could already see it as a holiday refuge for families who needed it, as Dewi had wanted her to do. Others deserved to see how life could be in this beautiful, wild place. Yes, she would make that happen for them.

The sun was high in the sky and only a few gobbets of cloud floated above the horizon, where the water blazed like a spilt slick of shimmering gold. A lone yacht was silhouetted against the expanse of blue and Nan stood, shading her eyes to watch its slow progress across the bay on this almost-windless day. The beach was quiet now, but school would finish soon, and the sand Would be covered with checked rugs, paddle boards and the air filled with the laughter of children, released for the summer.

She walked for an hour, over the headland and across all the separate covers until she reached Rhosneigr. With each step, she became more certain of her decision. For whatever real reason and with whatever warped motives, Robin had rescued her once, and let her follow her childhood dream in coming here. However hard it had been when they had first come to the island, when she looked ahead now, and imagined the future for her and the girls, it was good. Now it was her time to help him. If he had enough money, he could take the leap, as she had done, and leave his deeply unsatisfying life in Cambridge, waiting for crumbs from James Naughton, and follow his boyhood dream of being a painter, an artist. Those aspirations had been crushed by his brother Simon's death and meant that the weight of his parents' expectations rested solely on him. What a crippling burden that must have been. She hoped he would take the chance to be as free as she now felt. He deserved that.

FORTY-THREE

As the long, lazy weeks of June crawled past, Nan was busier than she had ever been. She had to wean the puppies, help Gwenno plant, harvest, box and deliver their vegetable crops, clear Dewi's farmhouse and begin to think about how best to convert the outhouse at *Coed Uchaf.* Any free time, she spent talking with Harri about how disappointing the past had been, for both of them, and how different they wanted the future to be. Harri listened, without interrupting or judging, and she loved him all the more for it.

One glorious July afternoon, Nan, Harri and Gwenno crouched in the reed beds around the estuary at Malltraeth watching wading birds tiptoe through the mud and herons wait, motionless, for fish to come near before stabbing them in a split-second flurry of beak and feathers. It was the last day of school, and they all knew their free time would be more limited from now on. Gwenno had packed a fabulous picnic, and they were soporifically full.

"I know it will take time to sort all the logistics, but life's too short to waste another second of it when we could be this happy," Nan said. "I really think you and Mim should come and live in *Coed Uchaf* once everything's finalised, Harri. Do you agree, Gwenno?"

"I do indeed!" she said, raising a large plastic glass of wine.

"Be prepared for Siân Williams and her nasty little gang to massacre us," Harri said. "People like that can't bear it when other people aren't as miserable as they are."

"I know, but I don't care. It's us that matters – us and our girls."

"I agree, but having been at the sharp end of gossip, it won't be plain-sailing, Nan."

"Cheer up, Harri, will you?" Gwenno said. "You both have a chance to start again, love each other and build something fabulous for you and your kids. Just get on with it!"

When both Harri and Nan saluted her, Gwenno threw a cork at them.

* * *

Ceri and Elin were ecstatic at the news that Harri and Mim were moving in.

"Can they come *tomorrow*? We'll be like the Three Musketeers, but The Three Sisters instead!" Ceri said. "Can we all have a puppy each? *Please.*"

"I'll see," Nan replied, knowing she stood no chance.

Mim seemed happy too, but when she asked her father if she had to call Nan "Mum", Harri looked troubled. "You need to be sure too. Let's think about that."

Later, he told Nan why.

"It's nothing to do with you, but if she's going to call you 'Mum', as I think I want her to, I need to know if she's mine, so that then when she calls me 'Dad', I know it's true in *fact*, as well as in my heart," he said. "I think we need to do a DNA test. If she's not mine, I'll know she is Idris'."

"*Was* Idris', my love, if that's how things turn out. She has always been your daughter, and always will be," Nan said.

"Thanks. It won't make a bit of difference to how I feel, but at least I'll *know*."

He told Mim that the cotton swabs he wiped inside first his, and then her mouth, were part of a doctor's check-up. Lying to her was difficult, but telling her the truth was impossible. Harri and Mim did not stay at *Coed Uchaf* every night at first, but a couple of nights a week, to make the change as gradual and easy as possible for Mim in particular. The little girl did as she was asked, but, at times, such as during a busy mealtime or a family movie-watching session, a shadow fell across her face when she thought nobody would notice. Nan did, and when they were alone, she asked what was troubling her.

"I always thought it would be just me and Dad," Mim replied. "I mean, I love you lots and *of course* I love the twins, but it will be *different* from now on, won't it?"

"Yes, it will, for all of us. That's why we're taking it slowly. What are you worried might go wrong? You know you can tell me anything, Mim," Nan asked. For a split second, she wondered if the little girl had somehow seen a DNA test on TV, so was now worried about why her dad had asked her to do one. Luckily, the reason was nothing so complex.

After a few moments wriggling in her seat, she replied, "I don't think my dad knows how to be happy. I worry he won't let himself be happy with you because he doesn't know how."

Nan let out a long, slow breath. "I worry about that too, so let's make sure we show him how, shall we, sweetheart? I think you and I could be world champions at being happy if we tried hard enough," she said, hugging Mim so tightly that she squealed.

* * *

On the day Nan and Harri told their mothers about their relationship, they made sure to ply them with large glasses of sherry beforehand. The two women had been friends in school, and wanted nothing but happiness for their children, but Harri was anxious about the whiff of disgrace that still hung about him like a pall. Eira still did not know the whole, sad story – chiefly because she had lived hundreds of miles away when Idris had died and was not in touch with Annie. Now, she needed to know it all, so he told his story clearly and truthfully, to complete silence.

"So you were the 'other man' in their marriage?" Eira said, when he had finished, clearly shocked. "Did you love her, Idris' wife?" Eira asked, looking directly at Harri.

Harri shook his head. "No, I didn't, and she didn't love me either."

"Then why did you take her away from him?"

Nobody spoke or moved, for several seconds, until Harri replied:

"Because I was weak and flattered to feel chosen, instead of him."

Eira nodded slowly. "That, I can understand, Harri."

Nan looked at her mother. Without doubt, Eira was referring to herself, to something she had experienced, but what could possibly have happened that bore any relation to what Catrin did to Idris? Just as she opened her mouth to ask, Eira caught her eye, swigged her sherry and put her empty glass down on the table.

"Anyway, I say that the past is gone, and we've all made our fair share of mistakes in it. Top us up, please!"

* * *

The result of the DNA test told Harri the news he had dreaded: he was not Mim's biological father. Devastated, he went back to his cottage, asking Nan to tell the girls that he was ill and refusing to answer any calls or even open the door. Mim was hurt and upset, so Nan kept her home from school, and they spent the morning curled up together with the pups squirming happily all over both of them.

When Harri returned to *Coed Uchaf* late that evening, Nan was glad all the children were in bed. She poured him a whisky, which he sipped in silence, but he left the sandwich she made him untouched.

"Oh, Harri, I'm so sorry," she said.

"It was my idea, and I needed to know, whatever the outcome. Mim is Idris' daughter, and Annie's granddaughter, and I feel they should know that. I owe poor Annie that, before she dies. Mim is the only family she has left. And I must tell my mam too."

"But you're not going to tell Mim, I hope?" Nan said. "She wouldn't understand, and finding out she has another dad – one who's dead, and she can never meet – would be awful for her."

"Agreed."

"But what kind of reception will Annie Hughes give you? She may still blame you for Idris' death."

Harri stroked her cheek gently. "I know, but these are my worries, not yours, *cariad*/love. I must face the truth in some way, after all these years of hiding away. Then, perhaps, I can start to properly heal."

Nan sighed. "OK, but you can't go and see Annie alone."

"No," he replied. "I will tell Mam the situation and ask her to come with me. I know she goes to visit her old friend from time to time, and she's on my side at least."

"Perhaps I could persuade my mother to come too. She really needs to see Annie while she still can. Dewi asked her to before he died, but she's reluctant to go on her own."

"Safety in numbers, I say, but we need to tell both our

mothers about the DNA results before we go and see Annie," Harri said. "I'm dreading it, but it has to be done."

"Are you going to go to your mum's now, to tell her? I think you ought to," Nan replied.

"No. Why don't we invite them both over later, kill two old birds with one revelation?"

Nan could not help but laugh at this, the very blackest of humour.

* * *

When her phone rang later that day, and she saw Robin's name on the screen, she let him wait for a few seconds. She knew why he was calling. Mr Davies had finally come through, Dewi's bequest had been formalised, and probate completed. She had emailed Robin that morning to explain her decision to alter their settlement more in his favour and to thank him for trying to help her stay at the farmhouse by making a huge sacrifice himself. Would his pride be wounded, thinking that she had done it to shame him, to make him feel like a loser who needed her help? She knew how he hated to be a source of disappointment. He'd spent his whole adult life trying in vain to avoid being that. When she eventually picked up, she heard only gulping sounds with the occasional intake of breath as Robin struggled to gain enough composure to speak.

"Nan, why did you do this? You don't need to do this. Dewi left that money for you, not to let me off the hook. I can't bear to think what he'd say about what you've done," he said.

Nan knew that, at that moment, every word she chose was vital, and the wrong one would see her carefully wrought plan collapse like a tower of sand.

"I've kept most of Dewi's money, Robin, for me and the girls. He left... instructions, for what he wanted me to do with some of it, but with the rest, I can easily buy you out. The farm is worth a lot and has quite a bit of grazing land still left that I can rent out."

"But why do you want to, after everything I did? I don't understand. I feel so guilty, and my parents are already furious with me, so ashamed of what I did to you with Rhian."

"I thought they'd be delighted you're shot of me at last!"

Her husband did not reply. Outside, above the still water, the lonely cry of a curlew cut through the silence like a knife through butter. Nan watched it reach the safety of its little flock scouring the banks of weed for food, and waited. Robin had something important to tell her, she could feel it coming.

"Not at all. I just think they wish I'd died, not Simon. Sometimes, Nan, I wish I had too, given the complete balls-up I've made of things," he said. "Perhaps I should grant their wish now."

"Stop it! Talking about suicide is a terrible burden to put on someone else, whether you mean it or not, Robin," Nan said, real anger in her voice. "Take those words back. I don't want to hear them, or anything like them, ever, EVER again! I'm giving you a *chance*, can't you see? A chance to live your life better, *be* better, do what you always wanted to do. Simon's death was not your fault, you hear me, and you do not have to atone for it anymore. It was a terrible, terrible accident."

Seconds later, an unmistakeable sound seeped from her phone. Robin was *laughing*.

"God, I'm so proud of you, Nan. Listen to you! I wanted to save you when we met, because you were broken, but I wasn't the right person: *you* needed to do it yourself, and you have!"

Nan felt the warmth of his words spread through her like a slug of the finest whisky. "Thanks. I guess I just needed to lead the life that was right for me, Robin. I'm doing that now, and you *let* me do it and I will always thank you for that, but now it's time for you to make some decisions about *your* life, Robin. You, not your parents."

Robin sighed. "James is on the verge of sacking me, so goodness knows what I'll do, Nan. My heart's not in it, not since I lost you and the girls, to be honest."

"We weren't what you needed, Robin, but the money I can give you now might help you do something better. You have a *choice,* don't you see? That's something I don't think you've ever really had before." She paused. Heart pounding, she went on, "Robin, I want you to use the money to paint, really paint – portraits, landscapes, abstracts, anything! Find a course, rent a studio, do what you have always wanted to do."

He laughed again. "You want me to be a bloody *artisan,* don't you?"

"I just want you to be yourself, love."

"I've never dared to do something really risky, or brave – just *stupid*, like leaving you."

Nan bit her tongue. This was no time for self-pity or blame. "It's water under the bridge, Robin. We are different people now. We must arrange for the twins to visit you too."

"I don't think they want to see me," he muttered. "They don't really like me."

Nan hesitated, before saying, "But perhaps they might, Robin, if you liked yourself."

FORTY-FOUR

For the whole of the night before Harri was to visit Annie Hughes, very heavy rain and fierce gusts of wind had whipped the sea into a froth and lashed the windows of *Coed Uchaf* relentlessly. These summer storms were infrequent, but vicious, a diluted warning of the ferocious ones that came later in the year. Harri claimed to have "heard nothing at all" during the night, but Nan saw dark shadows beneath his eyes and saw the restless tapping of his fingertips. Would Annie forgive him? It was a big ask.

Beti agreed to go with him into Annie's room, but Eira adamantly refused to go.

"It's better for everyone if I stay away. Too many people will alarm her," she said, but Nan knew that fear lay at the heart of her decision. Fear of what, she still had no idea.

The plan was that, if Annie heard Harri out, understood what he was saying and wanted to see her granddaughter, Nan would bring Mim to wave at the "ill old lady" from the garden outside her window to "cheer her up because she's sad". Harri remained adamant that Mim should not know the true situation, or who Annie really was.

"To have *three* Nains is a bit much for anyone to take in, let alone a small child," he told Nan. "I will tell her about Idris, and who he was, in my own time and after we've told our mothers. This is like a military operation!"

And in many ways, it had to be. Nan and Harri invited Eira and Beti for tea before they went to the care home so that they could tell them about Mim's true parentage, but they asked Eira to come first. Nan was surprised, but deeply proud of her mother's pithy, yet compassionate reaction to the news:

"It's good to hear the truth, not snippets of gossip, to be honest. I say what's done is done, the little girl is loved and good has come of it in the end. I must tell you that I had my suspicions but couldn't say. There's something of Annie about her – I saw it ages ago."

But it was Beti's reaction that stunned them all:

"I've known this news since the day she was born, son," she said, biting into a shortbread biscuit. "One look at your dark brown mop and her pretty blonde curls told me that, my boy."

Nan knew in an instant that Beti was right. How could she not have seen it too?

"What? But you never said anything," Harri gasped.

"What did you want me to say, as you struggled to get her to take a bottle, or sleep for more than twenty minutes, after Catrin abandoned you both? You were doing what needed to be done, and you loved that little mite from the off. You are her father and always will be. Idris is never coming back, and neither is her mother, thank goodness."

Harri put his head in his hands. "Mam, please."

"It made no difference to me, that she was Idris', don't you see? I love her just as much as you do, but I *have* always felt guilty that Annie doesn't know her son had a beautiful daughter, but whether or not to tell her was your decision to make, not mine. Today, we are going to put things right, *aren't we, Eira*?"

She looked at her friend defiantly. "No more excuses. You're coming with us."

Eira got up suddenly, as if standing to attention.

"*Reit*/Right, I may come, and I know I should come, but I do need to tell you something first, Nan. I'm sorry for all the soul-baring going on today, but there are things that need to be said, and I can only say them now. Tomorrow, I may not be able to."

Nan went as white as a sheet. "Mum, if you're going to tell me that Eric wasn't my real father I don't know if I..."

"No, girl. It's not that – unfortunately for you, he was. Just listen please – this isn't easy for me to say. It's about things that happened a long time ago, when I was much younger than you are now, isn't it, Beti?"

Beti nodded solemnly.

"So *Beti* knows what you're going to say?" Nan cried.

"Yes, she does, because she was there at the time," Eira said.

"Now *cau dy geg*/shut your mouth, Nan, and let your mother speak," Beti said. "Off you go, Eira. Time's pressing."

Eira folded her hands in her lap and began. "Nan, Annie Hughes and I were the best, the closest of friends. Me, Dewi and Annie went to the pub in Valley together every Saturday night, rain or shine. Annie could light up any room, she was so pretty, and full of dreams of going to live in London, getting away from the island. The very first night Eric arrived at the base, he made a beeline for her, and they were together all evening, dancing and laughing. Dewi told us that he knew his type, warned us both to leave him well alone, but it was too late for poor Annie. I didn't know the extent of his deceit then, but he made lots of promises in the next few weeks – ones he soon broke, of course. Eric was good at that."

"Did he promise to marry her?" Nan said. "Or did he... seduce her?"

"He did one so that he could do the other. She was not the

first and certainly not the last woman that man hurt, as we both know."

"Yes, we do," Nan said.

"But I hurt her too, Nan, because I took him from her. I remember the day I came here, to *Coed Uchaf,* and told Annie that Eric had chosen me to be his wife, instead of her. I knew she was sweet on him, but I stood right there by the old range, flashing my engagement ring, telling her 'not to fret' because 'there were plenty more fish in the sea' and that Eric and I were meant for each other. I truly thought he'd just flirted with her, led her on, you see. Later, I learnt that he'd done far more than that." She paused. "But I left her, my oldest childhood friend, broken, weeping, alone, in this kitchen. I can see her now, crumpled in a heap next to that old range. *Duw*/God, it was such a terrible, cruel thing to do."

Eira started to cry, a strange, high-pitched sound that made Shadow's ears prick up in alarm. For a long minute everyone listened to her, and watched her, until tears came and released her pain. "Yes, she forgave me, years later, when I knew everything, because she's a better person than I will ever be, but how can I forgive *myself?*" she cried. "The guilt stayed with me, like a rotten kernel inside a nut. I felt I deserved the misery your father inflicted on me, and I found it hard to trust or love anyone, even you, Nansi, my own child." She reached for Nan's hand. "Thank God I have a second chance now, thanks to Dewi."

Nan nodded sadly. "But Annie was pregnant with Dad's child, wasn't she?" she said.

"Yes, she was. But neither your father, or anyone else, knew that. I swear it."

"But Mum, what happened to make him choose you, not her, whether he knew she was pregnant or not?"

"I wish there had been a good reason for what he did, but he told me they had nothing in common, that she was 'too demanding'. Now I know why, of course – she was worried, terrified more like – and dreading telling him that she was pregnant, and he was probably finding her too needy for his liking." She paused and wiped her eyes. "But I believed him when he said I was 'more his type'. Why, I'll never know, because all I wanted to do was stay on the island, marry a farmer, have ten kids and be famous for my baking."

"And it was Annie that wanted to get away, but couldn't," Nan said. "That's so sad."

"Yes. It's all sad, Nan. Perhaps he chose me because he thought I would be easier to bully – I don't know, but choose me he did, and off I had to go to live in that awful suburb of that awful city. I was punished for abandoning my friend, with years and years of misery, and so were you."

Nobody spoke, and a hush as thick as treacle seemed to settle in the room. Shadow moved from one person to the next, nuzzling their hands with her wet nose to offer comfort the only way she knew how.

"So was Idris Dad's illegitimate son?" Nan said. "Did Tomos marry Annie when she was already pregnant?"

"Yes. He married her *because* she was pregnant. He was that kind of man. And they grew to love each other, so she was luckier than me in the end. Tomos never treated Idris any differently to his own son, who died so young: he was always just 'his bigger boy'."

"How ironic, that Dad could have had the son he always wanted, if only he'd been honourable and married Annie," Nan said. "And Idris was my half-brother... which makes Mim...?"

"... your half-niece!" Beti said. "And now she's coming to live with you! Incredible."

Nan felt something stir in her memory, like a bolt that has finally slid into place.

"Oh my God, Mum," Nan said. "When you and I visited *Coed Uchaf* that day, and you and Annie hugged and cried, you were saying sorry for betraying her, and she was telling you about Idris being Dad's son?"

Eira nodded. "Yes. It was the only time we could really talk. We'd come alone that time, remember? No wonder we both cried, with so many things unsaid, for so many years. She forgave me, straight away, said she'd had a good life with Tomos and was so proud of Idris. When Idris died as well, I couldn't bear it. I felt I had cursed her, somehow knocked her life off kilter, by being so selfish, so I stayed away after that."

Nan looked at her mother. "But what happened to Idris years later wasn't your fault."

"If it was anyone's, Eira, it was mine, and I need to know if Annie can forgive me, as she forgave you," Harri said softly. "So please, please come with us to see her."

A pause of several seconds. "If you can be brave enough to face up to the past, Harri, then I must too," Eira said, standing up and smoothing her skirt.

"We'll go together," Harri replied.

"We will. But remember, Harri – it doesn't matter who's your 'real' father or mother: it's the one that loves you, as you do Mim, that's the real parent. Dewi and Manon were far better parents to my Nan than me or her father were."

"You tried your best, Mum," Nan said.

Eira looked at her and Nan saw the pain in her eyes. "I tried to be the best mother I could be, yes, but that wasn't enough to protect you from him, was it? I can only hope you forgive me for that, in time."

"I already have," Nan replied, hugging her close.

Beti stood up and folded her arms. "*Reit pawb*/Right everyone, if all the dark secrets are out now, can we *please* go and tell Annie about Mim? After all the tragedies in her life, it might just bring her some joy at the end of it."

* * *

An hour later, as Nan and Mim were about to embark upon their sixth game of "hangman" in the care home car park, a text pinged into Nan's phone.

> A. listened, and I think she understood. She wants to see M. Bring her to the window please, the one that looks out onto the rockery.
> H. X

As they neared the window, Nan glimpsed a pale, thin face, haloed with white hair, standing quite still. Behind her, stood Eira and Beti, both supporting one of Annie's thin arms. Nan did not actually have to tell Mim that she should look at Annie, or to wave: the little girl did so anyway.

After a moment, the old lady raised a delicate hand and waved back.

FORTY-FIVE

There was always a brief pause after the schools broke up on Anglesey and before the holidaymakers invaded, like an intake of breath. Sometimes, it was a day or two, sometimes, a whole week, as term dates differed, but it was always a time when the island seemed to brace itself before the summer onslaught began. The beaches shone with smooth, white sand and all signs of the long, dark days and fierce winter storms were long-forgotten. The hundreds of noisy birds that had taken possession of clifftop crags and rocky coves, built nests and raised their young undisturbed seemed to know that change was in the air, and fat seal pups slithered off rocks to bask in less visible places. That year, the "calm before the storm" was a whole, luxurious week and the forecast was good for most of it. After the revelations of the last few days, everyone was very ready for a period of calm as they drove home to *Coed Uchaf* from the care home.

Harri announced that he would cook what he called a "celebration banquet" which involved nobody eating until 9pm and the kids being too full of crisps to eat anything by then. His relief at having spoken to Annie and starting to come to terms with him not being Mim's biological father was clear to all. The terrible strain of years of doubt and guilt had left his face, as if sloughed away, and he looked his true age, rather than years older. The next day promised to be equally eventful, as Nan had to sign her divorce papers in Gwenda's office later, so Nan was up very early. Robin had accepted defeat and agreed to take the money she had offered him to help him leave Naughton Consultancy and start his life again somewhere else. This filled her with a very slightly smug sense of pride. It felt so good, so very good, to be in control at last. Only one thing troubled her that morning. Mim had been very quiet since the visit to the care home. The little girl was unsettled, unsure of something, and Nan knew more than most how that felt. She would try and talk to her.

As the family slept, Nan pulled on some jeans, a T-shirt and some old red Crocs, fed Shadow and the pups, gulped down a coffee and headed out onto the cliff path. It was early, but the sun was already well above the horizon, lighting up a shoal of golden sparkles across the sea. She passed the burgeoning kitchen garden, buzzing with happy bees and her heart swelled with pride. Pulling the gate closed behind her, she walked under the ancient hawthorn tree that arched over it so protectively and turned left. She knew exactly where to go that day. To the place that she had first visited as a curious child, when everything that had happened, still lay ahead, like a wonderful story waiting to be written.

There were no other walkers out on the clifftop that morning as she headed for the burial chamber, and the only sounds in the still, warm air were the high-pitched peeps of sandpipers as they waded in the shallows. The climb up to the top of the hill was steep, the grass that topped it nibbled to a close fuzz by the colony of rabbits that emerged, shyly, only at dusk. Nan stood on the top of the rounded *twmp*/mound and spread her arms wide, as if embracing what lay before her. To her right lay a series of beautiful bays, fringed with marram grass and fretted with sea-slicked rocks. Each one was different and each one held so many memories. The nearest, Porth Nobla, was great for body-boarding with the girls, as waves were funnelled into the little cove and then crashed safely on the sand. The bay beyond it, Tyn Tywyn was where she and Robin had brought their girls as babies, to dabble their plump toes in the rock pools and point at scuttling crabs with their fat little fingers. Beyond, lay the weed-covered bay where flocks of migrating birds gathered to feed on the tiny creatures hiding in it and from which glorious murmurations of starlings began and ended. And there, in the distance, lay the golden expanse of Rhosneigr, where second homers would spend the summer "working from home" until they returned to their affluent lives elsewhere and left the locals to search for driftwood and walk in the winter wind and rain. They were never missed.

As she breathed in the beauty of where she lived, and where she would see her children grow up, Nan was thankful, above all, to the man who had let her come here, whatever his true motivation had been. He had indeed rescued her, though in doing so, they had lost each other. In the vivid fabric of her newfound happiness, there would always be a thread of sadness and of loss.

* * *

That evening, Harri came to find her sitting outside on the bench – *her* bench – sipping a glass of wine as the heat of the day ebbed. He had brought the rest of the bottle with him, running with condensation and perfectly chilled.

"How are you feeling? I assume you signed on the dotted line?"

She paused, and sipped slowly.

"I'm not sure. I feel different, but just the same, if that makes any sense," she said. "Robin sent me a text – 'Happy

Divorce Day'. Bit grim, but I wonder how he feels, on his tod in some room in Cambridge tonight?"

"I don't think he'll be alone for long," Harri said. "He'll find someone else to take under his wing."

"Rhian was tougher than I was; she left him."

"She didn't love him – you did," Harri said. "Catrin didn't love me either."

"And she wasn't the love of your life, was she, just as Robin wasn't mine?" Nan said.

"No, she wasn't, Nan."

They smiled at each other knowingly.

"We're stronger than ever now, but I want you to know that it's OK if, sometimes, we wobble a bit. Deal?" He held out his hand, and she shook it.

"Deal," she said. "We'll wobble together, if we wobble at all!"

The sun was beginning to set, turning the sky into a vivid collage of orange, yellow, red and purple that lit up both their faces.

"I'm a bit worried about Mim," Harri said. "She seems very... subdued. I hope I was right, not to tell her everything yet – about Idris, and Annie, I mean."

"I think you were. Such a lot's happened to her in a short space of time, remember," Nan said. "We've got together, you've both moved in here, she's suddenly part of a big, boisterous family. I'll have a chat with her, but we'll have to just take it one step at a time and answer her questions if and when it's right to."

"A *family*," Harri said with a sigh. "I've longed for one of those for so long."

A yell, from inside the house. "Mum! Tinker's done a big pooh on the carpet. It's soooooo disgusting!"

Nan got up. "Those puppies need to go to their 'forever homes', and soon," she said.

"But you said the girls could keep one each, remember. A promise is a promise."

"I know, I know. Wyn wants one, so that leaves only one to find a home for."

"Nan, before you go..." Harri said, his face taut.

"What's the matter? You look as if *you've* done a pooh too!"

He knelt down on the grass and grabbed her free hand. Everything suddenly seem to still around them, and Nan felt as if the world was holding its breath, just as she was.

"Nansi, I know you've only been Ms Brennan, and divorced for an afternoon, but will you marry me?"

She hesitated for less than ten seconds.

"Yes, I will – on one condition. Gwenno has to be my maid of honour, whether she wants to or not!"

"Fine, but good luck with getting her into any kind of frilly dress," Harri said, hugging her close.

FORTY-SIX

ANGLESEY, A YEAR LATER.

September is a fickle month on Anglesey, but the morning of the 19th, the day of Nan and Harri's wedding, was a glorious one, which was lucky as there was absolutely no flexibility in the timing. At Nan's insistence, they would marry in St Cwyfan's Church, "the church in the sea", because it was the place Harri had loved most as a boy and where they had first professed their love for each other.

"You need to overlay the sad memory of what happened to Idris there with a happy one – marrying me," she said. "It doesn't mean you've forgotten the past, it means you've accepted it as a part of your life, one link in the chain, but not the whole of it."

The tide would be at its lowest between 11am and 1pm, after which, things got riskier for those crossing over on the rocky causeway, so the service was set for noon precisely. It was to be a small gathering, as the tiny church could not accommodate many, but Eira and Beti had organised a party at the village pub for afterwards, and most of the local community was expected to come. Rumours of a "free bar", to be largely funded by Wyn, all but guaranteed it. Past gossip, mistakes and rumours were forgotten, borne away by good wishes for two people who clearly loved the island as much as they loved each other.

The bridal party gathered on the shore to walk over the causeway together at just after half past eleven. Harri, Guto and Emrys, the best man, had gone ahead with the vicar to turn on the gas heaters and the generator that powered the electric organ.

When everyone was assembled in an orderly line, Nan set off, her charity shop-bought ivory lace dress billowing in the warm breeze that made her look like a cloud crossing the sky as she picked her way across the rocks. Her three bridesmaids, Ceri, Elin and Mim followed on, happy to wear trainers now, but so excited about the satin pumps they were to change into for the service and the party later. Gwenno had been given free rein to choose her outfit as matron of honour, and she had gone for a silky, pale green dress, "to celebrate all the wonderful produce Nan and I have nurtured together", (or so she said, but in reality, because she simply looked stunning in it). Guto, the proud ring-bearer, was alongside his mum, followed by Eira and Beti who walked to the church arm in arm, and in wellies, "just in case". Wyn and his wife Josie and their four children were next, and Wyn had happily agreed to give Nan away. Last in the little procession came Ella, Nan's oldest Cambridge friend, with her husband Tarquin (who was dressed, as ever, in purple).

"So, you imagined all this, did you?" Ella said, as they all gathered at the top of the church steps. "Remember how I told you to *visualise* good things, and then they would happen?"

"Of course I did, Ella. That's why it's happening, I kept the faith," Nan replied with a wink.

As the girls slipped into their party shoes, they all heard Guto sing the first notes of the song Nan had asked him to sing as she walked towards being Harri's wife – 'Suo Gan'. As the trembling notes of the little organ wafted out of the open church door and the sounds of Guto's pure voice floated up into the sky, the three little bridesmaids fluttered into line behind Nan, and she took her cousin's arm and smiled at him.

"I never thought I would ever be this happy again, Wyn," she whispered. "After all the bad things that have happened, today I feel like I did when I was a child and came here. I wish Uncle Dewi and Auntie Manon were here now. Oh, I wish it so much."

"Well, if they were, they'd be telling you just how much you are loved, and how much you deserve all this, Nansi."

And when he led her into the church, and every one of those dear, kind faces turned to greet her, Nan finally believed him.

EPILOGUE

Almost exactly a year after their wedding, Harri and Nan's little boy was born. They called him Idris Dewi Parry. He came into the world in the kitchen of *Coed Uchaf*, surrounded by candles and dogs. Idris' three big sisters adore him, and particularly enjoy turning his mop of long dark hair into a crop of tiny pony-tails so that he looks like a very cute hedgehog.

Eira sold her house in London and bought a bungalow in Rhosneigr, from where she delights in shouting abuse at the Range Rover drivers who park in her cul-de-sac from behind her immaculately white net curtains. Every Wednesday, she collects Elin, Ceri and Mim from school, gives them tea and a sleepover at her house. There are always a *lot* of cakes. Eira and Beti take Mim to visit Annie fairly often, but she is deteriorating rapidly and vanishing into her memories a little more each time. Often, she says nothing, but simply looks at her granddaughter in loving wonder; her eyes, however, reveal a deep joy that was not there before.

Aled and Gethin Pritchard made a brilliant job of converting the outbuilding, and Harri added secret doors, shutters, beautifully carved banister rails and wooden four-poster beds to make the cottage like a fairy tale for the families that come to escape their troubled lives for a while. For some, it was the first time they had ever seen the sea, been allowed to stroke a friendly dog or watched a crab march unfeasibly sideways across the sand. Many of the children wept when it was time to leave, and so Nan and Harri have decided to convert his beachside cottage into another refuge home next year.

Robin resigned from his job, left Cambridge and moved to North Devon, where he is painting in a light, bright studio in Tavistock and doing very well. His parents disinherited him, but he is happy and lives with his young partner Tamsin, a yoga teacher. They have the fourth of Shadow's puppies and have called her Hope. Robin sees his daughters as often as he can. Between visits, he says that because the slate he painted when he and Nan moved into *Coed Uchaf* is still hanging in their kitchen, they know that he loves them all very much:

A fabulous family lives here.

Nan was called for interview by the Archaeology Department almost eighteen months after her initial application and offered the job of leading a youth project to connect local young people with their historical heritage. The Lottery Fund had doubled the salary offered. Now almost fluent in Welsh, and with Eira and Beti competing to look after baby Idris, she accepted the job. She loves explaining how the past has shaped what we see around us. The burial chamber, with its other-worldly carvings and rugged stone altar, is always a favourite site. Out of the corner of her eye, she sometimes sees a sulky teen surreptitiously leave an offering of flowers or pebbles out of respect for the past and the dead, who people it. Gwenno is in now sole charge of a thriving organic veg-box scheme and intends to expand further into soft fruit, and the draft plans for the school garden are awaiting approval at the council office. It could be a long wait...

For Nan and Harri, each day begins and ends with a walk – across the headland, along the beach or, on Sundays, a hike in Snowdonia, where they are learning to follow the sheep tracks into remoter places up in the mountains. The dogs circle the little family as they walk, nudging them with their noses if they slow down too much. In the kitchen, the heart of the home, Harri's beautiful driftwood carving of an elegant seabird, spreading its wings and finally flying free, has pride of place on a table next to the range. After a year-long sojourn nobody knows where, Fang the cat returned and the twins tell everyone that he went back to Cambridge, decided he didn't like it one bit, so came back home again.

Every time she hears her daughters say the word "home", Nan's heart fills with joy.

A LETTER FROM THE AUTHOR

Thank you so much for reading *The Forgotten Farmhouse by the Sea*. I hope you were swept along by Nan's story and have now fallen in love with the island of Anglesey, as I did many, many years ago. If you'd like to join other readers in hearing all about my new releases and some bonus content too, you can sign up for my newsletter.

www.stormpublishing.co/caroline-young

I really hope you enjoyed this book. If you did, and you could spare a few moments to leave a review, it would be hugely appreciated. Even a short review can make all the difference in encouraging a reader to discover my stories for the first time. Thank you!

My inspiration for this book was a seed planted in childhood. Anglesey has always been a part of my life, as my mother's family came from North Wales, and most childhood holidays were spent in a caravan on the island (often looking out at pouring rain)! Like Eira, my mum always longed to return, and eventually, she did. Having moved my own family here just over 20 years ago, the island's beauty and ever-changing moods have given me ideas for so many different stories. I know my mum would have been proud of the life I have built here, and be happy that she passed her love of this place on to me, as I have to my three daughters.

Thanks again for being part of this amazing journey with me, and do stay in touch. I have lots more stories to tell, and plenty more seabirds and strong women to celebrate!

Caroline

facebook.com/caroline.young.9250

ACKNOWLEDGEMENTS

For me, having a novel published has been a long time coming, and I must thank some of the people in my life who have never lost faith that it would happen one day. I am sad that my parents are not here to see it, as they always felt it was something I would do, but I thank them for giving me my love of Wales, and Anglesey in particular, which inspired this story.

Thank you to my chief cheerleaders and readers of early drafts – my sister Debbie, who loves this island as much as I do, and my dear friends Ag, Mel, Abby, Helen and Mel. Ann, Zoe, Rosie, Annie, Floss and Vicki, I thank you for never letting me give up. Extra special gratitude to my sea swimming partner Liz, who has bravely followed me into cold waters when it really wasn't sensible to do so. Kate and Paula, I am grateful for your unending support and unswerving belief in me, over our many years of friendship. Thank you, Idris, for reading through the text and checking my Welsh (which needed some serious polishing!).

More thanks to Janet, whose writing course I attended many years ago and who first made me believe that perhaps I could write well, and to Juliet, who has spurred me on through many disappointments and doubts. To my lovely editor, Kate Smith, thank you for championing my novel and my writing, and for sharing my love of the sea.

My biggest thanks, however, must go to Geoff and my three girls, Bethan, Rhiannon and Mari, who have witnessed the long and often turbulent journey that has brought me to this point in my writing life. I know how happy you are that my dream has come true, and that means more than I can say. May your dreams come true, too, however long you have to wait for that to happen.

Printed in Great Britain
by Amazon

39100409R00202